LADY ANNE'S QUEST

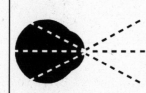

This Large Print Book carries the Seal of Approval of N.A.V.H.

LADY ANNE'S QUEST

SUSAN PAGE DAVIS

THORNDIKE PRESS

A part of Gale, Cengage Learning

GALE
CENGAGE Learning·

Farmington Hills, Mich • San Francisco • New York • Waterville, Maine
Meriden, Conn • Mason, Ohio • Chicago

GALE
CENGAGE Learning®

Copyright © 2012 by Susan Page Davis.
Prairie Dreams #2.
All Scripture quotations are taken from the King James Version of the Bible.
Thorndike Press, a part of Gale, Cengage Learning.

Thorndike Press® Large Print Christian Historical Fiction.
The text of this Large Print edition is unabridged.
Other aspects of the book may vary from the original edition.
Set in 16 pt. Plantin.

LIBRARY OF CONGRESS CATALOGING-IN-PUBLICATION DATA

Davis, Susan Page.
   Lady Anne's quest / by Susan Page Davis. — Large print edition.
      pages cm. — (Thorndike Press large print Christian historical fiction)
(Prairie dreams ; #2)
     ISBN 978-1-4104-7631-9 (hardcover) — ISBN 1-4104-7631-6 (hardcover)
    1. Aristocracy (Social class)—England—Fiction. 2. Large type books. I. Title.
  PS3604.A976L327 2015
  813'.6—dc23   2014047735

Published in 2015 by arrangement with Barbour Publishing, Inc.

Printed in Mexico
1 2 3 4 5 6 7 19 18 17 16 15

LADY ANNE'S QUEST

CHAPTER 1

October 1855

Halfway across the stream, the front wheel plummeted, and the wagon's whole front end jolted downward. Anne grabbed the edge of her seat and clung to it while trying to brace her feet against the footboard.

"I knew we should have gone to the ferry," her companion, Dulcie Whistler, cried.

Dulcie's husband, Rob, urged his saddle horse alongside them. "You all right?"

"Yes, but we seem to be stuck in a mud hole." Dulcie slapped the reins against the flanks of her team. The two mules leaned into their collars and strained to pull the farm wagon free of the muddy river bottom, to no avail.

"Miss Anne, you going to be all right?" Rob asked.

Anne gritted her teeth and nodded. "I can hold on for a while."

"Good, because the problem seems to be

on that side, and I don't think I'd best go around there."

His chestnut horse, Bailey, splashed through the water to the head of Dulcie's off mule. Rob bent over and grabbed the cheek strap on the mule's bridle.

"Come on, Rufus! Pull!"

His urging wasn't enough. The two mules continued to struggle until Anne was afraid they would exhaust themselves.

"Hey, Dan!" Rob waved to the young man who had accompanied them on this journey. "Tell the others to wait. Unhitch Smith's team and bring them up here, but keep to the upstream side." He rode back closer to Dulcie. "Don't worry, sweetheart. We'll double-team you out of there. Triple team, if need be."

Dulcie shook her head. "At least it's so shallow we won't drown if we fall in. I told you we shouldn't have tried to ford here."

"I know, but Mr. Perkins insisted. I don't think he's got much money, and the ferry costs a dollar. This time of year, you can usually get across here with no trouble." Rob looked toward the shore behind them. "Dan's getting the other team ready. You holding on, Miss Anne, or do you want to climb off?"

Anne unclenched her teeth. "I'm not sure

how long I can hang on." The wagon's corner sagged so steeply beneath her that her arm and leg muscles were already exhausted from clinging to the seat. And she'd thought her days of rough living on a wagon train had ended a week ago, when she'd rolled into Oregon City.

"Here comes Dan with the other team." Rob turned Bailey and splashed away from them, seeming to forget Anne's predicament.

"I'm sorry, dear," Dulcie said. "Can you hold on to me and pull yourself up higher on the seat?"

Anne grasped the offered arm and levered herself closer to Dulcie. Rob and his horse came even with them again.

"Dan's going to take you off," he told Anne. He went on with Mr. Smith following him and leading the second team of mules.

Dan brought his mount close to the wagon on Dulcie's side. "Can you climb into the wagon bed and get back here? If you get on behind my saddle, Star can carry us both."

Several thoughts flashed through Anne's mind, none of which could be expressed in a genteel manner. Dan thought like a farmer, with no concern for her feminine sensibilities. His very practicality irked her.

9

That and the fact that the young man whose suit she'd rejected a couple of months ago had once more inserted himself into her life without cause.

Dan had invited himself on this trip of about fifty miles, and she knew it was only so he could be near her, a circumstance she'd as soon do without. She wouldn't even spare a thought for the unimaginative name he'd given his horse. The placid gelding had a splotch on his forehead that horsemen referred to as a star, though in shape it was more of a blob. Now if he'd consulted Anne, she could have helped him think of a name with much more flair. Of course, flair would be wasted on a farmer.

Using all her remaining strength, she hauled herself up and over the back of the wagon seat, with a discreet push from Dulcie. All of her trunks had slid to the front of the tilted wagon box. She clambered over them, trying as best she could to keep her ankles hidden beneath the flounce of her skirt and to avoid Dulcie and Rob's one satchel, all of their bedrolls, a bundle of firewood, and the boxes of foodstuffs and cooking utensils. Once past the major obstacles, she clutched the side of the wagon and pulled herself precariously erect. Dan moved Star forward a step and reached for her. The wagon gave a sudden lurch, and Anne stumbled.

Dan caught her arm and steadied her. He looked forward and shouted, "Hold on, Rob! I'm taking Miss Stone off the wagon."

Too late. The combined teams of mules had thrown their weight into dragging the wagon free. Though Dan lunged to slide an arm around her waist and Anne leaped toward him, she tumbled into the foot-deep river.

She sat for a moment with the water swirling around her. Air ballooned her full calico skirt. It absorbed water and gradually sank to the surface, where the current tugged at it. Anne hastily clapped the sodden fabric against her legs and stared miserably up at Dan.

"Are you all right?" he asked with a grimace.

"I haven't broken anything, if that's what you mean." Anne regretted her curtness. Dan was a kindhearted soul, and her predicament wasn't his fault.

He started to swing his right leg over the saddle, but she shrieked, "Don't get down!"

"Why not?"

"The water will be over your boots. I'm all right." She scrambled to her feet to prove it and stumbled on the uneven river bottom. She was able to catch her balance, but her soaked dress clung to her in a mortifying manner, and the current continued to tug at her legs, skirt, and petticoats. Walking to shore would challenge her.

Dan settled back into the saddle and kicked off his left stirrup. "Well, at least let me pull you up and carry you to shore."

"No."

He frowned down at her. "Are you sure?"

"Positive." Anne could think of nothing that would induce her to give in. The thought of clawing up onto Star's back in her dripping costume made her shudder. The horse would hate having a wet bulk added to his load — and her drenched layers of clothing must weigh a great deal. Beyond that, the picture of herself holding on to Dan while the poor horse picked his way across the Long Tom only confirmed her instincts. With her eye, she measured the distance to the bank they'd left and then to the one ahead of them and set out for the far bank. Dulcie's wagon had nearly reached it, thanks to the extra team of mules.

Anne kept a little upstream, out of the mud the mules had churned up. The water deepened to mid-thigh, but the current wasn't too strong, and she waded against it, finally reaching shore.

"Sorry you took a dunking, Miss Anne," Rob shouted as she stumbled up the low incline.

Dan's horse lunged up the bank, and he dismounted and came to her side.

"I'm so sorry. I'll get a fire going straightaway."

Anne looked toward the wagon. "I need dry clothes."

"Of course." Dan's face flushed. "Mrs. Whistler will help you, I'm sure. We can hang a blanket. . . ."

They both fell silent and watched Dulcie drive the wagon up the slope. When it reached level ground, she called, "Whoa!" and the mules stopped, snorting and shivering.

"Good job," Rob told his wife. He turned his horse and trotted over to Anne and Daniel. "We may as well camp here. It will take several hours for the other five wagons to get across on the ferry. Miss Anne, we'll get you dried out in no time."

Anne nodded. Her teeth had begun to chatter. Though the October afternoon wasn't too cold, the breeze cut through her drenched clothing.

Dulcie hopped down from the wagon, hiked up her skirt, and ran toward her.

"Anne, you poor thing! Tell me what to get for you. Mr. Adams, get a move on. Start a fire over there, if you please." She pointed to a grassy clearing where others had camped recently.

"Yes, ma'am." Dan's chin sank nearly to his chest as he shuffled away, the picture of contrition.

Dulcie smiled at Anne. "Well, if he hopes to persuade you to marry him on this outing, he's not off to a very good start, is he?"

Anne grimaced. "He's a very nice man. I just —"

Dulcie patted her arm. "Don't fret about it, dear. He came at his own urging. Now, come over to the wagon, and I'll give you a blanket to put around you while I get your dry clothes out. Come. You're shaking."

Anne let Dulcie lead her to the side of the wagon. She'd traveled across the plains during the past six months on Rob Whistler's wagon train, but she'd only met Dulcie yesterday.

Yesterday — the turning point in Anne's life. She'd watched her best friend, Elise Finster, marry the wagon train's scout. Elise had been with her all of Anne's life. She'd helped care for her since birth, on Anne's father's estate in England. She'd even agreed to accompany her young mistress to

14

America after Anne's father died.

Though she was glad Elise had found love on the journey, Anne now felt abandoned. Logic told her that was silly. After all, she had insisted Elise marry Eb Bentley without further delay — in fact, had practically bullied her into it. She hadn't anticipated the emptiness that would descend on her as she journeyed away from her closest friend and confidante.

"Here you go." Dulcie pulled a dry petticoat and stockings from Anne's leather satchel. "Now, for a dry dress. Should I open one of your trunks?"

By the time they'd found a suitable traveling dress and all the accessories Anne needed, Dan had a cheerful fire blazing. To her relief, he crossed the stream again and rode off with the other families to help them ferry their wagons across upstream. She suspected his embarrassment had sent him on the errand. Dulcie and Rob set up camp while Anne changed behind her makeshift screen and dried her hair near the campfire.

"I'm going to make lots of coffee and a big pot of stew," Dulcie said. "If anyone else gets wet, or if any of the other women are too tired to cook, I'll have something to share with them."

"That's kind of you," Anne said.

15

Dulcie shrugged. "Folks have it hard on the trail, but you know that. I'm sorry we changed your plans for you. You weren't banking on making this trip with five other families — and Dan."

"It's all right."

Anne was mildly surprised to find that she meant it. Mr. Smith had approached Rob in Corvallis. He'd heard the wagon master was going south to Eugene, and he led a small group of families who'd arrived on a wagon train just days after Whistler's had come in. These five families wanted to go to the Eugene area, and they hoped Mr. Whistler would grant them his protection and the benefit of his knowledge of the area by letting them join his party.

"Some of those folks need all the help they can get," Dulcie said.

Anne laughed. "I'm afraid that's true. They're blessed to have Rob leading them, even though they don't have any more big mountains or hostile Indians to face." Although the short trip to Eugene had been planned to help her, she couldn't begrudge the Whistlers' kindness to a few strangers. She pulled her hair back and tied it with a ribbon. "How can I help you?"

Dulcie smiled at her across the fire pit. "You could get out the coffeepot and coffee. Rob brought a couple of buckets of water while you were dressing. Can you make coffee?"

"It's one of the skills I acquired this summer." Anne laughed. "It took awhile to master. In fact, Dan Adams and your husband were the victims of a few of my less successful attempts."

"I just love the way you talk." Dulcie's eyes went all dreamy. "Hard to think I'm out here camping with a fine English lady."

"Oh, you mustn't say that!" Anne glanced about, but no one else was near. "Dan doesn't know about my father's title, and I'd just as soon he didn't."

"I suppose it would discourage him if he found out."

"It's not *that* I'm worried about." Anne realized her words must sound a bit crass. After all, she didn't want to hurt Dan. "It's just that people treat me differently if they know."

Dulcie nodded thoughtfully. "I'll try not to, Miss Anne."

"Just Anne is fine. And thank you. I like the way you and Rob treat me. Let's not allow words to make a difference." She went to the wagon and pulled the coffeepot from the box of pans and kettles. Dulcie's small sack of coffee was stashed inside a biscuit

17

tin as a precaution against dampness, and she took the tin with her to the fireside. She measured the coffee carefully. Even though she would only be with these people another day or two, she did not want to bear their disdain for being a helpless lady who didn't know how to do anything useful. She'd had enough of that.

Dan stayed with the Perkins family as they waited for the ferry to return. Their wagon would be the last to cross the Long Tom River. After watching Dulcie's struggle, none of the others were willing to risk the ford. Loading each of the five wagons separately and waiting while they were deposited on the far bank took almost three hours. Dan regretted missing that time with Anne — yet he was glad to be out of her sight for a while.

He still couldn't believe he'd let her fall into the river. It wasn't truly his fault, but he still felt responsible. He should have told Rob he was about to transfer Anne to his horse. Before the incident, he'd already been low in her esteem. Now he'd sunk to the depths of a well, and the bottom felt mucky.

He should have stayed away.

He and his brother, Hector, had left the

wagon train at Oregon City after claiming their land. They'd gone on to Champoeg and found their acreage. It was beautiful — just what they'd hoped for. Hector had plunged into making the open land into a farm. Dan worked beside him, but his heart had flown elsewhere.

After a week, Hector had told him as they nailed down shingles on the cabin's roof, "Daniel, you need to forget that woman."

His harsh tone hurt. "That woman" was Anne, the most beautiful, graceful creature on earth. Dan had lost his heart before they'd even left Independence. Anne seemed to like him. After months on the trail and making himself as agreeable as possible to her and her companion, Miss Finster, he'd put his future in Anne's hands.

Proposing to her scared him to death. He'd blurted it out while they were dancing one night by the flickering light of a bonfire. The stunned look on her face had told him what her answer would be before she uttered a word.

He'd known he wasn't good enough for her. She might as well have said that, but she was too polite. Her excuse was her uncle. Anne had made the journey to find him, not to settle in Oregon. Certainly not to marry a man who planned to farm in

Oregon. Her goal was to locate her missing uncle and accompany him back to England, the land of her birth. Apparently Anne's father had died, and this elusive uncle was needed to head up the remaining family. Letters hadn't reached him, and Anne had undertaken the trip with a friend — an older woman who was also charming and ladylike — on a quest to find him. Without trying, Anne had captured and broken Dan's heart.

"I'm not sure I can forget her," he had confessed to Hector.

His brother sighed and laid down his hammer. "Then you'd best go after her."

Dan gaped at him. "What good would that do?"

"Maybe none at all. But if you declare yourself —"

"Did that."

"Again," Hector said testily. "If you lay it all out before her, and she still says no, well then, maybe you'll be able to settle down and work."

"I'm working."

Hector barked out a little laugh. "You've been pounding on the same shingle so long I'm surprised it hasn't splintered all to bits. That's the way it's been all week. Go on, Daniel. Marry her or get over it."

"I . . . don't know where she's got to now, Hec."

"You know she went as far as Corvallis with Rob and Eb. If she's gone on from there, they'll know where."

Dan swallowed hard. Star could take him to Corvallis in less than a day. "What about you?"

"I'll be fine while you're gone. I'll get this cabin watertight for the winter, and then I'll start breaking ground."

Daniel sat still on the roof with his hammer hanging loosely from his hand. Was there any hope? He didn't think so. Unless Anne had learned that her uncle was dead. That was what she'd feared most, she'd told him once. That Uncle David had passed away, and her arduous journey was for nothing.

She'd need some comfort if that happened. With a lot of prayer, maybe he could convince her that all was not lost — that God had brought her clear out here for another purpose, namely to become Mrs. Daniel Adams.

"You really think she'd listen to me?"

Hector shrugged and reached for another nail. "Maybe not. But if you don't go, you'll always wonder, won't you?"

"I suppose I will."

21

"Well, go on then. Come back here with Anne or ready to forget her and work harder than you ever have before."

Dan hoped he could find the drive and energy Hector wanted him to show on his return, because he wasn't optimistic about his chances with Anne. Why had he ever thought she might change her mind if she spent more time with him? So far, all he'd managed to do was ride Star along near the wagons and drop Anne in a freezing cold river.

As each wagon lumbered off the ferry, he instructed the driver to take it down to Rob's camp and set up for the night. By the time they got all of them across, darkness was falling. Dan's muscles ached, his belly growled, and he feared he was catching cold. Dulcie met him and the Perkins family with her full coffeepot in hand and invited them to come share the Whistlers' campfire and have supper. The savory beef stew helped take off some of the cold and the gnawing in his midsection, but watching Anne flit about the edge of the circle of firelight kept his stomach from settling.

She didn't ignore him; nor did she pay him special attention. Dan felt smaller and smaller as the others talked around him, planning tomorrow's travel.

"We should make Eugene by mid-afternoon," Rob said.

"We sure do appreciate your help getting down here safe," Mr. Smith said.

Rob shrugged. "Like I told you, I was coming anyway."

Dan finished his meal and handed Anne his empty plate. "Will you ladies need any more water or firewood tonight?"

"I believe Rob's taken care of everything," she said.

He nodded. "Well, thank you for the meal. It was delicious."

"You're welcome, but Dulcie made it."

Anne walked away with the dishes, and he watched her, an ache in his heart. If she didn't find this missing uncle of hers, she'd be all alone in the world. He'd heard her father had died a year ago. Her journey and the search for her uncle probably eased her grief, but how would she feel when it was over? She'd need something else to think about, that was sure.

He walked past Rob's wagon toward where he'd picketed Star. The bulk of Anne's steamer trunks rose dark in the wagon bed, and he smiled. How could a woman have so much baggage? His mother had owned three dresses: one for everyday, one for town, and one for church. Anne must come from a wealthy family back in England — she and her friend Elise both. Fine quality people, with enough clothes to outfit an entire normal school.

He scowled and turned away from the wagon. Maybe Anne would stay with Elise and Eb at their ranch if things didn't go well with her uncle. She'd certainly made it clear that she didn't want to become Mrs. Daniel Adams.

They broke camp early the next morning. Anne helped Dulcie with breakfast while Rob and Dan helped the other men hitch their teams. The sooner they took to the road, the better. Anne's hands trembled as she measured out the coffee. She made herself stop hovering over the Whistlers and Dan while they ate, but she was eager to snatch their dishes so she could wash and pack them.

At last they set out southward once more. They rolled toward the hills all morning. When the sun was high overhead, Rob called an hour's stop for nooning, to let the livestock rest. Anne fidgeted until the wheels rolled onward once more.

They'd just reached the hamlet in the shadow of Skinner's Butte when a cry from one of the wagons caused Dulcie to halt her team. Anne looked back to see the men congregating about the Perkinses' wagon.

A couple of minutes later, Rob rode up on his horse.

"Their axle is busted clean through."

Dulcie sighed. "At least we're close. But I surely did hope we'd reach Mr. Stone's house before dark."

"Well, we can fix it, but we'll have to completely unload their wagon." Rob shook his head. "Miss Anne, I'm sorry I let these people talk me into letting them come along with us. I feel responsible to see them safely there."

"Couldn't Anne and I drive on ahead and inquire at the post office as to where her uncle lives?" Dulcie asked.

Rob hesitated. "I promised Miss Finster — that is, Mrs. Bentley — that I'd look after Anne. Besides, Eugene is a pretty tough place, I'm told. I'm not sure you ladies should go there without an escort."

"I hate to lose the daylight," Dulcie said. "Odd how her uncle didn't give her directions."

That very thing had troubled Anne, too. She'd written her letter carefully, telling Uncle David she had come all the way from England to find him. But on Elise's advice, she hadn't mentioned the main reason for her journey. *I'm told you've moved to a farm near the town of Eugene,* she'd written, *and I'd like to visit you. I haven't seen you since I was an infant, and I confess I can't remember you, but I'd be delighted to meet you again and catch you up on the family news. Please send your reply to me at General Delivery, Corvallis. Your loving niece, Anne Stone.*

His simple reply — *Come on to Eugene. David* — had thrilled her and troubled her at the same time. Her uncle was an intelligent, well-educated man. Why hadn't he offered to ride down the river fifty miles to see her? And why hadn't he at least written more than those five words? Was he shocked to hear she was nearby? Was he embarrassed at what she would find? No, if that were true, he could have simply ignored her note and let her think it had gone astray. She had spent eight months trying to find him, and now she was within a few miles of his residence. She felt she would suffocate if they didn't press onward and put an end to her anxiety.

"Let us go on," she said to Rob. "We're this close. We can head into town and wait for you at the post office."

Rob's face twitched and tensed and wriggled. At last he said, "What if I send Dan with you?"

"Yes," Dulcie said quickly. "Or send him with Anne in the wagon. You and I could catch up quickly on horseback, if he'll let me ride his Star."

"Hold on," Rob said. "I'll ask him."

He rode back to where the others had begun unloading the Perkins family's belongings.

"I hope Dan will go," Dulcie said. "You've waited long enough for this."

Anne tried to sit still and not let her face show her anxiety.

Dan cantered Star to where they waited. "Miss Anne, you want to go on ahead to town?"

"Yes, if you're willing, Daniel."

He nodded. "Mr. Whistler says if you want to ride, you can take Bailey. He'll drive Mrs. Whistler on in the wagon after they get the Perkinses squared away."

Anne looked to Dulcie. Would she be disappointed to be left behind while Anne completed her adventure?

"That makes sense," Dulcie said. "You have a riding habit in one of those steamer trunks, I dare say."

"Yes, I do," Anne said. "Would you mind horribly?"

"Of course not. Get your outfit, and I'll help Dan put my saddle on Bailey."

27

In less than ten minutes, Anne was ready to ride, though she had to call Dulcie behind the bushes to help fasten her bodice correctly. Even though she'd survived the half-year trek to Oregon, she still depended on another woman to help her dress. That bothered Anne. From now on, any clothing she purchased would close in the front, and she would learn to sew more than buttons if it bored her to tears. She settled the matching hat firmly on her head and secured it with two long hat pins. Soft leather gloves and a crop completed her costume.

Dulcie gathered the dress, shoes, and bonnet she had discarded. "Don't you look fine, Miss Anne."

"Why, thank you." Would the other women think she was putting on airs, donning a velvet habit for her entrance to Eugene? She decided not to make the rounds of the wagons to say good-bye. From a distance, they would have fewer details to criticize. She pulled Dulcie to her for a quick embrace. "Thank you for everything."

Dulcie waved a hand through the air. "I'll see you in an hour or two. Mind you stay close to Daniel."

"I will."

"Of course you will. And if you're going on to your uncle's before we get there, leave word for us, won't you? Rob thinks there's a boardinghouse in town, and we'll try to get lodging there tonight. If there isn't a decent place, leave us a note at the post office."

"That sounds like a good plan." Anne walked to where Dan held the two horses. "I'm ready."

Dan's eyes widened as he gazed at her, and his face went pink under his short beard. She hadn't considered the effect her change of attire would have on him. She'd worn the habit a couple of times during the wagon train journey, but she wasn't sure Dan had seen her in it.

She mounted quickly, before he could get ideas about helping her, and gathered the reins. "Shall we go?"

"Yes, ma'am. Rob says the town hasn't had a post office long, but there should be a sign up."

They rode along at a smart trot. Bailey behaved perfectly, and Star kept pace alongside, snorting occasionally. A hill rose sharply from the level ground before them, and at its feet she could see several substantial buildings. Anne's spirits rose. The golden sun shone on a wide, lush valley that promised abundance. Being mounted on a decent horse added a thrill of well-being.

She'd always loved to ride, and her father had kept a stable of excellent hunters at Stoneford.

"Do you ever hunt?" she asked on impulse.

Dan frowned. "Well, sure. Hector and I plan to go after elk once we get our house tight."

Anne realized her foolish mistake. Of course he hunted game — several times he'd gone out with hunting parties from the wagon train. How could she think he'd understand she meant riding to hounds? She said, "Of course. How silly of me. I wish you success." She looked ahead to the cluster of houses and businesses that lined the main thoroughfare of the town. "Do you see the post office?"

Dan surveyed the street and pointed. "There." They rode to the small board structure, and Dan dismounted and came around to help Anne down from Bailey's back. He tied her mount to the hitching rail and offered Anne his arm.

Two men were leaning on the counter inside, deep in conversation with the bearded man on the other side. When Anne and Daniel entered, they fell silent and straightened, watching them. Heat flooded Anne's cheeks as she walked forward.

"You the postmaster?" Dan asked.

"Yes, sir. Postmaster, county clerk, and attorney at law. Help you?"

Dan said, "We're trying to locate a man named David Stone. I understand he lives near here."

The postmaster nodded slowly. "There's a fellow by that name south of here. Eight or ten miles, I'd say."

"Does he come in regular for his mail?" Dan asked.

"Haven't seen him for a while. I'd have to ask my wife if he's been in lately. I've been real busy, and a lot of days she's in here to wait on folks."

Dan nodded. "Well, if it's not too much trouble, could you please give us directions to his house?"

Anne felt a new glimmer of hope as the postmaster replied. She and Dan walked out to their horses.

"We can get there and back before nightfall," Dan said.

Anne cast an anxious glance down the street. "No sign of Rob and the others yet."

"That must be the boardinghouse." Dan pointed across the dusty street and down a few buildings. "We'll leave word there and speak for rooms."

"I may want to stay at Uncle David's

house tonight," Anne said.

"That'll be fine, if things work out well. But we'd best reserve a place for you in case they don't."

They trotted along swiftly, mindful of the time. Anne made polite conversation so far as was necessary, but Dan was a quiet man, so their words were sparse. She felt sorry for him. He was obviously on edge. A muscle in his cheek twitched now and then, and he threw her frequent glances, part longing and part panic. She supposed he dreaded handing her over to Uncle David and returning to his farm alone. She wished she could soothe his heart, but she had no comfort that wouldn't encourage him to think things she didn't want him thinking.

Her muscles ached as Bailey trotted over the rutted road. Her six months on the trail had strengthened and hardened her, but she'd hardly ridden a horse at all — not since the trading post at Schwartzburg — and her spine now felt each jarring step Bailey took.

After half an hour, she took pity on Dan and threw out an innocuous prologue to conversation.

"I shall miss Elise sorely."

"Oh yes. I imagine you will."

She nodded. "We'd grown very close."

Dan rode in silence for the space of two minutes before he commented again. "I believe you said once that you'd been friends a long time."

"Yes. I've known Elise since I was born." Perhaps this line of talk wasn't so innocuous after all. Anne didn't care to have Dan know that Elise had been her employee — her lady's maid, to be exact. Elise had served her mother for many years, but for the last three, since her mother's death, Elise had been Anne's closest companion, chaperone, and advisor. "We were planning to take a little house together back in England if things didn't work out with Uncle David."

She glanced at Dan. Was she revealing too much? He looked pensive, and she knew he was a thinking man. She did miss having Elise along to discuss things with. Dulcie was a dear, but she was a new acquaintance, and her thoughts seemed to go no deeper than what Rob would like for supper. Rob adored her, it was plain to see, and Dulcie oozed kindness. But sometimes one liked to share one's deeper thoughts.

"And if they did work out? What did Miss Finster plan to do if everything went well? Before she met Eb, I mean."

"She'd have gone home — that is, back to England — with us," Anne said.

"And lived with you?"

"Oh yes." She almost added, "She's lived with my family more than twenty years," but decided that would require further explanations, and so she fell silent. The road had wound through a forest but now came out in open farmland. That was something she could safely discuss with Dan. "The soil seems very rich here."

"Yes." Dan's expression perked up a little as he looked over the fields they were passing. The dark brown earth had been plowed, planted, and harvested, by the look of it. "They say you can get forty bushels of wheat to an acre in this valley."

"That's good, I take it."

"That's very good."

"Then you and your brother should be happy here."

Dan smiled. "Hector will, anyway. He has a sweetheart back East. He hopes to bring her out here next year. But we have to get the house built and the farm producing first."

"Your brother has a sweetheart?" Anne stared at him in surprise. "I never had an inkling."

"He's pretty tight-lipped about it. She's a

34

schoolteacher. When he told her about his dream of owning a successful farm out here, she agreed to wait for him. Hector's strongly motivated to make the farm succeed, you might say."

"Well, yes." She eyed him thoughtfully. "You should be helping him."

Dan bit his upper lip but said nothing.

Anne looked away. Dan was counting on persuading her to marry him. She could feel it. To pursue that goal, he'd left his brother alone at their new farm. It would probably be kinder to state the truth baldly: she liked him, but she would never consent to marry him. Anne wanted a marriage based on something more than friendship. She wanted a love so deep she knew she couldn't be happy with any other man on earth. It wouldn't be fair to a man like Dan to marry him. He would be good to her, she was sure. He would provide for her to the best of his ability. If she lived on his farm, she would probably be able to see Elise several times a year. But she would never know what it was like to truly love a man.

"That must be the lane up there," Dan said.

Anne looked ahead and saw a road diverge from the more traveled way they followed. They turned the horses in, and she scanned the terrain as far as she could see. A few seconds later, she spotted a small, roughly framed, wooden house with several fenced enclosures around it. A few cattle grazed in one pen, and a thin roan horse trotted along the fence in another.

"Is this it?" she asked.

"I think so."

Anne frowned. The unpainted house looked run-down. She saw no evidence of a garden. A clothesline off to one side caught her eye.

"Dan?"

"What?"

She swallowed hard and pointed. On the clothesline, a man's shirt and trousers hung amid linens, a skirt, two aprons, and a petticoat.

"Oh." Dan glanced keenly at her. "Is he married?"

"That's what I'm wondering. He didn't say." At least no diapers or children's togs flapped in the breeze. "Maybe we've got the wrong house."

"Maybe," Dan said. "If so, whoever lives here should be able to tell us where his place is."

The horses trotted up to the front stoop and halted. Anne sat for a moment, gazing at the door. Dan dismounted and dropped

Star's reins. The roan in the paddock whinnied and leaned its head over the fence toward them. Bailey snuffled.

Dan walked around Star and reached up to help Anne down. She touched the ground lightly and stepped away from him immediately. Though she was loath to approach the house, she didn't want Dan to think she enjoyed his touch excessively.

She was almost to the steps when the door opened inward. A stocky man filled the doorway, appraising her. His damp, straw-colored hair looked as though it had recently been in close contact with a pair of dull scissors. His beard was trimmed unevenly to about an inch in length. His waist was bigger around than his chest, and a pair of black suspenders supported his gray trousers. His shirt was a coarse, linen-and-cotton weave.

His calculating look spread into a broad smile. "Anne? Is that you? Why, h'aint you growed into a pretty thing?"

Chapter 2

Anne gulped. How could this man be her uncle? Impossible.

She sucked in a deep breath. Though he repelled her, she must use her manners and greet him warmly. He was now her closest living relative. Or was he? Could there possibly be two men named David Stone in the territory? Perhaps this was all a mistake.

Her stomach plummeted at the thought, but she pasted on a smile.

"Hello. I'm searching for Mr. David Stone. Would you happen to know where he lives?"

He laughed, a big, noisy guffaw. "Why, sweetheart, you're lookin' at him." He moved down onto the next step, and Anne backed away, into the solid bulk of Dan Adams.

"Daniel," she gasped.

Dan touched her back only for an instant, and she took comfort from that reassuring pat. He stepped around her, between her and the stranger.

"Howdy. Are you Mr. Stone?"

"Yes, I am," the other man said. He held out a meaty hand. "I'm this little gal's uncle. And who might you be, mister?"

"My name is Daniel Adams."

The man's eyes narrowed to slits as they shook hands, as though he was trying to categorize his guest, but Dan didn't offer more information.

Anne recovered at least a portion of her poise and moved up next to Dan. "I'm sorry, but you're not at all what I expected." She eyed the man. He was several inches taller than she was but not nearly as tall as Daniel. She gazed at his fleshy face, his flinty eyes, and his slicked-back, badly barbered hair.

She longed to bring out the miniature portrait in her handbag, but an inner restraint told her not to. This man could not be the same one who posed for the portrait twenty years ago. Or could he?

"You wrote that you wanted to see me and give me some news," the man said. "Come on in."

Anne looked at Dan. He arched his eyebrows, seeking her opinion.

"Well, I . . ."

"Come on." The man started up the steps again, beckoning with his beefy arm. "Millie's got supper ready."

Anne swallowed hard and looked to Dan again. He held out his crooked arm. She took it and walked with him up the steps and into the little house.

Her eyes took a moment to adjust to the dim interior. The house appeared to be divided into two rooms, and they had entered the kitchen. A cookstove stood to the right, with a stovepipe reaching up and bending to meet the chimney. A rough wooden table stood in the middle of the floor, and a woman came past it with her hands extended in greeting.

"So you're little Anne." She smiled broadly and seized both Anne's hands. "Oh my, what a lovely young woman you are." She threw the man a reproachful glance. "David, you should have told me."

He shrugged. "Didn't know. This here's Millie."

Anne found it hard to rip her gaze away from him and appraise Millie. The woman's thick auburn hair hung loose about her shoulders, and she wore lip rouge. Beyond that, the dim lighting left her in mystery, but her gathered and flounced dress looked to be of decent quality, unlike the man's clothing.

"Is this your husband?" Millie asked.

"No," Anne said quickly. "Dan is just a friend. He offered to ride down here with me, since I didn't want to travel alone." She eyed the stocky man as she spoke, hoping to shame him at least a little for not offering to go to Corvallis for her, but he only smiled and nodded.

"Well, let's sit down, folks. You must be hungry. Millie's been keeping a pot of stew simmering all day. We thought you might get here this afternoon."

Millie hurried to a bank of curtained shelves on the far wall and pushed the calico curtain aside. "I only set up for three, but you're welcome to join us, Mr. Adams." She turned with a tin plate and a thick china mug in her hands.

"Let me help you," Anne said.

"Oh no, that's all right. Sit right down." Quickly Millie laid another place setting for Dan. "Just grab that little bench by the window, Mr. Adams."

The four of them sat down at the table, and Millie began ladling out portions of stew. No one mentioned giving thanks for the food, which Anne found unsettling. The Stones had always been God-fearing Anglicans. She glanced at Dan, and he gritted his teeth then said, "Would you mind if I said grace?"

Their host stared blankly at him, but Millie said, "Go right ahead."

Anne closed her eyes. She'd never heard Dan pray before, but his quiet words soothed her.

"Dear Lord, we thank You for a safe journey and for the food we are about to receive. Amen."

"Amen," Anne whispered. She opened her eyes. Millie stood with the ladle in her hand, watching Dan as though waiting for a cue to continue serving.

"So you had a good trip down here from Corvallis?" the man asked.

"Well enough," Dan said.

He looked at Anne. "And did you come all the way across the country, or did you sail?"

"We came by wagon train," she said.

"Is that right?" He shook his head. His drying hair tumbled willy-nilly down his forehead. "Rough trip. Isn't that right, Millie?"

"It's bad enough." She handed him a bowl of stew. "Pass those biscuits around, David."

The food was more palatable than Anne had dared hope, and she ate two biscuits with apple butter and a large bowl of beef stew.

"Your stew is delicious," she said to Millie. "Thank you so much for feeding us."

"Yes," Dan said. "Mighty fine meal, ma'am."

"Oh, it's nothing." But Millie's smile said it was something. "What was the family news you hinted at in your letter to David, Miss Stone?"

"Oh." Anne hesitated, trying to recall the exact wording of her letter. "I assumed Uncle David would want to catch up on the family's doings. You see, my father passed away last year, about this time."

"Oh, that's a shame," Millie said.

"Your father?" the man asked.

"Yes. Your brother. He was —" Anne cleared her throat, uncertain as to how to approach the subject. "Well, as you know, he was the eldest, and he was . . . considered the head of the family."

"Mm." Her host's eyes narrowed, but he said nothing more.

Millie reached over and patted her hand. "There now, you must be feeling kind of blue."

"Yes, I do miss Father." Anne blinked back the threat of tears. "And then there was Uncle John. We tried to write to you, but the letter came back unopened."

"Uncle John?" Millie prodded.

"My father's brother," Anne said. "He was between Father and David in age."

"Oh, what a shame." Millie turned to David. "You've lost two brothers. What an awful blow."

"Yes." He swallowed hard and stared down at his bowl. "Well now. I guess that means some . . . some changes in the family."

"Indeed it does." Anne watched his face, waiting for him to ask about the peerage or the estate. Instead, he lifted his mug. "Got any more coffee over there, Millie?"

"Of course." Millie jumped up. "Miss Stone? Mr. Adams? Would you like more?"

"No, thank you," Anne said, but Dan handed her his mug with a grateful smile.

While Millie poured the coffee, Anne studied David. His gray eyes and blocky frame told her this couldn't be her uncle, but could she be sure? His shaggy beard meant nothing; his once-blond hair could have darkened over time. He could have gained weight, but would he have completely lost his refined British accent? She doubted that, though twenty years among rough Americans might contribute to the effect. And if a man wanted to blend in with those around him, he might make a conscious effort to lose his accent. But still, a man like that would have to be intelligent. This one seemed a bit dense. And Uncle David had surely been intelligent. Elise had adored him, and she'd often said how bright and personable David was as a young man.

If this were the same man, why didn't he seem to care that his two brothers had died within the last year and a half? Why didn't he realize he was now in line for her father's title? He hadn't even asked if she had siblings or if John had married and produced an heir before his death — or even how he'd died, for that matter. It didn't seem natural. She sent up a silent prayer for wisdom.

She noted Millie watching her as she carried the cups to the table. The gleam in Millie's eyes sent a warning through Anne. This woman seemed to have the cleverness David lacked.

"There you go, Mr. Adams." Millie set Dan's cup down beside his plate, smiling down at him. "It surely was kind of you to bring Anne all this way to see her uncle. David tells me that when he last saw her, she was only a baby." She tossed David a sharp glance, and he nodded vigorously.

I did say that in my letter, Anne thought.

45

"Still in her cradle. Sweet little mite." David reached for his mug. As soon as Millie gave it to him, he took a sip, then drew back quickly from the cup and blew air rapidly in and out of his mouth. After a few seconds he swallowed with a grimace. "Hot."

"Of course it's hot." Millie's snarl softened to almost a purr as she turned back to the guests. "We're so sorry that your papa and his brother passed on. Now, tell me about the rest of the family."

"Oh. Well, my mother is gone as well. She . . ." Anne glanced at Dan, but he was no help. He watched her avidly, but he couldn't guess at her inner turmoil. Anne hoped the depth of her distress didn't show on her face.

"Aw, that's terrible," Millie said.

Anne gulped, hoping fervently that Millie was not her new aunt. "Thank you. It's been three years and more."

"And do you have brothers and sisters?" Millie asked.

"No."

"Oh, so you're all alone now. What a pity." Millie looked over at David, as though expecting him to say something.

"Sorry," David said. He worked his mouth for a moment, contorting his face. "Get me some water, Mill. I burnt my tongue."

Millie got up and went to her worktable, returning with another cup, this one filled with water. "So, Miss Stone, you made this journey all the way from England to Oregon to find David, or did you come for some other reason?" Millie asked.

"Well, I . . ." Anne hesitated. "There was the matter of . . ." She glanced at Dan. He didn't know the whole of her mission, and she wished she'd explained it all to him on the way. How could she get around this now without either lying or giving away too much? If this man was truly her uncle, he had a right to know his own situation. And yet, if he *was* her uncle, why hadn't he figured it out by himself? Her father had told her more than once that David had struck out for America because he was certain he'd never inherit — being the third son set you free from family responsibilities.

"Speak up, girl," Millie said with a smile that seemed to Anne a bit calculating. "We're all family here. Well, except Mr. Adams, that is."

Dan cleared his throat and looked at Anne. His cheeks reddened above his short beard.

"Oh, maybe that's only a matter of time." David guffawed. "Is that the way the wind blows?"

47

"No," Dan said. "I'm only a friend, as Miss Stone said."

"I see." David smiled knowingly and turned his attention back to Anne. "Go on then. What brought you thousands of miles to see me?"

Anne's stomach seemed to drop away. She clenched her hands in her lap. "When my father died — well, there's the matter of his estate —"

"His estate?" David reached for another biscuit. "Did he leave you much?"

"David, that's rude," Millie said.

"Well . . ." Anne gulped and looked helplessly at Dan.

"Perhaps that's a private matter," Dan suggested.

"Well, it would be, but . . . well, my income is separate from your inheritance. . . ."

David looked up from the biscuit he slathered with apple butter. "*My* inheritance?"

"David inherits something?" Millie asked.

Anne nodded.

Millie's smile blossomed. "Well, speak up. What does he inherit?"

CHAPTER 3

"You mean my brother left me something in his will?" David grinned at Anne. "Now, isn't that the nicest thing you ever heard?"

"What is it?" Millie asked. "Money?"

Anne shrank in her chair. "Well, uh . . ." She looked to Dan again, as though casting about for a lifeline. What did she expect him to do? He had no idea what was going on.

Of course, there was that incident on the wagon train, where Anne's hired man had stolen a letter from her luggage. Wasn't it a letter from her missing uncle? And did that have anything to do with all of this?

"I'm sure the family's lawyer will contact you about it, now that Miss Stone has found you," he said.

Anne's look of gratitude made all of the heartache he'd endured in the last six months worthwhile. She smiled and caught her breath.

"That's right, Uncle David. Our solicitor

tried to locate you in St. Louis —"

"St. Louie?"

"Yes," Anne said. "Your last letter to Father came from there."

"Oh, of course." David gave a little laugh. "Been a while since I was in St. Louie."

"Yes. More than ten years. We all wondered where you'd gone. If you were still alive, even." Anne stopped and pressed her lips together.

"Well, you've found him now," Millie said heartily. "So just what does this inheritance amount to?"

When Anne hesitated, Dan said, "I'm not sure she can tell you that, ma'am. Doesn't the lawyer have to send official notification or something?" He eyed Anne keenly, hoping she'd see that he was offering her a way out if she didn't want to disclose any further information.

Anne seized the opportunity. "That's right. I felt like traveling, so a friend and I decided to come to America and look you up." She smiled a little too brightly for the paleness of her face, Dan thought.

"This friend?" Millie gazed at Dan.

"Oh no. Not Daniel. It was Elise Finster. Do you remember Elise, Uncle David?"

"Hmm . . . Elise . . ." He frowned and shook his head. "Can't say as I do."

"She was my —" Anne faltered to a stop and swallowed hard. "She's a good friend. She sailed to New York with me, and we made the trip west together."

"Oh. So where is she now?" David sounded a little nervous, and he glanced toward the door as if more British people were about to invade his home.

"She stayed in Corvallis," Anne said. "But she'd be delighted to see you again, if you wish."

Dan noted that Anne didn't mention her friend's marriage. She seemed to have grown cagey and was trying to keep from letting go of any more information than was necessary now. Maybe this was the time to get her away and have a long talk.

He shifted, as though about to rise. "Well, this has been a pleasant visit, and I'm so glad I was able to help Anne find you. But if we wish to get back to Eugene before total dark, we need to be going."

"Eugene?" Millie asked, her dark eyebrows flying upward. "You can stay here. No need to ride all that way tonight."

"Oh no, we have friends expecting us," Anne said hastily.

Dan jumped up and pulled out her chair as she rose.

"Now, wait," David said. "This inheritance. What do I have to do to find out more?"

"Perhaps I can come back tomorrow." Anne threw Dan a worried glance. "I can't tell you figures or anything like that, but I can bring you the solicitor's address in England so you can write to him."

"You mean you ain't got it with you?" David asked.

"Why, I . . ."

"We left all our luggage with our friends," Dan said. He could hardly believe an English gentleman — even one who had been in America for twenty years — would address a lady in such a manner.

"That's right," Anne said. "In fact, I borrowed a horse from them so we could ride out here quickly. But we'll come back in the morning."

"I can't persuade you to stay?" Millie stepped close to Anne. "Honey, we can make you a bed near the stove just as cozy —"

"Oh no, thank you. We have rooms waiting for us in Eugene."

Millie's smile disappeared. "Fine. Let me get your things." She walked to the pegs where Dan's hat and Anne's jacket hung.

David was still gaping at Anne. "I certainly

didn't expect to inherit anything from your father."

Anne's eyes narrowed. "You didn't?"

"Well, no. Why should I?"

"As I explained earlier, Uncle John is also deceased. He had no heirs."

"That was mighty nice of him, but how come you don't get it all?"

Anne drew in a deep breath but seemed unable to speak.

Millie came over and held out Dan's hat. Turning to Anne, she offered the velvet jacket of her habit. "Did your pa name David in his will and cut you out or what?"

Anne made a strangled sound.

"Nothing like that, I assure you," Dan said, taking Anne's jacket. He held it for her, determined to remove her from the house as swiftly as possible. "We promised our friends we'd get back before night, so we must go."

"Well, we'll be looking for you in the morning." Millie's voice had taken on a hard edge.

"Yeah, bring them papers with you. Address and such." David walked to the door with them and opened it.

Dusk had fallen over the valley. Dan led Anne to the horses and tightened Bailey's saddle cinch. As he untied the horse and turned the gelding toward Anne, her uncle followed them down the steps and grasped Anne's sleeve.

"There's more to this than you're saying, gal."

"Let go of me."

Anne's icy voice spurred Dan to action. He stepped up beside her and glared at her uncle. "Stand back, Stone. We'll bring everything necessary in the morning."

David glowered at him. "Make sure you do."

They cantered out of the dooryard and northward toward Eugene. Neither spoke until they'd gone nearly a mile. Anne slowed Bailey, and Dan let Star drop into a trot, too.

"Dan, I must apologize to you."

"Whatever for?" he asked. "Seems to me your uncle and aunt are the ones who need to apologize."

"I should have told you everything before we set out for this place. I deeply regret not doing so."

Dan's face softened. "Miss Anne, you have no obligation to me whatsoever."

She turned forward for a moment while she tried to collect herself. Her face burned. "That may have been true until today, but I owe you much for what you did in there."

Dan rode in silence for a moment, then said, "I'm glad I was along."

"So am I!" She looked at him in the twilight. "Daniel Adams, I can't imagine what would have become of me if I hadn't had you to lean on. At first, I thought it was just me. I was disappointed that my uncle wasn't all I'd expected him to be. Not just his appearance — though I'd imagined him to be taller, fairer, and more . . . shall we say, more fit? And his eyes. In the portraits we have of him, his eyes are quite blue."

"You might say they were blue," Dan said pensively. "Sort of grayish blue."

"Yes. Not at all the vivid blue in the paintings. I told myself, that is the painter's fancy. But I knew it wasn't. You see, my father's eyes were blue, and Uncle John's as well. At Stoneford there's a portrait of the three brothers. They sat for it when David was fourteen. And his eyes are the same shade as Father's and John's."

"Your eyes are brown," Dan pointed out.

"True. They say I favor my mother, which is a great compliment. Her hair was a rich brunette, and her eyes brown." Anne sighed. Now was not the time to get sidetracked in her memories. "But this man! He claims to be my uncle, but he can't be. His manner is vulgar, and his speech — what can I say? No Englishman of gentle birth would so forsake the language. It's not as though he hiked about the wilderness with trappers for twenty years. He ran a respectable business in St. Louis and then in Oregon City. People recalled his British accent."

Dan nodded soberly. "You believe this fellow is an impostor."

"Yes." Relieved to have said it, Anne huffed out a deep breath. "I see no other explanation. Add to that the fact that he knew nothing of the family's matters. He didn't ask after any family members, and he didn't seem to know the first thing about . . . well, about anything I hadn't put in my letter or mentioned after we arrived."

"I see what you mean. And that woman — she's a sly one."

"Isn't she?" Anne shuddered. "I can't bear to think of her presiding at Stoneford."

"This . . . Stoneford," Dan said. "That's your home in England?"

"Yes." She looked down at her hands, grasping Bailey's reins. The well-trained horse kept up his trot without urging from her. She'd given no thought to guiding him for the last mile. "Dan, I should have explained my family's situation to you. But you see, Elise and I had agreed before we left New York that it was best to keep it quiet. Other people didn't look at me the same way if they knew. . . ."

"It's all right," Dan said. "I believe in privacy."

"Yes, and I appreciate that. This wasn't really a secret, but it seemed more effective not to shout it about — sort of like your brother's fiancée. I'm sure if Hector had felt anyone needed to know, he'd have told them."

"Certainly he would."

Anne nodded. "So I'm telling you. My uncle David — whether he is this man or not — and I highly doubt that he is —" She hesitated, knowing their relationship would change forever when she uttered her next few words.

"Yes?" Dan said gently.

"He inherits everything — Stoneford and all its lands, the family fortune, and the title."

"Title?"

Dan's frown for some reason tugged at her heart like an infant's cry. He was so innocent, so guileless.

She swallowed hard and forced herself to say it. "My father was the earl of Stoneford. The title and the estate are passed down to male heirs only under British law. I, being a female, do not inherit."

"I . . . see."

Darkness had cloaked them so that Anne could still see his face, but indistinctly. What was he thinking?

"I had no brothers," she added.

"So your father's brothers are next in line."

"Exactly. Uncle John was next. Unfortunately, he died in battle unmarried. Uncle David had no way of knowing that. But it's up to him now, him and his sons — if he has any." She thought of the man they'd just left at the little farmhouse and shivered again.

"If that man is your uncle, I'll eat my hat," Dan said.

She smiled at that. "Thank you! For that and so much else you've done today."

"I could see how uncomfortable you were, and I knew something wasn't right. At first I wondered how you could have such a crude relative. It didn't take me long to see that you wondered the same thing and were having doubts about coming here."

Anne nodded. "That's when I decided not to tell him about the earldom or give him details about how to claim his inheritance. I wish I hadn't said a word about it, but I had, so it's too late. I'll have to go back tomorrow."

"We'll tell Rob everything. He'll go with us."

"Yes." That thought buoyed her. "He's a very smart man, and he reads people well. I've another card to play, too."

"Oh?" Dan asked.

"You know I had some dealings with the marshal in Oregon City."

"Yes. That fellow Peterson was trying to hunt down your uncle. I'm beginning to understand why."

"My uncle — my real uncle, I should say — is worth a lot of money to some people. What worries me most is that to some he's worth more dead than alive."

Dan pulled back on Star's reins. Both horses stopped, and Dan peered at her in the darkness. "Is there another brother?"

"No. But there is a cousin. He can't inherit unless David is proven dead."

Dan let out a deep sigh. "Now it makes sense. Anne, I'm so sorry."

"So am I."

He nudged his horse closer to hers. "We'd best hurry back to Eugene."

"I agree. As I was about to tell you, the marshal has a deputy there. Perhaps he would come out here with us and Rob tomorrow. If we act cleverly, I'm sure we can expose this charlatan."

"Yes, but we need to make sure before we leave town tomorrow that the person who owns this farm is really your uncle. There could be two David Stones."

"Yes, there is that."

"Well, let's get a move on. I don't like to have you out here in the open like this, now that I know your story."

Anne chuckled. "I'm in no danger. And I have a rather large, armed escort along."

"Well thank you, ma'am," Dan said, "but I disagree. You are the messenger who wants to alert your uncle to his new position and wealth. Remember Peterson? There may be someone else out there who would like you to give up the search."

CHAPTER 4

The boarders had long since eaten their supper when Anne and Daniel rode into Eugene, but the landlady had graciously set out coffee, crackers, cheese, and cookies for them and the Whistlers in her parlor. Dulcie's reaction to Anne's story was as Dan would have expected — she gathered Anne to her bosom and assured her that Rob would get to the bottom of things. Dan fully anticipated Rob to continue wearing his captain's persona, willing to take charge and face down the imposter.

Rob, however, surprised him by going out immediately to fetch the deputy marshal. While he was gone, Dulcie told them of how they'd at last untangled themselves from the pioneer families. Rob had spent a good half hour at the post office, talking to Eugene Skinner, the postmaster and founder of the city. One of their numerous topics had been where Rob could locate the deputy marshal for Miss Stone, so that she could check in with him as Marshal Nesmith had instructed her in Oregon City.

Rob returned with "Bank" Raynor in tow. The deputy stood only a couple of inches taller than Anne, and thin as a sapling, but his face — the part that showed above his gray-streaked beard — looked like a tanned hide. As he entered the parlor, he snatched off a disreputable-looking felt hat. He wore tall boots over whipcord breeches. A long hunting shirt hung down below his buckskin jacket. A sheathed hunting knife was mounted on his rawhide belt, and he wore a long-barreled pistol strapped to his side. Dan decided that Raynor was the man to have beside him if he ever came face-to-face with a grizzly.

After the introductions, Rob set a chair for the deputy strategically near the food, the fire, and Anne. It seemed prudent to Dan to keep in the background, so he eased around to the corner, where he leaned against the wall and listened to the conversation, but contributed only when asked a question.

Patiently, Anne told her story again, from the death of the earl back in England to the strange couple they'd found living at the farm south of Eugene City.

When she'd finished, Bank Raynor sat in silence for a long minute, gazing at her face. He'd downed a great quantity of cheese, at least half-a-dozen cookies, and two cups of coffee. Dan wondered if he was feeling sluggish, lulled by the warmth of the fire and Anne's musical voice.

"So, what should I call you?" he asked at last. "Are you 'your ladyship,' or 'countess,' or what?"

Anne smiled at him. "Miss Stone is fine, sir."

"And you can call me Bank."

"All right."

Bank moved slightly, making the smallest gesture with his coffee cup, and Dulcie jumped to refill it.

"So, Miss Stone, you have several indications that the man who claims to be your uncle is not really your uncle."

"That's right," Anne said.

"Is there any possibility that this is all a misunderstanding — that this is another individual with the same name? Stone is not that uncommon."

"I thought of that." Anne clasped her hands on her knees and leaned toward the deputy. Her earnest, beautiful face couldn't help but win him over, Dan thought. "If it were a mistake, surely he would have protested when he read my letter, saying I had arrived from England. Wouldn't he have written back asking questions? Suppose this other David Stone coincidentally had a niece in England, too. Wouldn't he balk when I told him his two brothers had died? I don't know as I mentioned my father's given name, Richard, to him, but I surely told him about my uncle John's death. I also spoke of my mother, and I mentioned a longtime family servant by name. Why didn't he raise questions?"

Bank shot a glance into the corner, surprising Dan. He'd almost felt invisible. As the deputy addressed him, he straightened his shoulders.

"You agree with that, Adams?"

"Yes, sir. Miss Anne mentioned several things that would cause a complete stranger — one with any integrity, that is — to say, 'Hold on, miss, you must have made a mistake.' But this fellow never did that. And he kept trying to draw more information out of her."

Anne nodded. "His companion, too. Millie. She seemed especially anxious to learn more about my family and my father's will. I wish I'd never mentioned that, but on our arrival I was so confused I wasn't sure how to proceed. As it was, I at least had the presence of mind not to give them any details about the estate or Uncle David's inheritance. But I did let fall that an inheritance from my father would come to him. I shouldn't have done that, but there it is. I was still sorting the facts and realizing that this man knew nothing about how English inheritance law works."

Bank nodded, stroking his beard. "And you first made contact with this man when?"

"Last week. I wrote a brief letter from Corvallis as soon as we arrived overland."

"Right. But you didn't tell him in the letter about the earl dying or his inheritance."

"No, sir," Anne replied. "I wanted to break it to him in person. And so far as I know, he still doesn't realize that my father was an earl."

Dan folded his arms and leaned back into the corner again. He was beat, and Anne had dark shadows beneath her expressive brown eyes. He hadn't taken the time yet to work out the implications of all he'd learned that afternoon. The woman he loved was a true aristocrat. He'd always known Anne was quality, but the daughter of an earl! How could he ever have imagined she might accept his suit? He shook his head. He and Hector would have a good laugh someday over his audacity, but right now his heart ached too painfully for him to see it as humorous. Maybe one day, Uncle Dan would take his brother's kiddies on his knees when they asked him why he was still a bachelor and tell them the tale of "The Lady and the Farmer."

Rob set his coffee cup on the side table. "Sure wish I'd known about this before I met Mr. Skinner yesterday. He seemed to know who Mr. Stone was and think well of him. Said he last came in for his mail a few weeks ago." He shrugged. "Miss Anne, maybe there's a way you could test this fellow to find out for sure how much he knows."

Bank nodded. "I was thinking the same thing. Trap him somehow into showing he's no kin to you."

Anne opened her handbag and reached into it. "I agree. I'd like to show you the portrait I have of Uncle David. I've shown it to Mr. Whistler before, but I don't believe Mrs. Whistler or Mr. Adams has seen it." She took out the framed miniature she'd carried from England to Oregon, opened the case, and passed it to Bank. "He was the youngest of the three brothers. Of course I don't personally remember him, since he left England while I was a baby, but I'm told this is a good likeness of him at the age of twenty — that is, about twenty years ago."

Bank studied the picture and handed it to Dulcie.

"Oh, he's a gorgeous boy," Dulcie said. "Those eyes! And lashes as long as a girl's." She passed the miniature to Daniel.

He looked down at it. The blond young man in the portrait was indeed handsome, with wavy locks and vivid blue eyes. Any young woman would swoon over him. Dan glanced over at Anne and met her gaze. "He's as unlike the man we met today as a bluebird from a blue jay."

Anne smiled. "Yes. Alike in a few general characteristics, but very different. I might have accepted that he'd gained weight and coarsened his looks through drink and poor food, but his manner of speech and gaps in knowledge clinched it for me. He's not my uncle."

Dan passed the portrait back to her and resumed his place in the corner.

"Well, an obvious way to trick him would be to ask if he remembers something and make the details wrong," Rob said. "If he agrees with you, he's lying."

Anne nodded. "Perhaps we can plan such a snare." She drew two envelopes from her handbag. "I also have the last letter my father received from him ten years ago. It's quite worn and tattered, I fear, but I ask you to put it next to this brief note I received in Corvallis and tell me whether the same person could possibly have written the two."

Bank carefully extracted the first letter and glanced at the flowing script that went on for two full pages.

"Is that the same one that was stolen from your luggage on the wagon train?" Rob asked.

"Yes, and I'm extremely thankful that you and the other men on the train were able to recover it for me."

Bank opened the second letter and grunted. After a moment, he held the two envelopes side by side. "Interesting. Not only are these addressed in different hands, but I submit that the person who addressed this second one is not the person who wrote the note inside it."

"I agree with you again," Anne said with a smile. "My guess is that David — or whatever his name really is — wrote the note, and Millie addressed it for him."

Bank passed the two letters to Dan, and he compared the handwriting, especially that on the two envelopes. "Something tells me that reading and writing are not his long suit."

"No. But my uncle David was an avid reader. In that letter to my father, he mentioned two books he had recently read." Anne placed the miniature back in her purse. "I should have seen it earlier. In fact, I did see it — or at least I saw clues that made me uneasy. But I didn't want to believe I was being deceived. I've looked so long and hard for him that I wanted it to be true. I wanted my search to have finally come to an end."

"Of course," Dulcie said. She reached over and patted Anne's shoulder. "I'm so sorry, my dear."

"Don't worry," Rob said. "We'll get the truth out of that scoundrel tomorrow."

Dan wondered whether they would. Maybe they could prove the man at Stone's farm was an imposter, but would that bring them any closer to finding Anne's uncle?

Anne rode in the wagon the next day, with Dan driving. Rob and Bank rode their horses just ahead of them. Much to Dulcie's chagrin, Rob had insisted she stay in Eugene City and make the acquaintance of Mrs. Skinner.

"We don't know what this fella will do

69

when we confront him," he pointed out. "We know he's slippery. I figure having to protect Miss Anne is a big enough worry for the three of us, without you being there, too. And if it comes down to needing support in this town, we'll need the Skinners on our side."

Dulcie huffed and rolled her eyes, but in the end she persuaded the landlady to prepare a small cake for her to carry to the Skinner house after the others set out.

Anne rode first to the county courthouse, at Rob's suggestion. They all hoped the people and records there could shed some light on the situation. The clerk behind the desk produced a copy of the deed to Anne's uncle's property.

"I remember him," the clerk said. "Tall, fair man with a British accent."

"Yes," Anne said, delighted to hear this description that coincided with her expectations.

"You should talk to Mr. Skinner. He's the county clerk. I'm just an underling. He'll know more about it, I daresay."

"I was hoping Mr. Skinner would be here today," Bank said. "Would he be over at the post office?"

"He might. Some days he's off on business."

Bank nodded. "Come, Miss Stone, we can stop in at the post office. I doubt Mr. Skinner can take the time to ride out there with us, but it would be good to at least get his take on this."

Dan went into the post office and came out frowning. "He's gone for the day. Rode up the valley — something to do with cattle."

"All right then, we'll proceed as we planned last night," Bank said. "You ready, Miss Stone?"

"Yes." Anne didn't really feel ready to confront the man at Uncle David's farm again, but she was glad she had three stouthearted gentlemen with her this time.

A low ceiling above them threatened rain as they rode southward. Anne wore her woolen overcoat, warm wool gloves, and a floppy velvet bonnet that covered her ears. Dan turned up his collar and settled his hat low on his head. He had leather gloves, but Anne thought he might do well with a soft muffler. Perhaps she would knit him one to show her appreciation for his support in this venture. Elise had taught her to knit, and while she couldn't tackle anything with size yet, a muffler should be within her ability.

They arrived at the small house as the first raindrops splashed down. Dan helped Anne down from the wagon. Rob eyed the nearby barn and dismounted.

"Wonder if we can put the horses under cover."

"Let's see what we get for a reception," Bank said.

They walked to the door, and Dan knocked. A moment later, Millie opened it. She looked at him and Anne, then past them to Rob and the marshal. Her eyes flared, but she stood back and opened the door wider, her expression neutral.

"Good morning. I see you've brought some friends."

"Yes." Anne walked into the house and spotted David standing near the table.

His face clouded as the men entered behind her. "What's this?"

"Hello." Anne smiled. "I hope you don't mind. I brought along my dear friend Rob Whistler. I mentioned him to you yesterday." She gestured toward Rob. "And this is Deputy Marshal Bank Raynor."

"Marshal?" David scowled at Bank, then looked back at Anne. "What did you bring him for?"

Bank stepped forward. "My boss — him being Marshal Nesmith, up in Oregon City — asked me to ride out here with Miss Stone and make sure everything went all right. Seems she had a little trouble up north of here when she tried to find you."

"Is that right?" David looked back to Anne. "You didn't tell me."

Bank said, "Well, somebody didn't want her to find her uncle. That fella's in jail now, but the marshal asked me to see that there weren't any shenanigans today."

David stared at him uncertainly.

Millie stepped forward. "Well, isn't that thoughtful of you? We had no idea Anne had so much trouble. Won't you all sit down? I think we have enough seats. Let me see. . . ."

A few minutes later, Anne and Millie were seated at the table with David and Bank, while Rob and Dan stood back to listen.

"Now, Mr. Stone," Bank began, "it seems you've been named as an heir in the will of Miss Stone's father. You can understand why we want to be sure you're the right man before she gives the information on how to claim that inheritance."

"Well, uh, sure." David looked to Millie, but she said nothing.

"So, I have here some information . . ." Bank took a slip of paper from the pocket of his hunting shirt. On it, Anne had written a few facts about her family the evening before. "Now, can you just confirm for me, please, your date and place of birth?"

"Uh . . ." David swiveled his head and again looked at Millie.

She gave a slight nod without changing the tight set of her mouth.

"Let's see . . . I was born . . . uh, that would be May 16, 1824."

As he spoke, Anne watched Millie. She closed her eyes briefly but otherwise didn't move. Anne knew the date was off by nearly ten years but didn't speak up.

"And whereabouts was that?" Bank asked.

"Oh, in England," David said more confidently.

"Where in England?"

"Mm, outside of London."

"Could you name a town, sir? Or a county at least?"

"Uh . . . it's been a long time. I'm not sure I remember."

Bank grunted and looked down at the paper. "And could you name your four siblings for me?"

"Huh?" David stared at him blankly.

"Brothers and sisters," Millie said. "He wants to know the names of your brothers and sisters."

"Oh." David ran a hand through his beard. "Well, uh, there was me and . . . me and Anne's father, and . . . hmm . . . well, there was John."

His gaze darted to Millie and then to Anne.

Anne tried to smile encouragingly.

"Uh, Millie, can you get me some coffee?" David asked.

"Certainly." Millie hurried to the stove and then bustled about between the cupboard and the table.

Anne rose. "May I help you, Millie?"

"Uh, sure. There's two more cups there. See if the other gents want coffee, would you?"

A few minutes later, David, Bank, and Rob sipped their coffee. Anne caught Dan's gaze as she resumed her seat. Dan nodded soberly.

"Well, then," Millie said, "maybe we can get on with the paperwork now. Is there something for David to sign?"

"Not just yet," Bank said. "Mr. Stone, it appears you don't know much about your family."

"Well, now, that's a fact." David smiled sheepishly. "You know, it's been a long time since I saw any of 'em."

"But still," Bank said. "You ought to know when you was born. Any man should know that."

"What'd I say?" David asked. "Don't tell me I gave you the date wrong."

"You certainly did."

"Well, what do you have? Maybe somebody copied it wrong."

Bank scowled at him. "I don't think so, but if you can tell me your mother's name —"

Millie shoved her chair back. "This is ridiculous. David's scatterbrained. So what? Does that mean he can't have what's rightfully his?"

"Not at all," Bank said. "I'm just not sure anything's rightfully his."

"Why, you!" Millie stood shaking and glowering at Bank. "It's not his fault that he's stupid."

"That's right," David said. "That old dun mare of mine kicked me in the head last fall. I can't remember half of nothing since then."

Anne managed to keep a straight face, but Bank let out a guffaw, and Rob barked a little laugh as well.

"Is that right, ma'am?" Bank asked Millie. "Did he take a kick to the head recently?"

Millie hiked her chin up. "Yes, he did. If I hadn't nursed him back to health, Miss Stone here wouldn't have an uncle to her name." She turned a malevolent glare on Anne.

"Well, then," Rob said with a deferential

glance at Bank, "perhaps you could answer a few questions, ma'am. Maybe you can tell us the name of your mother-in-law."

"Well . . ." Millie's mouth twitched.

"Her mother-in-law?" David said.

"Yes, I asked your wife if she could tell me your mother's name," Rob said.

"She's not my wife," David said with an injured air.

"Oh, pardon me," Rob said.

Millie's face had gone crimson, though with mortification or rage, Anne couldn't tell.

"And just what is your relationship to this gentleman?" Bank asked.

"I don't see that that's any of your business," Millie replied.

Rob smiled apologetically. "So you can't help him with the necessary information? That's too bad, ma'am, because if he really is entitled to something, it'd be a shame if he couldn't claim it."

Millie didn't speak, but her face shivered and squirmed until Anne thought she would explode.

"Well then, I guess it's time for us to hit the road," Rob said. He stood and pulled out Anne's chair for her.

Anne rose and cleared her throat. "Well, I, uh . . . I guess we'll be going." This was where she would ordinarily thank her hostess and assure her that meeting her had been a pleasure. For once in her life, Anne's manners didn't help her.

Dan held up her coat. "Come on, Miss Anne."

Bank rose, turned, and took a step toward David until their noses were only inches apart. "I don't suppose you want to tell us where the real David Stone is — the gentleman who owns this property?"

"I own it," their host said.

"Oh really? Can you show us a deed?"

"Well, uh . . ."

"You'd have to go to the county courthouse for that," Millie said. "He doesn't keep it in the house."

"Funny thing," Bank said. "We were there this morning. We saw the deed on file. And the man who owns this land was able to give them proof of his identity." He stretched up into David's face. "And he isn't you." He drew his pistol and poked it into the man's ribs. "You want to tell me who you really are?"

CHAPTER 5

"He's David Stone." Millie's voice was like granite.

"Really?" Bank didn't bother to look her way but kept staring into the man's eyes. "Ma'am, did you know it's a crime to abet a criminal?" He prodded their host. "Put your hands up. I'm taking you back to town."

Slowly the man raised his hands. "I didn't do anything. Millie —"

"As far as I know, his name is David Stone," she said. "I haven't been here that long, but that's the only name I know him by."

"Millie —"

"Don't talk," she snarled. "Are you completely daft? If you want to go to prison, go, but you're not taking me with you." She strode to the door, snagging a shawl from a peg on her way out.

The door slammed shut behind her.

"You want me to stop her?" Dan asked.

"Not unless she's stealing one of our horses," Bank said.

Dan hurried outside, and Rob followed.

"Miss Stone," the deputy said, "I'm going to truss this fella up and put him in the back of the wagon. That all right with you? If you'd rather not ride with him, you can take my nag."

Anne looked down at her full-skirted traveling dress. She hadn't brought Dulcie's sidesaddle along today. "I'll be fine in the wagon, so long as you search him first for weapons."

"No fear."

Anne nodded and staggered out the door. Her legs felt like rubber. Dan met her on the steps and offered his arm.

"Where is she?" Anne asked.

"She went to the barn. Rob's keeping an eye on her."

"Mr. Raynor plans to take the man back to Eugene."

"Fine by me." Dan went with her to the wagon and gave her a hand up.

The barn door opened, and Millie rode out on a chestnut horse. She cantered toward the road without looking their way.

A few minutes later, they set out with Dan driving and the man who claimed to be David Stone tied up in the back. Bank and Rob rode close behind them, watching the prisoner every step of the way.

As they drove, Anne's mind whirled. Had she set out on a fool's errand last spring? She remembered the tip Elise had received in St. Louis that had sent them across the plains in Rob's wagon train. Had they chased a false clue all year long? They'd questioned hundreds of people, inquiring for David Stone. With persistence, they'd located a few who remembered an Englishman — the accent had made him stand out. People remembered that and his genteel manners. Obviously this was not the man to whom they'd referred. Maybe he really was named David Stone, but she doubted it. And where was her uncle?

She backtracked in her mind. Where had they lost the real David's trail?

"Oregon City," she said softly.

Dan looked over at her. "What?"

"People in Oregon City knew my uncle. Two years ago, he was there, and he had the British accent and the refined manners. Those who knew him by sight looked at the miniature and said it was him. That's where we lost the trail."

"How do you figure?" Dan asked.

"Someone told us David had bought some

land near Eugene. I wrote to him in care of general delivery at the Eugene City Post Office. And I got back the note from this man and Millie. So was my uncle never here?"

"I'm pretty sure he was," Dan said. "From what the county clerk told us, the man who registered the deed to that land was the genuine article."

She sighed. "You're right. I was forgetting that. But if Uncle David bought the property, where is he now?"

"Maybe the marshal can get more out of the impostor when he's got him in the jail. Without Millie around to prompt him, he might actually say something relevant."

"True. Perhaps I should make another list of questions — like how long has this fellow been at the farm? And does he claim to own it outright? If so, how did he pay for it? We know Uncle David had means. He'd sold his business in Oregon City."

"And Mr. Skinner told Rob he knew Mr. Stone. I'm sure Bank can get Skinner to take a look at the prisoner once we get back to Eugene. That should settle it."

Dan had such a practical mind. That was a comfort. Anne settled more comfortably on the wagon seat. If she didn't look behind her on the way to town, she might be able to forget that they were transporting a prisoner who'd tried to claim her uncle's inheritance.

Millie Evans waited near the river for a good hour. Shouldn't take them longer than that to clear out. She let the bony mare graze and thought about her prospects.

If they'd left Sam alone, things would be fine. If they'd arrested him, she'd have to fend for herself — nothing new. But she'd want to get her stuff out of the house if she could and avail herself of any plunder she could carry. The rain had stopped, but not until she was thoroughly wet. She'd risk building a fire in the farm kitchen's stove and dry out.

When she judged enough time had passed, she put the bridle back on the mare and headed by farm lanes and wooded paths toward the Stone farm. She approached from the side and sat watching for a long time from beyond the corral before moving closer. The wagon and team were gone, and no saddle horses stood in the yard. Unless they'd hidden their mounts in the barn, the marshal and the rest were gone.

The cattle still grazed in the pasture. She'd expected Sam's horse to be missing, but the skinny blue roan cropped grass alongside the steers. They must have hauled

Sam off in the wagon, she decided. That wasn't good. Not that she cared — much. But she could use his roan for a pack horse.

She approached the back door of the house cautiously, not seeing any flicker of movement in the one window on that side. The stillness was creepy. She dismounted and hitched the mare securely. All she needed was to have her horse light out on her.

The quiet of the house felt even eerier than that of the barnyard. She checked both rooms to be sure. She wouldn't dare sleep here. The marshal might come back. He would probably send someone to tend the livestock today or in the morning. He wouldn't leave the cattle there for someone to steal. Or, if he was that stupid, Miss Stone would do something about it. She was probably the tenderhearted type that would hand-feed an orphaned bear cub until it got big and killed her. And anyway, she'd no doubt lay claim to all of David Stone's property in the name of protecting the family's belongings.

Just how extensive were they, anyway? That mysterious estate in England must be worth a lot, or his niece wouldn't have come halfway around the world to tell David he'd inherited it. Too bad there wasn't a way to find out.

In the bedroom, she grabbed her extra dress and petticoat and her heavy winter coat off the pegs on the wall and emptied the dresser drawers into a sack. Too bad the little plan she and Sam had cooked up hadn't worked out. He'd invited her to come cook for him when his rich boss went off into the mountains. Millie had conceived an idea that when Stone returned, she might convince him to keep her around for more than her cooking. He obviously had money. He had big plans for this farm and the improvements he'd make in the spring. Why shouldn't she be part of the plans?

Now all that was out of the question. She went back into the main room and looked around. Her gaze fell on the small desk against the wall. She went over and pulled out a handful of papers. She'd seen them all before — who could live in another person's house for a month and not take a look at the few papers in it?

Stone hadn't left anything valuable in the house, but maybe there was something that would tell her where he'd gone. She threw the mail Sam had picked up down on the desktop. She'd already read the two letters — one from some store in Oregon City and the fateful letter from his niece. Of course, they weren't supposed to open them. Sam wasn't even supposed to get them from the post office, but Millie had envisioned the possibility of learning something useful if they did. And so it had seemed.

She'd prodded Sam into answering Anne Stone's letter — and a fat lot of good it had done them. She'd figured they could trick the girl into giving her "uncle" a loan at the least. But instead of taking easy pickings from the rich man's niece, they'd gotten a posse.

Ah, there it was. From the papers, she plucked a note from an outfitter in Scottsburg. *The supplies you requested will be ready when you arrive in late September.* So Scottsburg was the jumping-off place for David Stone's new property. She could go there and pick up his trail, with or without Sam.

She put the papers back in the desk's pigeonhole and hurried to the kitchen cupboard. A couple of empty flour sacks lay folded on the bottom shelf, and she grabbed one and began filling it with foodstuffs. No sense leaving good food here. After packing two sacks with supplies, she walked slowly about the room, looking at the furnishings with fresh eyes. What would help her along the way? Stone had left Sam well provisioned but had only left him a couple of dollars for emergency cash. That was long gone.

She picked up the small, decorative lantern from the desk. It had always appealed to her. If she didn't find it useful, she could sell it. She also pocketed a pen that looked like it was made of silver and a couple of sheets of paper, which she folded up neatly. One just never knew what one would need.

An afterthought sent her back to the kitchen shelves. She added a tinderbox and a few candle stubs to her stash, along with a tin cup, a plate, a fork, two knives, a spoon, and a small kettle.

Did she dare spend the night in the barn? She could leave her horse saddled in case a fast getaway became necessary. And she'd have the bundles ready to strap to the roan's saddle in the morning. She'd better pack some oats for the horses, too. In some ways, she hoped Sam would get loose and come back. In other ways, she might do better without him. She reached for a second cup and stopped. She'd worry about Sam Hastings if and when he showed his face.

"You let him go?" Dan stared incredulously at the marshal. "I don't understand."

Bank sighed and polished the deputy

marshal's star on his hunting shirt with his cuff. "I didn't have enough evidence."

"He was impersonating another man."

"Got no proof."

Dan eyed him critically. "Last night you said all that about the county clerk knowing the real David Stone."

"Well yes, there is that." Bank ambled to the small stove that heated the room he claimed as his official office and the attached cell. He picked a tin cup off a shelf and filled it with coffee. "I guess what I should have said was we've got no proof that the man I arrested wasn't also named David Stone."

Dan huffed out a breath. "So now he'll go back to Mr. Stone's house and squat there? Miss Anne has no recourse?"

"Well, no, I told him he can't do that. See, Mr. Skinner came by this morning. He knew right away that this wasn't Miss Stone's uncle — that is, the man who owns the property. Don't know if you realized it, but Eugene Skinner's a lawyer."

"I think he mentioned it the other day."

Bank scratched his chin through his beard. "Yeah, well, he's a lot of things, and that's one of 'em. I asked him to come take a look at the prisoner. He did, and he said it wasn't David Stone. But the prisoner insisted he *was* David Stone. He didn't have any proof, but he stuck to his story. Mr. Skinner said he wasn't the same David Stone who bought that piece of property last year and came in once a month or so for his mail. He said he happened to know *that* Mr. Stone had bought some land up Scottsburg way and was talking about prospecting up there."

"I don't suppose he could have told us that two days ago when Miss Anne and I met him at the post office."

Bank shrugged. "He didn't know what was going on. Says he mentioned to his wife last night that two people was in looking for Mr. Stone — meaning you and Miss Anne Stone. But he wasn't sure if Stone was out to his farm or not."

Dan nodded. He guessed it made sense that Skinner had sent them to Stone's place without further explanation. He wouldn't want the postmaster broadcasting his private business to the world.

"Well, Miz Skinner told him that last week this other feller came in and took David Stone's mail." Bank started to take a sip from his cup then hesitated. "You want coffee?"

"No, thanks," Dan said.

"Right. Well, apparently the fella in question told her at the post office that he was

Stone's farmhand and was watching the place for the boss while he went to look at his new property. But Mr. Skinner didn't know that when he saw you."

"That just beats all," Dan said. "Did she know the other man's name? I assume he's the one you had in the jail overnight."

"He didn't give it, and she didn't ask." Bank lifted his cup to his lips.

"So we're supposed to believe that David Stone hired another man by the same name to watch his place for him."

"I expect he was lying when he took the mail," Bank conceded.

"Yeah. He could be lying so bad that he's done in David Stone and taken over his property."

Bank frowned. "Murder?"

"Could be, don't you think?"

Bank stroked his chin. "Guess I'd better ride out there again and talk to some of the neighbors. Ask 'em when they last saw Mr. Stone. The real Mr. Stone, that is."

"Good idea. And while you're at it, ask if they know who this other man is and if they've seen Millie about the place."

"Yup. I'll do that. But I wouldn't put any notions of Stone being murdered into Miss Anne's pretty head."

"Don't worry, I won't suggest it." Dan

crammed his hat onto his head and beat it for the boardinghouse. He'd have to tell Anne that Bank had let the impostor go. She wasn't going to like that news.

Millie huddled in the alley between the barber shop and a freighter's stable. Her auburn hair was hidden under a drab poke bonnet, and she wrapped her shawl close. She risked a lot, coming into town this morning, but much depended on knowing what the uppity Englishwoman and her friends decided to do next.

Adams came out of the jail and hurried down the street. She reckoned Bank Raynor was still in there, and she surely didn't want him to see her. Probably Sam was in there, too, warming the bunk in a jail cell.

She waited until Adams turned a corner and set out after him. His long legs carried him quickly, and she had to lift her skirt and hustle, which garnered her curious stares from several pedestrians. He entered one of the more substantial houses near the river. Eugene City was just putting down its roots, and most of the residents lived in cabins or small houses thrown together out of logs or whatever lumber they could get their hands on. This one looked a little more respectable. She walked closer and spied a small sign swinging from the porch roof. Rooms.

So, the so-called friends whom Miss Stone and Adams were staying with consisted of boarders. Unless they owned the boarding-house.

"Millie?"

She whirled around. Wobbling down the street toward her on unsteady legs was Sam Hastings.

"What are you doing here?" She grabbed his arm and spun him around. He nearly fell over and clutched at her, leaning heavily on her shoulder. "I thought the marshal had you locked up."

"So he did, but Mr. Skinner came in this morning early and told him he had to let me go."

"And you headed straight for the nearest saloon." Millie shook her head and un-tangled his arm from about her shoulders. "If you can't walk straight, I don't want to be seen with you. Where were you headed, anyway?"

"Over to the livery. I got no horse, and the marshal said he wouldn't take me back to the farm. Said I have to stay away from there. 'Course, I have to get my stuff. And my horse. Got to get old Blue. I'm sure Mr. Stone would want me to have old Blue."

"Old Blue's not at the farm," Millie said.

"He's not?" Sam stopped in the middle of the dirt street and blinked at her. "Where'd he get to?"

She seized his wrist and pulled him out of the way of an approaching wagon. "I've got him and the mare outside of town. I packed up some stuff, but I didn't take your clothes because I figured they'd keep you in jail for a while."

"Well, they didn't, but I can't stay at the house. I don't reckon Mr. Stone would want me to now, anyways." He scowled at her. "I shouldn't have let you talk me into trying to trick his niece, Millie. That ruined everything. I had a nice, soft job there. Plenty to eat, a roof over my head."

"Oh, stop whining. There's still money in this. I can smell it."

Sam shook his head. "Don't see how."

"You wouldn't. Just come with me. You can take Blue out to the farm and get your clothes. I'm going to stick around town and see if I can find out what Miss Stone plans to do next."

"Why should you care?"

"Because her uncle has money. Buckets of it. Enough to set us up for life, unless I'm mistaken."

Sam considered that, puckering his brow

93

and weaving on his feet with the effort of thinking. "Can't see how we'd ever get it now."

"You leave that to me."

"I can't believe Deputy Raynor let that thug go." Anne sat in the parlor of the boarding-house with Dan, who had summoned her from her room on his return from a consultation with the deputy marshal at the jail.

The landlady came to the door with a laden tray.

"Here you go, miss. Tea just the way you like it. And I put some muffins and a few sugar cookies on. This gentleman has probably worked up an appetite already."

Dan grinned at her. "Thank you, Mrs. Brady. Your baking can't be beat."

"I agree," Anne said. "Eugene City may be a little rough around the edges, but your table is fit for royalty."

Mrs. Brady flushed to the roots of her wispy white hair. She set down the tray and waved a hand through the air, smiling. "Oh, go on now. You folks would flatter me to death."

Anne smiled as the older woman backed out of the room with a little bow. Of course the tea tray would be extra on her bill, but she couldn't bring herself to forgo the

94

amenities. And Dan deserved it, after spending so much time sorting out her affairs with Bank Raynor. Two more months until she could draw more money from her trust; she'd already sent a letter by ship to the family solicitor, asking that he arrange for the bank at Oregon City to give her a payment early in January.

"Daniel, what do you think I should do?" She poured him a cup of the strong black tea and passed it to him.

"I assume you still want to find your uncle."

"Of course. That's my main purpose."

He nodded as he stirred sugar into his tea. "As I see it, he's away from home for an indeterminate period of time."

"Yes, but he should be coming back." She gazed at him bleakly across the tea table. She didn't want to voice the thought that Uncle David might be dead. No doubt Dan had thought of it, too, but she refused to give the idea credence. "Should I stay at his house, do you think?"

"Well, that depends. I'd think you have the right to if you want, and I can understand your desire to secure his property. But it's isolated. Mr. Raynor and Rob both seem to think a farm like that might be the target of thieves. Maybe even Indians who want to 'borrow' some beef."

Anne shivered. She certainly couldn't live out there alone. "I came all the way across the continent without having any run-ins with the natives. If you please, I'd rather not contemplate getting on their bad side now."

He chuckled. "I'm with you there. Well, you could stay here, I suppose, and ask Mr. Skinner to tell you when Mr. Stone next shows up to collect his mail."

That was out of the question, though she didn't say so. She couldn't afford to pay for her room and board until January. After that, it shouldn't be a problem, but in the meantime Mrs. Brady had to live, too. "I wonder what will happen to his cattle. The impostor said Uncle David hired him to tend things while he was away. Do you suppose he was telling the truth?"

"Your uncle wouldn't leave the place abandoned — not with livestock on it. Maybe that part was true. Anyway, Raynor said he'll go out there and see to the animals and talk to some of the neighbors. Maybe he can get a better idea of what's been going on."

"I'm glad to hear it. Maybe I should just stay put today and see what he finds out." Anne glanced uneasily toward the door. "Of course, I hate to keep Rob and Dulcie away from their home any longer than necessary. Or you either, Daniel."

"Don't worry about me. I'm here to help you see this through. And tomorrow's Sunday. We can attend church here in town and rest. Let's see what Bank turns up. Then if you want to stick around here for a while, you could tell the Whistlers it's all right for them to head on home. I'm sure Mrs. Brady would be considered an adequate chaperone for you if you stayed in Eugene."

"Well, I'll think about it. I do want you to know how much I appreciate your coming down here and giving up your time."

"Anne, it's my pleasure."

His deep voice and earnest gray eyes brought on a curious fluttering in her stomach. Anne sipped her tea, trying to analyze the sensation. She still didn't want to marry a man whose greatest ambition was to grow wheat. Not that farming was a dishonorable profession, but she was sure the life would bore her to tears. Still, if one was honest with oneself, Dan Adams was a handsome man, and in the months she'd known him, she'd found him kind, thoughtful, and reverent. A lady could do worse.

■ ■ ■ ■

By Sunday morning, Millie was ready to tear her hair out. Were these people going to just sit in Eugene forever? She'd spent two nights curled up in a bedroll in an unsuspecting farmer's barn outside town. The only decent boardinghouse was occupied by Anne Stone and her entourage. She and Sam could hardly show up there. And Deputy Raynor was watching the Stone place like a hawk. Sam had barely gotten away with his extra socks and gloves.

She and Sam had stayed outside most of Saturday, never remaining in one spot too long. But today was colder — a blunt reminder that November had arrived three days ago. She had a coat, but Sam's light wool jacket wouldn't be adequate for winter.

She picked wisps of hay from her hair and smoothed out her blankets. Why did she bother to worry about Sam, anyway?

He stirred and rolled over in the hay with a moan.

"Wake up," Millie said. "We need to get out of here. The farmer will be out to feed his stock soon."

Sam pushed himself up on one elbow and blinked at her in the dimness of the barn.

"What are we going to do today?"

"We're going to find out what Miss Hoity-Toity Anne's plans are."

"How do we do that?"

A good question. Millie rose and gathered her bedroll and extra clothes. "I have ideas. Hurry up. We'll go someplace where we can cook breakfast first. The same spot we ate supper last night."

"All right, I'm coming."

She walked on the spongy hay over to the edge of the loft and climbed down the ladder, balancing her load. She almost wished Sam hadn't gotten out of jail and found her. He was just slowing her down. Why should she always have to wait for her stupid brother? Even after all these years, Millie cringed at the words that had leaped into her thoughts. Her stepmother had beaten her soundly for calling Sam that. She was forbidden to ever say the word *stupid*. Now, when she thought it, she felt the sting of the switch on her legs — twenty years later.

She opened the back door of the barn — the small door beside the manure heap — and slipped out. Just as she closed it behind her, she heard another sound — the grinding of the big front barn door as its wheels rolled along the track.

She caught her breath and listened, her

ear to the crack she'd left between the door and the jamb. Was Sam still up in the hay mow or had he started down the ladder?

"Hey! What are you doing in here?" a man shouted.

"Me?" Sam asked. Millie could almost hear him gulp. "I–I'm not doing anything."

Stupid half brother.

CHAPTER 6

"We can't just go off and leave you here." Dulcie threw a pleading look at Rob over the dinner table. They'd just returned from the service at the rustic little church, and Anne had raised the question of the Whistlers going back to Corvallis without her.

Rob settled back in his chair with a sigh. "Now, sweetheart, Miss Anne is an adult. If she wants to stay and wait for her uncle, that's her right, and if she wants to head up into the hills looking for him, well, that's her right, too."

"But she's such a pretty young thing. She can't travel around mining country unchaperoned."

"I'll stay with her," Dan said.

"That's almost as bad," Dulcie replied. "I know you mean no harm, Daniel, but can't you see how it would look if Miss Anne traipsed about the wilderness with you?"

Anne decided it was time she spoke up.

"Dulcie, dear, I know you mean well, but I'm sure Dan is capable of protecting me." She flashed a glance his way and saw him flush with pleasure and straighten his shoulders a fraction of an inch. She would have to be careful not to imply more than she meant where he was concerned. "And Mr. Skinner says there are towns all along the road to Scottsburg. We should be able to find respectable lodgings when we need them, at least that far."

"I wouldn't be too sure," Rob said. "Some of those towns are just a handful of cabins with a post office for miners and trappers."

"Nevertheless," Anne continued, "I'm sure Daniel and I can reach Scottsburg safely. And from there we should be able to reach Uncle David's mine within a day's travel, and I'll have my uncle to defend my honor."

Rob shook his head. "That sounds good, missy, but we both know you've thought you were close to catching up with your uncle twice before and had to deal with disappointment. Supposing you get up in the Coast Range and he's nowhere to be found? Then what will you do?"

"We'll ride back to Scottsburg," Dan said firmly. "And if it looks as though we'll have to spend a night or more on the trail getting to the mine, we can perhaps hire a guide to take us. That's if I can't convince Miss Anne to stay in Scottsburg while I go and fetch Mr. Stone myself and bring him to her."

"No," Anne said, frowning, "I don't suppose you could persuade me of that."

Rob laughed. "You ought to have known better than to even think of it, Dan."

Dulcie leaned forward and shook an accusing finger under Anne's nose. "I know you're independent, but my question is this: When we get back to Corvallis, what will we tell Mrs. Bentley?"

"That's true." Rob rubbed the back of his neck, making a tortured face as he considered his wife's words. "Elise will be very unhappy. We told her we'd place you in your uncle's care or bring you back with us. No ifs, ands, or buts."

"Sounds like we'd better start practicing our 'buts,' " Dulcie said.

Anne chuckled. "Elise will understand. Won't she, Dan?"

He gritted his teeth. "Well . . . I don't know as she will. But I can't think of a better plan. Can any of you?"

"You'll take my horse," Rob said, and Anne took that as admission of defeat.

Dulcie nodded. "And my sidesaddle."

"Oh no, I couldn't," Anne said quickly.

Part Rob from Bailey, his favorite mount? She wouldn't think of it.

"I don't see that you have much choice," Rob said. "Unless you have enough cash to buy a horse, and I'm not sure you could find a sidesaddle if you scoured Eugene City for one."

"But —"

"We'll be fine with the team and wagon," Dulcie said. "You'll have to go through your trunks today, though, and pack up what you want for the journey. We'll take the rest back to our place and keep it for you until you come for it."

"That's very generous of you," Anne murmured. She couldn't think of anyone in England who would have shown her such kindness. "I promise I'll bring Bailey back to you safely."

"I'm sure you will." Rob cleared his throat and looked at his wife. "Well, sweetheart, do you want to set out tomorrow morning?"

"I suppose we should, though it's tempting to stay one more day," Dulcie said. "Anne needs time to sort through her luggage, and she might learn a little more about her uncle's doings."

"I'll repack this afternoon," Anne said.

Dan nodded. "I can bring the wagon over from the livery and load the trunks. And I'll make sure we have all the supplies we might need for the trip. Do you think we should take a pack horse?"

His question alarmed Anne. She didn't want Dan laying out money for her venture, and an extra horse was beyond her current means, especially if they planned to pay for rooms and meals along the way.

"We should do fine with Star and Bailey, especially if you think we'll find lodgings every night."

"Good," Dan said. "I don't expect we'll need a tent, but we might want to tote a couple of blankets just in case, and one kettle."

Dulcie laughed. "Anne, you'd better take a coffeepot and some coffee beans along for this young man. I've never seen such a coffee drinker."

"Well, Mrs. Brady makes it so well." Dan waved a hand in protest. "But you don't need to do that for me. I can go without coffee for a week if I have to. And we'll likely be able to find it wherever we stop."

Anne smiled and determined to slip a coffeepot and a small stash of ground coffee into her pack.

"Now, you'll want to head straight south to Cottage Grove first." Rob held out the map he'd asked the postmaster to sketch for him after church.

"Will we pass Uncle David's property?" Anne asked.

"Yes, you will."

She looked at Dan. "I'd like to stop in and see the neighbors Bank Raynor talked to, if you don't mind — the ones who said they'd look after the cattle until Uncle David returns."

"Certainly. We can go by David's house again, too, if you want."

"I don't see any reason to go there. Mr. Raynor said he looked around to make sure there were no valuables left in the house."

"If there were, that Millie probably pocketed them." Rob shook his head. "She was a sly one."

"Good thing I wasn't there," Dulcie said. "I'd have blacked her eyes."

Anne couldn't hold back a smile. "I'll miss you, Dulcie."

"Well, you'll see me again soon enough. I hope your uncle will bring you up to Corvallis, if only to get your trunks."

"He'll want to see Elise, I'm sure," Anne said.

"Good. I want to meet this famous English gentleman everyone's been talking about." Dulcie's eyes danced. "Imagine, meeting an earl out here in Oregon Territory."

Anne didn't deflate her spirits by explaining that her uncle wouldn't officially be the earl of Stoneford until he returned to England and claimed the title and the estate. She smiled at Dulcie. "I'm sure he'll be delighted to make your acquaintance. Yours and Rob's. After all, your husband saw me safely through many perils on the trail."

Dulcie reached for Rob's hand. "I almost wish I'd been along this summer. It might have been fun traveling with you and Elise Bentley."

Rob smiled at her indulgently. "No, darlin', you've told me a thousand times you don't want to make that trip ever again."

"It's true." Dulcie sighed. "When I first laid eyes on Oregon City, I said, 'Rob, please find a place where I can have a hot bath, and if I ever need to go East again, I'll go by ship, thank you very much.' "

Millie slipped behind a buckboard and ducked down. Dan Adams and his friend Whistler came out of the livery stable. She could hear them talking as they walked past her hiding place.

"Are you sure you and Anne have everything you want for now?" the older man, Whistler, asked.

Adams had a brace of saddlebags thrown over one shoulder, and Mr. Whistler carried a shotgun.

"Pretty sure," Adams said. "We don't want to take too much up into those hills and regret having to haul it."

"Well, Anne won't have to worry about her trunks. We've got them strapped down tight in the wagon. We'll take them right back to our place in Corvallis, and she can pick them up when you come back."

They reached the street and headed off toward the boardinghouse, and Millie could no longer make out their words.

Where was this wagon they were talking about, anyway? Adams and the tall trail master had driven into the livery ten minutes ago. Were they leaving the wagon right inside the barn overnight? They must be, with all their boxes and bundles in it — including the fine lady's kit and cargo. In the short time Millie had been observing Anne, she'd worn four different outfits, including two today alone. She'd set out for meeting this morning all got up in finery. Her hat matched her overskirt, and the lace on her bodice alone must have cost a month's wages.

Then this afternoon, while Millie had watched from behind a cedar tree on the edge of the yard, Miss Anne had gone in and out from the boardinghouse to the wagon and back with her bundles and frippery, wearing a brown dress of good quality wool, with black velvet-ribbon trim. Understated but elegant, just plain elegant. Four dresses were more than most Oregon women could lay claim to, and Millie could only imagine what lay in the steamer trunks Whistler and Adams had trucked to the livery in the back of the wagon.

She slid from behind the buckboard and flitted to the door of the barn. Cautiously she peeked around the edge of the door. The livery man was in there, feeding the horses fortunate enough to sleep inside. Soon he'd lock up for the night. Millie smiled to herself as she eyed the ropes wrapped around Miss Stone's trunks. Anything a man could tie, she could untie. It would just be a matter of coming back tonight when no one else was in the barn.

Hoisting her skirt, she hurried out to the street, watching out for familiar faces. She darted between two buildings and out behind them, toward the grove where she'd tied her chestnut mare.

In fifteen minutes, she'd reached the small sheltered meadow where she'd left Sam and Old Blue. Sam lay on the grass with his head on his saddle, while Blue grazed twenty yards away without so much as a hobble or a picket line to hold him.

"Why did you let the horse loose?" she cried.

Sam sat up and blinked as she jumped down in a swirl of skirts. "What? Old Blue will come to me."

To prove it, he rose, stretched, and ambled toward the roan.

Old Blue lifted his head, looked at Sam, and resumed grazing, but took a few short steps away from him, gradually swinging his hindquarters in Sam's direction.

"Oh terrific, now you won't be able to catch him," Millie said.

"Can, too!" Sam quickened his steps. Blue rewarded him by trotting a dozen steps away. He put his head down to the grass again but kept one ear cocked toward Sam.

"You are such a dolt!" Millie shook her head in despair as she opened her saddle-bag. "You'll have to give him some oats or you'll never catch him. Lucky for you I scooped up a handful that had spilled outside the livery in town." She took out a knotted handkerchief, plump with her loot, and carried it to him. "We're fortunate that farmer didn't find our horses out behind the barn this morning."

"Wouldn't be my fault if he had." Sam gazed at her with an injured air. "You're the one who picked the spot to leave 'em."

Millie ignored that. "Get that horse and tie him up. I'll get out our lunch. We probably would have been safer if we'd stayed at Stone's place last night. Live and learn."

Sam scowled at her. "You blame me for everything, but it was your idea to move around and sleep in barns. You said the marshal would find us if we stayed at Stone's."

"And so he would have. He was out there again yesterday."

"How do you know that?"

"I learned a lot this afternoon. That's the other reason I wanted to stay someplace closer to town. We needed to stick close to Miss Anne until we knew what her plan was."

Sam watched her as she laid the makings of a campfire. "Do we know it now?"

"Yes, we do." Millie used the plural pronoun loosely. She wasn't about to disclose to her stolid half brother — whom she considered to be little more than half-witted — everything she knew. For one thing, if Sam had another brush with the law, he'd probably spill it. If not, he'd forget the critical bits of knowledge. No, it was best to tell

111

Sam what he needed to know when he needed to know it. "Get that horse and then bring me some firewood."

"You gonna tell me our plan, Mill?"

"When you've brought an armful of sticks. Good, dry stuff, now. Don't bring me anything green. And don't call me Mill."

Why couldn't her mother have given her a pretty name — something flowing, like Victoria or Charlotte?

Sam carried the small bundle of oats toward the horse. Old Blue was curious enough to let himself be caught this time. When he was tied up, Sam trudged away toward the line of pine trees that lined the creek. Millie filled her one pot with water and considered her strategy. She definitely wouldn't tell him about the glorious dresses she was sure she'd find in Anne Stone's trunks. She'd think up an excuse to go back tonight. Maybe she could give Sam a simple errand to carry out while she went to the livery. If he noticed that she came back with an extra sack, she'd tell him she'd found some clothes and let it go at that. She'd choose carefully and leave Eugene with some assets for the days ahead.

But that was only a small part of Millie's plan. She needed her half brother to help her carry it out. Convincing Sam they should separate might be the most difficult part.

Dan looked up from fastening an extra strap on the pack he'd loaded behind Star's saddle. Bank Raynor was walking across the yard of the boardinghouse toward him.

"You folks heading out this morning?"

"Planning on it," Dan said. "You're out early."

Bank nodded. "I got a message last evening from Marshal Nesmith. Figured I'd best get it to Miss Stone before you headed out."

"What is it?" Dan tugged on the strap. Everything lay snug on Star's flanks. Way more gear than he liked to carry, though — he ought to have insisted on a pack horse.

"Seems there was a gent from New York who chased Miss Stone all the way out here. She mentioned him the other night — Peterson."

That grabbed Dan's attention. "Yes. Nesmith had him in custody when we left Oregon City. That was nearly two weeks ago."

"Well, he ain't there now."

"They've released him?"

"I'm not just sure what happened. All the marshal's note said was, 'Tell Miss Stone that Peterson is on the loose. She'll want to warn her uncle.' Now, mebbe you can make more of that than I can."

Dan puzzled over the message. "Not much, I'm afraid. I know who Peterson is, of course. I'm not sure we need to be concerned about him now that we're down here. But thank you."

Bank nodded. "Well then, that's all I came for. I hope you have a good trip, and that you find Mr. Stone in one piece."

"I appreciate it, sir."

"Right." Bank hesitated. "You watch out for Miss Stone, won't you, Adams? She's a pretty little thing. No bigger'n a minute, and I don't misdoubt she can take care of herself, but still — you don't want to put it to the test, do you?"

Dan nodded gravely. "I most surely will take care of her."

He smiled as he watched the old man walk away. Taking care of Anne would be his life's mission if he had anything to say about it. But he wasn't sure telling her that Peterson was out of jail would be the best way to do that.

Anne liked Uncle David's neighbors, the McIntyres, and wished she'd stopped in and met them the first time she'd approached her uncle's farm. They might have saved her a lot of worry.

"I told David I didn't trust that feller he hired," Mr. McIntyre told her, shaking his head woefully. Anne and Dan had dismounted in the neighbors' dooryard to inquire about David's situation. "He's trusting to a fault, though. Said Sam would be all right, and what could he do wrong, anyhow? David left him with a score of cattle at pasture and five acres he'd planted to winter wheat. That was all the man had to watch out for. David couldn't see any harm in it."

"That's because he didn't know Sam's sister would show up," Mrs. McIntyre added.

"If she *is* his sister." Mr. McIntyre winked at Dan.

"He's not smart enough to lure a woman out here unless she was related to him," his wife said. "If your uncle weren't so softhearted, he never would have hired Sam Hastings to begin with. That man couldn't find a quill if he had a porcupine in his lap. Say, speaking of Millie, Sam came over here and borrowed my sidesaddle for her shortly after she arrived. They never brought it back."

"I wonder if it's still over in David's barn,"

Mr. McIntyre said.

"I wouldn't count on it," Dan told them. "Millie lit out on horseback the day we took the deputy marshal out there. I expect she's still got it."

"Well, I'll take a look around when I go over to check the livestock."

"But you *are* sure Uncle David went up to the mountains?" Anne asked.

"Oh yes," Mrs. McIntyre said. "He'd bought that property up there and said he wanted to go look it over and see if it was worth doing some mining on it."

Her husband ran a hand over his chin. "That's right. He'd been studying up on it, kind of as a hobby. I saw him the day he pulled out. Had all his gear on a pack mule. Said he thought he'd do a little panning in the creek that ran by his land, and if he found some color, he might even get a sluice box."

That news relieved Anne. She would stop wondering whether Sam and Millie had done something awful to him.

"I wouldn't worry about him being gone several weeks," the man continued. "He was quite excited about it."

"Just like a boy," Mrs. McIntyre said. "But I expect he'll tire of it soon, now that it's getting colder. Can you folks stay to dinner?"

"No, thank you," Anne said. "I have news for my uncle that I really must get to him. We want to push on to Cottage Grove. Is there a hotel there?"

"Sure," said Mr. McIntyre. "Or you could spend less and get a better supper if you stopped with the Randall family. They're just past the feed store on the south edge of town. They take in travelers regular, and Mrs. Randall makes a fine chicken pie."

Anne looked up at Dan. "Sound good?"

"Sure does."

They set out once more at a quick trot. When they passed the lane to Uncle David's farm, Dan looked over at her with raised eyebrows.

"You sure you don't want to stop?"

"I'm sure." The cattle grazed peacefully inside the rail fence. She could see the barn's ridgepole in the distance. "The next time I see that place, I want Uncle David there, welcoming me to his home."

"All right, they're past Stone's place." From beneath the spreading branches of a pine tree, Millie peered at the retreating horses. "You wait half an hour. If they don't come back and no one else happens by, you can go fill out your supplies from the house. There's plenty of beans and cornmeal and raisins. Then follow along. We know they plan to spend tonight in Cottage Grove, so there's no hurry. When you get there, look around and find out where their horses are stabled. But whatever you do, don't let Adams or Miss Stone see you."

Sam scrunched up his face and wagged his whole body from side to side. "I don't see why you have to go on ahead."

"I told you. It's better if I get ahead of them. I'll see if I can get wind of David before they do. If I get to him first, I can soften him up and maybe find out what he's really worth."

Sam shook his head. "That don't make sense to me. Why can't we stay together and just follow them to where he's at?"

Millie sighed in exasperation. "Because, you dunce, you're going to slow them down, remember? So I can get a good head start on them. The longer I have to get friendly with ol' Uncle David before Miss Anne shows up, the better."

"She'll just tell him how we tried to trick her."

"Not if things go my way. Now, you do as I say. Slow them down, throw them off the trail — anything you can think of. Give me

118

time to find David Stone and learn whether his mining property is valuable. It could end up being worth more than his inheritance from his brother."

"Well, yeah." Sam's brow puckered. "I heard they're taking millions from the mines down Josephine way. I don't know why he didn't buy land down there."

"Because it's all bought up, no doubt. Now folks are sniffing around up this way, and he wants to get in on it early. You told me Stone is a smart man, right?"

"Oh, he's powerful smart."

"So he wouldn't get taken in by some swindler and buy worthless property. There's bound to be a little gold on it." Millie pushed the branches aside and walked back toward where they had tied the horses out of sight of the road.

"I don't see why he didn't just stay here and run his farm." Sam panted along behind her. "It's a nice farm."

"Sure, Sam. It's a wonderful farm."

Millie untied the mare's reins and led her out toward the road. By the time she was settled in the saddle, Sam was just coming out of the woods, tugging the roan along behind him.

"You're supposed to wait and make sure they don't come back," she said.

"Do I have to?"

Millie sighed. Sam was like a kid in some ways. "At least keep an eye out for the neighbors. If anyone comes along and asks what you're doing, tell them you came for your clothes."

"I got my clothes already."

"They don't know that."

"Oh yeah."

"And don't steal anything big. You know — that they could see."

Sam looked at her blankly as though the thought would never have entered his mind without her help.

"But get plenty of oats for Blue. Enough for several days."

"What about your horse?"

"We'll manage."

Millie turned the mare southward.

"Wait," Sam called. "How will I find you again?"

"If you ever catch up to David Stone, trust me, I won't be far away."

CHAPTER 7

Cottage Grove was a pretty little town on the edge of the Willamette River's Coast Fork. Anne imagined that every bedroom window had a lovely view of the mountains that folded in around it.

They found the Randalls' house without any trouble. The first man they asked pointed the way and declared, "You'll get some good eating there."

The sun was still higher than the hills to the west. It was a pity they couldn't keep riding for another hour or two. But they must bow to propriety on this journey if Anne hoped to face Elise and Dulcie again without shame.

"You'll have to bunk in with our boys tonight, Mr. Adams," Mrs. Randall said ruefully as she led them through the kitchen toward the stairway. "We've already got folks in the one guest room."

"That's fine," Dan said, but Anne felt bad

for putting him in that situation.

"Miss Stone can take our daughter's room," Mrs. Randall added. "Mary Lou can sleep in with us tonight."

"We don't want to inconvenience you," Anne said.

"Let's not fuss about that," the hostess replied cheerfully.

Mr. Randall piped up from the corner by the stove, "If you was married, you could share the same accommodations, folks."

Dan went scarlet to his hairline.

"There's truth in that," Mrs. Randall said with a chuckle.

Her husband guffawed. "We got a preacher right down the street."

Dan looked helplessly at Anne. She decided the best thing to do was laugh with them.

"How nice for you. Daniel and I have been friends most of a year now, but we've no matrimonial plans."

"That's right," Dan said. "This trip is purely out of necessity."

"Too bad," said Mr. Randall. "Mighta made a nice honeymoon."

Millie had stayed well behind the pair until they took their horses off the trail to give them water. She hurried past, well out of sight, and then lit out for Cottage Grove. She made good time, galloping the mare most of the way. While the horse rested and grazed outside town, she went into the general store, bought a slice of cheese, and pocketed a pot of lip rouge and a tin of peaches.

She didn't let the horse rest long, wanting to be certain she'd cleared town well before Miss Stone and Adams showed up. Her next stop would be the little town of Anlauf, at a distance of about twelve miles. As she rode out of Cottage Grove, the road left the Coast Fork, skirted a pond, and followed Pass Creek, upstream and uphill, toward the divide. The road was passable for wagons, but still rugged, and she kept a steady, slow trot when possible. On the steeper grades, the mare walked.

She passed a few cabins, but the farther she went, the more desolate the landscape became. Reports Sam had brought in about the Calapooya Indians flitted through her mind. Had they really taken to the warpath again? She scanned the forest on both sides of the trail. The tall firs towered above her. She could see between their trunks for a ways into the cool shadows. Were angry warriors lurking there?

Something moved ahead of her, and the

mare leaped to one side with a squeal. Millie's heart nearly jumped out of her chest. She kept her hands low, with tension on the reins.

Fifty yards ahead, two deer hopped across the road and disappeared into the trees.

She patted the horse's withers as the mare continued to prance and blow out air.

"Take it easy, girl. It was only a couple of deer. Settle down."

The mare crow-hopped one more time and minced forward with tiny, precise steps. As Millie's pulse slowed, she was able to breathe normally again, but she didn't trust the horse with a loose rein for a good ten minutes. At last they settled into a road-eating trot. Millie thanked her lucky stars she hadn't wound up in the dirt with a broken neck.

She should have taken Old Blue, but Sam would have come after her. He claimed the horse was his since David Stone had left it for him to use. Millie was stuck with the thin nag she'd picked up in Champoeg without benefit of a bill of sale. Poorest horse she'd ever stolen.

Anne came down to breakfast in the Randalls' kitchen looking beautiful, as always. She wore her blue velvet habit and an adorable hat that looked as though it had come out of a shop window in New York. Dan supposed it was the only modest outfit she had for riding, but it seemed a bit overdone for the wilderness. She looked rested, and her eager smile when she met his gaze set his stomach fluttering. If only she weren't so lovely, he could bear it better.

"Good morning," she sang out.

"Sit you right down, Miss Stone," Mrs. Randall said. She indicated a place at the table next to Dan, where she had set out white china plates with green ivy painted around the rims.

Dan held Anne's chair for her and resumed his seat.

"How was your night?" Anne asked.

He wished she hadn't asked in the hostess's presence. He glanced toward Mrs. Randall's ample back and shot Anne a rueful smile. "Fine. Just fine."

Anne nodded in comprehension and shook out her napkin before spreading it in her lap. There would be plenty of time later to tell her how the three boys had offered him their bunks, but Dan had insisted on rolling out his blankets on the floor. It had seemed the polite thing to do at the time. But he'd reckoned without the oak planks beneath him or Petey's incessant snoring.

Right now the prospect of eight hours or more in the saddle quelled all sense of adventure inspired in him by Anne's quest.

They finished their meal, and Dan rose to pay the hostess. Anne leaped up and followed him, opening her purse.

"Let me take care of it," Dan said softly.

"Oh no, I couldn't. In fact, I should be paying your way. This is my excursion, not yours, and you've given up much for my cause."

"Don't even think it." He smiled down at her. "It's a delight for me to be of service, Anne. I'm just glad you've allowed me to come along."

Her cheeks went a becoming shade of pink. "Thank you, Daniel. But you mustn't even think of paying my expenses. If you insist on paying your own way, at least let me keep my dignity and cover my own."

"Very well."

"My land, you folks are so polite it's painful," Mrs. Randall said.

Anne's flush deepened, and Dan regretted quibbling over money in front of the hostess.

"You've been most kind." Anne placed a few coins in the woman's hand and turned to the door.

Dan held out the money for his night's

lodging.

"She's a proud one, isn't she?" Mrs. Randall asked, watching Anne step through the doorway.

Dan pulled back in surprise. "Oh no, she's nothing like that. She only wants to be clear that she's independent."

"Oh, she's a real lady, anyone can see that, and I don't doubt she can stand on her own two feet. But she's not averse to leading you about the territory, now is she?" Mrs. Randall chuckled. "How far are you folks traveling?"

Caution counseled Dan, and he replied, "We're heading over Scottsburg way."

"Ah. Getting the steamer there?"

"I'm not sure yet. Miss Stone has business in that area."

Mrs. Randall nodded. "It's not so bad to marry a woman who knows how to carry out her own business, you know." Her smile indicated that she was just such a woman and Mr. Randall was a fortunate man indeed to have found her.

Dan managed a smile. "I'm sure that's true. Thank you."

The children came in from their chores and began to set up for their own breakfast as he left the house. He found Anne in the barn working diligently at a tangle of leather straps, with a determined set to her jaw. Her eyebrows were drawn into a lovely pucker.

"What's the trouble?" Dan asked.

"Our bridles are all jumbled together, and these reins are tied in about a hundred knots."

"The boys must have done it when they came to do their barn chores this morning." Dan bent over the mess and frowned. "I can't believe their father would allow it, though, and it must have taken some time."

"It's a fine way to treat their paying guests," Anne said.

She carried the bridles to the brighter light at the open barn door.

"Would you like me to do it?" Dan asked.

"No thanks, I'm getting it. Why don't you go ahead and saddle up?"

He left her working on the knots and walked to where she'd placed her sidesaddle the afternoon before, on a wooden rack attached to the wall. He pulled it down and frowned in dismay as the cinch strap, girth, and stirrup tumbled to the floor.

"What on earth?" He sighed and stooped to retrieve the pieces.

"What is it?" Anne called.

"Seems the little urchins undid every buckle they could find and loosened the straps." The trick would cost them a good half hour in getting started. Dan had a mind to go find Mr. Randall and complain. But that would take another ten minutes.

He set the saddle back on the rack and began threading a leather strap through the slot at the top of the stirrup. No doubt entered his mind that his saddle was in a similar fix.

At last they had everything put back the way it should be.

"Ready to start," he asked Anne, "or are you exhausted?"

She chuckled. "I'm ready to get out of here — I'll tell you that."

They led the horses into the barnyard. Mr. Randall came around the corner of his house and stopped short.

"I thought you folks were gone already."

"We had a few things to take care of first," Anne said with her usual pleasant smile. "We're ready to start now, though."

"Well, have a good trip." Mr. Randall lifted his hat and watched in puzzlement as they mounted and trotted out of his barnyard.

"Do you think we'll be able to make Elkton today?" Anne asked.

"I hope so. We'll have to see how things look when we get a bit farther along." Dan had hoped they could make it to the next village in time for their midday meal and then press onward to Elkton. "I guess a lot depends on the terrain."

The information he'd gleaned in Eugene City told him that the distance from Cottage Grove to a small settlement at a river junction was about fifteen miles, and from there to Elkton, on the Umpqua River, was nearly as far again, but through less hospitable country. Several hamlets lay along the first portion of the journey, but beyond them they would see only a few cabins among the forested slopes. The road would take them over and between some rugged hills as they approached the Coast Range. Dan didn't want to risk being caught out in the wilderness after dark.

The trail swung westward as they left town, and they rode away from the river. The road bore deep wagon ruts in some places, and they let the horses pick their way between them, but for the most part the footing was easy.

"We'll follow Martin Creek for a while," Dan said, "and then pick up Pass Creek. The road pretty much follows the rivers through the mountains."

"It's a lovely day for riding," Anne said.

Dan had to agree. He settled back in the saddle and decided to forget about the mischievous Randall kids and enjoy this time with Anne. He reminded himself that these few days might be all he ever had with her. When it was over, she'd go back to England, and he didn't think she'd shed any tears over him.

Her friend Elise had changed her mind and decided to stay. How on earth had Eb Bentley won her over? Maybe he should have had a man-to-man talk with the gruff scout. Perhaps Eb could give him a few tips on wooing English ladies.

After two hours on the road, they stopped to rest the horses.

"I think we'll reach Anlauf soon," Dan said.

Anne took a parcel from one of her bags and unwrapped four fluffy biscuits. "Mrs. Randall sent these along, and I have some raisins and cheese."

They sat down on the creek bank and watched the horses crop the grass.

After a few minutes of quiet, Anne smiled over at him. "This seems like when we were on the wagon train and stopped for nooning."

"Yes, only not so frenetic."

She laughed. "We had a few moments, didn't we? But Mr. Whistler claims our trip was singularly uneventful."

"I guess Rob ought to know." Dan took another bite of biscuit.

"I keep thinking about those people at Uncle David's farm," Anne said. "Sam Hastings and Millie."

Dan raised his eyebrows in question as he chewed.

"If he really was working for Uncle David, how did he expect to get away with impersonating him?" Anne shook her head. "I don't think Sam is very smart."

"Neither do I. We're well rid of him." Dan reached for his canteen.

"I wonder where he went after Deputy Raynor let him go."

Dan paused with the canteen partway to his lips. "Well, Raynor told him he couldn't stay at the farm." He shrugged. "It's not our worry now."

"I suppose you're right." Anne rose. "Do you think there's anything to see in Anlauf?"

"We'll cross the Territorial Road there. It goes on down to California."

Star jumped suddenly with a sharp squeal and kicked his heels at Bailey. Anne's horse responded with a snort and turned his hindquarters toward Star. The pinto gelding awkwardly hopped several steps.

Dan shot up off his log seat and called in

a low voice, "Take it easy, Star. Calm down, fella."

The pinto stood shivering near the edge of the creek.

"What do you suppose startled him?" Anne asked.

"I don't know. Maybe a bee stung him." Dan looked all around but saw nothing that could account for the horse's actions. He walked over to Star and patted the trembling gelding's neck. "What's the trouble? Hmm?"

"It's a good thing we hobbled them," Anne said.

"Yes. Let's move on, if you're ready."

She nodded. "If you think Star is calm enough."

A faint rustle came from a thicket. Dan peered at the bushes but couldn't make out any solid shapes among the thick branches. An eerie feeling crept over him. Eugene Skinner had said the Indians in these parts weren't too happy since the white settlements had mushroomed. Could there be angry Calapooyas watching them?

Another rustle, fainter, drew his gaze to the tree line. His chest tightened as a dark-clad figure slipped between the close-growing cedars. Best not to tell Anne. He reached for Star's halter. "Let's go."

■ ■ ■ ■

Millie trudged slowly into Elkton past noon of her second day on the trail, leading her horse by the reins. The worthless mare had thrown a shoe three miles back and limped so badly Millie knew she had to walk. It happened when they'd forded a creek. The horse had scrabbled in the rocky streambed and come out the other side minus a shoe. Millie blamed the horse for not being careful.

Stupid horse! She was glad she hadn't named her.

With any luck, she could pilfer a few coins and buy some lunch with it. But what was she going to do about the horse?

She turned and looked behind her. She'd gotten beyond Anlauf and stayed the previous night in a corn crib. She hadn't slept well and took to the road this morning feeling tired. The mare moved along well with a few stops for water and corn from the supply Millie had collected at her night's berth. She'd been pleased with her progress until their mishap while crossing one of the numerous creeks they encountered.

Ever since the mare lost that shoe, she'd feared Adams and Miss Stone would ride up behind her. But so far, she'd met only a few miners and a lone horseman coming from Elkton, and had overtaken a band of freighters heading there even slower than she was moving.

The freighters had called rude things to her and whistled. One had offered to let her ride one of his mules. Millie grimaced and shook her head as she remembered his boldness. Maybe she should have let her dignity slide and taken him up on it.

No, that wouldn't have ended well, she was sure. If she'd been alert, she wouldn't have let them see her at all. She had no doubt the freighters took particular notice of her and would be able to describe her minutely if anyone asked. She should have taken to the woods and worked her way past them without being seen.

"I really should have left you with Sam and made him give me Old Blue," she muttered.

The mare stretched her neck to the side and tried to grab a mouthful of dead grass. Millie jerked on the reins. "Oh, no you don't! Come on."

Elkton seemed a thriving community, compared to the hamlets she'd passed through earlier. Farms that held a prosperous air lay on the outskirts. The village itself boasted several large houses and businesses, a post office, and at least two houses with boards out front advertising ROOMS TO LET. A pocket of dwellings clustered near the point where Pass Creek flowed into Elk Creek. Beside a whitewashed, two-story house was a rail corral with a dozen or more mules and horses milling about inside. She decided that was as good a place as any to seek a new mount.

A three-sided shed sat at one side of the corral, but there was no barn. She couldn't see anyone about, so she led the mare over to the fence and tied her up. She was about to raise her skirt and duck through the fence rails when a door clumped shut. She looked under the mare's neck. A huge man had come out of the house and was approaching the corral. Worse, a short-haired, yellowish dog with a massive, square head trotted ahead of the man.

The dog barked fiercely. Her mare gave a squeal and jumped, crowding Millie.

"Help you?" the big man called. He clapped his hands together once, and the dog fell back, whining. "Sit," the giant said, and the dog plopped his hindquarters down in the dirt.

The man walked over and peered over the mare's back. "You want something, ma'am?" He towered like a rock formation, glaring down at her.

Millie swallowed hard and met his stony gaze. "Hello."

Slowly his sour face smoothed out to neutral then slid into a smile. "Well, well."

"I'm looking to trade my horse." It wasn't what Millie had planned, or the way she usually acquired a new mount, but sometimes a woman was forced to take extreme measures.

The man looked down at her mare. Millie retreated a step, so she could take him in without getting a sore neck. His bushy eyebrows tightened.

"This hoss right here?"

"Yes."

"She's lame."

Millie wanted to deny it, but that would be worse than useless. The mare stood with one foot — the shoeless one — tipped up and resting with just the tip of her ragged toe on the ground.

"She lost a shoe in the creek a few miles back."

The man grunted. "Bad place. People always cross there, but they should go upstream a ways. Well, I've got a ten-year-old bay gelding out there. He's healthy, but he's ornery. Or I've got a sixteen-year-old mare I could let go. She's sweet-natured, but she's on the thin side."

"Oh, I . . . well . . ." Millie hated being at a disadvantage. "Would you take my mare in trade?"

The man sighed. "I'll have to look her over." He took a step toward the mare's hindquarters, ran a hand down her flank, and stretched her hind leg out across his knee. After a moment he set the hoof down gently and straightened to his full height. Once again, Millie was startled by his size and backed up a step.

"I'll need a horse that will take a side-saddle." She wouldn't back down on that. She'd ridden the stolen mare astride all the way from Champoeg to Eugene City and vowed she'd never do that again.

He grunted and looked at the horse again.

Squinting against the rays of the sun, Millie studied the few horses among the mules in the corral. The bay horse didn't look bad at all. But where had all her confidence got to? She could usually talk her way out of any situation, but this time she wasn't so sure. Was it because he was so huge? Men didn't often intimidate her. She was smarter than most, so what was there to fear?

He moved around to the side where Millie

stood and ran a beefy hand down the mare's off hind leg.

"You traveling alone, missy?"

Millie felt a rush of apprehension, another rarity for her. "No, I've got a couple of friends coming along, but they had to make a side trip on an errand. They'll be along before dark."

He eyed her sacks and bundles, tied to the saddle. "Her horn's pretty torn up. It'll take a while for her to grow it out again. I'm not sure I can shoe her for a month or two."

"Uh, I wondered — uh — how much you're asking . . . if I trade my horse, that is . . ."

"I'll have to get twenty-five dollars for the gelding, besides your nag. The mare I can let go for less, I suppose. Hate to, but . . ." He shook his massive head. Even standing beside Millie on level ground, he was a foot taller than she was. "Well, I'll take ten for my mare, along with your trade."

Millie huffed out a breath. She had less than a dollar in her pocket. "I'll have to think about it."

His eyes narrowed. "You ain't got the money?"

"No."

"Well, maybe when your friends get

here . . ."

Millie considered her options. If she stuck around until after dark and stole one of his horses, he'd know who did it and set out after her. That was a hanging offense. Too risky. There might be a farm where the horses weren't too close to the house. She doubted that — there'd been too much talk about Indian trouble. Everyone would lock up their livestock at night and turn their dogs loose. She squared her shoulders.

"I don't suppose there's any place in this town where I could earn some money."

He smiled slowly and leaned toward her. "Well, now, that depends."

CHAPTER 8

Quickly Anne gathered the remains of their meal and tucked them away while Dan bridled both horses and put their hobbles in the saddlebags. They filled their canteens and mounted. All the while, Dan looked around, scanning the trees and the far bank of the stream. His anxiety made Anne want to gallop away from the spot as fast as Star and Bailey could run.

Instead they picked up a brisk trot and continued along the road. Dan's hand never strayed far from the butt of his rifle, where it traveled in the scabbard next to his right knee.

The road stayed within sight of Pass Creek most of the way. She enjoyed that at first, as the creek gave them a constant supply of water and provided some spectacular scenery as they wended their way through the hills. But now its babble covered other sounds she might have heard, and she wished they weren't forced to stay so close to it.

Dan stayed on edge, constantly watching, searching. He barely spoke to her until they began to pass a homestead here and there. She felt his relief as he relaxed in the saddle and smiled across at her.

"Almost to Anlauf."

A small village appeared between the high hills, and they approached the junction of their road with another that looked well traveled.

Dan slowed Star and waited for her to catch up. He pointed southward at the junction. "They say that road goes all the way to California."

Visions of gold miners and Spanish priests danced in Anne's mind.

"Of course, there're a lot of hostile Indians between here and there."

"Mr. Skinner said there's been fighting on the Rogue River," she said. "Is that near here?"

"It's a ways." Dan frowned, and she guessed that was because he had to give such a vague answer. Dan was a man of precision. No doubt he'd ask someone along the way exactly how far it was to where the hostilities raged and to the California border.

"Are we stopping here?" she asked.

Dan looked about, as though suddenly recalling the buildings around them. A grist mill rose by the edge of another large stream pouring into Pass Creek.

"Do you want to?"

"Not really. It's still quite a ways to Elkton, isn't it?"

"Yes. At least as far as we've already come today."

Anne stopped Bailey in front of what appeared to be a trading post. "Let's just stretch our legs for a minute and let the horses breathe."

Dan seemed agreeable. They didn't want to get caught on the isolated road to Elkton after dusk. Neither of them said as much, but the specters of Indians, wildcats, and ruffians hovered in Anne's mind. And there was always the question of propriety. She'd promised a number of people that she wouldn't be out alone with Dan at night. She wanted to be able to report to her friends later with a clear conscience. Not that Dan would try to take advantage of the situation. He was much too genteel for that.

Was that what made her categorize Dan as "unsuitable for husband material"? Was he just too much of a gentleman? The shocking idea brought heat to her cheeks.

She slid to the ground without waiting for Dan to help her. As she walked about, pretending to take great interest in the tiny town, she wondered why she should blush over a dull man. She sneaked a glance back toward where he stood beside Star, working at one of the rawhide strings holding his pack to the saddle. True, Dan didn't have an adventuresome spirit. But he wasn't as bland as she'd found him a month ago.

They left Anlauf behind and rode steadily for two hours, stopped for an hour to let the horses rest, and moved on toward Elkton. Where the road was overshadowed by huge pines, an eerie feeling swept over Anne.

"There's nothing like this in England. All the forests have been cut over and over for wood."

"I guess we've both seen a lot of new things since we joined the wagon train," Dan said.

Anne looked over her shoulder. As far back as she could see, something moved along the trail.

"Dan!" She reined Bailey in and swung around for a better look.

"What is it?" he asked.

"I'm not sure. I thought I saw a rider. But I don't see anyone now."

"Perhaps it was a deer crossing the trail."

"I don't think so. It looked like a grayish horse with a man on it, but it was way back there at the bend." She pointed.

Dan stared at the back trail for another moment, then turned Star. "Let's put a little speed on and get out of these woods."

Anne said no more but gladly urged Bailey into a canter. They rode side-by-side when the road permitted, and Dan let her take the lead when the ruts and washouts were bad.

They rounded a bend, and he pulled Star in, squinting at the trail ahead.

Anne rode up beside him. As far ahead as she could see, a line of pack animals plodded along the route.

"Freighters," Dan said.

"Can we pass them?"

"Should be able to." He glanced up at the bluff looming over them on the side away from the stream. "We might have to stay behind them for a while, but it won't be for long in any case. The town can't be far ahead."

As their horses trotted up behind the string of pack mules, the freighter who rode last in line swiveled in his saddle and looked back.

"Hello," he called.

"Good afternoon," Dan replied, riding

ahead of Anne. "Where you headed?"

"Elkton, then Scottsburg," the freighter said.

"How far out are we from Elkton?" Dan asked.

"Less than two miles."

"That's good to hear." Dan looked back at Anne. "Not much farther."

The freighter stared past him, and when he focused on Anne his eyes bulged. "What do you know? This must be our lucky day — two winsome women in one afternoon." He laughed and met Dan's gaze but sobered when he realized Dan wasn't amused.

"Sorry, mister. No offense to your better half. It's just that we saw a rather robust redhead ride past us a couple of hours ago."

"Watch your tongue," Dan growled.

Anne pulled gently on Bailey's reins and fell back a little. Dan could get information from the rough freighters. She would keep in the background until he came and told her what he planned to do. Perhaps once they got beyond this hill, where the road squeezed between the creek and a steep incline, they could pass the mule train.

Sure enough, he soon turned Star and rode back to her.

"He says there's a place up ahead where we can get up off the road and pass them

146

— where the hillside isn't so abrupt."

They rode at a walk for a few more minutes until the vista opened up ahead of them. The widening horizon promised open farmland.

"Come on," Dan said. "Let's get some speed up."

Anne urged Bailey to follow him, and they trotted off the path into the weeds and bushes. As they dodged between a few pines, she wasn't sure they were making much headway against the freighters. At last the ground evened out and they came to a farm with a hayfield bordering the road. They cantered along the edge, parallel to the long line of mules. More than thirty pack animals, all heavily loaded, made up the caravan. The drovers looked up one at a time, as she and Dan came into their peripheral vision. All of them stared at Anne, and she felt her face flush. Determined not to let them engage her in conversation, she gazed straight forward, at Dan's broad shoulders. He did make a magnificent figure on horseback. Why had she never noticed that before? She could almost see him riding to hounds at Stoneford. He would enjoy the chase — but she doubted he'd take to the social life in the aristocratic circles of England.

At last they were past the freighters. Dan kept to the field a bit longer, and she was glad he didn't take her up onto the road immediately in front of their leaders. It was embarrassing enough to be seen with her hair coming loose and fluttering behind her. She did hope they found decent accommodations this evening. Something told her the muleteers would get rowdy when the sun went down.

As they neared Elkton, fatigue set in. Bailey's easy trot had become jarring, and Anne would have given much to stop the motion of the horse. When at last the town appeared, she gazed around in disbelief.

"Are we there? Truly?"

"Yes." Dan smiled gently at her. "I know you're exhausted, but really, Anne, you've been a wonderful traveler. You haven't complained once."

"And we'll make it to Scottsburg tomorrow?" Her voice had a plaintive note she regretted, but Dan's smile only deepened.

"Yes, dear lady. I'll ask about it, but I'm sure it's only half the distance we've come today, though we'll follow the Umpqua, and they say it takes more turns than a screwdriver."

She stared at him for a moment before her tired brain caught up. She laughed. "I don't mind a twisty river, so long as we get there. Oh Dan, just think! Scottsburg tomorrow, and perhaps I shall see Uncle David the next day."

Cautious Dan couldn't exult with her. He gave a judicious nod. "Perhaps. For now, I suppose we'd best find accommodations."

"Oh look! There's a place serving food." Anne pointed to a one-story building with a crudely lettered sign: MEALS.

"Did you want to eat?" Dan asked.

"Let's find rooms first. Perhaps it will be a nice boardinghouse with supper included. But I'll admit I'm hungry, and I'll wager you'd like a cup of coffee and some hot food."

"I wouldn't turn it down." Dan jerked his head toward a man driving up the street in a farm wagon. "Why don't I ask this fellow if he knows where we can stay?"

Anne waited with the horses while Dan walked out to meet the farmer. The man halted his team in the street and talked earnestly for a couple of minutes, pointing here and there as he spoke. Dan took it all in, nodding at strategic points. He turned and jogged back to Anne while the farmer and his team clopped off eastward.

"He says there's at least three hotels or boardinghouses, all run out of private

149

homes. The freighters will probably camp outside the village, so we don't need to worry about them crowding us out. One of the boardinghouses is right over there." He pointed across the street and down a bit, to a graceful wood-frame house of three full stories.

"That looks respectable," Anne said.

"Let's go and ask if they have two rooms." Dan untied the horses, and they decided to walk, leading their mounts the short distance.

The cushioned rocking chairs on the front porch tempted Anne, but she allowed Dan to guide her inside. In the foyer, an impressive, walnut-railed staircase wound upward. A table served as a desk, with a box divided into pigeonholes mounted on the wall behind it. The furniture looked solid and functional. Anne did not aspire to elegance on the frontier, just comfort, and the cozy fire burning in a stone fireplace assured her she would find it here.

A middle-aged woman came through a doorway and smiled at them. "Stopping over, folks?"

"Yes." Dan stepped forward as she moved behind the desk. "We're in need of two rooms, if you have them."

She frowned. "Well, I've got one nice front

room you could have, but if you need another . . ." She peered past him at Anne. "Is it just the two of you, or do you have children?"

"It's just us." Dan's face colored beneath his stubble of a beard. The poor man! He was so shy, this must be quite a trial for him. Anne stifled a giggle.

"Well, we could put the lady in the front room," the landlady said, "but you, sir, would have to share with two of the miners."

"Oh well . . ." Dan glanced around at Anne. "What do you think?"

She walked over and stood beside him. "Might there be another place with more rooms?" she asked. "We thought we liked the look of your house, but Mr. Adams would prefer privacy, I'm sure." He hadn't squawked about sharing with the Randall boys in Cottage Grove last night, but Anne sensed that sharing a room with a couple of prospectors alarmed him. On the other hand, a gentleman like Uncle David would probably be classified as a miner in this situation, so perhaps bedding down in the same room with them wouldn't be too uncomfortable.

"Well, now, I've got a little room out back," the woman said. "It's not much —

just a lumber room, we call it. It's off the woodshed, and we store trunks there. My Jack put a cot in there when he came home last summer, because his room was full of argonauts. If you want to see it, sir, maybe you'd consent to sleep out there. I could make the lady nice and cozy in the front room, and we wouldn't charge you much for the shed."

"That sounds agreeable," Dan said. "Thank you."

"Let's go take a look. If you're not put off by the boxes and trunks, we'll make a transaction here."

"And do you serve meals?" Anne asked as they followed the woman out to her spotless kitchen.

She lit a spill at her cookstove and used the roll of paper to light a kerosene lantern. "I put breakfast on the table at seven. Other meals, you have to go elsewhere. But there's a couple of places where you can get good, plain food." She led them out the back door and through an attached room with slatted walls, piled to the rafters with split firewood. "Here we go. I'm Jenny Austin, by the by. I only let this room now and again, but it's all made up fresh." She opened the door and walked in, holding the lantern high.

The windowless lumber room was as clean

as the kitchen. Boxes, kegs, and a couple of trunks filled half the floor space. On the other side was a narrow bed bearing a quilt patterned with bright greens, reds, and whites. Nearby were a washstand and a crate set on end, with a calico curtain hiding the shelves of the improvised bedside table.

"It's not much, but such as it is, it could be worse."

"I'll take it," Dan said.

"Very well, then. If you want to bring in your things, I'll show the lady to her room." They followed her back through the kitchen. A tall, thin man wearing a vest and white shirt stood near the desk in the foyer.

"There's my husband," Mrs. Austin said. She introduced them and left the men to settle the registry and payment.

They were halfway up the stairs before Anne realized she should have given Dan some of her dwindling cash or else stepped up and paid Mr. Austin directly. She hesitated on the landing.

"Everything all right, dearie?" Mrs. Austin asked. "My Bill will bring your things up in a jiffy — or a couple of jiffies."

"I'm just tired, thank you."

"Well, you'll probably want the nearest eatery, then. Willis and Simpson's, near the bridge. The place doesn't look like much, but I'm told they've got a new cook and the pie's worth eating."

She led Anne into a charming room with rose trellis wallpaper and white muslin curtains. Mrs. Austin lit the lamp for her and spread back the covers. "There. If you want a fire, ask Bill when he brings your luggage. Or he can have one burning when you come back from supper. It's likely to rain tonight, and you don't want the damp to settle in your lungs."

"That's very kind of you," Anne said. "Would you please tell Mr. Adams I shall be down in ten minutes to go for supper?"

"I'll do that very thing." Mrs. Austin backed out of the room with a smile and shut the six-paneled door.

Anne almost felt as though she were back in St. Louis. The plump mattress under the crocheted bedspread called to her, but she brushed off her skirt and peered into the looking glass hanging over the maple dresser. The disarray of her hair alarmed her. If only Elise were here to dress it for her.

She took off her hat and removed the hairpins. It might take more than her promised ten minutes to repair this damage.

A tap at the door alerted her to Mr.

Austin's punctuality. She opened it to him and gratefully took her satchel from him.

Dan was waiting in a velvet-covered chair near the front desk when she descended the stairs a quarter of an hour later. He wore the same trousers he'd had on all day but had put on a fresh shirt and added a ribbon tie and somehow managed to shave in the brief time she'd allotted him.

"I'm sorry I've kept you waiting," she said.

"Not at all. Shall we go? A couple of other patrons came in from the restaurant and praised the new cook's venison roast."

"Indeed? I wonder what's brought such a masterful chef to this wilderness." Anne took his arm, and they walked out into the twilight. "Oh, the horses!" She glanced toward the hitching rail, where one sad-looking dun was tied.

"Mr. Austin assured me he would take good care of them."

"Good. Oh Dan, I need to settle with you about the payment for our rooms." She glanced up at him shyly from beneath the brim of her bonnet. This wasn't a subject a lady liked to broach.

"You mustn't think of that," he said. "We've discussed this before. Frankly, I was glad to have a chance to help out." He paused at the edge of the street and gazed

down at her with gray eyes so compassion-
ate that Anne almost blushed. "Anne,
forgive me for asking, but perhaps it's time
I did. Are you truly all right financially?"

"Oh Dan, please don't —"

Before she could say more, he held up a
hand. "I'm sorry. I know how you dislike
this type of discussion, but you've confided
in me that the family fortune is slated for
your uncle, not for you. I'm not a wealthy
man, but I am able to see us through this
expedition. If that would help you, just say
the word."

Her face must now be a deep shade of
scarlet that would draw unwanted attention.
She looked down as she tried to regain her
composure.

"Daniel, I appreciate your friendship and
your generosity. What you say is true, but I
should feel ill-bred and tawdry if I let a man
— even a gentleman such as yourself —
bear my expenses."

He grasped her hand where she'd tucked
it through his arm and squeezed her fingers.
"Dear Anne, I wouldn't want that. But
neither would I want you embarrassed if
your funds gave out on you. From here on,
I'll keep paying my own share, and you just
give me the sign if you need a bit of as-

sistance, all right? We won't speak of it again."

She wanted to be cross with him, but she couldn't. Instead, her love of words betrayed her into a tiny smile. "And what's the sign, I wonder?"

Dan's worry creases smoothed out. "Why, just tell them your hired man will take care of the bill."

"Hired man? You should be a butler at least."

"I'm afraid the people here wouldn't know what to do with a butler. Maybe your guide?"

"How about my friend?" She returned the pressure on his fingers.

"I like that. Shall we?" He nodded toward the low building with the crudely painted sign board.

"Indeed. I'm famished." She stepped eagerly with him toward the ramshackle restaurant. She wouldn't consider what her British friends would think of this place, or even Elise, who had traveled across the plains with her. In truth, the place looked a bit homey in a crude way, a welcome refuge for travelers.

"Mr. Austin told me just before you came downstairs that those freighters we passed earlier brought an injured man in." Dan

157

guided her out of the path of a wagon.

"Really? One of their men was hurt?"

"Not one of theirs. They said he'd passed them this afternoon, and then later they came upon him lying in the road. Apparently his horse had thrown him. The horse was off the road, grazing. But the fellow was out cold. They tossed cold water in his face and he woke up, but he appeared to be quite shaken, so they brought him in to town."

"Is there a doctor here?" Anne asked.

"Mr. Austin says there is — one the steamship owners brought in for their crews. I suppose he'll be all right."

A drop of water splashed on Anne's nose. "Oh dear, it's raining."

Dan seized her hand and pulled her the remaining few steps to the door of the restaurant.

Millie peered out the half-open kitchen door without losing a stroke in stirring her cake batter.

"You got that johnnycake ready?" Andrew Willis yelled. Her new boss seemed to have only one pitch to his voice, and it was aimed to carry over the roar of conversation in the dining room behind him.

"I just took it out of the oven."

"When will the next batch of stew be ready?"

"Not for another twenty minutes or so. The carrots are still crunchy." Millie leaned so she could see past him. If Anne Stone and Dan Adams showed up, she wanted some warning.

Andrew glowered at her, and Millie glared back. She could cook, but she couldn't work miracles.

"You should have started it an hour ago."

"How was I to know you'd have this many customers tonight?"

"They'll probably want some flapjacks and sausage then."

"You go ask them. Don't tell me what the clientele 'probably' wants."

He grimaced at her. "Oh, and one fellow wants jam for his biscuit. We got any jam?"

Millie stared at him. "How should I know?"

"You been cooking in here all day. You musta been through all the stuff." Willis stalked to one of the shelves, opened a small crock, and peered into it. "Ha!" He looked around, found a soup bowl and a spoon, plopped two scoops of preserves into the bowl, and strode back into the dining room, letting the door shut with a thunk.

Sweat streamed down Millie's face as she

poured the cake batter into the one pan remotely the right size. She slid it into the oven, mopped her brow with the hem of her apron, and checked the fuel in the firebox. As much as she hated to increase the temperature of the room, she tossed in a couple more sticks of firewood. At the worktable, she cut several slabs of johnnycake and put them on plates.

She'd thrown open the back door ten minutes after she'd been hired, but the occasional breeze that wafted in was no competition for the heat radiated by the cookstove. For six hours she'd slaved to satisfy Willis's burgeoning flock of customers.

She strode out to the back stoop and flapped her apron in front of her face for a minute. The air had cooled since the sun dropped, and a welcome breeze came across the Umpqua. Millie let it caress her cheeks. She didn't mind working when that was the only option, but she hated to sweat. That made it harder to present herself as a lady.

The liveryman had frightened her for a moment, she admitted to herself. She'd feared his idea for her employment was something indecent, and Millie had her limits.

"Andrew needs a cook, over across the

way," he'd said in a conspiratorial tone.

"A cook? For how many people?" Millie had stepped back to avoid his fetid breath.

"Oh, just everyone who passes through here." The man let out a big guffaw. "He ain't had a decent cook since Harry up and left for the gold fields."

"Harry?"

She wished she hadn't asked as she got a rambling tale of Andrew's business partner gone missing — otherwise known as Harry Simpson, formerly the best cook in Elkton. The liveryman walked over to the restaurant with her, making good on his promise to "put in a good word" for her. And when she'd earned ten dollars, he promised to trade his mare for hers.

Andrew Willis had hired her on the spot, and Millie had felt she had little choice, though the way he studied her figure made her flesh crawl. Every man in the rude café stared as well, and Millie had made one condition before she entered the cramped, untidy kitchen and donned Harry's abandoned apron.

"I'll not serve the customers, too. If you want me to cook, I can do that. Mister, I can cook up a cyclone for you. But I won't carry it out to the men. Someone else will have to do that."

"Someone else" turned out to be Andrew himself. Millie wondered that he didn't have a wife or even some neighbor women who would like to work as waitresses, but perhaps the town was too rough and tumble for women. Whatever the reason, she soon found herself cooking ten dishes at once and trying to eke out Andrew's supplies to fill all the orders he brought her.

The door to the dining room banged again, and she slipped back inside.

"What are you *doing*?" Andrew yelled. "We've got hungry people out there."

"Just catching my breath. I'm like to die in here. Oh, there's your johnnycakes."

Andrew looked at the prepared plates and grunted. "I need two beefsteaks and some biscuits. And have you made gravy yet?"

"Beefsteaks?" Millie cried. "I haven't seen any beef except that one bone you gave me to put in the stew when the venison ran out."

"Hmpf. Guess I need to get out to the springhouse and bring in more meat."

"I guess you do. Bring some more chicken, too, if you've got it. I've made three batches of fried chicken, and it's all gone." She placed her hands on her hips. "If this is how it is every night, how did you and Harry keep yourselves in supplies?"

162

"It's been powerful busy today," Andrew admitted. "Guess people heard about you. Harry's been gone a week, and I've been dishing up pretty poor fare. Thought I'd lost all my customers. But when I put the word out this afternoon that I had a new cook and she was making a dozen apple pies, that's when they started lining up at the door."

"Well, there's not much pie left." Millie glanced over at the pie and a half on the sideboard. "You got any more apples?"

"Oh sure. I got a lot of those from the orchard over where the Hudson's Bay Company used to have its fort. I'll bring some in. You've got plenty of coffee, right?"

"Two pots full."

"Well, can you serve that up while I go out and get the stuff you need?"

"I told you, I'm not serving the clientele."

"Aw, come on, Charlotte." She'd told him her name was Charlotte when he'd hired her, as a precaution in case Miss Stone or Mr. Adams or even Sam came in and heard her name. Now she was glad she'd had the presence of mind to do that, since the new cook seemed to be the talk of the town.

"All right, I'll do one round of coffee and pie, and I'll tell folks who haven't had their main meal yet that we're working on it."

Willis grinned. "You're a capital girl, Charlotte. And I wouldn't say it in front of Harry, but you're a really good cook, too." He dove for the back door.

Millie looked at all her pots to make sure nothing would boil over in her absence and checked the progress of the cake. She grabbed two pot holders, took a steaming coffeepot in each hand, and pushed her way through the doorway to the dining room, shoving the door with her backside.

Freighters and miners erupted in cheering and whistling as she turned.

"Hey, you're better-lookin' than Harry!"

"Are you Charlotte? Bring some of that coffee over here!"

"No, darlin', pour mine first. I'm parched."

Millie stared at the room full of rowdy men and sucked in a deep breath. "All right, gentlemen. I've got ten pieces of apple pie left in the kitchen. If you want to get a slice, put fifty cents on the table, and I'll pick it up as I come around."

The men didn't disappoint her, but anted up as she made the rounds, filling their chipped mugs.

"Hey, sweetheart, how much do you charge for kisses?" one miner asked her.

"More than you've got in your pocket."

When she'd picked up five dollars, she called, "Sorry, fellows, the pie just sold out, but if you come back tomorrow, we'll likely have more."

A loud wail drowned her last few words.

Quickly she filled all the cups pushed toward her, dodging a few straying hands and tossing off retorts to their comments. Soon both pots were empty.

"Okay, folks, I need to go make more coffee and take the applesauce cake out of the oven. Those of you who didn't get pie, may I suggest cake or gingerbread? Andrew will be back any second to take your orders."

"Aw, Charlotte, whyn't you take 'em?"

"Because Andrew can't cook, and you all know that. So while I cook, he'll take orders."

As she pulled open the kitchen door, the street door opened and a cold draft swept through the room. She looked toward it and nearly dropped both coffeepots.

Coming through the doorway, clad in a stunning green-and-gold satin dress and a darling velvet cape and bonnet, smiling up at her handsome escort, was Anne Stone.

CHAPTER 9

Millie ducked through the kitchen door and set down the empty coffeepots. She tore off her apron and tossed it on the worktable. Her pocket was heavy with the pie coins. She hugged it close to her thigh as she ran to the corner where she'd left her coat and sack of clothes. Her saddle and other gear were at the livery with her lame mare, but she hadn't wanted to take a chance of losing the dress she'd extracted from Anne Stone's trunk, so she'd brought it along to Andrew's place.

She almost laughed at the thought of elegant Miss Stone sitting down to eat dinner amid the boisterous crowd of miners in the other room. If she weren't in such a hurry, she'd stick around to see whether she actually ate at Andrew's or went someplace else.

She pulled on her coat, hefted the sack, and dashed for the back door.

166

"Whoa, whoa, whoa!" Andrew was coming up the back steps. He shot out an arm to stop her from piling into him and dropped a plucked chicken and a basket of apples. The apples thudded down the steps and rolled hither and yon.

Millie tried to shove past him, but Andrew's fingers clenched her wrist. "Where are you going, missy?"

She stared into his suspicious face for an instant. "I've got to go out back. *You* know." She made a face that she hoped would imply her urgent need to visit the little building a lady would never mention.

"With all your stuff?" Andrew's eyes squinted into slits. "Not running out on the customers, are you? We've got a lot of dinners yet to serve tonight."

She sighed and pulled her wrist from his grasp. "Look, I need to leave. I'm sorry — it's an emergency. Just give me what you owe me, please." She was glad after all that she'd run into him. She'd have slipped away without her pay, and she needed that.

"You ain't worked a whole day yet."

"Pretty near. I mean it, Mr. Willis. I need to get going *now.*"

"Why? What's happened?" He looked past her into the kitchen.

"Nothing, but if I'm not in Scottsburg by

167

morning, something awful will happen."

This didn't satisfy him any better than her earlier answers. He leaned against the doorjamb and studied her with an air of disapproval.

"You're lying. Why?"

"I'm not."

"You planning to ride to Scottsburg all by yourself? 'Cause the steamboat don't leave 'til morning. I know that for a fact."

She looked him over, wondering how big a fib he would swallow. So far she wasn't doing very well. And if he tried to collect money for the pies . . .

"All right, I'll tell you." She blinked several times and tried to conjure up tears. "I went into the dining room, like you said, and gave all the men their coffee. And some of them —" She sniffed. "Some of them said shameful things to me. Mr. Willis, I'm afraid of those men. Some of them have got no morals at all. Please let me go."

Andrew laughed. "You think you'll be safer on the road to Scottsburg than you were in my dining room? Girl, you're loony. What do you think would happen if one of them caught you a mile out of town, all by your lonesome? Besides, I won't let 'em bother you."

She achieved what she hoped was a pathetic quivering of her top lip. "I'm just so scared. And I'm nigh exhausted. I don't think I can cook anymore tonight."

"Well, you've got to. We have a business agreement. Come on, now. Fried chicken, more pies . . . I ain't paying you a cent until you do."

Millie let out a pent-up breath. "All right, but don't make me go out into the dining room again. I don't want them to see me."

"All right, Charlotte. Just you put your apron back on and get busy. I'll go deliver them pie slices and tell the ones still waiting to be patient. How do I know who gets the pie, now?" As he spoke, he picked up the things he'd dropped and placed them on the table.

"Oh, they'll know. Just ask who was promised a slice of pie." She dearly hoped they wouldn't tell him they'd paid her, but if they did, she guessed she'd have to hand over the five dollars.

Andrew loaded the tray and carried it into the dining room. The roar of voices and clinking of silverware on china burst through the doorway then quieted again as the door closed.

Millie looked longingly toward the back door. If she ran now, the liveryman wouldn't trade her a decent horse. She needed the pay Andrew had promised her. She couldn't think of anything more she could do to ensure that Anne Stone and Daniel Adams wouldn't learn who was cooking their dinner. Resolutely, she tied the apron around her again and picked up a limp, naked chicken.

The next morning, Millie crawled out of the hayloft in the barn behind a farmhouse before the sun rose and brushed all traces of her sleeping place from her hair and clothing. The rain had let up after midnight, and for a wonder she'd slept soundly. She hurried through the shadows to the horse trader's corral.

Her saddle was waiting for her in the flimsy shed, and she decided to go ahead and put it on the mare she was taking. If the owner came out before she was done, she'd pay him. If not, she supposed she'd have to go knock on his door and give him the money. She wished she dared to leave Elkton without paying for the horse, but that was too dangerous. He'd have the marshal on her for sure, and she couldn't stand for any delays now, nor too much scrutiny.

Just for a moment, she considered putting her saddle on the bay gelding, which looked to be in better shape than the mare, but she didn't have twenty-five dollars, and she'd never get away with it for less. The horse trader wasn't just big, he was shrewd. She threw one last wistful glance at the gelding. The horse she'd ridden into town got no notice. Millie was glad to be rid of it.

The liveryman arrived, rubbing the sleep from his eyes, as she tied her bundles to the saddle. She'd sneaked a small bag of oats from the farmer's cache last night and had slipped it into the sack with the dress she'd pilfered in Eugene City. At least her new mount would have a little nourishment later.

"Well, Miss Evans, you're about early." He frowned as he eyed the mare. "I guess this means we're doing business."

"Yes, sir, and I've got the money right here. Thank you kindly for recommending me to Mr. Willis."

His eyebrows shot up as she heaped his palm with coins and a few bills. "Well now. I heard there was big doings at Andrew's last night. I almost went over to see if I could get a piece of your pie."

"The pies sold out as fast as I could bake them."

"Do tell." The huge man slapped the mare gently on the withers. "She's a good horse.

Treat her well, and she'll do the same for you."

"Thank you," Millie said. "Say, there hasn't been a fella around asking for me, has there?"

The man shook his head. "You did say you had friends coming in, but nobody's been here inquiring for a lovely young lady."

"Oh, thank you." Millie smiled up at him, knowing she'd get a lot further with him if she played along with his attempts at flirtation. "He's my half brother. Light hair, beard, not nearly so tall as you are." She blinked at him, disgusted with herself, but determined to leave a favorable memory, since she had to leave *some* impression.

"Nope, haven't seen him, but if he comes along, I'll be sure to tell him Miss Charlotte Evans was here."

"Thank you." She almost told him Charlotte wasn't her real name, but then what if Anne Stone made inquiries and learned she'd been here?

She swung up onto the mare's back.

"Her name's Vixen."

Millie almost shouted, "I don't ever name horses." Instead she gave him a farewell wave and set out on the westward road.

David Stone crawled out of his wilted tent

and looked around at the sodden mountain-
side and the rushing creek. He hated rain.
His bay gelding, Captain, named in a fit of
nostalgia and yearning for his brother John,
plodded toward him. He looked black when
he was wet, and David regretted not having
built a shelter for the horse.

Captain came over and rubbed his damp
face against David's arm.

"Good morning." David rubbed between
Captain's ears absently while he considered
his course for the day. He'd have to make
the trip down to Scottsburg for more supplies if he wanted to stay up here to prospect
any longer. He and Captain both had survived on short rations for two days and
would have a very skimpy breakfast.

Maybe he should just pack up his tools
and go home. The rain swelled the stream
and made it hard to work the sluice box —
a difficult job for one man as it was. He
should probably go home and see if that
shiftless Sam Hastings had ruined his farm.

He walked back to the tent, with Captain
tagging after him. Stooping, he pulled out
his nearly empty sack of provisions.

"Here you go, boy." He'd saved the last,
shriveled carrot for his horse. Inside the tent
were his gold pan, spade, pick, and other
tools. If he was going to break camp, he'd

have to pack up everything. He hated to strike a wet tent. At least it wasn't raining this moment — but that didn't mean it wouldn't soon. He squinted up at the low clouds. "Well, Lord, shall we have a cup of tea, and I'll wait for You to speak?"

He always read a little scripture in the morning while his breakfast heated. Maybe God had a message for him today. Lately, he'd been feeling that his life was empty and hadn't a lot of point to it. He'd made money and lost it again, made friends and left them behind, fallen in love and climbed out again. He was forty-one years old, and this morning he felt ancient. He was so thin, he could count his ribs easily, and his left knee ached. The thought of riding all day with his foot confined to the stirrup made it hurt worse — but the prospect of standing in the icy creek wasn't much better.

How did he get to this place? Was he supposed to be this age and not have loved ones around him? He'd bought the farm near Eugene as a place where he could settle down. So why couldn't he feel settled?

Captain nuzzled him for more carrots.

"Sorry, old boy. I haven't got any more. You'll have to make do with what you can browse on." He hated not having decent feed for the horse. He took out a small sack of rolled oats and set aside enough to make himself a small portion of oatmeal, then sprinkled the rest among the weeds. "There. See what you can make of that."

While his tea water and oatmeal heated, David opened his Bible and read a psalm. *"LORD, what is man, that thou takest knowledge of him! Or the son of man, that thou makest account of him! Man is like to vanity; his days are as a shadow that passeth away."* Wasn't that the truth?

His thoughts strayed, as they often had lately, to England. Stoneford. His real home. Was it time to go back? What would he live on, other than his friends' kindness? He'd have no income there. If he sold his mining claim and his farm, he'd have enough to take passage to England, but not enough to set himself up once he got there.

Maybe he should write to his eldest brother, Richard. Why hadn't he kept up the correspondence, anyway? Laziness, he supposed, and the difficulty of making sure he'd get a reply when he'd moved around so much. Now it had been so long since he'd written that he was embarrassed to barge into John's and Richard's lives again.

He recalled the days he'd dangled Richard and Elizabeth's infant on his knees. Little Anne was such a pretty mite. She probably had several brothers and sisters now. John must be married, too. David hoped so — hoped they were both happy and fulfilled.

The water boiled, and he jumped up to fix his tea. Sometimes it was hard to come by out here. A mercantile in Eugene stocked it for him, but the traders in Scottsburg had offered coffee instead. The stock David had carried with him was running out, like all his other provisions, and of course he had no milk to put in it.

He picked up his Bible and read the next verse aloud. " 'Bow thy heavens, O Lord, and come down; touch the mountains, and they shall smoke.' " He looked out over the hills, with the clouds rolling close to their summits. " 'Cast forth lightning, and scatter them; shoot out thine arrows, and destroy them.' "

Thunder cracked, and on the hillside across from the ravine where the stream flowed, lightning split a gnarled cedar tree.

Captain left off nosing about in the dead grass and snorted, whipping his tail back and forth. Raindrops splattered on David's head, and he slammed the Bible shut. He dashed to the tent and placed the book inside. Poor Captain. The horse would have to fend for himself in the storm.

David ran back to the fire and grabbed his pot of oatmeal and his cup of tea. Captain trotted off toward the lee of a rocky outcropping. David crawled into the tent and sat for a moment, listening to the rain pelt the canvas. A gust of wind shook it so hard he wondered how long before the whole thing would collapse on him.

"Well, Lord, if that's Your opinion, I'd say it's definitely time to go down the mountain."

Millie arrived in Scottsburg late in the morning. She'd shaken off Andrew's pleadings and refused to come back to cook breakfast. She'd made a good trade, as far as the horse was concerned. The new mare moved along briskly through the wooded hills. She'd met several horsemen and a couple of farmers driving wagons eastward and passed more freighters and some drovers taking a small herd of cattle west. The mare didn't balk at bridges, and she had a smooth canter — overall, Millie felt she'd spent her ten dollars well, and she still had the pie money in her pocket.

If she could have afforded the time, she had no doubt she could have struck an agreement with Andrew Willis by which they both profited. But she didn't want to work hard all day in a sweltering kitchen. She wanted to take things a little easier and be ready to go out dancing in the evening, instead of needing to soak her feet and tumble into bed.

No, she had no regrets about leaving Elkton. One thing troubled her, though: where was Sam?

She'd seen no sign of him. Because of Miss Stone's presence, she hadn't dared peek out into the dining room again to see if he came into the restaurant last night. Before she went to the livery that morning to make her trade, she'd sneaked around to the stable behind the fancy boardinghouse. Sure enough, the horses Anne Stone and Dan Adams rode were in there. She was ahead of them now. She'd hoped to have a couple of days' lead on them, but she'd have to make do with a few hours.

But it would have been nice to see Sam for a minute. What was he up to, anyway? Not enough to hold her adversaries back, that much was obvious. Odd that he hadn't found her, though. Her lame horse should have told Sam she was in Elkton, and he could have located her if he'd hung around. She'd give him a piece of her mind next time they met.

A downpour broke as she reached the

outskirts of town. She pushed the mare into a canter and rode the last quarter mile squinting against the fat raindrops that pelted her face. The brim on her hat served only to funnel the water into a nearly steady stream that poured down her back and soaked through her coat. By the time she saw a sign for a hotel, she was bedraggled and uncomfortable.

She threw the ends of Vixen's reins toward the hitching rail and ran up the steps. She shoved the door. It flew inward and crashed against the wall. The desk clerk and three other men in the lobby looked up.

"Sorry." Millie gave the clerk a weak smile and closed the door. Suddenly out of the wind and drumming rain, she wondered if she was going deaf. The four men still stared at her. Not the entrance she liked to make. She dredged up a smile and strode toward the desk.

"May I help you, ma'am?" the clerk asked.

She hesitated. She didn't want to blurt out a request for the rates in front of the other customers. You never knew when it would be advantageous to make a gentleman's acquaintance, and she didn't want them all to know first thing that she was nearly broke.

"Uh, yes, thank you." She raised her chin

and hoped her disheveled auburn tresses held a hint of mystery, not complete squalor. "I wondered if you have a room free."

"Well, yes, we do, ma'am." The clerk turned the registry toward her. "That's a dollar a night."

"Oh." She kicked herself mentally for letting that give her pause. She had five dollars and seventy cents in her pocket, but she certainly didn't want the clerk to know that. With meals and care for the horse, that wouldn't last more than two or three days in this mining town. Her impulse to ask if they had a cheaper room might be a mistake, though. She picked up the pen. "I may wish to stay several nights."

"Of course. Our policy is, if you pay one night in advance, you can settle the rest when you leave."

"Perfect." With a flourish, she signed, "C. R. Evans." She didn't think Miss Stone and Mr. Adams knew her last name, and if they came in behind her, she doubted they'd recognize the name Evans. But sticking with the alias "Charlotte" that she'd used in Elkton seemed wise. One of the men who'd bought pie from her at Andrew Willis's establishment might ride over here.

"I have a horse outside," she murmured, in tones as like Anne Stone's as she could muster. "Do you have accommodations for my mare?"

"Yes, ma'am. I'll have somebody see to it. Fifty cents a night. Seventy-five if you want us to give him oats."

She nodded. "It's a brown mare with a sidesaddle — out front."

"Very good, ma'am."

"I shouldn't like the saddle to be ruined."

"We'll get her under cover right away, ma'am. Do you have bags?"

"Oh . . ." Millie couldn't think how she'd explain to the snooty clerk that she carried her clothes in a grain sack. "I shipped a valise that will probably come later when the freighter comes in, but there is a saddle-bag and a sack containing a gift for my cousin. If your man could just bring those to my room . . . ?"

He glanced down at the registry. "It'll be there before you get your bonnet off, Mrs. Evans." He smiled at her stupidly.

Was he making fun of her wet, drooping bonnet? It took Millie a moment to realize he was waiting for her dollar. Obviously he wouldn't put her horse under cover until she paid.

She took out the pouch her coins were in and held it below the level of the counter so that the clerk couldn't see how light it was.

181

She placed the money beside the registry.

The clerk smiled and whipped the coins off the surface like greased lightning.

"Thank you, ma'am. It's room 202, up those stairs. Just throw the bolt when you're inside, and use this key when you go out." He placed a substantial steel key in her palm.

Millie paused, observing through lowered lashes that the other three men lingered and threw frequent glances her way. Maybe she could wangle a free dinner with one of them.

She cleared her throat and said to the clerk, "My cousin is to meet me here, but I've learned today that he'll be delayed. I may have to wait a few days for him to arrive."

"Very good, ma'am. If you need anything, just let us know."

"Do you serve meals?" she asked.

"Yes, we do. That door" — he pointed to her right, beyond the staircase — "is our dining room. They'll be serving dinner in about an hour, and supper from five to eight."

"Thank you." She lifted her skirt perhaps an inch more than was absolutely necessary and made her way leisurely up the stairs, well aware of the four pair of eyes watching her. Either she looked so outrageous they couldn't believe her, or she'd kept enough of her usual poise and comeliness to fool them all into thinking she was a lady. Time would tell.

A thought occurred to her, and she almost cast it aside, but its attractiveness made her pause with one foot on the next-to-top step. She would do it! But not until she'd had a chance to clean up.

A half hour later she again approached the front desk, this time without the audience of loiterers.

"Ah, Mrs. Evans." The clerk's eyes lit in appreciation. Apparently her ministrations to her hair and wardrobe were successful. "How may I help you?"

"My cousin mentioned that he hoped to meet a gentleman here. I thought perhaps you knew him — a Mr. Stone."

"Mr. David Stone? The Britisher?"

Millie smiled. "He's the one."

"He often stays here. In fact, I shouldn't be surprised if he came in today — or very soon. Would you like me to give him your name if I see him — or your cousin's name?"

"Oh that won't be necessary. I'll let my cousin handle it when he arrives. Thank you very much."

CHAPTER 10

Dan felt like an utter failure. He'd gotten Anne halfway to Scottsburg when the heavens let loose on them. They'd taken shelter in a thick stand of pines, but even so they'd been soaked to the skin within half an hour. The fierce wind tore at them and made his teeth chatter. Anne stood between the horses, leaning against Bailey's side and shivering uncontrollably.

People in Champoeg said this rain would keep up all winter. No snow to speak of this side of the Cascades, but lots and lots of rain.

He leaned close to her and laid his hand on her arm. "Anne, I don't think this is going to stop. I want to build a fire."

"Can't we just mount up and gallop for Scottsburg?"

"I'm afraid you'll be sick if you don't get warm soon."

"Maybe there's a house not far away, and

they'd let us come in and get warm."

"Now that sounds like a good idea. Let me help you into the saddle."

Less than a mile farther down the road, they came upon a farmhouse with a snug barn and fields spreading behind it. With a prayer of thanks, Dan led the way up the lane, dismounted, and knocked on the door.

It was opened by a sturdy girl of about twelve who looked him over suspiciously then called over her shoulder, "Mama! It's a half-drowned man, and there's a lady with him."

"What?" A thin woman of about forty hurried over, wiping her hands on her apron. She sized him up in a glance and looked out at Anne. "Oh sir, look at you! Bring your wife in. This isn't weather to be out in."

As Dan went back to get Anne, he heard the woman tell her daughter, "Go out and get Billy and Felix. Tell them to put these horses in the barn and brush them down well and feed them."

The girl threw on a hood and shawl and scurried out the door and around the house.

Dan raised his arms to Anne, and for once she let the reins drop and fell into his embrace. Her lips were blue. "Let me carry you."

"No, please." A look of alarm crossed her

face. She gained her footing and leaned on his arm. "Thank you, Daniel. I shall be fine."

He hurried her inside, and the farm wife shut the door behind him.

"Is she ill?"

"Just chilled through, but I fear she'll be ill because of it."

"Bring her right in here. She can lie down on my bed." The woman pushed aside a calico curtain in a doorway.

"Oh really," Anne said, "I'll be all right, now that we're out of the wet and the wind."

"Still, you'd like to change, wouldn't you?" the woman asked.

"You're right. That would be nice."

The woman smiled and eyed her cautiously. "English, aren't you?"

"Yes."

"I'm Lena Moss."

Anne held out her gloved hand. "Anne Stone. And this is my friend, Daniel Adams."

"Oh." Mrs. Moss looked from one to the other of them in confusion.

"We're not married," Dan said quickly. "I'm escorting Miss Stone to see her uncle in Scottsburg. This driving rain caught us."

Mrs. Moss's expression went from scandalized to soft with compassion. "Well then, let's see if we can make you comfortable. Do you have extra clothing along?"

"Yes," Anne said. "In my valise."

"I'll have the boys bring it in."

A few moments later, young Felix brought Anne's bag in, and Mrs. Moss led her into the next room. Dan took off his coat and hat, hung them near the door, and moved toward the stove. It warmed the kitchen end of the long room, ticking merrily away, and a coffeepot and a kettle of water on its surface sent off steam.

"Help yourself."

He turned to find Mrs. Moss behind him, bearing an armload of Anne's wet clothing.

"Cups are in the cupboard yonder." She nodded toward a large cupboard topped with rows of shelves.

Dan took down a china mug and poured himself coffee. Mrs. Moss brought a wooden rack from a corner and set about spreading Anne's skirt, petticoat, bodice, and stockings to dry.

"My husband went to Scottsburg this morning," she said. "He'll be back directly, unless he's decided to wait out the rain."

"It's a raw day." Dan could well imagine the farmer taking refuge in a haberdashery or a café.

The three youngsters tumbled in at the

back door and bantered as they took off their wraps.

"Here, you!" Mrs. Moss shook a finger at them. "Stop that rowdiness, or you'll not have any cookies."

"Cookies?"

"Yes, Becky May Moss, but not for girls who charge in here behaving like hoydens."

Becky hung her shawl on a hook and faced her mother demurely. "Yes, ma'am. Shall I get a plate and offer them to our guests?"

"Now, that's better," Mrs. Moss said. She adjusted the position of the drying rack on the other side of the stove and walked toward the cupboard. "Give Mr. Adams some, by all means, and I expect Miss Stone would appreciate a few as well, once she's got her dry clothes on." She threw Dan a glance over her shoulder. "And you, Mr. Adams. When she comes out, please feel free to use our room. Your things are dripping wet, too, I've no doubt."

"I cannot thank you enough," Dan said. His wool trousers were beginning to steam and feel a bit too warm against his skin, so he moved his chair a little farther from the stove.

"I do hope the lady won't be ill," Mrs. Moss said. "She's just a bit of a thing, isn't she? Pretty."

"I brought the rest of the baggage up, Mama," Felix said. "It's in the woodshed."

"Well, bring it in here. Mr. Adams can't use it out there, now, can he?"

Felix opened the back door and lugged in Dan's valise and saddlebags. Billy shut the door behind him, giving Felix a playful tap as he passed with his hands full. Felix growled at him.

"That's enough," their mother said. "Put those things down and get your snack. And behave like civilized young gentlemen. Becky, you'll be setting the table for supper when you're done."

"Yes'm. Are they staying?" Becky cast an uncertain glance at Dan from the corner of her eye.

"Oh, we couldn't impose," Dan said quickly.

"Dear me, of course you could." Mrs. Moss brought a cast-iron frying pan to the stove. "The lady can't go on in this weather. You'll stay with us tonight." She eyed Dan archly, as though daring him to contradict her. "You, sir, will have to sleep upstairs with the boys. It's all right, though. They've got the chimney through their room, and you'll be warm. Miss Stone can take Becky's room."

Anne wouldn't like it one bit — being

189

delayed another night from finding her uncle. "But we can't —"

"Don't fret, young man. 'Twon't be the first time Becky's stayed in with us."

The curtain in the bedroom doorway pushed to one side and Anne appeared in an attractive but serviceable gray dress with black braid. She'd combed her hair and pulled it neatly up into a twisted bun.

"Thank you so much, Mrs. Moss. I feel 100 percent better."

"You're most welcome, my dear. I was just discussing our arrangements for tonight with Mr. Adams."

Anne looked at him with arched eyebrows.

Dan stood and grabbed his valise. "Mrs. Moss can tell you. I'll step into the other room and get out of these damp things."

"Sit right down, dearie, and have a cup of tea with sugar. Since you're English, I'll warrant you like it with milk in it."

"Yes, thank you."

"And we've oatmeal cookies and . . ."

Dan pushed the curtain back and made good his escape.

David let Captain pick his way down to Scottsburg as fast as the poor horse wanted to go. He was not only laden down with David's weight and that of his mining gear, but everything was dripping wet. On a sunny day, David would have stopped to see Whitey Pogue, a crusty old miner with a claim lower down on the same creek as his own, but in this foul weather, he decided not to make the detour.

An hour before sunset, he arrived at the stable of the Miner's Hotel, the best hostelry in town. David unloaded his horse and rubbed him down while Captain dove into a ration of crimped oats. He'd much rather see to it himself than wait for one of the hotel employees to care for the horse. They might not give Captain the attention he deserved for his faithful service.

At last, weary to the bone, David trudged across the muddy barnyard and around to the front door of the hotel.

"Ah, Mr. Stone," the clerk called out. "I thought you might come in today."

"Yes, it's miserable up there in the hills." David couldn't help but notice the attractive woman with auburn hair who glanced up from her reading when he entered. She sat in a niche to one side of the room, on an upholstered settee where patrons sometimes met for conversation.

He took his key from the desk clerk. "Thank you, Ed."

"I'll get your satchel out of the storeroom

and bring it right up. Will you be wanting a hot bath before dinner?"

David laughed, looking down at the mud-smeared clothing that clung to him. "It would be criminal not to, I fear. Bring on the hot water."

"And does your horse need care?"

"I put him up myself, thank you." David turned toward the stairs and was surprised that the woman he'd noted earlier had approached and stood near the newel post, watching him.

"Mr. Stone?" she asked.

"Yes."

"Mr. David Stone?"

"That's right."

She wasn't the prettiest woman he'd ever met, but she had an interesting face, and her hair shimmered in the lantern light, with red highlights in the brunette. Her dress was made of commonplace calico, covered by a silky shawl — an import if he wasn't mistaken.

"Do I know you?" he asked.

"Oh no, sir, but I heard the clerk speak your name. I'm visiting from Eugene City, and an acquaintance there mentioned you to me. She said you were over this way and it was possible I might meet you. I hope you don't think me too bold to approach you."

David chuckled. "Not if you don't think me too loathsome to approach in my present state."

She looked slowly from his face, which sported several days' growth of whiskers, down to his open coat and vest, his mud-spattered trousers, and his high leather boots.

"Oh no. Loathsome is not at all the word I would choose, sir."

To David's consternation, he felt the heat in his face. "Well, ma'am, you have the advantage of me. You know my name, but I haven't heard yours."

"Forgive me. I'm Charlotte Evans."

She held out a dainty, gloved hand, and he took it. The woman had a certain appeal — a forthright charm that many of the frontier women lacked. David studied her face for a moment. She'd used cosmetics, but with a light touch. Probably she was near thirty, but she had the assets to keep a man in doubt. And she seemed intelligent, something he liked in a woman but rarely had the opportunity to enjoy these days.

"Are you engaged for dinner?" he asked. "Perhaps we could discuss our mutual acquaintances in Eugene."

"Actually, I thought I was, but I'm not. My cousin was to meet me here today, but I've been informed he's delayed."

"Well then, Miss Evans, it would give me pleasure if you would dine with me. The hotel lays a creditable table."

"I should love to." She lowered her lashes and said softly, "Though it's Mrs. Evans. My late husband —" She broke off with a slight cough.

"I'm sorry. Forgive me."

"Don't distress yourself over it," she murmured. "James passed on five years ago, and I've begun a new phase of my life. In fact, that is why I'm here in Scottsburg. But perhaps that is better left to tell later. I'm sure you're anxious to get to your room."

"I'll be eager to hear about it. Shall we say in one hour?"

She bowed her head in assent.

David smiled as he hurried up the stairs. He hadn't expected a charming dinner companion tonight.

Millie spent the hour preparing for her dinner with Mr. Stone. Part one of her plan had worked to perfection. If only she had time to carry out the rest. She dressed her hair carefully, letting her curls tumble down from the bunch at the back of her head. She refreshed her powder and lip rouge with an expertise gained from years of experience.

Last, she wriggled into the gown she had obtained from the obliging Miss Stone. On her arrival at the hotel, she'd asked for two things — a hot bath and a flatiron to press her clothing with. She'd let go of a precious nickel to have the hired boy black her shoes. She'd have liked to have a prettier pair, but the hem of Miss Stone's gown was long enough to hide all but the gleaming tips of the only pair she had along on this journey.

She eyed herself in the mirror over her dresser, turning this way and that. She could think of no way to improve her appearance. She only hoped Stone's niece and Adams didn't show up at this hotel. They might — it seemed to be the nicest one in town, and the prices reflected that, as did David Stone's choice to stay here. The only thing she could imagine that would be worse than meeting Anne Stone in the dining room was to have Sam come bumbling in and claim her. Her masquerade with David would be over in a trice. She was glad her brother hadn't shown up yet — though she was a little concerned about him. Sam never learned how to take care of himself, and she despaired of ever teaching him.

Perhaps he was doing his job after all. So

far as she knew, Adams and Miss Stone hadn't ridden into town yet.

The other vital ingredient for this evening was a plausible story. She went over the tale she'd concocted in her mind. David Stone must believe every word she said, and he must sympathize with her. She mustn't make her plight sound too pathetic, or he wouldn't want to get involved. No, she must present herself as a strong, charming woman in difficult circumstances. One who didn't need rescuing but was not above accepting the hand of friendship. One who valued a smart, competent, independent man. That shouldn't be too difficult to put across to Stone.

The fact that James Evans had left her a widow, though inconvenient at the time, was now an asset. She'd just have to be careful not to divulge too much about James, how he made his living, or the manner in which he had died.

She gave her hair a final pat and picked up the silky shawl. She'd never owned one so nice, and her gown was beyond anything she'd ever seen, let alone imagined. It was just the tiniest bit tight, but not so bad it made her look bulgy, and she didn't suppose the gentlemen who saw her in it would mind. The shawl would help hide her flaws, too. She didn't own a nice purse, so she tucked the pouch with its remaining coins into the pocket beneath her skirt. Gloves, courtesy of Miss Stone, and a fan she'd acquired without benefit of a receipt from a shop in Eugene completed her ensemble. She glided down the stairs well pleased with herself.

As she'd planned, David Stone was already in the lobby, waiting for her. He paced across to the front window and looked out at the rain-drenched street, his hands shoved into his pockets. She'd picked a handsome one. Tall, with only a hint of silver in his light hair. He'd reached maturity, but he was still in mighty fine shape. She appraised him as she would a horse and knew she'd pick this one out of a herd. The fact that he had means was crucial. His fine looks were a bonus.

He turned and started back toward her, letting his gaze swing over the lobby and up the stairs. With satisfaction, she noted the exact moment he saw her. His eyes lit, and his smile made her shiver with anticipation. She'd succeeded in part two of her plan.

She continued down, and he met her at the bottom of the steps.

"Mrs. Evans, you look lovely."

"Why, thank you."

He nodded in appreciation. "I haven't seen a woman so well-turned-out since I left St. Louis — or possibly even New York. I must say, it's refreshing."

"You flatter me, sir."

"Not without cause. Shall we?" He crooked his arm and offered it to her.

Millie slipped her hand inside his elbow. "Delighted, Mr. Stone. This is such a treat."

"Oh, you've sampled the hotel's cuisine?"

"No, I meant finding a dinner companion who can carry an intelligent conversation. You've no idea what a dearth of good company I've undergone since I left San Francisco a month ago."

"Oh? You came up from San Francisco? I've been thinking of traveling down there. You must tell me about it."

"Mr. Adams!"

"Yes, Felix?" Dan was still shaving when the boy burst into the loft room he'd shared with Felix and Billy the night before.

"It's your horse, sir."

Dan's stomach tightened. "What about him? What's wrong?"

"When we got out to the barn, he was loose and had his head in the oat bin."

"Oh no." Dan grabbed the towel and quickly wiped the lather from his face.

"We don't think he ate too awful much," Felix said. "And I know for certain sure he was tied when I left him last night. I put him away myself, and I *know* he was hitched. Besides that, we've never known a horse could unhook the top of the grain bin and open it."

Dan reached for his shirt. "Is he acting ill? Standing back on his heels? Nipping at his side or anything like that?"

"No, sir." Felix looked up at him oddly. "There's one funny thing, though."

Dan continued buttoning his shirt. "What's that?"

"Your bridle and Miss Stone's. They're all . . ."

Dan eyed him sharply. "What about them?"

"They're all tied together. Knots everywhere."

Dan froze with his hand on his cuff button. "Knots?"

"That's right." Felix gulped.

"You kids didn't do that, did you?"

"No, sir. We wouldn't."

"I didn't think so." What in the world was going on? Dan finished buttoning his cuffs and slid his vest on. "Take me out there and show me, please."

Felix dashed down the stairs, and Dan followed.

Half an hour later, he entered the Mosses' back door with Felix. Anne was already seated at the kitchen table with Becky, eating a hearty breakfast of eggs, sausage, flapjacks, and dried blackberries. A china teapot sat near her plate, with a pitcher of cream and a bowl of white sugar nearby.

"There you are," she said with a smile. "I thought you were still asleep." She picked up her knife and fork.

"No, I've been out to the barn with Felix." Dan pulled out a chair next to her and sat down. "Anne, I think we should leave as soon as possible. Will you be able to pack up your things as soon as you've eaten?"

She sat still with the knife poised over a flapjack, looking at him with troubled brown eyes. "Of course, Daniel. Is something wrong?"

He sighed. "You remember Cottage Grove? The way our gear was all knotted together?"

Anne smiled wryly. "How could I forget? But wait." She frowned and cocked her head to one side. "We thought the Randall children had done it."

"Well, I don't think that anymore."

She studied him for a moment. "I see."

"It's almost identical to the other job, and I'm pretty sure the Randall kids haven't followed us here."

"I should think not."

Dan shot a glance at Mrs. Moss. She was cracking more eggs at her worktable, but she made no pretense of not listening. "It gets a bit more sinister, I'm afraid."

"Oh?" Anne asked.

"Star was loose in the barn, and the grain bin was open."

"Oh no. Is he all right?"

"We think so, but I'll have to watch him closely today."

"But who — ?" She glanced around. "Oh Daniel. I can hardly believe this is happening."

"Trouble with your horse?" Mrs. Moss asked.

"Yes. Your husband and the boys discovered it when they went out to do their chores," Dan said. "The odd thing is it's not the first time our tack has been tampered with like that."

Anne laid her knife down. "I'll go close up my luggage at once."

"No, finish your breakfast," Dan said.

"You eat, too, young man." Mrs. Moss shook her wooden spoon at him.

Dan smiled. "Thank you, ma'am, I will.

But then we'd best get on to Scottsburg."

"I'll fill your plate right now. Becky, run out and see if you can find me a few more eggs, will you?"

Becky rose, carried her dishes to the sink, and took her hood off its peg. When she was out the back door and their hostess was bustling about to fix his plate, Dan lowered his voice and leaned toward Anne.

"There's something I didn't tell you, and I probably should have." He glanced up. Mrs. Moss was approaching with a mounded plate. "Oh, thank you. That looks delicious." He straightened and shook out the napkin at his place.

She set the plate in front of him. "You're welcome. I'll step out for another jug of milk, if you want a bit of privacy."

Dan smiled at her. "That's very kind of you."

Mrs. Moss slipped out into the woodshed, and he looked into Anne's troubled eyes.

"What is it?" she asked.

"Bank Raynor told me the morning we left that Peterson was on the loose. He'd gotten a message from Marshal Nesmith to that effect. I didn't see that it would help things to tell you, but . . . well, I should have, and I'm sorry. I also should have been more vigilant."

Anne stared at him. "You think Peterson would play childish tricks like this? That makes no sense whatever."

Dan leaned back in his chair. "I admit, I struggled with that. But who else, Anne? Think about it."

"I don't know who else, but Peterson wouldn't hang about and tie our reins in knots. Cold-blooded killers don't fool around and play pranks. He wanted to kill my uncle, Daniel. Don't you understand that? To him, Uncle David is worth a lot of money — but only if he's proven dead."

CHAPTER 11

The ride to Scottsburg was mercifully short. Anne's habit was stiff from its soaking the day before. If only Elise were here — she would know how to clean it so that the velvet regained its soft pile. As it was, Anne didn't think she could stand to wear it in the saddle for a full day.

Mrs. Moss had given the name of a friend of hers. The widow kept a clean, respectable boardinghouse on a quiet side street of Scottsburg and charged less than the hotels. They found it without any trouble. Mrs. Zinberg welcomed them, smiling when Anne told her of her friend's recommendation.

"Oh, that's just like Lena. Isn't she the sweetest thing?"

"She took very good care of us," Anne said.

"She would. She's been extra kind since my William died. I'm moving up to Corvallis in the spring, to be with my daughter, but I'm getting by in the meantime."

"My dearest friend lives in Corvallis," Anne said. "I shall have to give you her name before we leave."

A gray drizzle threatened to become a steady rain, and Mrs. Zinberg hustled Anne inside. Dan carried in their bags.

"Why don't you get settled, and I'll take the horses to the livery stable," he told Anne.

Mrs. Zinberg said ruefully, "It's too bad for you to have to take them over there, but I haven't kept horses since William passed away. I'm afraid you'd find nothing for them to eat in the barn."

"It's all right, ma'am," Dan said. "I'm sure Miss Stone could use a rest."

"Shouldn't I go along to inquire about Uncle David?" Anne asked.

"It's raining again. I truly feel you're better off to stay where it's dry and warm."

"All right," Anne said uncertainly. "Just make sure they're talking about the right man, won't you?"

"I will. Tall, blond Englishman, right? Forty years old."

"Yes. I do hope you can find out where he is, or at least where his claim lies."

"Oh, this uncle of yours is prospecting?" Mrs. Zinberg asked.

"Yes, at least that's what we were told. He bought property near here and came to look it over. But he's been away from his farm more than a month, and we didn't know when he would return. I hope we haven't made a mistake in coming all this way."

"You go on, sir," Mrs. Zinberg said to Dan. "Ask at the post office. They should know if he's around here. I'll take care of Miss Stone for you, no fear."

Dan stood with his hat in his hand, waiting for Anne's approval. She sensed that it would hurt him somehow if she didn't let him do this for her.

"Yes, go," she said. "I'll be fine with Mrs. Zinberg."

Anne went upstairs to her snug room under the eaves and unpacked her satchel. Changing out of the itching blue habit into her gray dress lifted her spirits. Her hostess insisted on taking the heavy velvet riding dress and sponging it while she heated water for tea.

"You needn't," Anne said.

"But you'll want to wear it tomorrow if you're riding again."

Mrs. Zinberg was so matter-of-fact and Anne was so tired that she let her do it.

Anne sank into a well-cushioned rocker before the fireplace with a lap robe over her knees. As she watched the flames, she reviewed the journey she and Dan had made from Eugene to Scottsburg, but she could find no logical explanation for the pranks played on them. Peterson's intentions troubled her, but she couldn't see a way to find out his whereabouts.

When Mrs. Zinberg brought the tea tray, she smiled at the plump, graying lady.

"Thank you so much. This reminds me of home. We got a lot of rainy days in England this time of year, and I would often sit near the fire and read."

"Oh, you're from England?" Mrs. Zinberg seemed unduly surprised by that. "I thought maybe you were from Boston or thereabouts."

Anne chuckled. "No, but I'd like to visit that city sometime."

"Tell me about England." Mrs. Zinberg passed her a blue-and-white china cup and saucer. She then poured out her own tea in a mismatched white cup and brown saucer. Anne suspected she had been honored with the only remaining matched pair.

"Of course it seems the dearest place on earth to me," she said. "Though Oregon is very nice — in fact, the climate seems quite the same. Of course, you have more hills — and bigger ones."

"Very large ones east of here," Mrs. Zinberg said.

"Yes. I saw some of those." Anne chuckled at the memories of her wagon trip. "Bigger trees, too. Much larger. And I've never seen such vast fields of corn. Wheat, that is." She shook her head. "In England, corn is grain of any type."

"Really? Then what is corn?"

Anne smiled. "That is maize."

"Ah." Mrs. Zinberg laced her tea with sugar and offered Anne the bowl.

"No, thank you. Was your husband a farmer?"

"No, he was a surveyor."

Within the next hour, Anne learned much of her hostess's story, her ills and her woes, as well as a few fond reminiscences of her husband and their two daughters, now grown and gone.

At last Mrs. Zinberg rose. "There, if I don't get moving, we shan't have any supper."

Anne looked about the room. "Do you have a clock? Dan seems to have been a long time in town."

"I expect he stepped into one of the taverns for news of your uncle and met some new friends, as they say." She smiled, but Anne shook her head emphatically.

"Daniel isn't like that. He never drinks a drop."

"Oh. Then I suppose he may have had some trouble getting word of your uncle and is asking more people." Mrs. Zinberg frowned and headed for the door to the kitchen shaking her head.

Her air of disbelief at the same time amused and troubled Anne. If Dan *were* a drinking man, she'd have no trouble imagining the reasons for his delay. But he was so sober and dependable it was hard to think he'd gone astray from his mission. Looking about for a distraction, Anne found a few books on a shelf. She took down one by Dickens and settled again in the rocker.

An hour later, Mrs. Zinberg laid the table and sat down with her knitting. She and Anne kept up a sporadic conversation about knitting, yarn, travel, and literature. At last a quick knock came on the door, and the lady of the house rose to open it.

Dan came in, dripping rain on the rag mat.

"I'm sorry," he said. "It's coming down quite hard now."

"Don't fret about the floor," Mrs. Zinberg said. "Hang your coat over there and come get warm."

Anne sank back in her chair with a sigh. Until that moment, she hadn't admitted to herself how worried she was. She made herself breathe calmly while Dan took off his coat, hat, and boots.

Mrs. Zinberg shooed him toward the fireplace.

"Warm your hands while I put supper on the table." She scurried toward the kitchen.

Dan scarcely waited until she was out of the room.

"I've some news of Mr. Stone, but I fear our journey is not over."

"Oh? I had hoped, but not expected, to find him here."

"As did I. But I learned where his claim is. It's several miles up in the hills, by way of what I'm told is a very rough trail."

"Can we do it in a day?"

"I'm not sure. Probably." He sat down in the chair opposite Anne on the hearth. "But to go the distance and get back to town safely before nightfall — well, that is debatable. In fact, several gentlemen debated it at length."

She smiled.

"Anne, the oddest thing happened."

"Oh?" She sat up straighter and tried to rid her mind of cobwebs.

"I saw a blue roan tied up in front of a saloon this afternoon."

"Is that odd?"

Dan seemed at a loss for words, but shook himself. "It seemed so to me. This roan was a dead match for the one we saw at your uncle's farm."

Anne sat forward in the chair and stared at him. "Do you think it was the same horse?"

"It couldn't be." Dan held his hands out toward the fire and gazed at the flames. "Could it?"

"There are lots of blue roans."

"Yes, and we didn't see that one up close. But it's thin like that one."

"Well over sixteen hands, I thought at the time," Anne said uneasily.

"More like seventeen. This one, I mean. I stood next to it and thought what a fine horse it could be if it were fattened up."

"Black mane," Anne said.

"Tail like a crow's wing."

They looked at each other.

"There was no brand on this one," Dan said. "I looked him over pretty closely, I'll tell you. Dark socks on his hind feet, and stockings on the forelegs. All four hooves are black."

"What about his face?" Anne asked. "Any markings there?"

"No, just speckled salt-and-pepper, like the rest of him."

She frowned. "I don't recall any markings on the other one."

"Neither do I. He's nine or ten years old, judging by his molars."

"And we've no idea how old the one at the farm was," Anne said.

"No, but I'll know this fellow, Hastings, if I meet him on the trail."

"There, folks." Mrs. Zinberg bustled in, wearing her apron. "Supper's all ready."

Dan rose and held out a hand to Anne. She let him assist her in getting out of the rocker.

"It can't be the same horse," she murmured.

"No, it can't."

"There was that time on the trail between Anlauf and Elkton when I thought I saw a gray horse behind us."

"I remember," Dan said.

They didn't speak of it during supper, but kept up a pleasant conversation with their hostess. Afterward, Anne drew Dan back into the parlor.

"We must go to Uncle David's land tomorrow, no matter what the weather."

"I understand your concern," Dan said, "but I don't want to take you out in inclement weather again. If it's raining in the morning, I think we should wait."

"I don't suppose you inquired about the owner of that curious roan you saw in town."

"I did." He grimaced. "I went inside and asked the barkeep. He said he didn't know whose it was for sure, but most of the men in there were regulars who were known to him. However, a couple of strangers had come in within the last hour, and he said perhaps it belonged to one of them. Then he looked about as though expecting to see them, but apparently they'd left. And when I went back outside, the horse was gone."

Anne tapped her chin. "Perhaps he'd already left the tavern when you were there and stepped into one of the shops."

"That's probably what happened. I missed him." Dan shrugged.

"We must leave early in the morning," Anne said. "If we find Uncle David, we can stay at his claim with him overnight. If not . . . well, we'll just have to turn around and make our way back down the trail."

Dan sighed. "I'm getting to where I feel I know you fairly well, Anne."

"Oh, do you?" She smiled at that.

"Yes, and that's why I went to the mercantile and stocked up on a few provisions for the trail. There'll be no boardinghouse up in the mountains. I got enough rations to last us a couple of days, and a packet of lucifers. I hope you won't think it too bold of me, but I also purchased a cape for you. The shopkeeper told me the material sheds water well. Somehow they've woven some India rubber into it. Anyway, I thought you'd not be averse to another layer between you and the rain."

Anne hardly knew what to say in the face of his thoughtfulness. She couldn't offer to pay for the cape and other supplies — her funds were nearly exhausted and they might have a few more nights' lodging to pay for. Besides, it would hurt his feelings to suggest he'd acted improperly to buy her an article of apparel. She'd already wounded him enough by rejecting his suit. Why dash his fine spirits further by turning down a gift that could very well ward off illness?

"How kind of you. Of course I'll take it along. If we have another day such as we dealt with today, I shall find it my favorite piece of clothing, I'm sure."

"All right then. We'd best get a good night's rest. I'll load up our stuff at first light."

David smiled as the waiter set a slice of chocolate meringue pie in front of Charlotte and another at his place. Charlotte's expressive green eyes all but devoured the dessert.

"I'm sure I can't eat all of that," she said.

"It'll be fun to try," he assured her.

"Do you want this on your bill, sir?" the waiter asked.

"Oh yes, certainly," David said. He'd have to speak to the manager about the awkwardness of having the waiter mention the bill yet again when he was entertaining a guest. He supposed the man wanted to be sure he was paying for Mrs. Evans's dinner as well as his own — as if any man in his right mind would think he'd dine with a stunner like Charlotte and make her buy her own meal. Besides, he'd paid for her meal yesterday. He'd stayed in town an extra day, using the heavy rain as an excuse. How much of his behavior tonight was due to the lovely Mrs. Evans's presence?

She was prettier than he'd thought on first impression. Of course her cosmetics enhanced her natural looks, covering some freckles no doubt, and giving her eyes that smoky, adoring air. And her dress — it was as fine as any he'd ever seen in London. She'd certainly surprised him there. She was better gowned tonight than any other woman in the room — but of course, not that many women came to Scottsburg, and the farmers' wives usually dined at their own kitchen tables.

True, Charlotte had worn the same dress last night, but she'd explained that she'd come with only a small bag. The trunk she'd shipped seemed to have been delayed, and she contemplated shopping in the town's limited stores if it wasn't delivered soon. He might even stick around tomorrow and offer to escort her if the cousin didn't show up.

"Tell me more about your cousin," Dan said. "You mentioned that he's meeting you. What brings him here?"

"Oh, he's interested in mining. His work has something to do with geology. I'm not sure I understand it all." She chuckled and gazed at him from beneath her long, dark lashes. "What about you, Mr. Stone? You told me you have a claim nearby. How far away is it?"

"It's actually about two hours' ride downhill."

Charlotte laughed softly. "And uphill?"

"It can take me three or four hours. Have to baby the horse, you know, especially if he's loaded down."

"I imagine you're quite a horseman. How do our steeds compare to what's available in England?"

"It's been years since I was in England last, so I don't really know. There are some fine stables, of course."

"Now, did you live in the city or the countryside?"

"I usually stayed in the country. My father had a house in town — London, that is." David shrugged. He didn't like to talk about his family. People sometimes found that pretentious. "It belongs to my brother now. But I used to spend a lot of time there."

"London." Her eyes grew dreamy. "How I'd love to visit that city."

"Oh? I found it dull and full of smoke."

"Ah, men!" She smiled and took a bite of her pie.

To David's astonishment, the chocolate meringue had all but disappeared. Apparently Charlotte wasn't as stuffed as she'd claimed. His own piece was only half gone.

"Would you like more pie?" he asked.

"Oh well, uh . . ." She glanced at his plate. "No, I don't think so. Perhaps some coffee, or . . ."

He raised his eyebrows. Or what? Did she expect him to order wine? He wasn't sure they'd have it.

"I like a cup of tea after my meal," he said.

"So do I." She smiled and wriggled as though settling in for a long, cozy chat.

"You must tell me about your visit to San Francisco," he said.

She launched into a detailed and amusing description of the city, and David began to relax. She had obviously been there in person. Had he doubted her sincerity? He supposed it was just the old wariness from England — being skeptical of fellows who hung about wanting to be your best chum. That was one reason he'd never told anyone in America that he was the third son of an earl. Folks were never genuine with you once they knew that, and worse yet, people who wanted favors crept out of the woodwork.

But Charlotte seemed a nice enough woman. A bit forward perhaps, but who wasn't in these frontier towns? A widow with looks like hers wouldn't remain single long, and who could blame her for setting her sights on a likely prospect, a mature man with a bit of property — in short, himself? David was a bit taken aback by his own thoughts. Did she really only want to spend a pleasant evening with him, or did she aspire to something more permanent? And did he mind?

Years had passed since he'd let down his guard with a woman. But what was the harm? He'd lately pondered this very thing

— finding a nice woman and settling down. Was Charlotte that woman?

He wondered vaguely if there was a place that offered dancing and immediately ruled it out. The hotel offered no entertainment. There just weren't enough decent women here to support a club or an assembly hall. Probably the only dancing in Scottsburg took place in the saloons. So what entertainment could a gentleman offer a charming lady?

The waiter brought their tea and slid a slip of paper onto Charlotte's saucer.

"Begging your pardon, ma'am, but I was asked to give you that."

David scowled at him. "What is that, Philip? I told you this all goes on my bill."

"It's nothing like that, sir. Someone inquired at the desk for Mrs. Evans."

"Oh." David turned and craned his neck to see if anyone was searching the room for Charlotte, but he couldn't see anyone in the doorway to the lobby. When he turned back to the table, Charlotte was perusing the note, holding it below the edge of the table. "Is it your cousin?" he asked.

"I — well, I'm not sure. Would you excuse me just a moment? I'll go and speak to the desk clerk about this."

"Allow me to escort you." David pushed

his chair back.

"Oh no, thank you. I think I'd best tend to this myself."

She rose, and David stood. Unhappily, he stayed where he was as she walked toward the lobby. Every man in the dining room swiveled his head to watch her go.

"Can I get you anything, Mr. Stone?" the waiter asked.

"No. Thank you." He sat down with a thud and sipped his tea.

CHAPTER 12

"What are you doing here?" Millie dragged Sam around a corner into the hallway that led to the kitchen and the rear entrance.

"You said to catch up to you. Well, here you are, and here I am."

"Where have you been?"

"On the trail."

Millie sighed. Sam was duller than a butter knife. "Do you have any money?"

He laughed. "No. Where would I get money?"

"I expected you to be creative. I personally spent an entire day cooking to earn enough money to replace my horse. I almost got caught at it by Miss Stone and her toady, Adams. I'd like to know why you didn't slow them down."

"I tried, Millie. But they're smart. And besides, I got hurt. I fell off my horse."

"Oh, you poor thing." She gave him a cursory inspection. "You look all right now."

"Can I stay here tonight?" Sam asked. "I'm tired of sleeping in barns and hay-stacks."

"Are you crazy? This place costs a dollar a night."

"Aren't *you* staying here?"

Millie put her hands on her hips. "I *told* you. I stopped and earned some money."

"I could sleep on the floor at the foot of your bed." Sam's hangdog face made her want to scream.

"Oh, and how would that look?"

He shrugged and looked down at the floor.

Millie looked over his shoulder toward the lobby. The desk clerk was looking their way and frowning.

"Tell me quick — where are Miss Stone and Adams?"

"I lost 'em."

"What?"

"I told you, I got hurt, and it was raining, and I couldn't find out where they're stay-ing here. Last night, I tied their tack in knots to slow them down, but I didn't want to follow them too closely and get seen. When I got to town I thought they might be here, but their horses aren't in the stable. I checked two other places, too."

Millie did some quick thinking. Appar-ently Sam didn't know David Stone was here or that she was having dinner with his erstwhile boss. She reached into her pocket and took out four bits. "Here. This is all I can give you. It only leaves me a few cents. Get yourself a room someplace if you can for that, and something to eat. And then you'd better find out where they are!"

"I saw Adams once."

Millie raised her eyebrows and leaned toward his face. "I thought you lost them," she whispered in a tone she hoped conveyed danger.

"So I did, but after I'd looked and looked all over town, I gave up and went into a saloon. Spent my last half dime for a beer."

"And?"

"In comes Adams, bold as brass."

Millie folded her arms and drummed her fingers on the sleeve of her fancy gown. "I'm waiting."

"He walks up to the bar and asks the barkeep if he knows David Stone."

"What did the bartender say?"

Sam shrugged. "I don't know. I scooted out the door while Adams wasn't looking. You told me I couldn't let him see me."

Millie sighed. "I don't suppose you followed him when he left the tavern?"

Sam hung his head. "He came out real quick, so I hid around the corner. Mill, he caught sight of my horse and went over to it and looked it all over and petted it."

"Oh, that's just great."

"Really?" Sam asked hopefully.

"No, not really! You are such an idiot."

"Well, I figured I'd best make myself scarce, so I hoofed it the whole length of the street and back. And when I got back to where Old Blue was standing, Adams was gone." Sam smiled as though she should pat him on the head now.

"So you lost him again."

"Well, yeah."

"Sam, listen to me. You are going to find Adams. And where you find him, you'll find Miss Stone. You are going to find out their plans. If they're going to try to meet up with Mr. Stone, you're going to stop them."

"What about you?" Sam asked.

"I'll be waiting here, on the off chance that Mr. Stone comes into town."

"What if Adams and Miss Stone go up to his mining claim?"

"Then you follow them. You've got to keep them from getting to Stone before he comes down here."

"Whyn't you just go with me? We could find him together."

"No," Millie said. If she could just keep Sam busy and Anne Stone out of the way

224

for a few days, she might be able to reel in the rich uncle. "I think one of us should stay here. We don't want to miss him. You concentrate on slowing down Miss Stone and Adams. If that means you have to recruit some friends to help you, then do it."

"Friends? What friends?"

Millie clenched her fists. "Look, are you really this stupid? *Find* someone to help you."

"But . . . I've got no money to pay anyone, and I can't let Adams or David's niece see me."

"You'd *better* not let them see you. Now, excuse me. I have to get back to my dinner."

She flounced to the lobby in a swirl of skirts. Behind her, she heard Sam's plaintive, "Nice dress."

David was checking his pocket watch when she returned to the table. He jumped up when he saw her.

"I'm *so* sorry," Millie said. "I've kept you waiting much longer than I anticipated." She slid into her seat.

"Think nothing of it," David said. "I hope everything's all right."

She gave him a tight smile. "That was a friend of my cousin's. S–Stephen asked him to find me and tell me he should make it into Scottsburg tomorrow or the next day. I'm ashamed to say his 'friend' was a bit inebriated. He must have stopped at a saloon before he came here. It took some time to get the message out of him."

"I'm sorry."

The waiter appeared with a teapot in his hand. "Would you like more, madam? Sir?"

David looked inquiringly at Millie.

"Well . . . ?" She returned his gaze.

"Philip informs me that there is a charming view of the moon on the river from the steamboat dock," David said with a glance toward the waiter. "I believe there'll just be a sliver of moon tonight, but we may not have a rainless evening again for some time. Perhaps you'd like to see it."

"I should like nothing so much as to see a cloudless sky, Mr. Stone." This was going better than she'd anticipated. Millie waited for David to come around and hold her chair as she rose.

"You might want a wrap," he said.

"Of course. It will only take me a minute." She glanced about apprehensively as they entered the lobby, but there was no sign of Sam.

"I'll wait for you right here," David said.

Millie hastened up the stairs. Part three,

despite one snag, complete. Now for part four.

David was waiting, as promised, when she returned a moment later with her beautiful dress covered by her old woolen coat. She'd arranged the silk shawl over that, in an attempt to make it look less dowdy, and had freshened her lip rouge.

He offered his arm, and Millie mustered every ounce of charm she could find.

The brief walk to the dock gave their conversation time only to graze the top of Eugene society, for which Millie was grateful. Apparently David knew the Skinners and all the other pioneers intimately, and her own ignorance would soon be manifest if she couldn't distract him from the topic.

A thin, dark-haired man leaned against one of the dock's pilings, smoking a cigarette, but aside from him, the pier was deserted.

"Lovely night," David said as they strolled along the dock. A much-scarred river steamer was tied up alongside, but the decks were empty.

"And not too cold," Millie said. She wondered if she could have gotten away with just the shawl — and a warm arm, of course, if she shivered.

"There's the moon." David stopped and

gazed upward. Only the thinnest fingernail showed, but the stars glittered bright.

Millie gave the sight a proper moment of appreciation and looked back toward shore. "This is quite a pretty little town by starlight."

"Yes."

He was looking at her. She could tell, but she deliberately kept her gaze on the riverbank. The smoker tossed his cigarette in the water and ambled toward the center of town.

"You know, Charlotte, I was planning to return to Eugene tomorrow, but now I'm not so sure."

"Oh?" She looked up at him and blinked — only once, lest she overdo it and he think she was a flirt. "Is business keeping you?"

"Not really, but I'd like to be sure you're safe until your cousin arrives. And meet him if I can."

"Oh." She smiled. "That sounds like such a treat. I'm so glad we met, David."

He patted her hand and looked up at the moon again.

Was he shy? She hoped he wasn't the type who would take weeks to feel bold enough to steal a kiss. The whole fictional cousin business could get awkward if this dragged on too long. She couldn't get Sam to pose as her cousin, because David knew him. And last night he'd retired immediately after dinner, pleading fatigue. But really, she was quite pleased with the direction things were headed. She eased a little closer to him and dared to squeeze his arm the tiniest bit. David responded by pressing her hand against his arm ever so slightly.

Hadn't she heard somewhere that English men were cold fish? This one might take some work.

The town was just stirring when Anne and Dan made their way to the ferry and crossed the Umpqua. For once the sun shone, half-hearted and cool. Dan prayed it would last.

He entrusted the horses to the ferryman and stood with Anne by the rail. As the south shore approached, she looked back at the town.

"The sheer size of this land continues to astound me," she said.

"Yes, there's room for everyone," he said, but immediately he thought of the Indians lashing out against the encroaching whites not so far to the south.

"It's no wonder so many have come here from Europe," Anne said. "The prospect of owning land . . . for so many that's an impossibility in England."

Her troubled face led Dan to wonder if she felt guilty for being born into the noble class. In a similar fashion, he felt twinges of remorse when he considered how many Indians had been displaced for homesteads. Hector brushed that aside, insisting that things were the way they were, and the Adams boys could do nothing about it, so they might as well take advantage of the situation. But Anne was like him. They could not bear their cultural burdens lightly.

"Do you think Uncle David is safe?" she asked as the ferry drew close to its mooring.

"Of course. Why wouldn't he be?"

"Well . . . there's Peterson."

"The postmaster said your uncle came to fetch his mail about a week ago."

"That recently?" She turned toward him eagerly, her lips parted.

"Yes. I should have told you last night, but it slipped my mind. He said David's been in two or three times in the last month, and then went back to his claim." Perhaps they should have waited in Scottsburg for him to return. If he'd tried harder, could he have persuaded Anne to wait at Mrs. Zinberg's house and let him make daily inquiries for her uncle? Dan strongly doubted that.

Star balked a little when it was time to step off the ferry. He wasn't usually afraid of bridges or rough spots in the road, but today he seemed a little skittish. Bailey, on the other hand, was as dependable as his master and stepped off as calmly as Rob would have.

Dan checked all the straps and buckles on Anne's saddle before giving her a hand up. She wore her velvet habit again, with the new cape snubbed behind the saddle's cantle with her blankets. He'd insisted they bring their bedrolls and camping gear in case they spent a night on Stone's claim with him, but they'd left some of their clothing at Mrs. Zinberg's, lightening their loads.

"How far is it?" Anne asked.

Dan pointed up the valley. "About eight or ten miles overall. We're to take this road for two miles, then turn off to the right and go up into the hills. The postmaster said it wouldn't be too rough, but I found another fellow who goes up there a lot — has a claim not too far from David's — and he said the last two or three miles make a rugged climb. He said to take our time so the horses aren't worn out when we hit the steepest part."

Anne set her jaw. "Then we'd best be going." She looked back toward the ferry slip. The boat had shoved off and was a third of

231

the way back across the river. On the far shore, a horseman already waited for it.

They rode along for a half hour, saying little except for Anne's occasional exclamations over the lovely scenery and Dan's fretful observations on the clouds rolling in.

As they approached a stream, they halted their horses at the edge and stared at the scene before them. A log bridge decked with sturdy planks appeared to have fallen into the creek on the far end of the span.

"That's odd," Dan said. "The ferryman didn't say anything about a bridge being out."

"Yes." Anne pondered the logistics of it. "I'm no expert, but if it was washed out, wouldn't someone in Scottsburg have told us there was flooding?"

"Yes, and it wouldn't have gone down this quickly." Dan looked upstream and down. "I suppose we'll have to go along that path and see if there's a ford nearby."

They turned their horses onto the narrow path along the creek bank. Twenty minutes later, Dan found a spot where they could descend to the streambed and cross safely. The water was only a few inches deep, though it flowed swiftly. On the other side, they made their way back to their path and at last came to the far end of the bridge.

Dan dismounted and examined the supports. "It looks as though someone sawed right through the beams here."

Millie got up earlier than she wanted to. She had things to do if she intended to maintain the lifestyle she was growing accustomed to until she felt confident of asking David for a small loan without offending him.

The mercantile, perhaps. There were several small shops in town, but down near the steamer dock a large establishment catered to the miners and farmers. She'd go there first — that or a place where she could get breakfast for less than the hotel's exorbitant prices. She hurried down the street, wearing her calico dress and wool coat. She didn't want to look too prosperous this morning, or to stand out in any way, though most likely an auburn-haired woman men seemed to find handsome would not go unnoticed. With that in mind, she'd put her hair up and added a hat.

She found a bakery where several men were lined up to get rolls and pastry. She got in line. They all eyed her surreptitiously. This wouldn't do. She needed to go unwatched, if only for a few seconds. She left the line and gazed at the cakes and bread loaves in the case near the window, pretending to have trouble making her choice. When the line was down to one man, she stood behind him.

"There you go." The baker handed his customer a brown paper parcel, and the man gave him a few coins.

Millie watched closely, but no change was handed back. Her disappointment hit a new low. The smell of the baked goods had her stomach rolling, and she'd hoped for a bun or two. She had only a few pennies left in her pocket.

"Help you, ma'am?" the baker asked.

"Oh, I — no, thank you. I changed my mind." She scurried out the door and stood panting on the sidewalk. It would be easier to pick a pocket, but she hated doing that.

"Morning."

She whirled toward the voice. A tall, thin man with a dark mustache nodded to her from where he leaned against the wall of the bakery.

She nodded and turned away.

"Didn't I see you with David Stone last night?"

Millie's heart lurched. She looked about, but no one else seemed to have heard. She eyed the man closely. The smoker from the dock? That must be it. She took one step closer.

"You know him?"

"Not personally."

"What is your interest in him?" she asked.

The man opened his jacket and reached into an inner pocket, coming out with a cigarette. "What's yours?"

Millie's heart paused and went on, faster. "None of your business. Good day." She turned away, but he leaped to her side and fell into step with her.

"On the contrary, I think we should have breakfast together and discuss it."

She eyed him askance. What was his game? Still, breakfast without having it added to the hotel bill . . .

"Are you buying?"

He smiled. "Of course."

Chapter 13

By noon Anne was certain. They were hopelessly lost in the rolling hills, and the temperature had dropped at least ten degrees since they left the ferry and detoured to avoid the damaged bridge. The clouds tightened overhead, obscuring the sun and threatening another bout of severe weather.

"Dan?" She urged Bailey forward and tried again, calling toward his rigid back, "Daniel!"

He turned in the saddle, a worried frown not hidden quickly enough.

"Perhaps we should go back and seek better directions."

Dan wheeled Star around and rode back to her. He stopped and eyed her sadly. "I'm afraid it's too late. Anne, I'm sorry, but I've no idea how to get back to Scottsburg."

They sat for a minute, looking around. The trail they'd been following had petered out, and Dan had tried to find his way back to it, but Anne didn't recognize anything she could see now. The wind snaked between the hillsides, and the bushes shuddered. A clap of thunder made the horses jump.

"I'm afraid we're in for it," Dan said.

"Should we go downhill until we find a stream?" she asked. "They'll all flow into the Umpqua eventually, won't they?"

"I . . . suppose so." He looked so contrite that she wanted to comfort him.

"It's as much my fault as yours," she said. "We probably went the wrong way back at that fork where I said to go right."

"Well, someone ought to mark these trails." Dan winced. "I'm sorry, that sounded rather petty, didn't it? I'm not usually a whiner."

"No, you're not."

The clouds let loose, and the rain dumped on them in huge drops so thick they might have been poured from a giant vat.

"Quick! Get to the tree line," Dan shouted.

Star bounded away. Anne loosened her reins, and Bailey cantered after him.

When they reached the verge of the pines, Dan jumped down. He helped Anne alight and then walked between the trees, pulling Star behind him, shoving branches aside.

When they were well out of the open, he dropped Star's reins and came back to help Anne.

"Here, bring Bailey up near Star. I think they'll stay together. We'll get into the tightest thicket we can find and sit this out."

"Shouldn't we tie them up?" Anne asked.

"They ought to stay — they're both well trained. And if you tie them up and the thunder scares them, they'll likely break whatever you tie them with. We'd have to unbridle them and put the halters and lead ropes on to make them completely secure."

"All right." Anne could see that Dan was near his limit of patience, which was considerable. Still feeling guilty for losing the trail, no doubt. She let the reins fall.

Dan fussed with the knots on her saddle strings. "You'll want the cape now." He fumbled at the rawhide strings but couldn't untie them. "Bother." He shoved his hand in his pocket and came out with a folding knife.

"No, wait," Anne said. "Let me. I have fingernails." She didn't want to return Dulcie's saddle to her damaged. It took her a couple of minutes, but at last she got the knots loose. The rain continued to pelt them. Though the fir trees slowed it down, she would still be soaked again in a matter of minutes.

Dan grabbed the cape and shook it out, then wrapped it around her shoulders. "Come on!" He seized her hand and yanked her away from the horses.

"I thought I saw a big cedar over there." Anne pointed, and Dan veered the way she indicated. They crashed through buck brush and around firs. At last she spotted the down-slanting branches of an incense cedar, with dark, flat needles making a canopy near the ground.

"Under there," Dan said.

Anne looked back. "I can't see the horses."

Dan hesitated and craned his neck, looking. "Do you want me to bring them closer?"

A lightning bolt cracked and struck a tall fir tree not far away. The top splintered and crashed to earth. Immediately, thunder boomed so loud Anne's ears throbbed. She clapped her hands over them.

"No!"

"Then get under cover."

She hauled in a deep breath and dove under the lowest branches. The cape tangled about her, and she had to wriggle about to adjust it. She found she was almost able to sit up in the dim hideaway. Dan rolled in and fumbled about until he half-sat, half-lay on his back beside her. Neither of them spoke as the rain lashed the forest and the thunder rumbled, now distant, now frighteningly close. Anne drew up her knees and rested her head on them, closing her eyes.

After several minutes, the rain seemed to slacken.

"Anne, can you ever forgive me?" Dan asked.

"There is nothing to forgive. I forced you to bring me on this expedition." She raised her head and listened. "I do worry about the horses, though."

Dan sat up. "I'll go check on them."

"Please take this marvelous cape." She unfastened the button at her throat.

"Oh, I couldn't."

"You must. I shall come with you if you don't."

He chuckled and accepted it from her. "Don't know as I can put it on in this small space." He crawled outside, and Anne shielded her face as the swaying branches released a shower of droplets.

Dan was gone a good ten minutes, and the rain picked up again. She was thankful for what shelter she had, but her habit was damp through, and her feet were like ice. She began to fret about Dan and wondered how far he'd had to go to find their mounts.

After one especially loud *crash-boom* of thunder, the branch that formed their doorway lifted and Dan crawled in, hauling the soaked cape behind him.

"They've worked their way down in a draw, but I think they'll be all right. The wind is probably milder down there."

"How far away are they?" Anne asked.

"Not that far. It just took me a few minutes to pick up their trail and follow them."

"Dan, you're shivering."

"Aren't you?"

"Here, let's not get grumpy."

"I'm sorry." He ran a hand over his face and sighed. "Anne, I've let you down."

"No, you haven't."

"Well, we differ in opinion on that. But I've got to get you back to Mrs. Zinberg's before dark. What would you say to striking out as soon as the lightning stops?"

Another flash punctuated his words, and they both waited for the thunder. It came just seconds later. Anne looked over at Dan. She could hear his teeth chattering.

She reached out for the edge of the cape. "Look, the outside of this is wet, but the inside feels pretty dry. What if we drape it over us, like a traveling robe? You need to warm up a little, Dan. I'm afraid you'll go hypothermic — is that the word?"

"I don't know, but I do feel as though I might freeze to death. I've got the lucifers in my pocket. If I thought we could build a fire. . . ."

"Well, come closer."

He didn't move.

"This is no time to be shy," Anne said.

Dan unbuttoned his jacket and slid over next to her. He folded back the side of his coat nearest her. She leaned closer and felt his warmth.

"Pull this cape up over your shoulder and put your arm around me."

"Anne —"

"Oh hush. It has nothing to do with — with anything other than survival." Her face flamed, but in the semidarkness, he wouldn't see that, and it actually felt good to have one part of her warm. She peeled off her soggy gloves and set them on the ground next to the tree trunk.

Hesitantly, Dan raised his arm and enfolded her.

"I fear my habit is so damp I won't be much help to you."

"No," Dan said in a strangled voice. "You're warm."

"Good." She very daringly slid her arm around his middle and laid her head against his chest. The pounding of his galloping heart rivaled the thrumming of the rain.

They sat in silence for a long time. Dan stopped shivering. Perhaps ten minutes later, his chin came down and rested gently on the top of her head.

Anne wondered if he was asleep. His pulse was still quite rapid, and she decided he wasn't. She'd told herself this was necessary, but now she wondered if he'd been right to object. Was she leading him on? She wished Elise was here to advise her. Dan was an honorable man, and she'd intended no harm. He was so warm and comfortable now, and his strong arm about her lulled her into thinking everything would be all right.

Some time later, Dan stirred and Anne jerked awake.

"What is it?" she asked.

"The rain has slacked. It's still very gray out, though. I wonder if the sun won't set early today. I'd best go for the horses."

"Let me come. I need to stretch my legs."

"All right, but you must put the cape on."

By the time they'd crawled out of their den, the front of Anne's habit was drenched again. She said nothing about her discomfort and donned the black cape.

"This way." Dan reached for her hand.

"Oh, I left my gloves in there."

"I'll get them." He dove into the hideaway again and thrashed about a bit, then appeared at the opening. "Here you go."

Anne tried to pull the sodden gloves on, but they resisted, so she shoved them into the pocket of her skirt.

They trudged through the woods in twilight until they came to a steep-sided ravine.

"Hold my hand," Dan said.

They slipped and slid down the incline.

"Where are they?" Anne looked all around, but saw no sign of the horses.

"They can't have gone far. I expect they went downhill." Dan pointed in the direction the ground sloped.

"Daniel?"

"Yes?"

"What will we do if we can't find them?"

"Please don't talk that way, Anne."

"All right."

Dan set out with a determined stride, and she followed, but she soon lagged behind him. She shoved through some underbrush, and a rope of vine maple snagged her shoe. She went down, floundering in the bushes. As she struggled to rise, she thought she heard a horse's snort, up the slope a bit to her left. She squinted into the darkness.

White patches. It had to be Star.

"Dan!"

"What is it?" He was fifty yards or more away.

"I think I've found them."

"Where are you?"

"Here." She tried to spot the white blotches again and began to labor up the side of the ravine.

A dark apparition darted from behind a tree between her and the place where she'd seen the horse.

Anne shrieked and fell back. "Daniel!"

The figure raised an arm over its head. "Horse mine!"

"I don't get it," Millie said. "What is it you want with David Stone?"

Peterson smiled and shook his head. "It's a business matter."

She sipped her tea. If she was going to spend a lot of time with an Englishman, she needed to learn to like tea. She'd eaten an enormous breakfast and managed to sneak a biscuit into her handbag while Peterson had left the table to get an ashtray. She didn't like him. At least not yet. She didn't trust his dark, calculating eyes and his thin, black mustache. But he held a certain fascination. Intelligent men always drew her. What exactly made him tick?

"Well, it's a business matter for me, too. I

can't do anything to make David upset with me or to cause him to think poorly of me."

"Oh, I guarantee he won't think anything of the sort after I see him."

She eyed him suspiciously. Did Peterson know about this inheritance thing Anne Stone had mentioned? That must be it. He was going to tell David about the estate. She wasn't ready for that. Earning David's trust and admiration before he knew he was a rich man — well, a richer man — was crucial to Millie's plan. He had to believe she'd loved him before she knew about his finances.

"I don't know," she said. "What's in it for me?"

He drew on his cigarette and blew out the smoke. "Money, of course."

She frowned. He would offer that — the one thing she was desperate for just now. Unfortunately, to carry out her plan to set herself up for life, she needed cash enough to make a show of not caring about money.

"How much?"

"Twenty."

She let out a grim chuckle. "You're dreaming."

"Fifty then."

"Why don't you just walk up to him in the hotel lobby and tell him you want to speak to him?"

"It's important that we have privacy when I confer with him."

"Ah." She frowned and reached for her cup again. Seemed to her, Peterson could just tell David he needed to speak to him in private, but she didn't suggest that. For some reason he didn't want David to know he was here before the meeting took place. Sounded fishy. Still, she didn't want to talk her way out of this deal before she decided she didn't want it.

"How do I know that what you say to him won't be detrimental to me and my cause?"

He smiled. "And what exactly is your cause, Mrs. Evans?"

She gazed across the table at him. Frankness might be the best order of business — cut through all the chitchat.

"I want to marry him."

Peterson's mustache twitched. "I see." He picked up his coffee cup and took a sip.

Millie plunged ahead, hoping she hadn't ruined her plans as well as his. "Does that affect your business with him?"

Peterson's eyes narrowed to slits, and he set the cup down precisely in the middle of the saucer. "Not a bit."

"Tell me exactly what you want me to do."

"Take him away from the hotel — somewhere out in the open. The evening would be best."

"A little stargazing?" she asked.

"Perfect." He flicked his cigarette over the ashtray.

"And you'll just . . . materialize and tell him what you want to tell him?"

"Something like that."

"Why didn't you approach us last night? You saw us out walking."

"I had to be sure of my man. Now I am."

Millie leaned back and surveyed Peterson. He was too clever by half. She smiled. "The thing is I'm not sure that your business won't affect mine. Could you wait a day or two?"

"I hardly think so."

She sipped her tea again, thinking about it. Peterson was a man who played his cards close to the vest. He wasn't going to spill everything to her. But if she let on that she already knew his business, maybe she'd learn something.

"Is this about the business in England?"

His eyebrows rose.

"You know," she said in a cajoling tone. "The *family* business."

He gazed at her thoughtfully. "I've never been to England. What's going on over there?"

248

Millie clamped her jaws together. She was a fool. Now he'd suspect something. But if he wasn't here about that, what did he want?

This whole thing with David could explode in her face. If that happened, she'd need means to get away quickly.

"I'll need a hundred," she said. "In advance."

"Did you get a good look at him?" Dan held Anne by her arms and forced her to meet his gaze. "Was there only one?"

"Y–yes. He had garish black-and-red paint on his face, and — and feathers in his hair."

"What was he wearing?"

"A buckskin jacket and — oh, I don't know. Some sort of trousers."

"But there was only one Indian?"

Anne's teeth chattered as she nodded. "Oh Daniel, what will we do? He's stolen our horses."

Dan looked up the slope. He couldn't leave Anne here alone and run after the fellow. The Indian might have friends nearby. Dan had seen nothing but had heard faint hoofbeats retreating as he ran to Anne's side. He had to make a decision, and he only had one chance to make the right one.

"We walk the way we were going to go when we had the horses — downstream.

Come on." He turned her away from where she'd encountered the savage and put his arm firmly about her waist.

"We c–can't just abandon Star and Bailey. Dan, I promised Rob I'd bring Bailey back in good shape."

He kept walking and pushed her along with him. "What do you suggest? We can't go and fight a savage for them."

"But — all our things are on the saddles."

Dan took two deep breaths before he answered. He tried to make his voice cheerful. "Not all. Only a few things, really. Most of our stuff is at Mrs. Zinberg's."

Anne planted both feet solidly, and he had to stop walking. "Those horses and the saddles are the most valuable things we have right now. How can I repay Rob and Dulcie? Dan, my money is nearly gone until January. That's another six weeks. More than that." Tears flowed down her cheeks, joining the drops of mist that gathered there.

"Anne, dearest, you mustn't."

"Mustn't what?"

"Distress yourself. Rob and Dulcie will understand. The critical thing right now is finding shelter before dark. We can't stay out here all night."

Anne looked around, shivering. "N–no. We can't." She looked up at him, and for a moment he thought she'd regained control of herself. But her face crumpled, and she let out a sob. "Oh Daniel."

He folded her in his arms, and they stood in the darkening ravine. The rain spattered down gently on his hat and her cape and the trees. Would it turn into a violent downpour again? If he didn't find shelter for Anne soon, she might collapse.

She was a plucky girl. She'd sailed the Atlantic for her uncle and crossed the Rockies for him. She'd even faced down some unscrupulous men. But Lady Anne Stone seemed to have her limits. That came almost as a relief to Dan. Perhaps she wasn't impossibly above him, after all.

He held her a minute longer, thinking of their options, but he couldn't see a better plan than the one he'd stated. And every moment they waited, the darker it got. Could it possibly be that late in the afternoon?

"Anne, dearest, listen to me."

She gulped a few more shallow breaths then straightened slightly. "What is it, Daniel?"

"We can't go after that Indian and get the horses back. He's gone. I'm sorry about that, but we need to get started. We can't stay here, so we have to walk. Come. We'll follow the ravine."

"All right." She hiccupped. "I'm not sure how far I can walk, but I'll try."

She staggered along, and Dan held her up, willing her to keep going. The rain soaked them. Questions hammered him. Should he look for another sheltered spot? Should he stop and try to build a fire? How could he have been so stupid as to leave the horses unattended, with all their gear, including his rifle? The prospect of being out all night with temperatures in the hills plunging even lower — possibly below freezing — kept him moving.

Anne's steps dragged. Dan uttered the same phrases over and over. "We can do it. Don't give up. Come on. A little farther."

After perhaps an hour, they struggled down a rocky incline to the bank of a small stream. The ground was muddy in the bottom, so they had to stay up the slope a little ways, which made for awkward footing. Anne leaned into him, and Dan walked on the downhill side. They followed the rippling water, and around each bend he expected the view to open up and to spot a town, or at least a house or two. This brook had to dump into a larger waterway soon, didn't it?

The stream curved and wound through

the woods, never seeming to widen. The shadows multiplied and darkened. Dan's mutterings began to sound nonsensical to him. Anne staggered and fell.

Dan stopped on a bed of orange pine needles and caught his breath. Anne sat crumpled with her dark cape and muddy blue skirt spread around her. He leaned over her.

"Come, Anne. We have to keep going."

"I can't."

"Yes, you can. Come on." He tugged on her arm, but she pulled away.

"Just leave me, Dan. You can go faster without me. I'll wait here for you to come back with help."

"No. I can't do that. What if the Indian came back?" He pulled at her hand, but it slipped out of his and fell to her side.

Anne looked up at him with a stricken expression. "He said, 'Horse mine.' What if he only took one of them, Daniel?"

Daniel huffed out a breath. Maybe he should have gone up the hill and followed the thief. It was too late now, though. Anne wouldn't last going all the way back there, and he surely wouldn't desert her out here in the wilderness. He'd made a mess of things. Her reputation was no longer a high priority, and when it came down to it, neither was finding her uncle. He needed to get her back to Scottsburg alive.

"Anne, I'm not leaving you."

CHAPTER 14

Anne stared up at Dan. Rain pelted her. It hit his hat and collected on the crown. When he leaned toward her, a stream of water ran off the brim and onto the ground between them.

What was it he'd said? She only wanted to rest. If they couldn't get out of this icy rain, she would pull her cape around her and roll up right here on the ground and not move until . . . sometime.

"Anne!" He prodded her shoulder.

She rolled away from him.

"Anne Stone! Shame on you! You're not a child. You know full well that I can't carry you, but I'll try if you don't get on your feet and walk."

"I can't."

Dan's face hardened. "Your father would be mortified if he could see you now. Didn't he teach you to have more grit than that?"

She opened her eyes just enough so she

255

could see him beneath her lashes. Dan had never talked like that before. He was the perpetual gentleman. Night was falling, and his face showed up pale in the dim light. He was worried, not angry. Worried about her. She opened her mouth but nothing came out.

"All right, I'll carry you then." He stooped and clamped an arm around her back, pushing the cape in and groping for her waist. When his other hand touched her thigh through her skirts, she jumped away from him.

"What? Stop!"

"You won't walk, so I have to carry you."

"No, wait." She held out her hands in protest. "Give me a m–minute."

"You've had a minute. Come on, Anne. It's getting colder. You get on your feet, or I'll throw you over my shoulder. Which is it?"

She exhaled heavily and reached for his hand. Dan pulled her up.

"Good girl. Let's go."

He propelled her onward, along the bank of the stream. She trudged beside him, moving slowly. Her legs were stiff, and her feet were going numb, but she didn't dare stop. Something in his gray eyes and rock-firm voice had told her that he would make good on his threat. Dan would pack her home or die trying.

The stream wound downward, around a bluff. Dan was walking in water, lurching a little as he pulled her along. The rain pounded harder, and Anne kept her head down. She could barely see her feet in the darkness.

"I smell smoke."

She stopped and raised her chin. "What?" She turned her head and stared stupidly at Dan.

"Wood smoke. Someone's got a fire going. Come on." He squeezed her hand and dragged her forward.

Anne tried to hasten her steps, but her legs wouldn't obey her brain. They staggered onward until they rounded the bluff. Dan gave a whoop.

"Look! A cabin!"

Anne could smell the smoke now. She squinted where he pointed, and sure enough, a sliver of light came through the trees.

"Jump up."

"What?"

Dan positioned his arms. "Jump up and let me carry you across the creek. The cabin's on the other side."

"I can walk."

"I don't want you to get your feet any wetter. Come on. Let me."

He stooped, and she reluctantly put her arm around his neck. It felt heavy in the wet, freezing garments. Dan found strength somewhere to lift her and lurch across the stream. She feared he would drop her the way he had a week ago when they crossed the Long Tom, but he made it without stumbling. On the other side, he set her down on a rock and tottered up the bank. At last they stood at the door of a crude log cabin.

"Anybody home?" Dan called. He pounded two weary thuds on the door.

From within came a cautious voice.

"Who wants to know?"

David hurried up the steps to the post office and pushed open the door.

"Mr. Stone! Good afternoon." The postmaster whirled around to search the rack of pigeonholes behind him.

"Thank you," David said. "I guess you know what I want."

"Ha. If I could give people what they want every day, I'd be a very popular man." The postmaster turned and handed him an envelope. "That's it this time."

"Hmm." David took it. Nothing from Sam

Hastings, but he'd asked Sam to send him a note every week to tell him how things were going at the farm. He'd been here a month, but he'd had no word from Sam.

"Someone was in here yesterday, asking for you."

"Oh?" David asked absently as he scanned the envelope. "If they come in again, tell them I'm staying at the Miner's Hotel."

"I'll do that."

He tucked the letter in his pocket and went outside. Must be an assay report on the ore samples he'd sent to San Francisco. He would wait and open it in his room. Now for some shaving soap, and then he'd stop in the stable to check on Captain. Or perhaps he'd go there first and take a look at the letter in the stable, away from prying eyes. Its contents might make a difference on his timetable. If the yield from his claim looked promising, he'd stay to put things in motion. If not, he might just sell out now and go back to Eugene. He had an idea he might invest in a stagecoach line between Eugene and Oregon City.

Of course, there was Charlotte Evans. He wouldn't mind seeing her again tonight. He hadn't figured her out yet. Her auburn hair and green eyes had attracted him straightaway, and she'd come to dinner gowned like a duchess. She was hands-down the prettiest woman in Scottsburg, but she lacked a high-gloss polish.

For the frontier, her manners were passable, and he wouldn't ordinarily demand more than that. In fact, the woman he'd almost married in Missouri came from an unpretentious background. He'd never told her about his own pedigree. She'd loved him — or so he'd thought — and he had been ready to settle down. He wouldn't ask more of someone else, and yet . . .

Charlotte implied somehow that she was a tad above her neighbors. She wasn't snooty exactly, and he hadn't seen yet how she acted around other women. He *had* seen the way she held herself when she knew men were watching her.

Maybe seeing her in the company of other women was a good idea. He wished he had friends here in town — besides miners and dockhands — and someone was throwing a party. He could tell a lot about a woman from the way she carried herself at a social event.

He'd seen a couple checking in to the hotel last night when he'd gone downstairs to ask for some hot water. Perhaps he could "run into" the man in the lobby, and later in the dining room, he could introduce

Charlotte. It seemed like a decent plan, and he became more aware of the people around him as he hurried down the street. He saw a few women, but most were hardened frontier wives. None that could hold a candle to Charlotte.

He frowned as he entered the dim stable. Whom did he think he was kidding? Would he dangle after Charlotte Evans if he met her in London? If he stood her beside Elizabeth Stone, his brother's wife, or even her lady's maid, Elise Finster, Charlotte wouldn't measure up. And if he were honest, she wasn't a woman he would consider taking home to Mother, if Mother were still on this earth. Charlotte had that worldly wise edge, like a woman who knew what was what but wanted him to believe she was innocent. When he was with her, that trait was easy to overlook. Should he be watching his back?

Dan had never been so glad to hear a crotchety old man's voice before.

"My name is Daniel Adams, and I've got a lady with me. Our horses were stolen, and we're lost. Can you help us, please?"

After a pause, the old-timer called, "Are you lyin'?"

Dan pulled back and stared at the crude

door. "No, I'm not lying. Why would I do that? We're freezing to death out here!"

"Let me hear the lady."

Dan looked at Anne. She blinked up at him, her lips trembling.

"What does he want?"

"Tell him your name. You can do it."

"I'm Anne Stone. Please, sir. We're like to die out here."

A thud came from within, and the door creaked open. Dan stood eye-to-eye with an elderly man whose flowing white beard resembled a frozen waterfall. His alert blue eyes peered at them from beneath white tufts of eyebrows.

"Well, lookee there. I've never had a lady grace my hearth before. Come in, missus. Do enter and be welcome." He stood back.

Dan grasped Anne's elbow firmly. "In you go." He gave her a little boost as she levered herself up the step and over the threshold. The old man slammed the door behind them and dropped the bar in place. The heat coming from a blazing fire shocked Dan.

He pulled off his gloves and turned to unfasten the hood of Anne's cape. He threw it back, revealing her porcelain face and the ridiculous blue velvet hat that had no business out here in the forest.

"Mm, mm," said the old man. "Ain't she just the purtiest? To what do I owe this honor?"

"It's like I said," Dan replied. "An Indian stole our horses, and —"

"Are you sure?" The old man's eyebrows sprang higher.

"Well, I didn't get a good look at him, but he scared Miss Stone half to death."

"Miss Stone?" The codger peered at Anne. "You kin to that English feller up the mountain?"

"I suppose I am," Anne said. "Do you know David?"

"Know him? I've shared a beaver tail with him." He held out a hand to Anne. "Here, missy, come right over to the fire. You look cold enough to skate on."

Dan unbuttoned his coat with aching fingers. "Sir, we're much obliged. I think we'd have been in serious trouble if we'd had to stay out all night in this cold rain."

"Name's Pogue — Harlan Pogue, but folks call me Whitey." He stroked his luxuriant beard and winked at Anne. "They used to call me Blackie when I was younger. Can't figure that out."

Anne smiled and held her hands toward the fire. "Well, Mr. Pogue, Daniel is right. I believe we owe you our lives."

"Whitey, I told ya. Look at you. Shaking all over." The old man dragged a short bench over. "Sit yourself down."

While Dan removed his wraps and helped Anne get off her cape, coat, hat, and muffler, Whitey bustled about. He filled his coffeepot, threw more wood on the fire, and straightened the blankets on his bunk.

"There now, folks, in a few minutes we'll have some hot coffee for ya. Can't say as I've got any fancy eats, but there's some cornmeal porridge I can slice and fry with side meat."

"You don't have to feed us," Dan said.

"Oh? You got vittles?"

"Well, no. I'm afraid our supplies went with our horses."

"There you go. We'll have us some porridge and side meat after a bit." Whitey peered at Anne's face, frowning. "You feeling better, missy?"

"Yes, sir. Thank you." The color was returning to Anne's face.

"That's good." Whitey plopped down on the edge of his bunk. "I don't got any dry clothes I could offer you."

"We'll be fine," Dan said. His trousers were drying out, and his boots began to steam. He drew his feet back from the fire. He suspected Anne's heavy skirts and petticoats would take longer.

"This horse thief," Whitey said. "What exactly did he look like?"

Anne hesitated then gave him her sketchy description.

Whitey shook his head. "Don't sound right, and I know most of the red men in these hills."

"There's fighting south of here," Dan said. "Is it possible some of those Indians have moved up this way to get away from it?"

"I s'pose." Whitey shrugged. "I'm sure sorry that happened to you, missy. And you was out looking for your uncle, you say?"

"That's right. I haven't seen him since I was a baby." Anne gave him a shaky smile. "I've been trying to find him for nearly nine months now."

"Well, you're not awful far from his claim," Whitey said. "It's uphill and east of here. Tell you what. I could take you there tomorrow if it ain't raining so bad."

"Would you?" Dan asked before Anne could respond. "I'd be happy to pay you for your trouble."

Whitey waved a hand at him. "No need for that. I'd like to see Stone again myself. He tells capital stories." He leaned toward Anne. "So what brings you to find him now, missy, if you haven't bothered for most of your life?"

Anne smiled wearily. "My father passed away last year, and I've no close family left but Uncle David. My family had tried to write to him several times, but we hadn't heard from him for ten years. So I decided to look for him."

"And quite an adventure she's had," Dan added. "She made the wagon trip from Independence, and a swindler tried to bilk her, and now she's been robbed by an Indian and nearly frozen to death."

"Yup, that's quite a tale," Whitey said. "Well, we won't be too comfy tonight, all three of us in this little shack — more cozy than comfy, I guess you could say. But you'll be warm, and I'll put something in your bellies, and in the morning we'll see if we can find Mr. Stone."

"Can we get there on foot?" Anne asked.

"Oh, it's a rugged climb, but you don't look too spindly. I think you can do it."

Anne chuckled, and the sound lifted Dan's heart. She could laugh, and less than an hour ago she was ready to give up and die. Later when she was helping Whitey wash their dishes in a chipped enamel basin, he brought in wood and water then sat listening to her banter with the old man. Whitey was obviously delighted.

Why had he ever set out from the farm in Champoeg? Dan wondered. He wanted to blame Hector, but he couldn't. His brother hadn't forced him to saddle Star and ride out. He wasn't sorry, yet . . . Dan couldn't imagine watching Anne sail away to England. He wanted to help her find her uncle and straighten out the whole mess about the inheritance, but losing Anne again might crush him.

She laughed, a musical sound that pierced him because he knew that he wouldn't hear it much longer. Dan squeezed his eyes shut. He should have stayed away and left her in Rob and Dulcie's care. Because once again, Anne was going to break his heart.

"It's chilly tonight," David said as he and Charlotte stepped out onto the front porch of the hotel. "Are you sure you want to walk?"

"I had my heart set on it." She looked up at him from beneath lashes that for some reason looked longer and more luxuriant than they were last night.

"I wouldn't want you to take a chill. And besides — there's no moon to see tonight."

She sighed heavily. "I suppose you're right. But the hotel offers so little entertainment."

"Perhaps we could scare up another pair and play cards." David steered her adroitly toward the door. "There was a couple just sitting down when we left the dining room. Perhaps they'd join us."

He could tell Charlotte wasn't completely mollified. What was going on? She seemed more insistent than a woman who just wanted to snuggle up to him would be. Although he hadn't done much snuggling lately, David was certain he hadn't forgotten how, and the woman involved was usually much more compliant than Charlotte.

They walked back through the lobby, and he looked around for likely companions for the evening. A thin man was reading a newspaper, and two other men sat in the nook to one side, smoking cigars and laughing. None of them struck him as what he was looking for.

"Perhaps they have a small parlor we could sit in," Charlotte suggested.

David almost offered the sitting room of his own two-room suite and changed his mind. He didn't really want to entertain a woman in his hotel suite, for one thing. Past experience had proven such action could be risky. For another, he happened to know that his was the only suite the hotel offered, and Charlotte might get her nose out of joint if she knew about it. The hotel usually opened it for David when he visited, and in times of great overcrowding — like the days when a new mine opened and the investors came to see it — they would put a bed in the sitting room and rent it as two separate rooms. He suspected it sat empty most of the time, waiting for the establishment's wealthier patrons to return.

Although Charlotte had seemed reluctant to go back to the dining room, she presented a charming attitude when David led her to one of the tables.

"Good evening, folks," he said.

The man and woman eating looked up in guarded surprise.

"Hello," said the man, standing. "Stone, isn't it?"

"Yes. We met this afternoon. This is Mrs. Evans." He looked at Charlotte. "Mr. and Mrs. Packer."

They all exchanged their how-do-you-dos.

"I hope you'll pardon us," David said, "but we had planned to go out this evening and the rain has discouraged us. We wondered if you by any chance would be interested in joining us for a quiet game of cards or just conversation."

The couple looked at each other. The woman's eyebrows rose, and he gathered she was passing the decision to her husband.

"Might be interesting," Mr. Packer said.

David smiled at the woman. "We wouldn't want to intrude on your plans."

"It sounds lovely," Mrs. Packer replied.

"Good. Why don't we wait for you in the lobby?"

"Perhaps the desk clerk could scare up a card table for us," Mrs. Packer said.

The gleam in her eyes made David wonder what he'd gotten himself into.

The next morning Whitey shared bacon, oatmeal, and coffee with Anne and Dan. When they'd eaten, Anne insisted on washing the dishes while the two men packed a small amount of gear.

Whitey tucked several small items and some jerky into a dirt-colored pack and added a long-barreled pistol. Then he strapped on a sheath that held a wicked-looking knife. Last of all, he hefted a shotgun and nodded at Dan.

"You got a pea shooter, Daniel?"

"No," Dan said. "My rifle was on my saddle, and I didn't bring a handgun."

"You orta have one," Whitey said. "Can you hit the broad side of a saloon?"

Dan smiled. "I reckon."

Whitey nodded and held out the shotgun.

"Take this, then. I'll use my Colt if need be." He turned and looked at Anne, who was hanging up her rag of a dish towel. "Aw, I hate to take you out of here, missy, because I know the likes of you isn't apt to grace my cabin again. But" — he slapped his thigh — "I promised I'd take you up to David's claim, and so I will. Let's get crackin'."

They set out in the chill of dawn, but the sun soon made its way up over the hills to the east. Walking kept Anne warm, and within an hour, she paused to shed her cape. Dan rolled it up and carried it under his arm.

The path became steep, but Dan and Whitey made sure she found good footing. They came out in a clearing from which they could see all the way to the Umpqua.

"See the smoke yonder, from all the chimneys in town?" Whitey asked, shaking his head. "I don't wonder the natives are put out with us. Afore you know it, the forest will be all stripped off these hills."

"How far now?" Dan asked.

"We're more'n halfway." Whitey turned and picked up the path, which was little more than a deer trail.

They went downhill for a short ways and along a hillside.

Dan stopped and said, "I smell smoke."

Whitey swung around and stared at him. "You got a good nose, boy."

Dan smiled. "That's how we found you last night."

"It's true," Anne said. "Dan smelled your chimney before we saw the cabin." She sniffed the air. "I think I smell it, too. Is there a cabin up here?"

"Don't think so. Lot of claims," Whitey said, "though most fellas don't stay in the hills all winter. Most of them are packing up by now." He peered through the trees on the slope below them. "Well, let's move along quiet-like and see what we see."

He walked stealthily, lifting his booted feet high, and Anne almost laughed aloud. She looked at Dan, and he grinned. "When in Oregon, do as the locals do."

Anne followed Whitey, trying not to make a sound.

After a few minutes, Whitey stopped and looked back at Dan. "You still smell it?"

"I think so, but my nose may be getting used to it."

"There be a stream down in the draw." Whitey waved vaguely down the slope ahead of them. "I'm thinking someone's camped there."

Dan passed the cape to Anne and lowered

his shotgun to the ready position. The two men crept closer, dodging from tree to tree. Anne held back a ways, but stayed within sight of them. Before long, Dan and Whitey stopped and took cover behind two trees. They peeked out and then conferred in whispers. What on earth were they looking at? She glanced over her shoulder, but saw nothing alarming there, and moved closer to the men. The babbling of a small stream reached her, but no other noise beyond the soft wind in the boughs above her.

Whitey was making signals to Dan, pointing and then making a circle with his finger. Dan nodded and slipped off through the woods to the left. Whitey tiptoed forward and a little to the right.

Anne crept closer and hid behind the tree where Dan had stood. She peeked cautiously between the branches of the bushy pine. Below her, on the bank of the stream, a man bent over a campfire. Grazing nearby were three horses. Anne could barely contain her excitement as she surveyed Bailey and Star. They looked fine, as did the rangy blue roan that cropped the dead grass near them.

She sucked in a breath and studied the man. His shabby buckskins looked familiar, but this was no Indian brave with feathers in his hair.

"Put your hands up," Whitey yelled from behind his tree.

The man jumped, dropping his tin cup into the fire, and whirled around.

"Easy now," Dan called from the other side of the clearing. "We've got you surrounded, mister. Put your hands nice and high, where we can see them."

Slowly the man complied. Whitey stepped out from behind the fir tree and walked toward him, holding his Colt pistol in both hands, trained on the man's chest.

"Just stand still now. You got any weapons?"

The man shook his head, then said something too low for Anne to hear. Whitey reached out and unbuttoned the man's jacket.

Dan came up from behind with the shotgun pointed at the man. "I got you covered, Whitey."

The old man pulled a knife from the prisoner's belt and patted his pockets, then stepped back.

Anne couldn't stand it any longer. She ran forward, gazing at the man's face.

"Dan, that's the man from Uncle David's farm."

"Thought so." Dan edged around to

where he could see the prisoner's face, still aiming the shotgun at him. "All right, Hastings — and don't try to tell me your name is Stone. We know better. What are you up to?"

CHAPTER 15

"What happened last night?" Peterson asked.

He and Millie had met at the café for breakfast again, though he hadn't asked her to. She'd gone there thinking he might show up. The food was good, and no one from the hotel was likely to see him here. Sure enough, as she tucked into flapjacks, eggs, and sausage, with a generous side dish of oatmeal, he slid into the chair opposite her.

"He wouldn't go out in the rain, hard as I tried to get him to go," Millie said.

"Hmpf. Didn't know he was such a namby-pamby."

"Well, a gentleman doesn't like a lady to get soaking wet and catch her death of cold." Millie picked up the pitcher and poured sorghum over her stack of pancakes.

Peterson picked at his eggs and biscuit. He left half of it and gestured to the waitress for more coffee. After she'd poured it and left the table, he leaned toward Millie.

"You'd better get him out there tonight. I'll be waiting."

Millie shrugged. "If it doesn't rain again."

"If it does or if for some other reason you don't hold up your end of the bargain, you'd best think about paying me back my hundred dollars."

"Can't," she said blithely.

"What, you spent it already in this miserable place?"

"Part of it."

His eyes narrowed. "Yes, I noticed you had some new fripperies last night. Well, you'd better keep our deal in mind. Because I don't like to be burned in a business deal."

He got up and tossed four bits on the table.

Millie watched him walk away. She liked him less the more she saw of him, but she was in it now. She picked up the coins and put them in her purse before waving to the waitress.

"Yes, ma'am. Can I help you?"

"The gentleman had to leave, and I told him I'd settle up. How much was our breakfast?"

"That'll be thirty-five cents, please."

Millie opened her purse and fished around until she had the right change. "Thank you." She put the coins in the woman's hand and added a nickel. "Oh, that's for you." She smiled and hurried out to the street.

"You know this mangy critter?" Whitey asked.

Before Anne could speak, Dan answered. "We've met. He claimed he was Miss Stone's uncle, but she knew that wasn't true. Apparently he's followed us all the way from Eugene and stolen our horses."

"What do you need three horses for?" Whitey asked.

"Wait a minute," Anne said. "He can't be the man who took them. He's not an Indian." She stared at Hastings's sandy hair and scruffy beard.

"I'm thinking in the near dark with some war paint, he might pass," Dan said, squinting at Hastings. "Take a look below his right ear, Anne."

She moved around and stepped closer to Hastings. Dan raised the shotgun an inch as a warning to the prisoner.

She studied Hastings's profile and gulped. "It looks like red paint in his beard. But how —"

Hastings actually cracked a smile. "It warn't hard. I covered my face and beard with the stuff and scrunched my beard down into my coat collar. A little soot in my hair and a couple of feathers, and I fooled you, didn't I?"

Anne blinked at him. Was the man insane? She turned helplessly to Dan. "What do we do now?"

"We take our horses back," Dan said.

"But what do we do with him?"

"We'd best take him down to Scottsburg and turn him over to the law," Whitey said. "Stealing horses is a hanging offense, ain't it?"

"Wait just a second." Hastings still held up both hands, and he spread them in supplication. "I wasn't really *stealing* them."

"What are you talking about?" Dan asked. "You *did* steal them."

Hastings's hangdog look raised Anne's ire. "You're insufferable."

"I was just trying to keep you away from David."

Anne stared at him. "Whatever for?"

Hastings's mouth worked, but nothing came out. He lowered his hands and stared at the ground.

"We almost died last night," Dan said. "Miss Stone was overcome by exhaustion and cold."

"Sorry," Hastings muttered.

Anne stepped closer. "Look at me, Mr. Hastings."

Slowly the man's gaze rose until he looked her in the eye. "I'm sorry, ma'am. Truly. I never intended to hurt you."

"Then why did you do it? Why don't you want me to find my uncle?"

"That should be obvious," Dan said. "He doesn't want us to tell Mr. Stone that his employee tried to defraud us and him. I wouldn't be surprised if when he gets back to his farm, your uncle finds that this man has squandered most of his resources."

"That ain't true!" Hastings looked so pained that Anne feared he would leap on Daniel — or burst into tears.

She exhaled deeply. "I hate to give up our quest even for a few more hours, but I think Whitey's right. We need to escort Mr. Hastings into town."

"I could take him," Whitey said. "I'll tie a noose around his neck and make him walk while I ride the horse."

Anne grimaced and looked at Dan. That sounded like an accidental suffocation waiting to happen, and she didn't like it one bit. If Whitey didn't strangle the man, Hastings might manage to escape. "What do you think, Daniel?"

"I hate to say it, but I think we should all

go back to Scottsburg."

"We're not far from David's claim," Whitey said.

"He ain't there."

They all swiveled toward Hastings.

"What did you say?" Dan asked.

"I said David Stone ain't at his claim no more."

"Where is he?"

Hastings huffed out a big breath. "Down yonder in Scottsburg, I reckon. But I ain't supposed to tell you."

Anne frowned at him. "Are you saying my uncle is in Scottsburg now?"

"Uh . . . well . . ."

"I demand that you tell me." Anne clenched her fists. "What do you know, Mr. Hastings?"

"Well, I rode up to his claim first thing this morning, and he wasn't there. Just got back when you folks come by so neighborly." He eyed Whitey's pistol and Dan's shotgun. "I reckon he's down to Scottsburg. Or I s'pose he mighta gone back to Eugene, but I h'ain't seen him."

"We missed him," Anne said. The disappointment hit her hard. How many times could this happen?

"How can that be?" Dan asked. "I inquired at the post office."

"Easy to do out here." Whitey spat tobacco juice off to one side. "If David went down to Scottsburg yestiddy, he might be heading back up to the claim today. Too bad to be so close and not have a look. You might miss him again."

Dan nodded. "We should go up there. What do you say, Anne?"

Determined to eliminate the risk, Anne agreed. It took them less than a half hour to get to the claim. Anne stood beside the stream and gazed at the marks left by David's spade as he dug out dirt to sift for gold. His fire pit held cold ashes, and the flattened rectangle nearby showed them where his tent had stood. She could even see where his horse had cropped the grass.

"Told ya he warn't here," Sam Hastings said.

"Shut up." Whitey glared at him.

Sam shrugged. "I'm just sayin'."

"Well, don't say no more." Whitey looked at Anne. "What you want to do now, missy?"

She looked helplessly to Daniel. "Do you think it will do us any good to go back and ask around town for him?"

"I don't know what else we can do," Dan said.

"Maybe we should leave some sort of message here for him." The thought that she might miss him again depressed Anne horribly, and she was resolved not to lose a chance to make contact.

Dan rummaged in his saddlebags, but no one had any paper.

"Maybe we could write a message on this scrap of leather," he said.

Anne used a charred stick to write a few words on the leather. "Uncle David, looking for you. Anne Stone." She wrote the date and rolled up the improvised note. Dan tied it with a rawhide thong and tucked it firmly between two rocks on the fire ring, sticking out so that anyone building a fire there couldn't help but see it.

"There. If some skunk doesn't decide to chew on it, it should stay there." He stood and smiled down at Anne. "Ready to go back to town?"

"Yes." She hugged the black cape about her and took one last look over the valley. "I'm glad I saw this place, anyway." She turned to Bailey and sent up a silent prayer of thanks for the safe return of the horses.

"Mind if I ride along?" Whitey asked. "There's things I could use from the store."

"Wait a second," Hastings said. "Are you going to make me walk all the way to Scottsburg?"

"Why not?" Dan asked.

"We should get there before dark if you don't dawdle." Whitey grinned at Anne and put his foot in the blue roan's stirrup.

What was it about the river that Charlotte found so fascinating? David ambled along with her, not in a hurry. Did she only want to get him out of the hotel, away from onlookers? Personally, he'd enjoyed their evening with the Packers last night. He'd thought Charlotte was having a good time, too, but she'd avoided committing to another session of cards tonight.

He didn't object to stargazing with a pretty woman. And his sporadic doubts about Charlotte were dim just now. She'd come down to dinner tonight in a new dress — plainer than the elegant one she'd worn on previous evenings, but perfectly suitable for the frontier hotel. She'd told him she'd found it in the mercantile. She seemed like a nice woman, and she was definitely intelligent. Perhaps he could learn to overlook her foibles. If she could put up with him, too, they might make a go of it. The fact that her cousin had yet to appear in town niggled at him, but that wasn't Charlotte's fault.

The road to the docks was the most traveled in Scottsburg, and the freighters kept it in good repair. This time of night, the riverfront was quiet except for a couple of saloons that fronted on the water. Shouts and raucous music wafted on the cool breeze. A man leaned against a piling on one of the smaller docks, smoking a cigarette. David had the feeling he'd seen the fellow before.

He led Charlotte away from that end of the road, heading instead for the steamer dock.

"I do love the night sky," she said, looking dreamily up at the velvety canopy.

"What do you like best about it?" David asked.

"It lets me think of things I never think about in daylight. Things I scarcely believe are possible at other times. But under the stars, I can think about anything . . . and forget things, too."

"What sort of things?"

Charlotte lifted her shoulders and shook her head slightly. "You know. All the sad things. Like being alone now and having to plan the future."

"You're going to live with your cousin and his wife, aren't you?"

"That's just a stopgap. Oh, they're nice enough, but I don't want to stay with them forever. You'll pardon me, won't you, if I say they're a bit provincial?"

"I'd pardon far worse things than that."

Her laugh rippled out over the water. "David, you make me feel so clever."

He smiled and paused when they came to the dock. "Would you like to walk out on the pier again?"

"I should like it above all else." She looked up at him coyly. "Well, not *all* else, but above most things."

The minx. She was the most outrageous flirt he'd known outside a saloon. And this talk of her lonely state and unsettled future — was that meant to draw on his chivalry and lure him in? He still liked her, but he wasn't sure he wanted to be caught, even though he longed for permanence.

"I'm sure you'll find a place you enjoy. And your cousin's household may surprise you. They may have connections you find very amicable."

"None so amicable as you, I'm sure." She squeezed his arm a little as they stepped onto the dock. "Oh David, I confess I shall miss you when I've left here."

Her burgundy lips assumed a pout that he found at the same time attractive and annoying. He'd never minded if a woman teased him a little, but tonight Charlotte seemed to go about it with almost grim purpose.

"Where did you say your cousin lives?" he asked as they strolled out onto the dock, the sound of their footsteps lost in the swirl of the river.

"Did I not tell you? It's in Salem. He assured me in his letter that he would meet me here, but now I wonder if I shouldn't have taken another ship and sailed farther north." She waved a hand in dismissal. "No matter. I shall stay here until he arrives now that we've set the place. And I'm fortunate to have such sympathetic company while I sit in this rather irksome town."

"You've made my stay more pleasant, as well."

"Have I, David? That gives me great satisfaction." She said the words almost seductively, peering up at him with a smile.

He felt suddenly uncomfortable. Charlotte's veneer had worn a little thin. He'd decided she was straightforward to the point of bluntness. Now he didn't think so. She had plans that she hadn't stated, and he had serious thoughts about how much more time he wanted to spend with her. He shouldn't have walked out with her tonight — not that there was anything sinister in it, but she obviously hoped their relationship would not end soon. He turned toward shore.

"It's a bit chilly out here, don't you think?"

"Oh, let's not go back yet. I should be ever so warm if you'd just lend me your arm, David."

He heard her words subconsciously, but his mind had homed in on a figure on shore. A man walked up the road toward the end of the dock they were on. Was it the same fellow who'd been smoking down below? Perhaps they'd better wait until he passed before heading in.

"David, what is it? You haven't heard a word I've said."

"Oh, it's nothing." He glanced down at her and back toward the shadowy form on shore. The man had paused where the dock met land. He held something up. David's heart stopped for a moment as he realized the man held a pistol, then it went on beating at breakneck pace.

"Charlotte, my dear, I'm afraid we're about to be robbed."

"What? You can't mean it." She looked toward shore. "Oh no, David —"

A spark flickered near the man's hand, and something whizzed past David's ear, then a loud *pow* reached him.

"Get down!" He threw an arm about

Charlotte and took a step back. They were trapped at the extreme end of the dock. David shoved her down onto the planking.

As he bent to shield her, something whacked into his arm and he heard another *pow*. Next thing he knew, he was falling off the edge of the dock, flailing as he plummeted into the icy water of the Umpqua.

CHAPTER 16

Millie screamed and stared at the man on the shore. She whirled and grabbed the post at the end of the dock and peered down into the swirling water.

"David! David!" Nothing answered her but the rush of the river. A desolation and fear she had never known swept over her, quickly replaced by fury. Its heat rose from deep in her belly and mounted to her neck and face. She clenched her fists and ran along the dock.

Peterson met her about halfway. Millie charged into him and pummeled him with her fists.

"What were you thinking? Why? Why did you do that?"

Peterson caught her wrists and held them firmly. "Easy now. Did you see him in the water? Where is he?"

"I don't know. You monster! Why did you shoot him?"

Peterson laughed. "What did you suppose I wanted from him?"

"I thought you wanted to talk to him. Do you mean to tell me that you had me bring him out here so you could *kill* him?"

"Could you please lower your voice?"

"No. I'll tell everyone who will listen."

"No you won't."

Millie stared into his dark eyes. "You promised he wouldn't think ill of me after you . . ." She caught her breath and ripped her hands free so she could hit him again. "I hate you. I hate you!"

"Talk is cheap, Charlotte."

He caught her hands again and squeezed them so hard it hurt. Millie stood still and stared up at him.

"Let me go," she said between clenched teeth.

"Why should I? You're in this with me, my dear. It's your choice. You can help me . . . or not."

She took a step back, but Peterson held tight to her hands. Tears bathed her face, and it annoyed her that her hands weren't free to wipe them away.

"Just tell me why," she managed.

"If there was any other way, I assure you, I'd have found it. But Stone is only valuable to me if he's dead. It has to be this way.

And we need the body."

Millie gasped. "What on earth do you mean?"

"The death certificate, woman! Come on. Help me find him and drag him out of the water. Then you can call the authorities and tell them whatever you like." He walked quickly along the edge of the dock, staring down into the water on the downstream side.

"I'll tell them, all right. I'll tell them you shot that man in cold blood."

"No, you tell them anything but that. Because if they come after me, I'll tell them how you took money to lure Stone out here. Do you understand?"

All the strength drained out of Millie, and she almost fell to her knees. In a flash she did understand. Her lungs squeezed, and a weight crushed her heart.

"Yes."

He nodded. "Then get ahold of yourself and help me. We can't let his body float off down the river."

They both walked to the extreme end of the dock and gazed downward.

"The water's not running that fast, is it?" Millie asked after an awful moment of silence.

Peterson peered out away from the dock

and let his gaze track downstream. "I can't lose the body."

She said nothing but waited for him to speak again. He scanned the water continually. Millie began to think about trying to elude him. Could she outrun him to the end of the wharf? Doubtful. And if he caught her trying to escape, what would he do? He'd already killed a perfectly nice man and seemed to have no compunction about it. No one seemed to have heard the shot but her. At least, no one had come to investigate. He could kill her as easily.

And what would she tell the constable if she did get away from him? That she'd seen a man shoot another man, but there was no body and no evidence of the crime? If she named Peterson, he would deny everything and cast aspersions on her . . . or slip out of town before Millie finished telling her tale.

"Show me the exact spot he went in," Peterson said.

"Right here." She moved to the side of the wharf but turned half toward him, suddenly suspicious. What if he pushed her in? His only witness. But he seemed completely focused on finding David.

"I've got to get a boat." He stroked his mustache. "Can't have him floating all the way to the coast."

"I doubt you'll find him," Millie said. "The current probably pulled him under. He may never be found."

"I *have* to find him. I suppose the body could be caught under the dock."

She swallowed hard. "You can't just let him . . . disappear? He's been off at his mining claim. They might think he went back there. We could pack up his luggage and —"

"Stop babbling! I told you, I need a death certificate or all is lost." Peterson dashed along the dock, his shoes thudding on the planking.

Millie walked slowly toward shore. Peterson seemed to have forgotten her. He raced along the shore road toward the saloons. He'd said he needed a boat. No doubt he planned to poke about underneath the dock, in the eerie darkness. Well, he could do that alone. She turned in the opposite direction, though the road led past a looming warehouse and some shabby houses. She would take the long way around to the hotel.

David lay in the water on his stomach, hugging a piling about halfway along the length of the dock. The frigid water made his entire body hurt, but his arm was the worst. He touched it once and gritted his teeth. Clean through the muscle, he hoped. He concentrated on keeping his hold.

Above him, far away, he could hear their voices. First Charlotte's screams, then their feet thudding on the decking above him as he tried to maneuver his way beneath the dock and toward the riverbank. He felt his strength ebbing. As he shoved off from one piling and caught the next, it was hard not to be swept from under the dock and downstream. His head spun, and he clung to the piling. He must be losing blood, not to mention body heat.

He'd splashed into the water off the end of the dock, and somehow his momentum or the current had pulled him beneath it. He'd panicked at first, thinking Charlotte was alone and unprotected up there with a murderer. Then he'd heard her questions. "Why did you do it? Did you have me bring him out here so you could *kill* him?"

So. She was in some scheme and knew the gunman. But why? One thing he knew for certain — he wouldn't come out of hiding until they were gone.

As they walked along the dock and apparently searched the water for him, he grew weaker. Would they come down here and get into the water to search beneath the dock? He shifted his good arm lower, so that it was completely beneath the surface, just in case someone looking over the edge could glimpse the piling.

He heard the man's voice. It must carry some way — was there anyone else about to hear this thug?

"I've got to get a boat." And then, "I need a death certificate or all is lost." The heavier footsteps thudded toward shore.

It didn't make sense to David. He closed his eyes and tried not to lose his grip on the slimy post. Why would anyone need a death certificate? He opened his eyes. To prove he was dead, of course. But why? For whom? How could he be of value dead? There was his property, of course. But would someone kill him for an undeveloped farm and a not-too-promising mining claim? Did this man know something he didn't?

The voice sounded cultured but cold. Not like a backwoodsman or a hardened criminal. Who was he? David racked his brain for anyone who might hate him or even somebody who'd hold a grudge against him, but nothing came to him.

The lighter footsteps moved above him. Charlotte was still there. Should he let her know he was still alive? What would she do? She'd apparently betrayed him willingly, though perhaps in ignorance of the assassin's purpose. But David didn't have enough confidence in her to trust her again. He gritted his teeth and prayed in silence.

"I've got a place I can lock him up," the constable said. "Won't be the first horse thief we've kept in Fisher's icehouse until the judge said we could string him up."

Sam Hastings's face blanched.

"I'm not sure we want to go that far," Anne said quickly.

"Well, ma'am, did he or didn't he steal your horses?"

"He did," Dan said. Anne was obviously having second thoughts about turning the slow-witted thief over for justice. "Is it possible he could spend some time in jail for this, or even perform some labor in compensation?"

"You want him to work for you instead of hangin'?" The constable scratched his chin through his beard. "I dunno. Have to wait and see what the judge says, I reckon."

"We would plead for . . . for clemency. Wouldn't we, Daniel?" Anne turned her eloquent brown eyes on him, and Dan couldn't refuse her.

"Surely. We don't want this man executed."

"Thought you said he put you in mortal

danger. Look, either you press charges, or you don't."

Anne plucked at Dan's sleeve and pulled him toward the door. "Excuse us, Constable. We need a moment to confer."

Dan followed her outside, where Whitey waited with the horses.

"We can't let them hang him, Daniel," she whispered.

"Well, Anne, it seems to be the standard penalty for his crime."

"What's that?" Whitey asked.

"They'll hang Mr. Hastings if we file a complaint against him for taking the horses."

Whitey spat tobacco juice between the roan's front feet. "Yup. That sounds about right."

"But . . ." Anne turned to Dan, her face contorted in dismay. "That makes us directly responsible for his death. We can't do that."

Dan hesitated. "What do you suggest?"

"Let's ask Constable Owens when the judge will make a ruling."

They went back inside and put the question to the constable.

"Well, now, I don't expect he'll be here for another fortnight. He only comes once a month."

Dan arched his eyebrows at Anne. Her tense facial muscles had relaxed.

"And you'll keep him locked up until the judge comes?" she asked.

"Yes, ma'am."

"Well then, Daniel, I see no reason why we can't get a good night's sleep and consider this again tomorrow, do you?"

"I . . . guess not."

"Might be a good idea," Constable Owens said. "Let me know when you decide. I'll hold him meantime, just so's we know where he is."

"You can't do that, can you?" Sam cried.

"I can, and I will."

Dan took Anne's elbow and guided her outside before anyone had third or fourth thoughts on the matter.

"It's too late to ask at the post office tonight," he said. "Let's go back to Mrs. Zinberg's and inquire first thing tomorrow."

"What about Whitey?" Anne looked over to where the old man stood beside the roan, scratching under its forelock.

"I suppose we should put him up for the night at a hotel," Dan said.

"It seems only fair — after all, he put us up last night, when we sorely needed it."

"All right. Shall we install him in town or take him with us to Mrs. Zinberg's on the chance she has an extra room?"

Anne smiled. "That depends. Are you will-ing to chance rooming with Whitey again if she doesn't?"

Dan laughed. "Could be worse, I guess."

Anne leaned toward him and whispered, "He's getting awfully fond of that horse."

"Yes. I suppose he'd like to have a mount of his own. But we can't just let him take it, even if its owner is a thieving rascal."

"I'll bet Hastings stole that horse from Uncle David."

"I hadn't thought of that," Dan said. "We can ask him tomorrow. But for now, let's go. It's getting cold again, and if we stay out much later, we'll frighten Mrs. Zinberg when we pound on her door."

He led Star over toward the roan and said, "Whitey, what do you say to accompanying us to our boardinghouse? We'll straighten all this out in the morning, and you can go home if you like, but we'd like you to have a good night's rest and a hearty breakfast first."

Whitey's eyes glittered. "That's right neighborly of you, son."

David's head cleared as he left the water and clawed his way up the bank. He'd said it was chilly before, but now he was soaking

300

wet. The cold wind off the mountains could be lethal. Could he make it to the hotel?

Charlotte had finally left the dock, cursing as she went — not a section of her vocabulary she'd shown him before. What other talents were buried in the deeper layers of her personality?

He lurched onto the road and considered staggering the quarter mile to one of the waterfront saloons. Better not. That would attract attention. The assassin was looking for his body. The honorable David Stone would stay dead.

Down the road, a man came out of a saloon and strode up the boardwalk. David hobbled into the shadows. His arm hurt worse by the second, and he held on to it. He supposed he ought to be thankful it wasn't worse.

The cold air penetrated the layers of his wet clothing. If he didn't get inside soon, he'd be in even worse trouble. When the pedestrian had passed, he left his hiding place. By alleys and back streets, he made his way toward the hotel. Each painful step was a trial. His mind raced while his body plodded, slower and slower.

A man wouldn't need legal proof of his death to jump his claim. In that situation, it would be better if his body were never found. The thug could just squat on the land and prospect. He could probably even get away with impersonating David if he stayed away from those who knew him in Scottsburg, or perhaps he could claim they were partners.

So what was this business arrangement Charlotte had gotten into? From the sound of things, she hadn't expected a murder attempt. The man had tricked her into luring him out where he could fire the fatal shot without an audience. But the gunman's plan included the filing of the proper paperwork. Whatever for?

Now, if this were England . . .

But the assassin wasn't British. Still, the thought wouldn't go away. David hugged himself, shivering violently. He hobbled through another alley and came out in the yard between the back of the hotel and its outbuildings. Should he get his horse and flee without telling anyone what happened? He'd freeze to death before he reached the next town.

He stopped and leaned against the wall of the hotel's woodshed, his left hand clamped over his wound. He should see a doctor. Or would that prove fatal? Someone wanted him dead.

His thoughts veered back to England. This

might make sense there . . . but only if he were next in line to inherit an estate . . . say, Stoneford. A chill more bitter than that imposed by water and wind swept over him. This couldn't be connected to the earldom, could it? His teeth chattered, and he tried to clench them together, but he couldn't stop shaking. If he didn't get inside soon, the thug would get his wish. Sucking in a breath, he reeled toward the hotel's kitchen door.

Locked. David didn't think he had enough strength to get around to the front entrance. He fell against the door and raised his bloody hand to pound on the panel.

"Dear God," he ground out, "have mercy."

He lifted his left hand again and thudded his fist against the door. A rattle within startled him. He managed to draw back just before it opened, so that he didn't fall in.

"Help me," he said.

The rotund cook stared at him for a moment.

"Good heavens! Mr. Stone!"

David collapsed on the threshold.

CHAPTER 17

"Can you hear me, sir?"

David opened his eyes and blinked up at Ernie Bond, the hotel's cook. He reached out a shaking hand. "C–can you help me, Ernie?"

"What do you want me to do? You look half frozen."

"Help me get to my room."

"Yes, sir. Let me get Mr. Reed."

"No," David said. "Don't tell anyone."

Ernie swallowed hard and looked around the kitchen.

"I'm not sure we can do it without help, sir. We can go up the back stairs, but you've got the suite on the third floor, and that's a lot of steps."

"Then set me a chair by the s–stove. If I get warm, m–maybe I can walk."

Ernie bustled about and returned to give him a hand in rising.

"Easy, now. You all right?"

David groaned and pulled himself up, putting all his weight on Ernie's arm. They hobbled to a chair Ernie had positioned a yard from the big iron cookstove, and David sank into it.

"I've got a little coffee left. Let me get you some."

A moment later, Ernie held out the cup. David's fingers stung and prickled as the feeling began to return. "Can't —" He rubbed his hands together and grimaced.

"What happened to you, if you don't mind my asking?" Ernie said.

"Fell in the river."

"Bad place to be this time of year." His gaze fastened on David's sleeve. "You're bleeding, you know."

"Shot."

Ernie's eyes widened. "You need a doctor."

"Is there one?" At last David's hands stopped prickling and began to feel hot as the blood rushed through them. He reached for the cup.

"Oh yes. Doc Muller. Lives down the way. I could send the — No, I guess you don't want me to tell anyone. That's what you said before."

David nodded. "If I can get to my room, we'll see what's what." He clasped his hands around the thick china cup and sighed at the comfort of its warmth. Slowly he raised it to his lips and took a sip. The coffee was very warm but not hot.

"I can make a fresh pot," Ernie said. "I was about to close up the kitchen for the night. . . ."

"Don't bother," David said. "This is fine." He took a bigger gulp.

"Let's get that wet coat off you." Ernie took his cup away and worked at David's coat buttons. "You're lucky you survived."

David knew he was right, but his mind was too numb to form a prayer of thanks. The pain when Ernie tugged on his right sleeve jabbed him into sudden and complete alertness. He sucked in a breath and held it while the cook eased the coat off his other arm and dropped it on the floor.

Ernie moved away and returned with a heavy damask tablecloth. "I don't have a blanket. Put this around you."

"I'll get blood on it."

"You're shaking all over, Mr. Stone. Don't worry about the blood."

The weight of the dry cloth did feel good. Ernie gave him back his cup of lukewarm coffee, and he sipped it. As David thawed, other discomforts began to make themselves known. His feet ached, and his temple throbbed. He put his hand to it and winced. Had he hit his head on the dock when he fell? Maybe he'd stumbled going up the riverbank and didn't remember.

"We ought to do something about that arm," Ernie said.

David tried to look at the wound, but just moving his shoulder hurt more than it was worth.

"It doesn't seem to be bleeding much now, if that's any comfort." Ernie pulled the damask cloth over the injured arm.

"Probably the veins froze."

Ernie laughed. "When you think you can walk, I'll help you upstairs. Then I really should look at it or else get Doc Muller." Ernie looked toward the dining-room door. "Sometimes Mr. Reed comes out here in the evening. If you don't want him to see you, we need to do it soon."

"All right."

David handed him his coffee cup, and Ernie set it aside. He walked around to David's left side and stooped over.

"Put your good arm around my shoulders."

Even using his left side sent shafts of pain through David's body. He hung on to Ernie and pushed himself up. His head swam, and he stood still for a moment, gasping.

"All right?" Ernie asked.

"Yes."

"This way."

They staggered across the kitchen. David never should have sat down. Now his muscles had stiffened.

"My coat." They stopped and looked back. His sodden jacket lay in a heap behind his chair.

"I'll come back for it. We've got to get you out of sight."

Ernie half dragged him up to the first landing. David appreciated his not asking who had shot him or why — not that he could have answered the questions. Ernie seemed like a sharp-witted fellow. He understood the urgency.

A door opened down the hallway. David gritted his teeth.

"They won't see us unless they come down to this stairway," Ernie whispered. "But if anyone asks, I'll just say you came in drunk."

"Did I have a hat?" David asked.

"No."

"Must have lost it in the drink." Too bad. He liked that hat — and it would have helped shield his face. They swung around and started up the next flight of stairs.

When they reached the top, Ernie opened

the door. David heard footsteps in the hall, coming toward the staircase. After a moment, they faded away.

"That was one of the geologists in 210," Ernie said. "He went down the main staircase."

"Did he see you?"

"I don't think so."

"Well, at least he didn't see me. That would make him stare."

"Yes. A fat man helping a scarecrow wrapped in a tablecloth to his room."

David laughed out loud. He couldn't stop chortling, until he shook all over.

"Hey, it wasn't that funny." Ernie eyed him askance from about six inches away. "Let's get you on down the hall."

"At least it wasn't someone I know," David said.

"Yes, like that pretty Mrs. Evans."

David's blood chilled. "If she asks about me don't tell her you saw me tonight, whatever you do."

"Does she have something to do with this?"

"Just play dumb."

"Got it."

At last they reached the door to David's suite. He patted his pockets, afraid he might have lost the key in the river, but he found it, with a sodden wallet, a few coins, and his pocketknife. He handed the key over, and Ernie opened the door while David leaned against the wall.

Inside his bedroom, he dropped the table-cloth and let Ernie help him strip off his wet clothing.

"That wound looks nasty. You'd best let me fetch the doctor."

David hesitated. "The fewer people who know about this the better."

"Yes, but you could die from infection while you're keeping your head down." Ernie took the clean handkerchief David supplied and tied it about the wound. Just his touch sent a fiery pain through David's body, and tightening the knot made him gasp.

"All right," he said, "but help me get warm first." The rooms were chilly, but while David pulled on long underwear and woolen trousers and a shirt, Ernie lit the fire on the hearth.

"You should go to bed and sleep."

David shook his head. "I can't stay here."

"Why ever not?"

"The person who did this might come looking for me here."

Ernie frowned. "Is there somewhere else you could go?"

"I'll have to think about it. I have a few acquaintances in town but none I'd call close friends."

"Well, I'll run for the doctor. Lock your door and wait." Ernie turned to go.

"I really don't want to sit here that long."

Ernie swung around. "I've got an idea. You could ask to switch rooms."

"Hmm, could we do that with no one else knowing?"

Ernie's slow smile gave him hope. "There's a small room under the attic stairs that is only rented out when everything else is full. I can get the key easily when Reed isn't looking."

David's mind raced. "But if all my things are gone, he'll think I skipped out without paying."

"Well, you can't stay here if someone's trying to kill you." Ernie frowned at him. "What do you suggest?"

David sank down on the edge of the bed, pressing on his wounded shoulder. If it didn't hurt so much, he could think.

"You're right. I need to get out of this room. But maybe we can leave my things here, at least overnight, and see if anyone comes around asking for me or tries to break into the room. What do they do if a hotel guest disappears without paying?"

"They'd pack up your things and hold on to them for a while, in case you came back, or in case a family member claimed them."

"Well, that's not going to happen."

"Won't anyone know you're missing?"

"I haven't kept in touch with my family for a long time." Not for the first time, David regretted not writing to his brothers more often.

"Tell you what," Ernie said. "If you think you'll be all right for ten minutes or so, I'll see if I can get Doc Muller. After he fixes you up, I'll help you get into the little room under the stairs. We'll take your wet things and just enough for you to get by on — so that it looks like you left all your stuff and disappeared."

"Yes. And I'll leave enough cash lying about to pay my bill."

"Oh, Mr. Reed will be very pleased if you do that," Ernie said.

David nodded. "Of course, there'll be something in it for you, too, Ernie."

"No need, Mr. Stone. I'm not doing this for pay."

"I know, and that tells me you're the sort of man I'd like to count among my friends."

Ernie ducked his head. "I'm honored, sir. Now I'd best get moving."

"My pistol," David said.

"Where is it?"

"In the bottom drawer." He nodded toward the dresser.

Ernie got it out and brought it over to him. "Is it loaded?"

"Yes. I want it handy while you're gone. I suppose I'll have to leave it behind when we move, though."

"Why?" Ernie asked. "No one can say you didn't have it on you when you disappeared."

"I like the way you think. All right, see if you can get the doctor. After that we'd better get me moved."

Ernie left, and David lay back on the pillow with the pistol lying on his chest and pointed toward the door. He wished the door was locked, but even if he made it over there now to lock it, he'd have to get up again when Ernie returned and unlock it. That might be too much for him. He'd have to depend on the gun if anyone else came before Ernie got back.

The temptation to close his eyes was too great. Slipping into semiconsciousness felt delicious. The pain in his arm still maintained a constant presence, but he was able to push it aside now that he lay prone and could relax.

His eyelids flew open. What was he doing?

He couldn't go to sleep. An assassin wanted to kill him, and he'd flown back to the first place the man would look for him. He forced himself to sit up. His head cleared a little, and he tried to stand but lurched and nearly knocked over the nightstand.

He got as far as the chair and clung to the back, panting and fighting a blackout. The fire was burning down, but he didn't think he had the energy to build it up again. He summoned another ounce of resolution and took two shaky steps to the dresser. Most of his valuables had been in his pockets tonight, but a few other things must go with him to the new room. He gathered a minimum of clothing, leaving enough to make it look as though he was still using the room. Most of the small gold nuggets he'd gleaned at his claim had already been cashed in, but he pocketed a small pouch he'd left covered by his extra shirts. The extra ammunition for his pistol would go with him. He'd better leave his rifle, much as he hated to. Charlotte or the killer might know he had one, and he certainly hadn't been carrying it the last time they saw him. His mining gear represented less of a loss. What about Captain?

He sank down in the armchair near the fire and pondered that. How could he keep his favorite horse without arousing suspicion? Captain was stabled out back in the hotel's barn.

His head throbbed now, and his arm screamed as though a hot iron seared it. Maybe Ernie or the doctor could help him figure that out.

When the door opened, he jerked awake. He'd slumped down, and the pistol had slid between his thigh and the chair's arm. As he fumbled for it, Ernie entered and spoke.

"Here we are. How are you doing?"

"All right, I guess." David gazed past him to the doctor.

"This is Doc Muller," Ernie said. "Mr. Stone."

The blond man looked to be ten years younger than David, well fed, and self-assured. He stepped forward with a black satchel in his hand and a rueful smile on his face. "Mr. Stone, I understand you met with an untoward happenstance."

"Nothing happenstance about it. The blackguard meant to kill me."

"Ah. Would you like to lie down while I examine the wound?"

David looked to Ernie. "Can we go down the hall first? I'm afraid they'll find me here."

"Of course."

Ernie scouted the hallway, then helped him up. Dr. Muller stood watch while they lurched along to a door tucked under the attic stairway. The cook seemed to have picked up a skeleton key on his outing, and they were soon inside. Ernie drew the drapes first thing. The cot wasn't made up, and he quickly spread a quilt on it.

"I don't want to bleed all over the bedding," David said. He looked around, but besides the bed, the room held only a washstand, a narrow dresser, and a stool.

"I'll go for some sheets," Ernie said. "Then I'll get your wet clothes while Doc sees to your arm."

"Oh, and I left a small bundle on top of the dresser. Bring that, too, please." David sank onto the stool. He was putting Ernie to a lot of trouble, but the cook remained cheerful.

"I may as well get that cloth off and take a look while we wait," Dr. Muller said.

"Better lay this down." David handed him the pistol, and the doctor set it on the edge of the washstand.

David nearly screamed when the doctor began to unknot the handkerchief Ernie had tied around his upper arm. He clenched his teeth and tried to think about England — Stoneford's fields would be damp and dreary this time of year, and the trees would have shed their foliage, but if he were there, he and Richard and John would be out hunting. Some different it would be from hunting in Oregon, though. The thought of donning a pink coat and setting off after a fox seemed almost ludicrous compared to the elk hunt he'd had last year. And no one hunting in the Oregon woods would wear something as bright as the scarlet material his pink coat was made from.

He managed to lie still while Dr. Muller lifted his arm and probed the wound.

"Seems to have gone in here and out here. That's good — we don't have to remove it. It did a job on your muscles, though."

"I'm thankful it's not worse," David said without unclenching his teeth.

"I'll clean it up and then bandage it well, but you've got to understand, a wound like this is prone to infection within."

"Do whatever you have to, Doc."

"You'll want it checked frequently. Of course it will be sore for several weeks. But if the skin around it becomes hot and swollen, and if it looks redder than normal, that means it's infected. You don't want to let it go if that happens."

"What can you do?"

The doctor sighed. "The best cure is to

prevent it in the first place. So I will hurt you tonight to make sure it is thoroughly clean. This isn't a method many of my peers use, but I've found that patients do much better when I follow this procedure."

The door swung open, and Ernie came in carrying his things from the suite. "Here we go, Mr. Stone." He set the bundle on the dresser and dropped the wet clothes on the floor. "I'd better run down to the kitchen for your coat."

By the time he returned again, the doctor was cleaning up and putting his instruments away.

"I ran into Mr. Reed," Ernie said as he closed the door. "He asked why I was here so late."

"Is he suspicious?" David asked.

"I don't think so. I told him I wanted to start dough rising for breakfast. That means I'll have to come in extra early in the morning, but I don't mind."

"Is everything set in my old room?" David asked.

"Yes. I looked around in the sitting room as well as the bedchamber. Everything looks as though you stepped out for the evening and will return any moment. I made sure there's no blood or other telltale signs. And I soaked the tablecloth we used in cold water. It came out rather well."

"Thank you," David said. "Where's my soggy wallet now, Ernie?"

"Right here, sir."

"Good. Would you please give the doctor two dollars from it? I've explained to him that I shall disappear as a hotel guest."

"That's right," Dr. Muller said. "I'll come and check on you tomorrow, but I shan't inquire for you at the front desk."

"If you come straight to the kitchen, I'll let you come up the back stairs," Ernie said. "No one will be the wiser unless one of the waiters is in the kitchen then."

"I'll make it a point not to come at meal-time." The doctor pocketed the money Ernie gave him. "Thank you for paying promptly, sir. You're in the minority there. I assure you your location is safe with me."

Dr. Muller cracked the door open and went out, carrying his black bag. Ernie locked the door behind him, and David sighed.

"I can never repay you, but I'll make a down payment, Ernie. There's a little pouch in my bundle over there. That's for you."

"Oh Mr. Stone, I told you —"

David held up his good hand. "I know, but I want to give you this. It's a collection of small nuggets from my sluice box, and it should be worth about a hundred dollars. Don't say that's too much. It's not, and I have enough cash to get me home when I'm done here. But there's one other thing we need to take care of."

"What's that, sir?"

"I do want to pay the hotel bill. Perhaps we could leave enough money on the dresser in the suite to cover it? Then when Mr. Reed begins investigating my disappearance, he'll find it."

"Hmm. What if someone else goes in there first and 'finds' it?"

"The shooter, you mean?"

"Whoever. The cleaning woman, even. And once your absence is noticed, a lot of people will wonder what became of you. If Reed calls in the constable . . . Well, it wouldn't be the first time cash disappeared during an investigation, now would it?"

"What do you suggest?"

"You could put the money in an envelope with a note saying you plan to check out tomorrow and wanted to settle up in advance."

"Would that work? Reed would know it wasn't at the front desk when he left for the night."

"We'll leave it in the suite, then. Can you write a note if I bring you paper and pen?"

"Maybe." David yawned. He was tired out, but in addition the doctor had given him a powder to help him sleep. "Best be quick about it, or I'll be out cold." His brain was so numb he couldn't come up with a better plan.

Ernie hesitated. "Sir, don't you want me to stay here tonight? You need to rest."

"They won't find me here. You said no one uses this room most nights."

"That's true."

"Go on. What would your wife say if you didn't come home?"

"Wife? That's a good one."

"Still, I'll be all right. Leave me my pistol. I'll lock the door behind you."

"Let me take your wet things and get them dried and aired so you have a change in the morning. I might be able to do something about the bullet holes, too. . . ." Ernie held up the bloody shirt and shook his head as he surveyed the tattered sleeve.

"Don't bother," David said. "Just dispose of it discreetly."

"Well, sir, I could pick up anything you need at the haberdashery tomorrow. Too bad you have to leave so many nice things behind. . . ."

"Yes. I'll get on all right without them, but I wish there was a way to give some of it to you. Oh, that reminds me. Captain."

"Captain?"

"My horse. He's in the stable. I'd hate to lose him."

Ernie scratched his chin. "What if he sort of . . . checked out . . . before anyone knew you were missing?"

"Hmm. That might cause the assassin to believe I'm still alive."

"It might. Is it worth the risk?"

"What will happen if we leave him there?"

"Well, if we didn't leave the money to cover the bill the way we talked about, you could just leave the horse. Reed would probably sell him to pay your bill."

"My horse and gear are worth more than that, and besides, he's a good horse." David stifled another yawn.

"All right. I'll get the paper for you to write the note, and then I'll get the horse from the stable and take him and your wet clothes home with me. If nobody sees me, you're in good shape. I'll keep Captain until you're ready to travel again."

Ernie helped David get as far as the door, placed the pistol in his hand, and went out. David leaned against the jamb for a minute, listening to his new friend's retreating footsteps. He slid the bolt. He was just about to turn away when he heard soft footfalls in the hallway. He held his breath, wishing he'd doused the lamp. He heard a door open and close quietly, then more footsteps, so gentle he'd almost have said they were stealthy. Then all was quiet.

He stood there for a good five minutes — until his legs turned to lead. He couldn't stand any longer, even leaning against the woodwork. He staggered to the table and blew out the flame in the lamp, then lurched to the cot and lowered himself onto it with as little noise as possible.

CHAPTER 18

Millie topped the second flight of stairs and stood for a moment on the landing to catch her breath. Which room was David's? He'd let fall last night that he was on the third floor. She didn't think many guests were staying up here. She tiptoed along the hall, studying the numbers painted on the door panels, mentally boxing her own ears for not discovering his room number.

At the opposite end of the building, across the landing and at the far end of the hall she was exploring, a door creaked. She stepped back against the wall and peered toward the sound. A man had just gone through a doorway down there, but where had he come from?

She hastened along the carpet runner, crossed the landing with a glance down toward the floor below, and glided on into the other wing. Two lamps turned low threw just enough light in the corridor to guide her.

At the extreme end of the hall, the door on the left seemed the most likely candidate for the one the man had escaped through. To her surprise, small, neat letters on it proclaimed a discreet STAFF ONLY. Millie turned the brass knob, and the door swung inward on an uncarpeted landing. She'd discovered the back stairs.

With a sigh, she closed the door again. The man she'd seen was no doubt a hotel employee. This wasn't helping her. She needed to find out where David had been staying. After a moment's thought, she went to the nearest numbered door — 306 — and knocked softly. No sound came from within. She tapped again, louder. Still no response. She tried the knob, but the door was locked.

She moved on along the hallway. On the third door she tried — a room close to the landing, a man's voice called from within, "Yes?"

Millie froze, every sense a-tingle.

A moment later, she heard a bolt drawn, and the door opened about six inches. A gray-haired man wearing dark trousers, an undershirt, and suspenders peered out at her.

"May I help you?"

Millie clapped a hand to her cheek. "Oh, I beg your pardon. I was supposed to meet my brother, and I thought he told me that his room was 303. I must have gotten the number wrong. Please forgive the intrusion." She fluttered her eyelashes and pursed her lips, on which she'd recently replenished her rouge.

"Oh well, certainly." The man hesitated. "Er, what does your brother look like?"

"He's a tall Englishman." She immediately realized her mistake and added hastily, "That is, he's spent a lot of time in England, and he's picked up the accent. That's what most people notice about him first."

"Hmm, I think he said good-day to me this morning — he seemed to be on his way out then."

"Oh, I've seen him since then, but thank you." Millie smiled and moved on toward the landing.

"You'd better ask at the front desk," the man called after her. His door closed.

She lingered on the landing. Was it better to disturb other guests and let them see her seeking a tall Englishman — and she needed to revise her story if she chose that option — or to inquire at the desk? She didn't want anyone connecting her to David's disappearance. Yet several other guests had seen them dining together this evening. Maybe it would be wise to ask about him. That would imply that she didn't know he wasn't in his room and healthy as a horse.

She hurried down the two flights of stairs.

A new clerk was on the desk — a younger, red-haired man who looked to be scarcely into his twenties. He stared brazenly at Millie as she descended the last few steps and strolled toward him.

"Well, hello," she said. "Haven't seen you before."

"I'm the night clerk. M–may I help you, ma'am?"

"Oh dear, I didn't realize how late it was. Mr. Stone had asked me to meet him for coffee when I returned from my evening out with friends, and I don't see him here in the lobby. He hasn't by any chance left a message for me, has he?"

"Uh . . . What's your room number, ma'am?"

"It's 202. Mrs. Evans."

He turned away and scanned the bank of pigeonholes behind him. "Nope. I don't see anything in your box."

She sighed and fluttered her lashes. "Perhaps he gave up on me. Let's see, he's way up on the third floor, isn't he?"

"Mr. Stone? I . . . uh . . . I think so." The

clerk consulted the registry on the counter. "Oh, he has the suite. He's the English fellow."

"Yes." Millie's mind whirled. David had a suite? She hadn't even known the hotel possessed such accommodations. "Maybe he intended to have coffee served in his sitting room."

"Well, he hasn't asked for room service tonight, at least not since I've been here, but that's only the last hour or so."

"I'll go up and see if he's waiting for me. Uh, what did you say the number is?"

"He's in 304, but I can run up and check if you want, ma'am."

"Oh, that's all right. I shall have to go up to my room anyway, and if he's not in, I'll simply retire. Thank you very much . . . uh . . . what was your name?" She gave a smile she hoped dazzled the gangly young fellow, and he practically melted before her eyes.

"It's Ronald, ma'am."

"Oh please, Ronald. You may call me Mrs. Evans."

"Yes, ma'am."

She could feel his gaze on her as she sauntered to the stairs. She went along to her own room and gathered assorted hairpins, a nail file, and a pair of tweezers. One way or another, she was going to get into that suite.

Anne couldn't sleep. As much as she wanted justice, she wasn't sure that execution would be justice in Sam Hastings's case. The more she thought about it, the more certain she was that he hadn't acted alone.

"I ain't supposed to tell you," he'd said.

According to whom? she wondered. And hadn't he claimed he wasn't really stealing the horses but was only attempting to keep her from finding David? She'd assumed he meant because he didn't want her to reveal his attempt to impersonate her uncle. But would he follow her all this way for that? David would find out eventually. What good would it do Sam Hastings to keep her away from him for a while?

"If I don't find Uncle David, he'll never know I'm within ten thousand miles of here," she said aloud. Instead of trying to stop her from tattling on him, was Sam's goal to keep David from knowing about her?

She thought back over the two visits she and Dan had made to the farm when Sam pretended to be her uncle. She sat up in bed. The key to the puzzle was obvious — why hadn't she seen it before?

She threw back the bedclothes. In the

interest of saving the horses, she'd packed light, which meant she hadn't brought her dressing gown. That meant she had to get completely dressed before she left her chamber. Without another woman to help lace her corsets, that took some engineering, but ten minutes later she surveyed herself in the mirror and decided her appearance lay within the bounds of propriety. She opened her door and tiptoed along the hall.

As she passed the room where Whitey had settled for the night, snores penetrated the pine door panels. Mrs. Zinberg's room was downstairs, for which Anne was thankful. She pulled up before the door to Dan's room and looked over her shoulder. Only a little light spilled through the casement at the end of the hall, and she was alone. Feeling slightly decadent, she tapped softly on the door.

"Daniel? Daniel, it's me. I need to tell you something."

She was about to knock louder when she heard him turn the knob. He stared out at her.

"Anne?"

His tousled hair gave him a boyish look that she found adorable by starlight, and she smiled.

"What is it?" he asked.

Suddenly she realized anew how scandalous her behavior might seem.

"Oh! I thought of something. I'm sorry to wake you."

He smiled and opened the door wider, revealing that he was still dressed. "You didn't wake me. I couldn't sleep, and I was pacing the floor, thinking about what happened today."

"Me, too. Dan, don't you see? Sam Hastings wasn't in that bit of chicanery alone."

He stared at her for a long moment, then inhaled through his nose. "You're right. Of course. I should have seen it at once. The question is —"

Anne nodded. "Where's Millie?"

Whenever she got a new corset, the first thing Millie did was to sew a small pocket into it. Secure banking at its best. As she dressed in the morning, she patted the satin garment with satisfaction. She still had sixty dollars left from what Peterson had paid her — after a lavish shopping spree among Scottsburg's none-too-satisfactory retail establishments — and last night she'd added another ten.

She'd surprised herself when she shed a few tears for David into her pillow. It would have been grand to marry such a suave, handsome, wealthy man. Alas, that was not to be. From his room, she'd lifted his last gifts to her — a lovely little carved box containing a pair of onyx cuff links, a small Bible, and two five-dollar bills. She'd burned the envelope the money came in and the accompanying note: "I'll be checking out early. This should cover my bill. David Stone, #304."

Now wasn't that convenient of him to leave that before stepping out last evening? One would almost think he'd had a premonition that he might not return.

Poor David! She was still furious with Peterson and a little bit frightened, but she would never let him see that. In fact, she planned to be miles from Scottsburg before that shifty character was even out of bed. Too bad. She'd enjoyed this hotel. It was nicer than she'd expected in this rough river town, and so far she hadn't paid a cent. Two of her dinners went on David's bill, and thanks to him and Peterson, she had plenty to pay for her accommodations. She briefly considered skipping out without paying at all, but decided against that. She'd run up quite a bill, and it might be enough to make the manager set the constable on her. Of course, the constable would have his hands full with the disappearance of the hotel's most affluent guest. . . .

Her thoughts kept coming back to that. The shot in the moonlight, and David pitching over the edge of the dock into the river. Peterson's harsh words, and her aching emptiness. She was alone now, as she had been most of her life. It was up to her to distance herself from Peterson, who was obviously a very dangerous man.

A fleeting thought crossed her mind of Sam — where had he wound up? Was he still up in the hills, chasing Anne Stone and her stuffy bodyguard? She'd decided that's what Dan Adams was. Anne didn't give him enough encouragement to make him a lover or even a sweetheart. That girl had no passion. Millie could teach her a thing or two under different circumstances.

She sighed and settled her new hat on her upswept hair. Scottsburg needed a decent milliner, but this would suffice for now. When she got to San Francisco again, she'd buy a proper hat.

The hotel's breakfast was classier than what she'd gotten at the café with Peterson, though it cost nearly three times as much. Since she was paying this morning, she may as well stay here and enjoy it — and avoid the possibility of seeing Peterson again. That cook they had out back knew what he was doing. She'd take a leisurely breakfast, then pack her things in the new leather traveling bag she'd purchased, pay her bill like a decent lady, and collect her mount from the stable.

She opened the little carved box and gazed at the cuff links. Why had she taken them? She supposed she could sell them for a dollar or two in a pinch, but that wasn't the reason. David had worn them their first evening together. When did she get sentimental? That attitude could get her in trouble. He'd planned to check out this morning. Did he intend to tell her last night, or would he have simply left without saying good-bye? She closed the box and tucked it into the drawer with her fine new underthings and extra gloves.

The leather-covered book was smaller than any Bible she'd seen before. Compact, for him to carry about when he traveled, she supposed. She hadn't thought too much about him being a godly man, but he had quoted something she was fairly certain came from the Bible as they walked toward the river last night — something about the heavens and God's glory. Mostly he seemed to favor Shakespeare and Edmund Burke for his quotations, but in any case, he was quite the scholar. The books in his farm-house had told her that, and she'd expected him to be a little owlish, but he'd turned out to be far more dashing than she'd imagined.

Yes, he would have made a good husband. She'd never have had to worry about where the money for the tax bill would come from or struggle for the perfect word on any occasion. She could have tapped David for either at a moment's notice. She sighed and put the Bible in with the cuff link box.

When she opened her door, she took the precaution of looking down the hall first and waiting until the two men headed for the stairs had gone down. She didn't want to speak to any more people than necessary this morning. As she crossed the landing to the head of the stairs, she glanced up toward the third story. David's empty suite lay up there. Such a pity — she'd really liked him. But it was time to move on. She would have breakfast and then make one last purchase before leaving Scottsburg. With Peterson at large, she'd feel safer carrying a gun. A small lady's weapon, of course. She'd seen one in a shop yesterday and wished she'd bought it then.

She went down the stairs, avoided the desk clerk's gaze, and entered the dining room, knowing every eye was upon her. More than a dozen men were having their breakfast, and all seemed happy to have a pretty woman to look at while they did.

"Good morning, Mrs. Evans," the waiter said pleasantly.

"Won't you join me?" a smooth male voice asked.

Millie whipped around.

Peterson smiled. "I hoped I might see you again this morning. My table is right over here."

CHAPTER 19

"I'm sorry I can't just let you have the horse," Dan told Whitey. "Until we see what happens to Hastings and perhaps determine whether the animal really belongs to him, I think we'd better keep it in Scottsburg."

"Makes no nevermind to me," Whitey said, but his mouth drooped behind the fluffy, white beard. "If you don't mind, I'll tag along when you go into town. Got no hurry to get back up to my cabin."

"We'd be delighted to have your company a bit longer," Anne assured him.

They enjoyed a hearty breakfast at Mrs. Zinberg's house.

"Not every woman knows how to fry an egg to perfection," Whitey said with a big smile for the widow.

"Oh Mr. Pogue, you flatter me."

"No harm in flattering one as deserves it."

Dan glanced over at Anne, who didn't try very hard to hide her smile. Was Mrs. Zinberg actually blushing? Maybe he ought to pay attention — the old man seemed to be a master of flirtation.

"I'll be going to worship service this morning," the widow said. "You folks are welcome to attend."

Startled, Dan realized he'd completely lost track of the days. He turned to Anne. "Would you like to attend church?"

"Very much."

He nodded. "I admit I was planning to check at the post office today, but that will be closed."

"Maybe we could inquire at some of the hotels before church," Anne said. "Mrs. Zinberg, what is the best hotel in Scottsburg?"

"Oh, that would be the Miner's Hotel."

"Hands-down," Whitey agreed.

"And there are several other boarding-houses," Mrs. Zinberg said, "but all the mining company investors and government officials stay at the Miner's Hotel."

"Let's check there first," Anne said. "And if you can tell us where some of those boardinghouses are, we'll try them if my uncle's not at the hotel."

"Mr. Adams, there's a small matter I'd like to speak to you about."

"Yes, ma'am?"

She looked a little embarrassed, and Dan

wondered if she'd heard him and Anne talking in the middle of the night and jumped to conclusions.

"Well, perhaps I shouldn't mention it on the Lord's Day, but after hearing about your misadventures over the last two days, I did wonder if perhaps you wouldn't be in the market for a revolver."

Dan eyed her in surprise. "It wouldn't be a bad idea. I wished I had one when that thief made off with my horse and my rifle."

"Well, I have my husband's revolver, and heaven knows I would never use it. I don't even know how to load it. If you're interested in looking at it. . . ."

Dan glanced at Anne, who was calmly sipping her tea. She didn't seem to have a problem with him buying a handgun, or with him and their hostess doing business on Sunday. "Thank you, ma'am. I'd be happy to look at it."

The transaction was soon completed to both Dan's and Mrs. Zinberg's satisfaction. She allowed that she could use the extra bit of money more than she could a weapon.

Half an hour later, the travelers took their leave. Mrs. Zinberg all but simpered when Whitey bowed over her hand.

"If things don't work out for you in town, Mr. Pogue, you're welcome to return here for luncheon. I'll have plenty."

"Why, ma'am, that's a delightful invitation. I may avail myself of that."

Dan turned away to adjust his saddle's cinch strap. He never would have guessed the old miner had a deep vocabulary and courtly manners up his worn flannel sleeve.

They rode together to Constable Owens's house.

"Good morning, folks. I expected you to come around."

Dan swung down from the saddle and gave Anne a hand.

"How's the prisoner?" he asked.

"Fine when I took him his breakfast. A little chilly, but my wife had sent over two blankets, and he had a coat. He's all right."

"We've decided to see if we can find Mr. Stone," Dan said. "He may be able to help us settle some questions. We'll come back here later and tell you what we learn."

"All righty. Say — have you checked the Miner's Hotel?"

"That's where we're headed," Dan said. He felt like the model of incompetence. He hadn't checked the Miner's Hotel their first day in town, but he should have. Had David Stone been two blocks away, and he'd missed him? But he'd asked the postmaster and been told David hadn't been in for a week. More likely he'd returned to Scottsburg right about the time Dan and Anne left to ride up to his claim.

He gave Anne a boost into Bailey's saddle and then mounted Star. They set out without any more words, but he could almost hear Anne's thoughts — how close had they come to running into her uncle on the street? Dan had led her on a wild goose chase that nearly ended in tragedy for nothing.

The hotel sprang into view — a large, three-storied house with rambling porches and lots of windows. It looked comfortable and more substantial than places miners and dockhands would stay.

In the lobby, a dignified man of about forty stood behind the desk, checking a guest out of the hotel. When the customer left, Dan stepped forward, with Anne and Whitey on his heels.

"Hello. We're here to see Mr. David Stone. This young lady is his niece, and we were told he may be staying here."

"Oh yes, Mr. Stone is a frequent guest," the clerk said. "I'll send someone up to see if he's in his room."

"Thank you," Dan said.

The clerk nodded as he came from behind the desk. "Would you like to sit down while you wait? We're serving breakfast now. If you'd like, you can order coffee in the dining room."

Anne shook her head.

Dan said, "We're fine, thank you. We'll wait out here."

The clerk went through a doorway, and Dan guided Anne to a settee in the shadow of a folding screen. Whitey found a straight chair a short distance away and dragged it over. He plunked down in it opposite them.

"Well, it'll be good to see ol' David again," Whitey said.

Dan smiled at the old codger's designation of a forty-year-old as "ol' David," but Anne's face remained sober. She folded her gloved hands on her lap, but her gaze darted about the lobby. The clerk returned to his post a minute later, and he appeared to be busy with some papers.

"I do hope we find him in," Anne said. Anxiety lined her lovely brow.

Dan reached over and patted her hands. "I hope so, too. You've been through a lot, and this meeting is long overdue."

Five minutes later a boy arrived at the desk, red-faced and panting. He spoke in low tones to the clerk, who glanced their way, picked up something, and left the room with the boy.

Dan had a bad feeling about that, but he didn't say anything to Anne. Instead, he asked Whitey how the prices were on foodstuffs in the area. A grandfather clock in one corner ticked off the minutes, until he wondered if they would be late for church. At last the clerk reappeared, coming down the stairs this time, and walked across the lobby to where they sat.

"I'm sorry, but it seems Mr. Stone is not in his suite."

"Oh." Anne stared at him blankly.

"But he *is* still staying here?" Dan said.

"Oh yes. I'm sure he's only stepped out for a while."

Dan stood and stepped closer to the clerk. "Miss Stone has had an arduous journey to find her uncle. She is his nearest relation, and she's come to break news to him concerning a death in the family. If Mr. Stone has engaged a suite, would it be possible for you to allow her to wait for him there?"

"Oh, I . . ." The clerk eyed him doubtfully then looked over his shoulder. Two men stood near the front desk looking annoyed. "I must go and help those guests check out. But I couldn't let you into the suite without permission from Mr. Reed."

"And who is Mr. Reed?" Dan followed the clerk as he set off across the lobby.

"He's the manager, sir. He should be here soon, and I'll let him know your request."

"Thank you." Dan walked back to where Anne and Whitey waited.

Millie doctored her coffee carefully and avoided meeting Peterson's gaze. Had she actually thought him attractive on their first meeting? He made her skin crawl.

"Now, as I see it, there are only two possibilities," he said in a low, businesslike tone. "Either his body washed downstream and has yet to be found, or he escaped alive, in which case it behooves the two of us to find him."

Millie contained her snort to a dignified *hmph.* If Peterson expected her to stay in Scottsburg, he was suffering delusions. The only thing it behooved her to do was to leave town as quickly as possible. And she could guess why Peterson wanted to find David — to finish off the job he'd botched the first time.

Was it possible that David was still alive? She sincerely hoped he was.

"If he came back to his room last night, he may be upstairs this minute," Peterson said. "Or he might have found a doctor. I'm sure I hit him. We need to inquire as to whether there's a physician in the area."

"Why don't you do that?" she asked in sugary tones. "But if we're going on with this charade, shouldn't I raise an alarm?"

"And have the authorities out looking for his corpse? Hmm, that might actually be to my advantage. I tried half the night to find him on my own, and I couldn't. There must be people hereabouts who know the vagaries of the river. But how will we explain to them that we think he's in it?"

"I don't know, but if David is still alive, I certainly don't want him coming back and finding me placidly eating breakfast with the likes of you." She drained her coffee cup and pushed back her chair.

"Wait," Peterson said. "I need to know what you're going to do — where you'll be."

"I'll leave you a note at the front desk."

"But I'm not staying here."

"You're not?" Millie asked.

"No. I only came in for breakfast and to see you."

"Where —" She stopped. What did it matter? She didn't intend to see him again. She shook her head. "I'll see if I can find out whether he came in last night." And what Peterson didn't know wouldn't hurt him. No way would she tell him she'd picked the lock on David's door last night. She turned and strode quickly toward the lobby. He couldn't jump up and pursue her without causing a scene — one Millie would make sure the hotel staff noticed.

Two steps into the lobby were enough to pull her up short. Five yards straight ahead, the hotel manager was in earnest conversation with Daniel Adams and Anne Stone.

"It's very irregular," Mr. Reed said. "We don't usually go into a guest's room uninvited or allow visitors to do so."

"But he's her uncle," Dan said.

"I'm sorry, but I have to ask: do you have proof of that?"

Dan looked at Anne. He wanted to get tough with the manager, but the request was reasonable. Anyone could waltz in claiming to be a relative of a guest and use it as license to ransack a room.

"I have a picture of him." Anne delved into her handbag and brought out the miniature. "It was painted when he was young — about twenty years old."

She opened the case and handed it to Reed.

"I also have a letter that he wrote to my father some time ago, when he lived in St. Louis."

Reed eyed the portrait and pressed his lips together. "Hmm. This does bear a resemblance to Mr. Stone."

Anne took the miniature back and gazed at it for a moment before closing the case. "You see, Mr. Reed, my father died less than a year ago. David is his younger brother, and he has no idea about my father's death. I went to St. Louis hoping to find him there, but I learned he'd moved to Oregon. Sir, I've been searching for him all this time. Please, if there's anything you can do to help me . . ."

Her vibrant brown eyes, along with her plaintive story and her charming appearance, would persuade any man, Dan thought. Sure enough, Reed seemed to waver. At last he shoved a hand into his pocket.

"All right. It's not real proof, but you look like a respectable woman. I don't mean to cast aspersions on you or to imply that I think you are not what you seem, but one has to be careful. Out here people frequently misrepresent themselves, and it's my duty to protect our guests."

"I understand perfectly," Anne said. "In fact, I appreciate your diligence. I assure you, I would not take unfair advantage of your kindness. I bear my uncle only good-will, and this reunion means a great deal to me."

Reed pulled a large bunch of keys from his pocket. "All right, since the clerk has already checked Mr. Stone's rooms, I suppose we can go up." He shot Dan a glance.

Of course. That was why the clerk had hurried off after the boy had spoken to him. Probably dashed up the back stairs to scout out David's suite. That way, if the guest had passed out drunk, or if he'd died in the hotel room, the visitor wouldn't bear the shock of discovery.

Anne followed Mr. Reed up the stairs, and Dan followed as closely as her trailing skirt allowed. Whitey came last, gawking about at the carved woodwork, gilt-framed paintings, and hanging lanterns. At the first landing, as they walked around to mount the next flight, Reed looked back at Dan. "And this man is with you?"

Anne and Dan both glanced at Whitey.

"Oh yes, sir," Anne said. "He's a friend, both of mine and of Mr. Stone's. A mutual acquaintance who has been of great assistance to me."

Reed arched his eyebrows as though in doubt. "Very well."

They ascended to the third story, and he headed for one of the doorways leading off the corridor. A man carrying a covered tray came down the hall. He was already halfway along it, and he hesitated, then ducked his head as he passed them.

"Ernie," Mr. Reed said in surprise, "what are you doing up here in the middle of our breakfast hours? Shouldn't you be in the kitchen?"

The stocky man flushed slightly and looked down at the tray. "Oh yes, sir, I'm usually right there, but one of the guests was ill and asked for a tray."

"The waiter should have taken it."

"He was overwhelmed with folks in the dining room wanting this and that. It will only take me a moment."

Reed frowned. "We'll discuss this later. Deliver that and get back to your station."

"Yes, sir." Ernie glided down the hallway and exited through a door at the far end.

Mr. Reed knocked on the door to the suite, waited a moment, then put a key to the lock. He swung the door open and entered, looked about, then turned to Anne.

"Come right in, Miss Stone. I'm sure you'll be comfortable here. The clerk has already checked the bedchamber to make sure he hadn't simply overslept, but let me just make sure. . . ." He stepped through the connecting doorway. Dan heard a door open and close — probably the wardrobe.

"Well, he's certainly not here," Reed said

with a frown as he reentered the sitting room. "His things look undisturbed. I'll check with our housekeeper, though."

"Why is that, sir?" Dan asked. "To see if the room has been cleaned already this morning?"

"Well . . . er . . ." Reed cleared his throat. "I noticed that the blankets are not on the bed."

They all stood in silence for a moment.

"What does that mean?" Anne said at last. "Did someone forget to make up the bed?"

Mr. Reed's forehead furrowed. "I'm not certain. I'm sure Mr. Stone *had* blankets. Perhaps he spilled something on them — coffee, or . . . or . . . Well, as I said, I will check with the housekeeper to see if she knows anything about it. If you folks would please make yourselves comfortable, I'll return when I find out anything. And if Mr. Stone comes in, we'll tell him that he has visitors."

"Thank you," Dan said.

By the time Reed was out the door, Anne had gone into the adjoining room. Dan went and stood in the doorway. She walked slowly over to the dresser.

"His razor is here, and a couple of papers." She turned away as though stifling the urge to open the drawers.

"Mr. Reed looked in the wardrobe," Dan said.

Anne strode to the walnut armoire and flung the doors open. Inside hung a wool jacket, a pair of plain twill pants, three shirts, and a droopy felt hat. She reached out and touched the sleeve of the coat.

"It looks as though he certainly planned to come back."

"He's probably down the street getting a newspaper," Dan said.

Whitey had come to the doorway, too, and he spoke up. "Like as not, he's over to the tavern right now and we missed him on the way."

Anne smiled faintly. "I dare say."

Dan said nothing. Anne couldn't know her uncle's habits and vices, and it might be true. The saloons out here might stay open on Sunday, too, as vile as that seemed. From what he'd gathered in the past weeks, Westerners didn't observe the Sabbath as strictly as most folks did back East — especially in mining towns.

Anne continued to scan the room and stepped to the washstand. "Daniel."

"What is it?"

"Could you come look at this please?"

He stepped over beside her. "What?"

"There are no towels. You know Mr. Reed

commented on the bedding."

"Hmm. Maybe the housekeeper took away all the dirty linens but didn't bring the clean ones yet."

"Then why did she not take the sheets? That is very odd, taking the blankets but not the sheets."

Dan looked over at the bed. She was right about that.

"And Daniel . . ."

"Yes?"

"Please look closer at the rim of this wash-bowl."

Something in her tone put him on the alert. He stooped and peered at the edge of the large, white porcelain bowl. A small red-dish smear on the rim set his pulse racing.

"Do you think . . . ?"

Anne grasped his arm. "Yes, I do think. Look there." She pointed down at the floor and stepped back, holding her skirt against her legs.

Dan bent down and stared at the dark spot not much bigger than a half dime. Cautiously, he reached out and touched it with the tip of his pinky. He rose and walked to the window and examined his finger.

"I'm not sure, Anne. It appears to be dry, whatever it is."

She took out a handkerchief and picked

up the water pitcher. "There's no water in here."

"Could be he washed and shaved before he went out this mornin'," Whitey said.

Anne ignored him. "There are a few drops in the bottom." She wiped the interior of the pitcher with her handkerchief, set down the pitcher, and knelt beside the stand. She dabbed at the spot and looked at her handkerchief. "I don't want to take it all."

She rose and walked over to Dan and held it up to the light. "There. I'll eat my two best hats if that's not blood."

CHAPTER 20

David startled awake when a key turned in the lock. He aimed the pistol at the door, but when the knob turned, it didn't open. A soft tap followed.

"It's me."

The bolt was still in place. David sat up and shook off the cobwebs.

"Hold on."

When he stood, his head reeled. He lunged for the door and stood leaning against it, panting, until the swirling blackness receded.

"Ernie?" he croaked.

"Yeah. Lemme in. Quick."

David fumbled with the bolt and opened the door. The cook squeezed in with his arms full of dishes and shut it.

"Man, you look awful."

"Thanks." David hobbled back to the bed and sat down.

"I can't stay. If the boss sees me up here

again —"

"He saw you this morning?"

"Yeah. And get this — he was taking some people into your suite."

David's stomach dropped. "Really? Why?"

"Not sure. I heard someone was looking for you."

"Because I was shot at?"

"I dunno, but I saw a really pretty girl and two men. One was an old coot with a white beard, and the other guy was younger. Tall, decent looking. He'd shaved this morning, if that counts."

David rubbed his own stubbly chin. "Not sure if it does or not. Can you get my razor?"

"Not now. Those people are in there waiting for you."

"What on earth?"

Ernie shrugged. "I'll see if I can find out anything, but the boss will get mad if he sees me outside the kitchen again, and we start serving dinner soon. I brought you some more water and a sandwich and some cake. If there's any fried chicken left from dinner, I'll bring you some of that later."

"Thanks, Ernie. I forgot to ask you this morning about Captain."

"He's fine. He gets along great with my old nag. But listen, you've got to keep quiet, you hear me?"

"Absolutely."

"Good. 'Cause if Reed finds out someone's in here . . . Well, I wouldn't want to be around when he found out."

"The woman who was with Mr. Reed, it wasn't Mrs. Evans, was it?"

"Who?"

"The woman I had dinner with last night. She's a guest here — reddish hair, tall and regal looking."

"Hmm, no, I'd say not. I didn't want to look too close, on account of Mr. Reed being with them. She had dark hair and a fancy hat. Very handsome young woman. In her early twenties, I'd think. Fresh, young face."

"Well, that's not Mrs. Evans. She's a bit more mature. I wonder who it could be."

"Like I say, I'll see if I can find out more without stirring up suspicion. Maybe Elwood or Ronald on the front desk can tell me something. Now, I'd better vamoose. It's Sunday, and we serve a big dinner."

David managed to get to the door with him and throw the bolt as soon as Ernie left. He lay down again and stared up at the ceiling, wondering about the mysterious trio down the hall in his suite.

"You go on up to his room and knock on

the door," Peterson said. "Make sure some other people see you going up there. Then you need to talk to the manager. Tell him Stone promised to meet you at eight last night and he never showed up."

"Some of the hotel people saw us leave together around seven."

"All right, tell them that when you returned he had to go out on an errand but he promised to meet you again downstairs in an hour. He didn't show, and after a while you gave up and turned in. But then he didn't come down to breakfast this morning either. You're concerned, and he's not answering your knock."

"What good will that do?"

"Oh, come now, you can be persuasive. Insist that they open the door. Prove to the manager that Stone isn't there and most likely didn't come in last night."

Millie cast another glance toward the lobby. What would she do if Anne Stone and her friends came into the dining room? She supposed she could try to keep her face turned away and then sneak out after they were seated. Maybe she could hide her face with her fan.

"All right?" Peterson asked.

"I'm sorry, what did you say?"

"Insist that the hotel staff call the authorities in to look for Stone. Convince them that something awful has happened to him."

"And what if someone mentions you? A score of people have seen us together this morning."

"Tell them I'm an old friend who just got into town, and you wanted David to meet me. I'm staying at a boardinghouse down the street, if that helps. Go on, now. I'll inquire about a doctor."

"All right." Millie stood and grasped her purse and gloves. She dreaded going out to the lobby again, but there seemed no other choice. She walked slowly toward the doorway. A glance over her shoulder told her Peterson was paying the bill and would be right behind her. She peered out into the lobby.

She saw no sign of Anne and Adams. Her knees almost buckled, her relief was so strong. Now if she could just get her luggage and slip out without Peterson seeing her, he would think she'd gone up to David's suite. She might have ten or fifteen minutes before he came looking for her.

Too late. He'd turned around and was striding toward her. Millie scooted toward the staircase. At the first landing, she paused, hoping Peterson had gone outside so she could end this charade and go straight to her room to pack.

He was leaning against the newel post, looking up at her. He touched a finger to his temple in a mock salute. Millie lifted her skirt a couple of inches and started up the next flight of stairs. That man was driving her insane. She had to get away from him — away from Scottsburg. If David was dead, Peterson could implicate her. And if the Englishman was alive, she doubted he'd want anything to do with Charlotte Evans now.

Three steps from the top, she pulled up short. People had come to the head of the stairs, intending to come down. She started to flatten her full skirt and then caught her breath.

"Aren't you . . . Millie?" Dan Adams asked, staring down at her.

Anne Stone's mouth opened, and her eyes went round. "Yes, she is, and unless I'm mistaken — Daniel, I believe that dress belongs to me."

Millie glanced down at her full skirt of fine polished cotton. Though she'd purchased two new dresses, she'd chosen to wear this one today. It remained the finest dress she'd ever owned, and she felt beautiful and confident when she wore it. Except when standing face-to-face with its rightful owner.

She whirled precariously on the stairs, held up her skirts, and barreled down to the landing. Without a glance to see if they followed, she ran around to the next stairway, dodged a drummer coming up with his sample case in hand, and ran down to the lobby.

She half expected to find Peterson waiting at the bottom, but he was nowhere to be seen. She flew past the astonished desk clerk and out the door. Gasping for breath, she ran along the porch of the hotel and down the steps at the side. Around the corner of the building, she dashed toward the stable. A plague on corsets!

She stumbled into the barn and looked around in the dim light. No stable hand was there to get her horse. With a sinking feeling in her stomach, she remembered telling the clerk yesterday that they could turn Vixen out into their pasture. She didn't have time for this.

She looked back at the hotel. No one had come after her yet. She ran as fast as the constrictive undergarments would allow. In front of the establishment, several horses were tied to the hitching rail. One tall, speckled gelding with a coal black mane and tail caught her eye. He looked almost blue from a distance. She hurried over to him. Sure enough, that was Sam's saddle. Well, if her brother had come here looking for her, he'd get a surprise. She untied the roan's reins, sucked in as much air as her lungs could grab, and stretched her foot up to the stirrup.

She stood with one foot high off the ground, gasping and trying to summon strength to pull herself into the saddle. Behind her the front door of the hotel opened and banged against the wall. She didn't look back, but leaped upward and swung her right leg over the saddle without regard for modesty.

"Go, Blue!" She wheeled him and galloped off down the road.

CHAPTER 21

David leaned most of his weight on the sash of the tiny window in his room. He could see down to the street in front of the hotel. The sun was out, and he wished he could let some air into the stuffy little room. He shoved upward on the bottom sash with his left arm. The effort sent pain screeching through his shoulders and into his injured right arm. He ground his teeth and made one final push. The sash shot upward, and glorious air flowed in.

He hung on the narrow windowsill, gulping in the good mountain air. Now that he'd had time to rest, he had second thoughts about bringing in the authorities. He'd wanted to stay dead, so far as the shooter was concerned. But wouldn't he be safer with the U.S. Marshal on his side? A deputy marshal lived in Eugene. He doubted there was one this far from civilization, but there ought to be at least a constable in Scottsburg.

A wagon and team drove past the hotel, and he pulled back a little. No sense in letting the world see him hanging out the third-story window. Below and to his right, several horses were tied to the hotel's hitching rail. The one on the end was a tall, leggy roan that reminded him of the one he'd left at the ranch for Sam Hastings to use.

He heard the front door open, but the porch roof obscured his view, and he couldn't see who came out. Footsteps pounded on the porch and receded. Must have gone around to the side.

Two men came out of the hotel and ambled down the street toward the center of town. David stayed at the window, ignoring his headache and the searing pain in his arm. The breeze caressed his face. He'd deemed it prudent to leave his shaving equipment in the suite, but maybe Ernie could pick up another razor for him.

No. He was going to come out of hiding. As he straightened, a woman ran full tilt around the corner, from the stable area. She paused for a moment then hurtled straight toward the hitching rail. A moment later, she'd untied the blue roan's reins and vaulted into the saddle in a whirlwind of skirts and petticoats. Spunky gal. She tore off down the street, clinging to the horse like a burdock, her auburn hair glinting in the sun.

He caught his breath.

Charlotte.

What was she doing? That couldn't possibly be her horse. A lady like Charlotte would have had a sidesaddle. In fact, he'd seen her horse in the pasture yesterday. It was a none-too-fine brown mare.

Below him an old man with white hair and a beard long enough to drag in his soup hobbled down the steps and yelled, "Hey! Come back here, you!"

David stared down the street where Charlotte's escape was now just an echo of hoofbeats. The old man turned and lunged back toward the front steps.

David staggered away from the window. He couldn't take any more of this lurking in a corner and not knowing what was happening. Charlotte stealing a horse? If she'd lure a man to his death, he supposed she wouldn't be beneath snatching a horse. And what about those people in his suite? Who were they? More assassins?

He grabbed his shirt and eased it on over his bandaged arm. The doctor had said he'd come back today, but David couldn't wait any longer. He was getting out of this box of a room and reclaiming his life.

"That is most definitely blood," Anne insisted. "We found it on the floor in my uncle's bedchamber, and there was a trace of it on the washbasin as well."

Mr. Reed, who had been summoned from somewhere deeper in the building, shrugged. "So he cut himself shaving this morning. I fail to see —"

"We both know he wasn't in his room this morning," Anne said.

"Yesterday then."

Anne stamped her foot. She was tired of gentility and courtesy. The desk clerk was worse than no help, and now that he'd found the manager, she was still being put off. "Why can't you be reasonable?" She turned to Dan. "Daniel, please get the constable. I've had enough of this nonsense. We're going to find out what's going on here, one way or another."

"Oh, I'm sure there's no need for the constable," Reed said quickly.

"What else would you recommend doing?" Dan asked. "It seems likely that Mr. Stone was injured. If he never came in last night. . . ."

"But Mr. Stone is an unpredictable man.

He'll come here for a day or two and then go off to his mining claim. When he comes back, we open the suite for him again. Next thing you know, he'll be off to Eugene or who knows where."

Reed glanced toward the desk clerk, as if for confirmation. The young man, who leaned on the counter chewing a wad of spruce gum, nodded emphatically.

"But you saw him last night," Anne said.

"Well, yes," Reed replied. "He had supper in our dining room with Mrs. Evans."

"Mrs. Evans?" Anne asked. "Who is she?"

"Room 202."

"You mean she's a guest in this hotel?" Dan asked.

"That's right, sir. She's been here three or four days. Proper lady, I assure you."

"And she's acquainted with my uncle?" Anne frowned at him. This was the first she had heard of a woman connected to David.

"I wouldn't know if they were acquainted earlier, ma'am, but they've dined together the last several nights."

"I . . . see." Anne glanced at Dan, unsure how to proceed.

Dan cleared his throat. "She's not the same woman who ran out of here a moment ago, is she?"

"I couldn't say, sir," Reed said. "We've

had some supplies delivered, and I was out in the kitchen."

"It was her," the desk clerk said laconically.

"I knew we should have stopped her," Anne said. "How could she have come by that dress? I'd hate to think she and Hastings robbed the Whistlers when they left Eugene."

"Oh really," Dan said. "Do you think they'd go so far? I mean . . . dresses look alike."

"That one was custom-made in Paris last winter, and I haven't seen the same material since we crossed the Atlantic. I'm saying it was my dress, Daniel. Not that it *looked* like my dress, or that I think it *may* be my dress. That was my dress — one I left in my trunk on Rob Whistler's wagon in Eugene. And now that Millie person has it."

Dan held up both hands. "All right, I'm convinced. I'll go for the constable."

Anne felt some mollification but also some shame at behaving so forcefully in public. Her intention was to learn the truth, not to humiliate Dan.

"I'll get him for you," Whitey said. He'd hung back during their conversation, but now he stepped forward. "It looks like it may be a while before you find ol' David, and I expect I ought to get back up to my cabin. But I can swing by the constable's and let him know you need him over here."

"Thank you," Dan said. "That would be very helpful."

"Yes, Whitey. Thank you very much." Anne held out her hand and squeezed the old man's fingers gently. "We so much appreciate your help and hospitality."

The old man nodded and ambled toward the door. Just as he reached the threshold, it occurred to Anne that they hadn't decided what to do about Sam Hastings's horse. They couldn't let Whitey ride off with it. Maybe he was shrewder than she'd realized — offering to fetch the constable and then head home while she and Dan were too distracted to think about the dubious ownership of the horse.

"Dan, do you think —"

Whitey's piercing yell cut her off.

"Hey! Come back here, you!" He shot back inside and scrambled toward them. "Somebody done stole my horse!"

As David reached for his jacket, a soft tapping came on the door. His heart accelerated. He stepped over to the door and waited, listening.

"It's me." Another tap.

He threw back the bolt and opened the door. Ernie ducked inside and closed it.

"Those people — they found blood on the floor in your room. I must have missed a spot when I cleaned up."

"Oh great." David grimaced. Now what?

"They're talking to the manager, insisting he call the constable in."

"Well, I was thinking I'd get out of this room anyway. The question is, should I sneak away or should I reveal everything and trust the constable to protect me? I'm not too confident right now, knowing the man who tried to kill me is still out there."

"I don't know." Ernie looked down at the pitcher of water in his hands, as if suddenly realizing what he carried. "Oh, I brought this as an excuse. And I have to get right down there. The dining room is open. But that woman keeps claiming you're her uncle, and —"

"What woman?"

"The one who was in your suite. She insists she's got to find you, and if Mr. Reed won't do something, she will." Ernie walked across the room and exchanged the pitcher of water for the half-empty one on the washstand.

"She said she's my niece?"

"That's what I said." Ernie turned and

scowled at him.

"Did she give a name?"

"I don't know. I only heard a tiny bit myself, and the rest I got from a waiter. It's chaos down there right now, which is why I figured I could dash up the back stairs and warn you. They're making a to-do about the blood, and now some guy is claiming his horse was stolen."

"I think I may have witnessed that," David said.

"Really? So what do you want to do?"

"I think it's time I met this woman who claims to be my niece."

Ernie grimaced. "I'd love to see that, but if Reed sees me outside the kitchen . . ."

"Can you send someone to help me get downstairs?"

"How about I just help you back to your suite? Then when they come up to look at the blood spot . . ."

David clapped him on the shoulder. "You're a genius."

Ernie helped him into his jacket, and David pocketed his wallet and pistol. "All right. Let's go."

He hobbled down the hallway, leaning just a bit on Ernie. When they got to the suite, the door was ajar. Ernie peeked inside.

"Guess they left it open."

"All right," David said. "Go on down the back stairs. I'll be fine."

"You sure?"

He nodded. "No one's going to shoot me in front of Mr. Reed."

Ernie gritted his teeth. "I guess not. Let me know how it turns out, will you?"

"I sure will."

Ernie disappeared down the hall, and David walked slowly to the settee. He lowered himself to the cushions then took out his pistol and laid it on the seat beside him.

Before long he heard voices and footsteps approaching.

"I assure you, if he were injured seriously, Mr. Stone would have notified us," the manager said in his most pompous voice. "The fact that he is not in his rooms should tell you —"

Reed came through the doorway and stopped short, staring at David.

"Mr. Stone."

"Hello, Mr. Reed. What's all the fuss about?" David didn't feel like rising, but he could hardly remain seated when a woman entered the room just behind the hotel manager. He pushed upward with his legs and left arm, striving to control his facial expression and not give away his pain.

Reed approached with his hand extended.

"Oh Mr. Stone, you've no idea how happy I am to see you. How happy we *all* are."

"Uncle David?"

He looked at her then and stood still. She was the perfect image of her mother, Elizabeth. Her dark hair was pulled back in sweeping waves under a stylish hat, and her sweet, heart-shaped face took him back years, to Stoneford, leaving him no doubt that she was indeed his niece.

"Anne? How can this be?" He took a faltering step, and she met him in the center of the carpet and grasped his hands.

David ignored the pain and gazed down into her eager face. Could this be the dark-haired little sweetheart he'd bounced on his knee a score of years ago? The achy longing for England and Stoneford that he thought had faded to nostalgia reared up and called to him.

"Uncle David, I've looked so hard for you!" She burst into tears, and he did the only thing an uncle could do. He drew her into his arms, clenching his teeth against the fiery pain it caused him.

"Anne, my dear, I can't imagine how you ever found me. But —"

He looked beyond her and Mr. Reed, hoping to see his elder brother accompanying her. What he wouldn't give for a chat with

Richard right now. His brother would know exactly what to do when one was pursued by an assassin and the woman one felt an attraction for turned out to be a blackguard.

Instead of his steady, practical brother, a grave young man hovered, watching Anne with obvious concern, but holding back to permit her a measure of privacy in the reunion. An older man, one with white hair and a long beard, stood in the doorway scowling, his face ruddy against the cottony beard. Whitey Pogue. What was the crusty old miner doing here with Anne?

"You must sit down and introduce me to your friend," David said. "Mr. Pogue and I are acquainted already." As an afterthought, he turned to the manager. "Mr. Reed, could we please have a tea tray and some refreshments sent up?"

"Of course, sir. I must say I'm delighted to find you looking so well. We were all worried when you didn't appear this morning. I hope you'll forgive me for opening your room to your niece."

"I'd expect you to do no less."

"Thank you. I'll go down to the kitchen and speak for a tray now."

Reed bustled from the room, dislodging Father Time from the doorway to do so.

Anne, meanwhile, had excavated a handkerchief from her reticule and was wiping her eyes.

"Sit down, dear," David said tenderly. "Tell me what has brought you here and how the family is doing."

"Oh Uncle David!" Her tears spurted out again, but she sat and arranged the skirts of her blue velvet riding habit. It looked as though the outfit had seen a great deal of the countryside lately, what with a film of dust over it and dried mud spatters along the hem. Even so, she looked more charming than any of the women he'd seen lately on the frontier — with the possible exception of Charlotte Evans, about whom he would reserve his opinion until he'd had more time to consider her precipitous flight on the stolen horse.

That thought brought him full circle to the white-bearded man, and David gazed at him. "I say, Whitey, was that your horse that was taken from the rail out front not ten minutes ago?"

Pogue's face went redder, and he blustered, "It most certainly was. That hussy jumped on him and took off without so much as a fare-thee-well. Took my saddle and all the stuff on it, too."

"And one of my dresses from Angelique in Paris, unless I'm mistaken," Anne said, "though I can't for the life of me understand how she got hold of it."

"How bizarre," David said.

Whitey turned his hat around in his hands, watching Anne for a cue. "I was about to go fetch the constable for Miss Anne anyhow, because she thought you'd been kilt or somethin'."

"Oh? I'm sorry I caused you such distress," David said. "As you can see, I'm alive and well. Mostly well, that is. Won't you gentlemen be seated, please?"

"How rude of me." Anne jumped up again. "Uncle David, it gives me great pleasure to introduce Daniel Adams. Dan has been a good friend and a pillar of strength to me since Independence, Missouri."

"Indeed." David eyed Adams openly. Anne was obviously indebted to the fellow. Was she in love with him? And did Richard know about him? This bore looking into.

Adams took a seat in an armchair and shuffled his long legs until he at last appeared to be comfortable. Whitey hesitated, sticking close to the door.

"That horse, Miss Anne. Shall I get the constable anyway, even though Mr. Stone ain't done in?"

"Oh, I . . ." Anne looked doubtfully

toward Adams. "What do you think, Dan?"

"It wasn't our horse, Whitey," Dan said softly, as one would tell a child not to take the biggest biscuit. "Perhaps we should tell Constable Owens, but the man who owns the horse is the one he's got locked in the icehouse."

"Yes, that horse belongs to Mr. Hastings, like it or not," Anne said.

"Hastings?" David frowned at her. "Not Sam Hastings from my farm in Eugene?"

"The same, sir," Adams said. "He followed us here and tried to keep us from finding you."

David felt rather stupid as he stared at them. "But . . . whatever for?"

Anne looked uncertainly at Adams, then back to David. "We're not really sure, except that he tried to impersonate you when we arrived at your farm, and we think he was afraid you'd be angry when you found out."

"What?" David's jaw dropped, and he made himself close it. "I don't understand. Sam? Impersonating me?"

"It's quite a tale, sir," Adams said.

"Shall we send Whitey for the constable while you tell it?"

"That may be best," Anne said.

"I'll get right over there." Whitey turned

to leave but whirled back for a moment. "Glad you ain't dead, David." He slipped out the doorway.

David put a hand to his forehead and laughed. "How did you link up with that old fellow? He's quite the character, you know."

"We gathered that," Anne said. "But he took us in when I was near freezing to death."

Adams shifted in his chair. "Yes. I truly believe Anne might not have survived the night in the mountains if we hadn't found Pogue's cabin. He was generous to a fault with his limited resources."

"That sounds like Whitey." David gazed down at his niece. "Now, suppose you begin at the beginning. What induced you to leave England?"

Anne's bittersweet smile told him her news would not all be pleasant. He reached for her hand.

"It's all right, my dear. Why don't you give me the worst of it right now? We'll fill in the gaps from there. Your parents — I hope they are well."

Her eyes shimmered as she raised her chin in resolution. "I'm afraid not. Mother's been gone three years now, and Father . . ." She drew in a ragged breath. "Father died about a year ago. I've been hoping to find you ever since."

"Oh, poor Anne. I'm so sorry to hear this." David felt the burning of tears in his eyes. How horrible for the girl to have lost both parents in quick succession. His own affection for Richard ran deep, and he'd been fond of Elizabeth as well, but he had all but cut the ties with his family these last twenty years. For Anne, however, the loss was incalculable.

"We sent letters." She swiped at a tear with her handkerchief. "Mr. Conrad, the solicitor, was quite diligent about it, but we couldn't learn where you'd gone when you left St. Louis. So I set out in March with Elise — do you remember Elise Finster?"

"Why, yes, I believe I do. She was employed at Stoneford, was she not? A pretty German girl."

"Yes indeed." Anne's smile broadened. "She'll be so pleased to hear you remember her. Anyway, she came with me. We found you'd gone to Independence."

"So you followed me there?"

"Yes. Again we were disappointed."

"My dear, dear girl. I'm so sorry I neglected to write and tell Richard where I'd gone. That was remiss of me. It was unconscionable."

"Well, we got a hint that you'd removed to Oregon, so we joined a wagon train."

He laughed involuntarily. "You and Elise?"

"Yes. It was arduous — and very educational."

"Quite." He chuckled again. "I can't quite take all this in. You and Miss Finster, driving an ox team?"

"We used mules. It was on the wagon train that we met Daniel and his brother."

David again surveyed Adams.

"Daniel and Hector were very helpful to us and became good friends," Anne said. "They took up farming near Champoeg."

Adams nodded gravely.

Anne continued, a little breathless, "And then Elise got married, and Daniel offered to accompany me to your farm."

"Elise married . . . who? Your brother?" David turned a questioning gaze on Adams.

"Oh no, sir, she married the wagon train scout, Eb Bentley," Adams said.

"Yes, and you'll like him, I'm sure," Anne said. "I do hope you'll be able to go to Eb's ranch in Corvallis with me and see Elise."

"Well, I . . . of course I'd like to see her. But today's events prompt me to think I should return to Eugene quickly and see what's going on at my property there. I've obviously stayed in the hills too long."

"Oh, the deputy marshal asked your neighbors to take care of your cattle," Anne said quickly. "That was after he arrested Sam Hastings for fraud. But he had to let him go. . . ." She shook her head. "I'm telling things all out of order. I'm sorry. But the thing that's most important, Uncle David, is the thing I most urgently need to tell you. The whole purpose for my journey, in fact."

"I . . . don't understand." What could be more important than telling him of Richard's death? And what urgent purpose would retain its urgency for a year?

"It's . . ." She inhaled deeply and reached for his hand. "It's Uncle John, I'm afraid."

"John? What —"

It hit him suddenly, like an arrow out of nowhere. The thing he'd always considered so unlikely as to be impossible had happened.

"John is dead," he said.

The confirmation stared at him from her liquid brown eyes.

"Yes, dear uncle. In the Crimea, a year ago last summer. I'm afraid this means you are now earl of Stoneford."

CHAPTER 22

David rose and shoved his hands into the pockets of his trousers. He walked to the window overlooking the street and stood gazing out for a long moment.

Anne looked uneasily at Dan. The slight twitch of his lips was less than a smile, but still an offer of sympathy. They waited together, united in their knowledge. The pain and confusion that faced David now would bring some men to their knees.

The silence was broken by the desk clerk, who stood in the open doorway, bearing a laden tray. He puffed a bit, and his face gleamed red, with beads of sweat standing on his brow.

"Coffee and refreshments."

Dan jumped up and strode toward him. "Thank you. Let me take that."

The clerk passed the heavy tray to him with a sigh and closed his eyes for a second. "Thank you, sir. Oh, and I am to tell Mr.

Stone that his horse is not in the stable."

David swiveled from the window, his eyebrows arched. "I beg your pardon."

"Your horse, sir. The stable man says it was missing this morning. He thought you'd gone out and taken him yourself, but apparently not. Did you? I mean, perhaps you left him somewhere."

David smiled. "Yes, that's exactly what happened. Thank you — you may pass the word that my horse is accounted for."

The clerk nodded but didn't move. David walked across the room and placed a coin in his hand.

"Thank you, sir." The clerk left then, and David closed the door.

"Anne, my dear, would you pour the — Oh, bother, he said coffee, not tea. Do you mind?"

"I can stand it." She leaned forward and arranged the four cups. "I suppose Whitey will be back."

"And perhaps the constable with him," Dan said. "Shall I send for another cup?"

"Oh, let's wait and see what develops. He may have gone back to Mrs. Zinberg's for dinner. Uncle David? Milk and sugar?"

"I've gotten used to drinking it black since I'm so often in places where the accompaniments aren't available. Thank you." He took the cup and saucer she offered and sat down next to her.

"Daniel." Anne poured milk into his cup as she spoke then held it out to him.

Dan smiled. "Thank you."

Anne felt her face flush as she met his gaze. The simple fact that she knew how he liked his coffee and fixed it that way for him spoke volumes about their closeness. What must Uncle David think of them? She must make it clear very soon that she and Daniel had no romantic attachment.

"Care for a biscuit?" Dan didn't comment when she used the English word for cookies. When both men had chosen one from the plate, she set it down. Settling back on the settee with her cup, she eyed her uncle gravely.

"Now, what would you like to know first?"

"The peerage — the estate. If I decide not to claim it, what happens?"

"If you made a legal declaration to that effect, it would pass to Randolph."

"That fop?"

Anne cleared her throat, trying to keep a burst of laughter from escaping. "Uh, yes, that is what I'm told."

Uncle David shook his head. "I always thought you'd have brothers. And if not, why John . . ." His troubled blue eyes met her gaze. "I guess John has no heirs, or you wouldn't be here."

She smiled. "As much as I enjoy being in your company, I confess I should probably never have set out on this trip if the family had an heir safe at home. To my loss, I might add. Uncle, we live in a very small world at Stoneford."

"Yes. I found that out myself when I crossed the Atlantic. We make assumptions . . . however, to the point. Why should I go back?"

"But . . ." She'd never considered that he might not want to or that he would not consider it his duty to assume the earldom. "Do you love your life here so passionately?"

The bleak prospect of returning alone to England stretched before her. How could she go home without him? What life would she have there now? She couldn't imagine Merrileigh welcoming her at Stoneford, or that she would want to live under Randolph's protection. Even the cozy existence she'd imagined with Elise was no longer possible.

A sharp rap drew all their eyes to the door. Dan stood and walked to it.

"Who is it?"

"Constable Owens."

Dan opened the door and shook the man's

hand. "Good to see you again, sir. Thank you for coming."

"Mr. Adams. I understand you and Miss Stone have another matter to discuss with me?"

"Yes, we do." Dan led him over to the settee.

David rose with some effort. Anne wondered at the grimace on his face. Was her uncle in pain? Perhaps that bloodstain was due to more than a shaving cut after all.

"This is Miss Stone's uncle, David Stone," Dan said.

"Oh sure, I've heard about you." Owens reached out to shake David's hand.

"No disrespect, sir," David said, "but I'm not shaking hands just now. I've got a bum shoulder."

"Oh. Sorry." Owens looked down at Anne. "Good day, Miss Stone."

"How do you do," she murmured.

The men sat down, and Owens said, "Now, what's this about a stolen horse? Whitey Pogue claimed some woman rode off with the roan he rode in on yesterday."

"Yes, that's true," David said. "I saw her jump on it from my window."

"But it didn't belong to Whitey," Dan added. "The man we brought to you — Hastings — had it."

"However," David said, "the horse actually belongs to me. I left it for Hastings to use when I left my farm in Eugene. Apparently he followed my niece over here in hopes of keeping her from finding me."

"Indeed?" Owens gazed at Anne with renewed interest.

"That appears to be true." Anne leaned toward Owens and spoke earnestly. "We told you yesterday how he'd stolen our horses in the hills and left us out there to wander in the cold and rain."

"Yes. You found Pogue's cabin and spent the night there."

Anne nodded. "Now it appears that Hastings wasn't acting alone. When we met him at Uncle David's farm, a woman was in residence with him."

"What?" David's eyebrows shot up. "I assure you, that was not the case when I left Eugene."

Anne reached over and patted his hand. "I'm sorry, Uncle. We haven't had time to tell you the full story yet. When we reached the farm, Sam Hastings pretended to be you, and this Millie woman served us dinner. I thought she was his wife at first, but now I have my doubts." She felt her cheeks color, but there was no varnishing the truth. "And when we arrived here this morning looking for you, here was this Millie coming up the stairs wearing one of my dresses that I had left in Eugene with friends. Somehow she's gotten hold of my luggage, I'm afraid."

"Yes," Dan added, "and she ran out of the hotel and jumped on Sam Hastings's horse and rode off."

David clapped a hand to his forehead. "Charlotte."

"Charlotte?" Anne asked.

"She told me her name was Charlotte Evans. I'm afraid I've been duped."

"Would you care to tell us about it, sir?" Owens asked.

"It's embarrassing to admit it, but I believe she set out to charm me. We dined together several evenings here at the hotel." His face hardened. "But there's more to it. It's not simply a couple of petty thieves hoping to lift my wallet or even take over my property. Charlotte wanted to walk last night, and we went down to the river. We stood on the steamer dock for a minute or two, and I was shot at."

"Shot at? Oh Uncle David, that's horrible. Who would do that?"

"Not Sam Hastings," Dan said. "He was locked up in the icehouse."

Owens nodded. "I can testify to that."

David stood and with difficulty began to

remove his jacket. "I almost sought you out last night, constable, but I decided to lie low and let the gunman think he'd succeeded."

Anne leaped up and helped him ease the sleeves of his jacket off. She gasped and stared at David's right arm. Beneath his shirt a bulk of extra fabric bulged, and a reddish brown stain had seeped into the white cloth of his shirt.

Dan jumped to his feet. "How bad is your wound, sir?"

"Not so bad I can't travel." David folded his jacket over the arm of the settee and resumed his seat. "One of the hotel staff brought a physician in last night to see to it, and I moved to another room so that I wouldn't be easily found if the assassin came here. That's why I wasn't here when you arrived this morning. My shoulder hurts, but I think I'll survive."

"The hotel staff?" Anne's eyes flashed in anger. "You mean they *knew* you were here all along and lied to us?"

"Only one," David said. "Don't blame Mr. Reed. We were very careful that he should not find out. You see, the man who tried to kill me is still out there, and I thought the fewer who knew my whereabouts the better."

"Probably true," Owens said, "but if I'd known, I could have gone looking for him. Do you know the man who shot you?"

David shook his head. "It was dark, and I saw him from a distance. But he was thin and agile. I think perhaps he was the same fellow I noticed loitering earlier. I wondered about him at the time — regular skeezicks of a fellow. I can't be sure he's the one who pulled the trigger, but if it was, he had dark hair and a mustache. Tall."

"A mustache?" Anne cried. She whipped around to look at Dan, and he nodded.

"That sounds like Peterson. Mr. Stone, I'm afraid there's more to this tale than you've heard yet." Her uncle eyed him levelly, and Dan felt suddenly that he was looking at a man of rare intelligence. David Stone might have chosen a simple life, but he was capable of running empires. Another small notion nagged him — should he address Stone as "my lord"? Dan shook off the thought. Here in America, people didn't bow to lords.

"All right, suppose we enjoy our coffee and you tell me about this Peterson." David chose a cookie from the serving plate.

"Mr. Owens, won't you join us?" Anne

asked. We have an extra cup."

"Thank you, ma'am." Owens took a seat and accepted the coffee from her.

Dan sat down again. "I'll let Anne tell it, as she's privy to more details than I am."

"All right," she said. "Elise and I hired a man in Independence to drive our wagon for us. His name was Costigan. Later we found he'd pilfered your last letter to Father. I was carrying it with me on the wagon train. Costigan was also lazy. We fired him, and the wagon master ran him off the train. We puzzled over what his interest was in you. When we reached Oregon City, we found out. This other man, Peterson, had hired him to stop me from finding you. Peterson took a ship and arrived in Oregon about the time we did. He was asking about in Oregon City for you when we encountered him."

David sat in silence for a minute. He sipped his coffee and set the cup down. "Is this Peterson British?"

"No," Anne said, "but well you may ask. I have no proof, but I believe someone in England hired him to prevent you from claiming the peerage. Costigan was just a minion that Peterson hired. Peterson is the main one to be wary of — and even he is not the man behind the plot."

"So who is?" David asked.

Anne winced. "I don't know, but I have suspicions."

"My cousin Randolph?"

She let out a long sigh. "Who else would benefit from your death?"

David smiled grimly. "After I was shot last night, I heard the gunman say to Charlotte — that is, Millie, if what you've told me is correct — that he needed to find my body. I'd pitched into the river, you see."

"Oh Uncle David! How awful."

David squeezed her hand. "There, now. I'm sitting here with you, aren't I? The thing is, he told the woman he needed a death certificate and that I wasn't any good dead without it."

"So you're the fellow," Owens said with a mirthless laugh. "I got hauled out of bed about midnight by George Kidder. He's got a saloon down near the river. Said a fellow came in there yelling how a man had fallen into the river and they needed to find him and haul him out. George's place emptied out, and they had boats out, up and down the waterfront looking for this chap who'd gone in the drink. By the time I got there, folks were giving up and going back to their beer. I tried to locate the man who'd given the alarm at the start of it, and no one could point him out to me. I figured it was a mistake, or a cockeyed joke pulled by some inebriated lout. Either that or it was too late and the body would wash up downstream."

"How terrible," Anne said. "I'm glad you made it ashore, Uncle David."

"So am I, and that I eluded the man who started the whole thing." He shook his head. "I suppose it was that Peterson you mentioned. My question right now is whether or not Charlotte was in on it. She seemed shocked when he fired at me, but was she putting that on?"

"She's very good at dissembling," Anne said. "Daniel and I thought she might be the brains behind the impersonation after we'd met her and Sam Hastings. He didn't seem smart enough to think of it, much less carry it off."

David burst out laughing, and they all watched him, a bit uneasy. After a moment he sat back with a sigh. "Forgive me, but the thought of Sam actually claiming to be me — it's preposterous."

"I doubt he could read half the books on the shelves in your farmhouse," Anne said. "By the way, was he supposed to be living in there?"

"Yes, I told him he could stay in the house and be comfortable. Didn't expect him to move a doxy in the minute my back was turned, though."

Anne's face flushed.

"I beg your pardon," David said.

"Well, sir," Dan ventured, "this whole thing has turned out to be quite serious. We thought Sam and Millie were amateur confidence artists hoping to get their hands on a bit of your money. You see, Anne had hinted at an inheritance from your brother Richard, and I suppose Millie picked up on that and thought she could lay hold of it — or some of it."

"That may be," Anne said. "And when she saw that it wasn't forthcoming in cash, she set out to find you and wriggle into your good graces."

"Is that what she was doing? Call me an idiot, but I was quite taken with her at first. She was pretty and had charming manners. Not timid, but a bit outspoken. And she dressed very well."

"In my clothes." Anne's lip curled. That point obviously rankled her as much as anything else.

"But when did this turn into a murder plot?" Dan asked. "They must have connected with Peterson somewhere."

"Yes," David said.

"He might have gone to them in Eugene

and hired them the way he did Costigan," Anne said.

Owens stood. "We can speculate all day, folks, but it seems to me I'd best start looking for this Peterson chap. You don't think he stayed in this hotel?"

"He could have," David said.

"I'll ask. And if not, I'll start checking other hostelries."

"He didn't stay at Mrs. Zinberg's," Dan said as he got to his feet, "although Anne and I took Whitey there last night."

"And do I understand that you have Sam in custody now?" David leaned forward as if to rise, but Owens held out a hand to stop him.

"Don't get up, sir. Yes, I've got him locked in Fisher's icehouse until these two decide whether or not to press charges against him for horse stealing."

"I'd say not," Anne told him. "I mean, the horse is gone now, anyway. I'm sorry about that, Uncle David."

"It was a good horse, but if Charlotte's made off with it . . ." He shrugged. "I don't understand that. I thought she had a horse of her own stabled here."

"A quick getaway, I'd guess," Owens said. "And if she knew the horse and recognized it, she may have rationalized that it wasn't a crime to take it."

"Well, let's free Hastings, then," Dan said. "I'd hate for him to hang for this, even if he is a dimwitted scoundrel."

"Mr. Adams, would you mind going with me?" Owens asked. "Since you and Miss Stone brought Hastings in, I'd like you to sign a paper saying you've decided to drop the charge against him. That way I'm in the clear if anyone objects later to my letting him go."

"All right." Dan walked over to Anne. "You'll be all right for a short time with your uncle, won't you?"

"Of course."

David patted the pocket of his jacket. "I have a little Colt .44 insurance here, in case that fellow shows up again. And I feel bolder now that Constable Owens is on the lookout for him."

"I'll be back soon," Dan said. "Anne, I think it would be best if you lock the door while I'm gone." He didn't mean to alarm her, but with Peterson attempting to murder her uncle, he couldn't stress caution enough.

He walked over to the constable's house with him and waited impatiently while Owens got out the paperwork. He signed his name and put his hat on, declining Mrs.

Owens's offer of coffee.

"I'll go right over and release Hastings," Owens said. "What do I tell him about that horse?"

Dan sighed. He wanted nothing more to do with Sam Hastings, but he felt in some measure responsible. He had let Whitey ride the roan and hated to spoil the old man's pleasure in it, but he probably should have left the horse in Owens's care when they delivered Sam. The icehouse was at least half a mile away. He didn't want to leave Anne for very long with only her injured uncle to protect her.

"Tell him Millie took the horse."

"Millie."

Dan shook his head impatiently. "They said she was registered at the hotel as Charlotte Evans, but she was with Sam at David Stone's farm last week and called herself Millie. He knows her well, by the look of things. Just tell him. She had a brown horse in the hotel's pasture. Maybe he can use it until they meet up again." He had no doubt Sam and Millie *would* meet up again — if Millie saw a reunion as advantageous to herself.

"All right," Owens said, "but it's an odd way of doing things."

"This whole thing has been odd," Dan

replied. He went outside and strode back to the hotel.

He passed quickly through the lobby, hoping to avoid Reed, the desk clerk, and anyone else who was curious about David Stone and the beautiful young woman who had come to see him. He took the stairs two at a time and reached the top of the second flight panting. At the door to the suite's sitting room, he paused and knocked.

"Anne, it's me."

A moment later the bolt was thrown and the door opened. Anne's eyes were bright and her cheeks scarlet.

"Dan, come in quickly. I saw him in the lobby."

"Who?

"That man. Peterson — he's here."

CHAPTER 23

Anne locked the door again and hurried across the carpet to the door of Uncle David's bedroom. Dan followed her, peppering her with questions.

"Are you sure? I didn't see him. Did he speak to you?"

"Yes, I'm sure, and no, he didn't speak. I went down to get some fresh water, and I saw him. He ducked into the dining room, but I am certain it was him. I couldn't mistake those calculating eyes anywhere, even if there are other men with mustaches like that."

Uncle David was leaning on the dresser, pulling clothing from the top drawer and tossing it into the valise Anne had set next to him on the floor.

"Adams, we've got to leave." He shoved the top drawer closed and tugged on the drawer pull for the second.

Anne stepped forward to help him open

it. She suspected his wound was giving him more pain than he admitted to. "Here, Uncle David, let me do your packing. You sit down and rest."

"Should I go back and get Owens?" Dan asked.

"No time," David said. "We need to slip out of here before Peterson realizes it."

Anne threw Dan a glance trying to convey her concern. "Are our horses still tied out front?"

"Yes. They were when I came in. I could send word to the stable to have your uncle's horse ready."

David moaned.

"What is it?" Anne asked. "Are you ill?"

"No, I just remembered. I sent Captain home with a friend last night for safekeeping — or so I thought. I don't even know where Ernie lives, though."

"Ernie?"

His blue eyes took on a harassed air, and the fine lines at their corners deepened. "He's the cook, downstairs in the kitchen. He helped me last night — maybe saved my life. I thought I might stay in hiding longer, so I had him take Captain away. Didn't want the assassin who shot me to take him, or for Reed to sell him when I disappeared."

"I can go ask this Ernie where the horse is

now," Dan said.

"Hold on," Anne said. "This Peterson is only one man. Why are we letting him scare us so badly?"

"Because he shot your uncle in cold blood and wants to finish the job?" Dan asked.

"We should be able to outsmart him. Besides, if we're going back to Eugene, we need to get the rest of our things from Mrs. Zinberg's house."

"True." Dan frowned. "If we rode back to Eugene on horseback, we'd be vulnerable to attack at any point along the way."

"But where else could we go?" Anne asked. "You and I don't need to go back to Eugene. We could go right to Corvallis. But Uncle David may want to get back to his farm." She turned uncertainly to her uncle. "You wouldn't be any safer at the farm than you are here."

"That's right," Dan said. "We need to deal with Peterson now. I'll bring Owens back. He went over to release Hastings. If we —"

"There'll be a steamship embarking in the morning for Portland and Oregon City," David said. "If we could get on it without Peterson's knowledge, we could get away without riding through the wilderness where he could ambush us. And much as I hate to admit it, I'm not sure I could stay in the saddle for two or three days."

"You're not really fit to travel." Anne laid her hand across his forehead. "You feel overly warm right now. I think we should fetch the doctor."

"He said he'd come by today," David said. "Of course, if he goes to that room where I was last night, he won't know where I've gone."

He took a step toward the connecting door and staggered. Dan jumped forward and grabbed his left arm. "Sir, you need to sit down. It's all well and good to carry out heroics when you're healthy, but this is not the time. You need bed rest and a doctor to care for that wound."

"The man is ruthless," David said, but he let Dan lead him to the bed and sank down on the edge with a low moan. "Perhaps you're right, but . . . I can't bear to think of Peterson getting his way."

"He won't come and attack you in this room while Daniel and I are with you," Anne said.

"But he's waiting for me to leave the room. He's frustrated that he didn't get me last night. He might shoot me in a crowd now. He may be willing to take that risk if it's the only way he can get to me."

Anne watched Daniel. He seemed deep in

thought. "What do you think, Dan?" she asked softly.

"Well, I think your uncle is right about Peterson's intentions and his resolve. But we should be able to stop him. And if Owens can't catch him, we can at least find a way to stay safe here until David is strong enough to travel."

"Perhaps the steamer is the best idea," Anne said, though she remembered with apprehension her seasickness on the voyage from England. "He wouldn't expect that."

"I don't want to lose Captain," David said.

"And I don't want to lose Bailey again." Anne placed her hands on her hips. "Dan, why don't you go down and speak to the cook and find out where Uncle David's horse is? And perhaps you could inquire discreetly about taking horses on the steamboat?"

"I'll see what I can find out, but I hate to leave you here with that scoundrel in the building."

"Just go down and see Ernie," David said, easing back onto the pillow. "Then we can decide what to do. And go down the back stairs."

"Where are they?" Dan asked.

"Go out the door and turn left. Past the main stairway, and all the way to the end of the hall, on the left again. They go right down into the kitchen. Ernie should be there."

Anne went over and lifted David's feet and slid them up on top of the quilt. "You rest. I'll finish packing while Dan goes." She nodded at Dan and he slipped into the sitting room. She followed.

He'd paused by the hall door, waiting for her.

"Lock it behind me. I'll speak to you when I come back."

"All right," she said. "Don't let that monster see you."

Dan shrugged. "He may have seen me already. I didn't notice him when I came in, but I was avoiding looking directly at anyone. I didn't want Reed or one of his lackeys to stop me and ask questions."

"All right. Just hurry back."

He left, and she bolted the door and tiptoed back into the bedroom. David appeared to be sleeping, with his left arm across his eyes. She wished she had a blanket to put over him. No one had learned what happened to the missing bedclothes, but she suspected Ernie had carried them to her uncle's new room the night before.

Quickly she emptied the dresser and armoire, folding his clothing into the valise.

He had a variety of clothes — well-worn work clothes and presentable dinner wear. The nicest coat and trousers weren't high-toned formal clothing, but nice enough for any restaurant in Scottsburg or St. Louis, for that matter.

Dan was gone a good ten minutes. When he returned, she was waiting near the door.

"I found Ernie," Dan said. "He's happy to hear that Mr. Stone is feeling better but was dismayed when I told him you'd seen Peterson lurking about. He doesn't know the man, but I told him it was the same person Mr. Stone believed shot him. Ernie took me to the door between the kitchen and the dining room and let me peek out at the diners."

"And?"

"He's there all right, eating his luncheon. Brazen of him, don't you think?"

"Decidedly." Anne drew him further into the sitting room but kept her voice low. "I think Uncle David is asleep. I've packed all his clothing, but I haven't gone over this room for personal items. Dan, what shall we do?"

"Oh, that's the other good thing. Ernie says he can bring Captain — your uncle's horse — around to the inn's stable tonight. I was thinking that perhaps the three of us could get away to Mrs. Zinberg's and spend the night there. In fact, we might smuggle you out through the kitchen quite soon, and you could ride out to her house and tell her I'll come later and bring your uncle."

"What would you and Uncle David do in the meantime?"

"I'd stay here with him until the doctor sees his arm, and I'd also send an alert to Owens. Maybe he could pick up Peterson on some pretext or other and hold him until we get away."

"And ride for Eugene? I really don't think Uncle David could bear the strain or the jolting."

Dan gritted his teeth. "Well, this Ernie chap is very knowledgeable. He doesn't think we could take our horses on the steamer. But he says we could get a bigger boat in Reedsport and take the horses on board if we paid extra. He said boats leave there for the Columbia quite often."

Anne considered that. Uncle David would be sailing farther from his farm, but if she could get him to Eb and Elise's ranch, he could recover in peace. Elise would help her care for him, and she could return Bailey to Rob Whistler.

"I think I like that plan, though I confess I'm prone to sickness when at sea."

David awoke in a haze. Dr. Muller sat in a chair beside the bed, leaning over him, and was unbuttoning his shirt.

"Sorry to disturb you, Mr. Stone. I'm glad your niece is here to help you. But she tells me you intend to travel soon, and I'm not sure you're ready. Can I have a look at your arm, please?"

David tried to sit up. His whole body was sore, but his arm felt like molten lead and his head throbbed. He clenched his teeth and tried again, letting out a soft moan.

"Let me help." A young man stepped around the bed to the other side. It took David a moment to place him. Anne's friend . . . Adams, that was it. He wondered if Adams hoped to marry Anne then slapped himself mentally. Of course he did! The young pup was besotted with her, though he managed to keep a rather cool exterior. But he'd followed her hundreds of miles for what? A bushel of trouble? No, he was in love with Anne, no question.

Between Muller and Adams, they got his shirt off without making him sit up, but the pain in his arm now eclipsed everything else.

Muller handed something to someone

else. Anne.

"I want him to take a teaspoon of this dissolved in water. Can you fix it, please, Miss Stone?"

"Yes." She left the room, for which David was grateful.

The doctor deftly untied the strips of cloth holding the bandages in place. When he pulled them off, a different pain screeched up David's arm.

"Well, now, that looks as though an infection is starting." Muller shook his head. "I'll have to cleanse it again. I'm sorry, sir."

"I think we'd better forget about riding out of here tomorrow," Adams said.

"I should think so," the doctor replied. "Now, don't you worry, sir. I've got your niece fixing something that will help with the pain. I shan't poke around too much until you've got that in you."

Dan stood in the hallway talking to the hotel manager and Constable Owens.

"I'll check all around town and see if I can find out where this so-called gentleman is staying," Owens said. "Meanwhile, Mr. Reed, if he's seen hanging about this hotel, you call for me, and I'll come run him in."

"Yes," Reed said. "We must protect our guests. Mr. Adams, I assure you, if I'd known someone meant to harm Mr. Stone, I'd have called in the constable at once. And to think the gunman was right here in our dining room this morning."

"Don't you fret," Owens said. "I'll raise a posse. We'll scour this town."

"Oh, and you'll see to the extra rooms for Miss Stone and me?" Dan said.

"Certainly, sir." Mr. Reed bowed slightly and turned away.

"Well now, gents." Up the stairs came Whitey Pogue. "You still here, Adams?"

"Whitey, I thought you went back to your cabin," Dan said.

The old man lifted his hands and shoulders in an elaborate shrug. "Got no horse now. It's too far to walk this afternoon. Reckon I'll wait until morning."

"Well, if you don't mind sharing, you can bunk in with me here tonight. I'm going to move our stuff from the boardinghouse so that Miss Stone can be nearer her uncle."

"Sounds dandy," Whitey said. "They got good, big rooms here — bigger'n my cabin, hey?"

"Yes," Dan said with a smile. "What did Sam Hastings say when you told him about Millie taking the roan?" Dan asked Owens.

The constable snapped his fingers. "Meant to tell you, but all this talk about an assassin drove it plum out of my head. He said that Millie person is his sister."

Dan stared at him. "His sister? They surely don't look alike."

"Well, half sister, he told me. He said he guessed it was all in the family, and if she took his horse, he could take hers. He set off for the hotel's stable, and that's the last I saw of him. Didn't see any reason to stop him."

Dan shook his head. "Wait until I tell Anne. We misjudged those two, at least on that score." He looked about the hallway and the stair landing. "I do hate to leave Anne here alone. Perhaps I should go get our luggage from Mrs. Zinberg while the doctor is still here."

"I could fetch it," Whitey said. "Reckon I could get everything using your horse, Dan'l?"

"You fellows work it out. I'm going to get some men together and start looking for Peterson." Constable Owens strode toward the stairs.

Dan decided Whitey might be safer transporting the baggage than he would be, since Peterson knew him by sight. He gave the old man plenty of money to cover their bill with Mrs. Zinberg and a note from Anne to the widow, detailing the packing of her belongings.

He returned to the bedroom in time to help the doctor clean up and settle the patient comfortably.

"He'll be out for some time," Muller said. "I gave him a hefty dose of laudanum. The fool thinks he can get up and take on thugs and ride off to Eugene. Well, he needs to stay put for at least two more days. I'll come by first thing in the morning and look at that arm again, but if the infection spreads, he may be here a long time."

Anne refused to leave her uncle's bedside, so Dan went downstairs and asked for a tray for her. He'd had no lunch — only a couple of cookies off the tea tray, but the dining room was deserted and the desk clerk told him he couldn't be served until five o'clock. When the clerk wasn't looking, he ducked through the dining room and peeked into the kitchen.

Ernie hovered over the huge black stove, stirring pots, and a boy of about sixteen sat on a stool peeling a mound of potatoes.

"Mr. Adams," Ernie said, looking up in surprise. "I hope Mr. Stone is all right."

"He's got a slight infection in his wound."

"Dear me. I hope it's not serious." Ernie shook his head.

"I'm not sure. The doctor seemed concerned, but I don't think he wanted to worry Miss Stone too much. And speaking of the lady, she's had no luncheon. Well, none of us has. They said at the desk that we're too late —"

"Nonsense. I can make you some sandwiches. How many people?"

"Two, I guess." It was probably safe to assume Mrs. Zinberg would feed Whitey something when he got to her house, and David would most likely sleep the afternoon away. "Just Miss Stone and me."

"Mudge, get some pie and a couple of apples," Ernie said to his helper. The boy laid down his paring knife and hurried to obey.

"We're taking rooms here until Mr. Stone is able to travel," Dan said.

"Probably best." Ernie swiftly sliced a loaf of bread and set about smearing it with mustard. "Anytime you want a tray, just let me know."

Dan sat down on a stool near the stove, glad to have found an ally in Ernie.

Millie loaded a tray with a coffeepot, two dishes of venison stew, and half-a-dozen slices of pie and shoved open the door to the dining room. She quickly delivered the stew and began making rounds about the dining room, refilling coffee mugs and selling pie to men who'd thought they would skip dessert.

Now that her prospects of marrying a rich English gent had fizzled and she no longer feared discovery by Anne Stone and Dan Adams, she'd figured Elkton might be a good place for her to pause. She was tired of running and scrambling and hiding. Andrew Willis was happy to have her back, and word of her return spread swiftly through the town. The dining room was packed for every meal, with freighters and miners forming a line outside while they waited for tables to free up.

With Millie in charge, Andrew had left on a three-day trip to Eugene to lay in more supplies. Millie's first actions had been to hire a waitress and a dishwasher. She met the waitress, Virginia, halfway around the dining room.

"You got any more fried chicken?" Virginia asked. "I've got four more customers who are hankerin' for it."

"I'll go dish it up." Millie handed her the coffeepot.

"Send Stubby out to collect dirty dishes, too," Virginia said. "I don't have time. The customers are still three deep outside waitin' to get in."

Millie hurried back to the kitchen. Where were all these men coming from? She supposed a lot of them were headed to the goldfields farther south.

"Stubby! Go pick up the empty dishes. Quick now." The grizzled man whom she'd hired for the job hated to carry the heavy trays of crockery, but Millie had warned him he'd have to during their busy times. If he couldn't do the work, she'd hire someone younger. That had shut him up.

She put the money she'd collected for pie carefully into the two-gallon crock Andrew used for a cash box and shook her head. Andrew was such a trusting fellow. If she were of a mind to steal all his receipts for the day, it would be easy. But she'd promised herself she wouldn't do that.

She wasn't exactly sure what had happened to her between the Miner's Hotel in Scottsburg and here, but something was going on inside her. She'd decided first off to quit making her living by pilfering merchandise and cadging meals from men. Maybe it was the stolen dress that started her thinking she'd like to be honest. Anne Stone lived the way Millie wanted to live — but she'd never lifted a man's wallet and fled town in disgrace. Millie wanted what Anne had — dignity. Respect. Dare she think that someday she might attain self-respect?

Two nights ago when she'd checked into a boardinghouse at Andrew's insistence, she'd unpacked the small bag she'd gotten away with. David Stone's Bible and cuff links were in the bottom of it, along with her lip rouge and frilly garters. A wave of shame had swept over her — a rare occurrence in her lifetime. She had stolen a man's Bible, of all things. Was it for sentimental reasons?

She'd opened the cover and seen "David Stone, Esq." written in neat script. Esq. Esquire, she supposed, but what did that mean, anyway?

Out of curiosity, she'd sat down on her lumpy cot and flipped through the leatherbound little book. The tiny print made her bring the lamp closer, but she discovered several underlined places in the text. She browsed through the book, skimming the lines that he'd underscored. It made little sense to her — random thoughts that she supposed he'd found interesting. At last she'd laid it aside and gone to bed, exhausted from riding half the day and cooking the other half. Her last thought before drifting off to sleep had been that someday she ought to return the Bible. And the cuff links. And maybe even the ten dollars she'd stolen from his room. No, maybe not that. He would never miss it.

Now the thought came to her again as she arranged fried chicken and heaps of potatoes and squash on the heavy plates. She had stolen, and she ought to return the money — that and the pie money she'd taken from this restaurant a week or two ago. She owed Andrew five dollars. He'd never realized it and had gladly taken her back to work for him. He knew he was better off with her here in the kitchen, and she would make a pile of money for him. So why was her conscience bothering her about it?

Stubby dragged in, sagging under the weight of his laden tray. "Miss Virginia says hurry up wid the chicken dinners."

Millie arranged the plates carefully on a tray so that they wouldn't slide and lifted it to her shoulder. She shoved the door open and swished into the dining room with a big smile on her face. Men lingered for dessert when a pretty woman served them with a cordial manner. That was why she'd hired Virginia — a pretty farmer's daughter — over the more experienced older women who'd applied.

She caught Virginia's eye across the room, and the waitress pointed to the table of men waiting for their dinners. Millie wended through the close tables, her skirts brushing the men's chairs.

"Good stew, Charlotte," one of them called.

She smiled. "Thank you kindly."

"You can come cook for me anytime you get tired of this place," another said as she passed.

"Thanks — I'll keep it in mind."

She reached the corner of the room and lowered the tray to the edge of the table, balancing it there while she set off the plates one at a time.

"Mmm, that looks downright edible, sweetheart," one of the customers said.

"Enjoy it." She smiled at them all without making eye contact with any of them. "Save room for some of my walnut cake." She lowered the tray so that it was flat against her side and headed back toward the kitchen door.

"Millie?"

She whirled toward the familiar voice.

"Millie! Can't believe I found ya!" Sam shoved back his chair and stood, blocking her way. "I shoulda known nobody could make such good biscuits but you."

"Thank you. I'm working here now." She glanced at the other two men sharing his table and didn't like the look of them. Friends, or was Sam just sharing a table with strangers in a crowded restaurant? One had thick, dark hair and black eyes that raked over her. Had she seen him before? She looked away.

"Really?" Sam said. "You took a job? How long for?"

"I don't know yet. I might stay here. I like it, and my boss is real happy to have me cooking for him."

"Hey, Charlotte, how about some more gravy?" a man at a nearby table called.

Virginia sidled up to her. "I've got six more orders. You need to send this fella packing and get into the kitchen."

Millie bristled. "Don't tell me what to do, Virginia Shaw!" She looked back at Sam. "We close around nine o'clock. If you come back sober, I'll talk to you then."

Sam blinked at her guilelessly. "Sure, Millie. I can do that."

"Millie?" Virginia asked, peering at her vulturelike.

Millie whirled and headed for the kitchen, squeezing between the tables and laughing at the men's remarks.

Once in the kitchen, she stood for a moment breathing deeply. She hadn't counted on meeting up with Sam again, at least not this soon. She'd only been here a few days and hadn't really gotten herself established yet. As a good cook in high demand, she could earn a high wage here. She could be comfortable at the boardinghouse and put away a nest egg without having to do anything illegal. Andrew Willis would pay her well as long as she produced a lot of good food quickly.

Not only that, but when she'd taken Old Blue to the liveryman to see if he'd board her horse for her at a reasonable rate, he'd not only agreed at good terms, he'd done a little flirting with her. Millie had the feeling the pick of the men of Elkton was hers, if she wanted it, to say nothing of all the miners and freighters passing through.

But Sam didn't fit into that plan. He'd come to her rescue a couple of months ago when she was down and out. Flat broke with no place to live, she was lower than the bottom of a mine shaft. She'd tracked him down at the farm where he worked and happened on a convenient circumstance. Sam's boss was away and had let him live in the farmhouse and tend to things while he was gone. Sam had invited Millie to come and cook for him temporarily. She'd moved in and taken over the household, bullying her brother into doing whatever she wanted and taking advantage of David Stone's supplies and the spending money he'd left Sam.

Now she felt a little guilty about that. Oh, it was far from the worst thing she'd ever done — and those things she felt even guiltier about. But she didn't want to connect with Sam again for any length of time. It would be too easy to fall back into his lazy attitude and her thieving ways. That was what she'd been — a thief. No denying it. And she wanted to change, to become something better. She could see now that she'd have to take up an entirely different lifestyle to do that. Elkton offered her a chance, and she was determined to make a go of it.

"Hey, you better check them pies," Stubby said.

As Millie shook herself out of her reverie and strode toward the stove, Virginia poked her head in at the door.

"Here's my orders — got nine now. Six for stew, three for fried chicken."

"Don't know if I've got that much stew."

"Better make more. They're still coming in the door."

Millie glanced at the clock on the shelf over the flour bin. "It's after eight o'clock. Just tell 'em they're too late and we're out."

Virginia screwed up her face like she'd

been eating a sour pickle. "You got enough for these orders?"

Millie set a stack of soup plates on her worktable near the stove and started ladling stew into them. "Two, three, four . . . There's only enough for four."

"How much chicken?"

"Maybe six — your three and three more. After that we're down to pie and gingerbread."

Virginia trounced out the door without commenting on "Charlotte's" other name.

Somehow Millie made it through the next hour. When she was done cooking and dishing up food, she helped Virginia serve coffee and pie. They both carried heaps of dirty dishes to Stubby. At nine she put the CLOSED sign on the door, and at last the dining room began to empty. Sam and the dark-haired man sat at their table long after they'd finished eating, drinking cup after cup of coffee. Millie wished they would leave. She busied herself in the kitchen, tidying up and setting out what she'd need to start cooking lunch tomorrow.

She'd drawn the line when Andrew urged her to cook breakfast, too. Two meals a day was plenty, she'd told him. He'd work her to death if she'd let him. She'd worked from ten to ten the past two days, and she would soon be exhausted. As soon as Andrew returned, she'd have to sit down with him and thrash out some more favorable terms. And if he wanted to serve breakfast, he'd have to cook it himself or hire a morning cook.

Virginia hung up her apron, stretched, and said, "G'night. See you tomorrow."

"Is my brother still out there?" Millie asked.

"Who?"

"The fellow who wanted to speak to me."

"He's your brother? I didn't know. I tossed him out, along with the other stragglers. Sorry."

"Doesn't matter," Millie said. "You about done, Stubby?"

"Almost."

Millie picked up a dish towel and helped him dry the last rack of plates. At last he was ready to go, and she let him out the back door and locked it behind him. Then she took the money from the crock and put it in a cupboard with a lock. She got her coat, blew out the lanterns, went out the back door, and locked it behind her.

It was cold outside, and she pulled her coat closed. Walking around the corner of the building, she headed for the street and her boardinghouse. Two men detached themselves from the shadows at the front of the restaurant. Millie's heart pounded, but she stood still, realizing that Sam and his companion had waited for her.

"You done for the night?"

"Yeah, Sam. Where you staying?"

"We's camping down the creek."

She eyed the shadowy form behind him, sure it was the dark-haired man who'd been at his table. "Who's we?"

"Me and Lucky and a couple other fellas." He jerked his head toward the other man, and suddenly Millie remembered where she'd seen Lucky before. He'd been a chum of her husband, James's — one Millie hadn't cared to get to know too well.

"You wanted to talk," she said to Sam, ignoring Lucky. "You can't come to the place I'm staying this late."

"Can't we talk here? I was hoping I could wait for you inside, but that Virginia girl said we had to leave."

"What do you want to talk about?"

"I'm going with Lucky and the others. I want to know if you want to come with us."

Millie frowned. "Come with you where?"

"We're not sure yet, but Lucky thinks maybe over Fort Boise way."

"What do you want to go there for?"

Millie's suspicions grew wings and began to fly.

"Looks like as good a place as any," Lucky growled.

"And nobody knows us there," Sam added.

"So?"

"Lucky thought your cooking was tops. He and the boys think it'd be terrific if you wanted to come see to us."

"What does that mean, 'see to you'? You want me to cook and clean house?"

"Well, we don't have a house," Sam said.

"Mighty good eats, ma'am," Lucky said. "Your brother says you have other talents, too."

"Other talents? What are you talking about?" She turned her fiercest glare on Sam.

"You know," Sam said in soft, wheedling tones. "You're slicker'n anyone I ever saw at liftin' a wallet."

She stared at him, then at his shadowy companion. "No."

"Aw, come on, Millie. I told them about you, and they're counting on you. We'll need decent meals if we're going to make our living as road agents."

"Road —" She looked from Sam to Lucky and back. "No. Absolutely not. I'm done with crime, Sam. This is it right here for me. I'm staying here and working at the restaurant. I'm going to make an *honest* living. So forget it. And don't come around here bothering me again."

"Sounds like your sister needs a little persuasion." Lucky pushed past Sam and stood less than a foot in front of her, holding her stare. "Me and the boys'll take real good care of you, ma'am. That's a promise."

Millie ran her hand down her skirt until she could feel the comforting shape of the derringer she'd bought in Scottsburg. "No thank you, Mr. Lucky. That's final."

She was afraid he would insist, but Sam edged around him. "Come on, Millie. Please? We won't make you do anything you don't want to."

She strongly doubted that. "No, Sam."

"Then at least give Old Blue back. The constable in Scottsburg said you took him."

"Why should I?"

"Because Blue is my horse. And my stuff was tied to the saddle, too."

Millie almost protested, but the guilt that had plagued her for the last few days won out. If they got down to brass tacks, Old Blue belonged to David Stone. Did she want to start her new life with a stolen horse?

"What are you riding?"

"That horse you had — the plug of a brown mare."

Fair enough, Millie decided. She'd paid the asking price for the mare, and that was money she'd earned. Vixen wasn't as good a mount as Old Blue, but Millie didn't plan on fleeing the authorities again anytime soon.

"All right, I'll take Vixen back."

"What? You named your horse?"

"Oh, be quiet, Sam. Where is she?"

"Yonder." He jerked his head toward the hitching rail in front of the restaurant.

Millie sighed. "Wait here and I'll go get Blue for you."

"We might as well come with you," Lucky said, low and definite. Millie had a feeling not many people said no to Lucky.

She took a deep breath. "No. Stay right here. The lady I'm rooming with doesn't want to see any men hanging around. Sam, you wait here if you want to trade."

She walked out to the street and looked back. The two men were nearly invisible in the shadow of the building. At least they'd stayed put. She wouldn't trust that Lucky from here to the porch pillar. Above her, the sky was clear for once. The stars glittered like tiny lamps, lighting her way to the boardinghouse. Instead of going in, she walked around to the barn and went inside. Blue and the horse that belonged to the couple that owned the place whickered. Millie went to Blue's stall and patted his nose.

"I'm sorry, boy, but I've got to give you back to Sam. You were good for me." She put the saddle on him with Sam's bedroll still tied to it, bridled him, and led him out of the barn.

She had the assurance that this was right. She was giving the stolen horse back to Sam. From now on, settling Blue's ownership would be between him and David. Maybe if she started doing small good things, she could eventually become a good person. In fact, she would put a dollar out of her pay in Andrew's crock. If she did that every week for five weeks, she'd have paid back the pie money she took from him the first time she'd worked for him, and he would never notice. That would add to the "good" side of her behavior ledger. And she would read some more in the Bible tonight. What could be more virtuous than that?

She ignored the little guilt gnome that tugged at her sleeve to remind her that the Bible was stolen, too.

Back at the restaurant, Lucky and Sam

emerged from the shadows. Sam untied Vixen and walked toward her. Before she could say anything, Lucky stepped up beside Sam.

"Your brother and I talked it over, ma'am, and we think you need to come with us."

Chapter 24

Millie's heart sank and hit bottom. "He's my half brother, and it doesn't matter what *you* think. I'm staying here."

Lucky's hand snaked to his hip, and he drew his revolver so fast she barely had time to shove her hand in her pocket.

"Mount up, Millie." His voice had a steel edge now. Sam hung back, looking worried but saying nothing.

Millie's pulse raced. "Give me Vixen," she said to Sam.

He moved forward and held out the ends of the mare's reins. She put Blue's leathers in his other hand, at the same time pulling out her derringer.

She whirled on Lucky, who stood only five feet away.

"I'm pretty good with this little peashooter, mister. If you still want your friends to call you 'Lucky' after tonight, you'd best mount up and ride out of here."

His eyes narrowed. Sam gasped, but Millie didn't spare him a glance, knowing Lucky could get the upper hand quickly if she let anything distract her. They stood for a moment glaring at each other over their guns' muzzles.

Lucky laughed softly. "She's a hard one, all right, Sam. Who'd have thought it to look at her? All right, Miss Millie, you win this round, but I won't forget it."

"Neither will I," she said.

Sam gulped and held out the mare's reins. "If you ever need a friend, Millie, come find me. And we'd still like to have you cook for us."

"Don't count on it." She took Vixen's bridle and turned the mare to shield her from Lucky's view as she led her away. After a few steps she heard their horses moving and looked back. Both men were mounting. She hustled Vixen along to the corner and got off the main road before they passed.

After two days of bed rest, David seemed stronger. Anne had hardly left the suite, sitting with her uncle's pistol in her lap whenever Dan went out. The cook, Ernie, came every day to see how David was doing, and Dr. Muller came at least once a day to examine his wound and monitor his progress. Whitey, seeing no benefit to wandering about town when he had no money to spend, had left them to hike back to his claim.

On the third day, David awoke grumpy.

"How long do you expect me to lie in bed?" he asked Anne. "Bring me some clothes. I want to get up and go down to breakfast with you."

Anne rose and went to his dresser, where she'd put the clothing she'd unpacked after they'd realized he couldn't travel. "I don't think you're quite ready for two flights of stairs, but perhaps we can have our breakfast at the table in the next room."

She laid out his smallclothes, trousers, and shirt.

"Where's my razor? I want to shave."

She smiled at that. "Get dressed first, Uncle David. Call to me when you're ready, and we'll see. Oh, and don't tumble off the bed trying to put your socks and shoes on. I can help you with that."

"I'm not an infant."

"Indeed." He sounded like an earl in that moment — one whose dignity had been questioned. She checked the water pitcher and went into the sitting room, closing the connecting door.

Dan's distinctive knock came at the hall

430

door, and she let him in.

"Owens and his men haven't found a trace of Peterson. Once he left his boardinghouse, he simply disappeared."

"He probably rode out of town quietly that night." Anne glanced toward the bedroom door. "Uncle David is dressing. I must stay in case he needs help, but we'd like breakfast here. Have you eaten?"

"Not yet. I'll go down and speak for it."

"Thank you. We all need to eat a good meal. If the doctor approves, we may be able to leave today."

"Do you think so?" Dan asked.

"I don't think we'll be able to keep Uncle David down much longer. He wants to shave."

"He feels like a sitting target here," Dan said. "Do you really think Peterson would stick around?"

"You saw his persistence. He followed my uncle thousands of miles. I don't think he'll give up just because Owens is looking for him."

"I suppose you're right. Personally, I feel safer in here with walls around us and an officer of the law nearby. Well, I'll go down and ask for room service."

"Actually, I wouldn't mind a bit of exercise," she said. "If you don't mind staying here and playing valet if needed, I can order breakfast and then stop by my room to freshen up."

"All right. Just be careful, Anne."

She smiled. "I will. Did you want anything in particular this morning?"

"Eggs, maybe, and some flapjacks."

She went out and listened for the bolt to slide, then went down the stairs. At the second-floor landing, she peered over the railing and surveyed the lobby before continuing on her way. Peterson *must* be gone. At any rate, he wouldn't come back here where people would recognize him. But would he hire someone else to keep watch for him? The memory of Thomas G. Costigan on the wagon train brought an uneasy shiver. Anyone she met in the hotel might be in Peterson's pay, ready to pass the word to him when David left his quarters.

Anne had barely left when the bedroom door opened and David came out, walking slowly toward the table and chairs near the window. Dan rose and stepped toward him.

"Let me help you, sir."

"Thanks, but I need to practice using my legs. Can you help me get set up to shave, though?"

"Are you certain you want to do that?"

"Completely. But I'm not sure I can stay on my feet long enough to do it or have a steady hand if I'm swaying back and forth. Maybe you could put the basin of water and soap and razor on the table out here and prop up a small mirror so I can see what I'm doing."

"I'll get the one hanging over your wash-stand. Have a seat."

Dan waited until David had lowered himself with a sigh onto one of the chairs. Quickly he gathered the things he'd asked for from the bedroom, along with a couple of towels.

"Anne went down to order breakfast," he said as he reentered the sitting room. "By the time you're finished, it will probably be here."

Anne returned fifteen minutes later, wearing a fresh gown and with her hair cascading down the back of her neck in a most becoming style. Dan didn't know how she did it, staying up most of the night in her uncle's sitting room in case he needed her, but she managed to look so beautiful each day that she took his breath away. How he would go on without her when they finished this odyssey and she shooed him back to the farm, he couldn't imagine. He'd have to insist she sleep this afternoon. If David wanted to leave when his niece hadn't had a full night's sleep in days, he'd put his foot down.

An hour later, with breakfast done, the doctor came with an ebony cane for David to use to steady himself and took him into the bedchamber to check his wound. Anne and Daniel waited in the sitting room. Anne sat still on the settee with her hands folded in her lap while Dan paced from the window to the door and back, over and over. He wished he could remain as peaceful as she did. The confinement chafed on him, as did the uncertainty of their situation.

At last she broke the silence. "Dan, I know you want to get back to the farm and help your brother. Why don't you leave me in Uncle David's care? You've seen how much better he is."

Dan wheeled from the window and strode over to the settee. He sat down beside her and looked earnestly into her eyes.

"I can't do that. For all we know, that killer is still out there, just waiting for your uncle to leave these rooms. I wouldn't walk out and leave you in such a perilous situation." She lowered her eyelids, and he regretted speaking so frankly. "Besides, what makes you think I'd rather be puttering around the farm with Hector than here with you?"

Anne's eyes flew open wide for a moment then she looked away. "You didn't plan to be gone so long."

"No, but nothing could make me happier than staying by your side. I could wish the circumstances were less trying — that your uncle was well and that you could both travel on and resume your lives. But that would mean separation. Dearest Anne, please don't think ill of me for mentioning it. I've tried not to speak of this too often, because I know you don't share my sentiments."

"I won't say I do not care for you, Dan."

He was silent for a moment, unwilling to trust his voice. He sat back and cleared his throat. "That at least is a comfort. But I'm not sure you mean to give me hope."

"Hope is such a fragile thing. But I've discovered it fluttering inside me, even as I failed time after time to find my uncle." She started to move then hesitated. He eyed her cautiously, and at last she reached over and touched his hand. "Your presence has meant a great deal to me. In fact, your solid determination to finish the quest for the simple reason that it mattered to me has worked a slow, quiet course in my heart, until I find the prospect of parting company with you distressful." She looked away and whispered, "I believe we need hope. All the hope we can get. It's precious, don't you think?"

He turned his hand and clasped hers, not too firmly lest she pull it away. His heart thudded. "Precious indeed. Thank you."

The bedroom door swung open.

"Well, I can't say I approve," Dr. Muller said as he entered, "but Mr. Stone insists on traveling. His wound looks better — not so red and swollen. I believe we've got the infection licked. I'd rather see him rest a few more days, though."

Dan glanced at Anne. "Perhaps we could persuade him that Miss Stone needs rest herself before we move on."

"I'm fine," Anne said. "The fact that he's better gives me strength. I'm willing to leave now if that is what he wants."

Dan nodded. "I can check on the steamers and see when the next one leaves."

David insisted on paying Dr. Muller generously, in case they did not meet again. Dan went down the stairs with the doctor and parted from him on the street. He strolled at a quick pace to the waterfront. No large boats were docked, so he ambled down to where two men were stacking crates on the end of the largest dock.

"No steamers today?"

"Should be coming in this afternoon," one of the men said.

"And going out again . . . ?"

"Tomorrow morning."

"Thanks." Dan started to turn away then swung back to face them. "How big a boat is it? Will they take horses?"

"Doubt it. The deck area's pretty small, and they usually have it crammed with freight."

Dan walked slowly back to the hotel. He didn't want to leave Star behind, and he was sure David wouldn't want to part with Captain, either. As for Anne, she was committed to returning Bailey to Rob Whistler.

They reacted about the way he'd expected. After more discussion, he saw Anne to her room, where she promised to nap. David insisted he could fend for himself, so at about three o'clock, when the steamer's whistle sounded, Dan headed back to the landing.

He watched the passengers disembark and several men go aboard to make arrangements to have their cargo unloaded. When the dockhands started working, he made his way among them and up the gangplank.

The captain wasn't difficult to find. He

stood just outside the pilot house, his blue eyes sharply watching the activity around him while he talked to two Scottsburg business owners.

Dan approached him and waited for a break in the conversation about freight.

"Help you, sir?" the captain asked.

"Yes, I wondered if you're heading out for Oregon City tomorrow."

"That's the plan, yes, sir."

"Would you take three passengers?"

The captain scratched his chin. "Could. Not much of a load going from here."

"And do you take horses?"

He frowned. "Look around you, man."

Dan gazed at the limited deck space on the small, squatty sternwheeler.

"It can get pretty rough between here and the coast. You crowd three horses in here with passengers and cargo, and it can turn into a muddy ride. Then you get into open water, and you can't guarantee a thing. I have not slings to secure large animals with."

"So you wouldn't?"

The captain shook his head. "Don't care to risk it. Sorry."

Dan swallowed hard. "Not even from here to the coast? We might be able to get a bigger ship there."

"No doubt you could, but no, I won't take

438

'em on my boat."

Dan nodded. "I understand. Thank you."

Discouraged, he plodded back to the hotel. In his mind, he ticked off several options. They could sell the horses, which didn't seem agreeable to any of them. They might leave the horses in Scottsburg, to be retrieved later, but when? They could ride back to David's farm in Eugene, or to the coast, both of which promised to be dangerous.

He entered the lobby and headed for the stairs. As he passed the desk, the clerk said, "Hsst. Mr. Adams."

Dan paused and looked at him. "You wanted to speak to me?"

"Come closer, sir."

It was almost a whisper, and Dan was instantly alert. He walked over to the desk and said clearly, "Any messages for me?" He lowered his voice to a whisper. "What's up?"

"There's a man sitting yonder — don't look."

"I understand. What about him?"

"He asked for Miss Stone."

Dan tensed. "Is he a guest here?"

"No. I told him we couldn't give out information about our guests, like you said. He went out, but a little while later I went to get something, and when I came back he was sitting over there with the newspaper in front of his face. I ignored him. We've got no rule about people waiting for guests in the lobby, but . . . well, I thought you'd like to know."

"Thank you."

Dan walked deliberately over to the stairs and mounted them without looking toward the man indicated by the clerk. When he reached the first landing, he rounded the corner and paused long enough to look down and toward the sitting area. A young man with sandy hair and a heavy beard and mustache stared up at him over the top of an open newspaper. When he saw that Dan had noticed him, he averted his gaze to the paper.

Dan strode along the second-floor hallway to the far end. He looked over his shoulder then opened the door to the back stairs and ran lightly down them to the kitchen.

Ernie and his helper looked up in surprise.

"Mr. Adams," Ernie said. "I hope nothing's wrong upstairs?"

"No, our friend is gaining strength. But I wonder if I could ask a favor of you." He explained about the stranger watching the front entrance.

"I can go out through the dining room

and see if he's still there, but if Mr. Reed sees me, he'll get upset." Ernie scowled. "He thinks I should stay in the kitchen all the time."

"I'll go," his helper said.

Ernie's face brightened. "Sure. We'll send Mudge."

His helper whipped off his apron and handed it to Ernie. "What do you want me to do?"

"You heard me describe the fellow in the lobby?" Dan asked.

"Yeah."

"Just see if he's still out there and tell me what he's doing."

Mudge walked out through the empty dining room. Dan and Ernie, peeking through a crack at the partially opened door to the dining room, had a limited view of the lobby beyond.

"Where'd he go?" Ernie asked after a half minute.

"Looked like he went over near the stairs," Dan said.

Half a minute later, Mudge breezed back in.

"Well?" Ernie asked.

"He wasn't sitting there, so I asked the desk clerk. He said the fella went up the main stairs after you did, Mr. Adams."

Dan looked at Ernie for a second then dashed up the back stairs. At the second-floor landing, he paused to calm himself and stealthily opened the door to the hallway. Halfway between him and the main stairway, a man leaned with his ear against the door of one of the guest rooms.

Dan strode down the carpeted hall.

The sandy-haired man whirled. His eyes popped wide and he backed away, but Dan was too quick. He grabbed him by the lapels and shoved him against the wall.

"What do you think you're doing?"

CHAPTER 25

David held his revolver trained on the scruffy man Adams had herded into his sitting room while Adams tied the fellow to a chair.

"What will we do with him?" Anne stood by wringing her hands.

Adams secured the knots he'd tied and stood looking at David. "He admitted he was hired to find you."

"Did Peterson hire him?" Anne asked.

"Someone did. He wouldn't say who."

David stepped toward their prisoner and aimed the gun pointblank at him. "I'm tired of this. Who's paying you? Give us a name."

"I don't know," the man sputtered. "He said he'd pay me a dollar a day to watch the hotel lobby and try to find out your room number and tell him if you ever left the room. He wanted to know if you planned to leave Scottsburg. It was more than I'd made panning for gold, and it sounded like easy

443

work, so I took it."

"What did he look like?" Anne asked.

The man strained against the cords Adams had tied him with as though he wanted to move his arms when he talked. "I don't know. He was about forty, I'm guessing. Thin face. He had a mustache."

"A little pencil mustache?" Adams asked.

"Yeah. Skinny fella. Wore a suit like a dandy."

"We'd best turn this man over to Owens," David said.

"What? I didn't do anything!"

"You're in the employ of a killer," Adams said.

The prisoner's face blanched. "I swear I didn't know. I thought he just wanted to get in with Mr. Stone. I had no idea he wanted to harm anyone." He looked up at David. "No offense, mister, but he said you wouldn't give him the time of day and he had a business deal he wanted to talk over with you. He wanted me to tell him where you'd be, so he could find you outside the hotel. Said they wouldn't let him wait around the hotel anymore."

"More like, the constable is watching to see if he comes here," David said.

"So what do we do now?" Anne asked again. "I could go for Mr. Owens."

444

"We need to leave this town," Adams said. "If we stay here, Peterson's going to find a way to get to your uncle. But we can't —" He broke off and glanced at the prisoner. "Let's not discuss it in front of him."

"All right, I'll guard him," David said. "Get Owens, and we'll be rid of this baggage."

Adams hurried out, and Anne went over and locked the hall door behind him. The prisoner's eyes followed her every move.

"Why don't you go lie down?" David said.

"I don't think I care to be alone right now."

David could see the sense of that. With the certainty that Peterson was still about, lying in wait for them, sending Anne to her own room down the hall might not be the most brilliant plan. "At least sit in my chamber," he said.

Anne threw an uneasy glance at the prisoner and nodded. "All right. I shall think about our options."

All was quiet until Dan came in twenty minutes later with Owens in tow. Anne came and stood in the connecting doorway.

"Well now," the constable said, looking over the prisoner. "Billy Harden. You went bust on your claim, I heard. What are you up to now?"

"Nothing," the prisoner said. "I swear." The version he gave the constable squared with what he'd told them before.

Owens leaned toward him with glinting eyes. "Where's this man at now, Billy?"

"I don't know."

"But you had a way to report to him. Where were you going to meet him?"

The prisoner was silent for a moment. "Will you let me go if I tell you?"

"No."

"But, Mr. Owens, I didn't do nothing."

"Maybe it was all in ignorance — that wouldn't surprise me a bit," Owens said, "but now you know that man meant to harm Mr. Stone. So tell me what you know."

"What do I get if I tell you?"

"You don't get strung up, that's what you get."

Billy stared at Owens. "You can't hang nobody without a judge says so."

"Oh, can't I?"

Anne looked horrified, and David threw her a surreptitious wink. Owens wouldn't have the stomach to lynch a prisoner, but they couldn't have Anne ruining his strategy by protesting too heartily. His niece had been through a lot, but it seemed she was still tenderhearted enough to spare a criminal.

"He gave me two bits and said to go to the Big Tree Saloon tonight, down by the river, and he'd find me."

"Hmm." Owens frowned at him. "You giving it to me straight?"

"Sure am."

Owens gestured to David and Adams to join him, and the three stepped out into the hall.

"I'll try to get him over to the icehouse without a lot of people seeing me, but it'll be hard to take him out of this building unnoticed, especially if someone's watching."

"There's stairs for the staff that go down into the kitchen," Adams said. "You could take him that way and out the back."

"Good. I'll lock him up and see if I can get wind of this Peterson." Owens shook his head. "Persistent, isn't he? I was sure he'd left town. He must have a big payday riding on killing you, Mr. Stone."

"I hate to think it, but it seems you're right," David said.

Owens untied the prisoner, and Adams showed him the back stairway. When he returned, David told Adams and Anne, "We need to sit down right now and decide what we're going to do. Personally, I don't want to depend on Owens to catch that thug

Peterson."

"I agree," Adams said. "What I didn't have a chance to tell you is that the steamer is too small to take horses on the deck. The captain wasn't open to it, and I could see why. But Anne and I don't want to give up our horses, and I know you don't either, sir."

"We could head out for your place in Eugene," Anne said doubtfully.

"Too risky," David said. "He could bushwhack us anywhere along the way."

"How about this," Adams said. "I could go back to talk to the captain again and make it look like I was buying tickets on the steamer. If I asked him nice, he might put it about that we were taking his boat tomorrow. He's going down the river and up the coast to the Columbia, then to Oregon City."

"And what would we really do?" Anne asked, her eyes bright.

"Start out tonight when it's full dark and ride to the coast. If Peterson figures out we left on horseback, he'd probably expect us to ride east. But we go west instead, and follow the river road to the coast."

"What's the point, other than to confuse him?" David asked.

"We could get a bigger ship at Reedsport

or Gardiner, board it with the horses, and sail to Oregon City. A steamer would get us there in less than two days."

"Then you'd be nearly home, and Uncle David and I could ride down to Corvallis to Eb and Elise's ranch," Anne said. "I like that plan. Can you stand to be away from your farm a little longer, Uncle David?"

"That doesn't matter much. It's staying alive I care about."

Anne's face sobered. "Maybe we ought to stay right here until Owens catches Peterson."

"We've done that and he hasn't even laid eyes on the fellow," David said. "How long do you think we should hide in this hotel? It's been days already."

"Your uncle's right," Adams said. "Peterson is staying out of sight. Unless he makes some big blunder, we're at his mercy. He could wait forever, though I don't think he would. I wish I knew where he's hiding."

"Must be boarding somewhere," David muttered. "But I don't want to stay here any longer. Let's get out of Scottsburg."

"All right," Adams said. "I'll go have a word with the steamboat's captain."

Ernie sent the dishwasher up with a tray of sandwiches and coffee at one o'clock. "Did anyone see you in the hall?" Dan asked when Mudge set it on the table in the sitting room.

"I don't think so."

Dan put fifty cents in his hand. "I'd like you to go out to the stable with me after we've eaten. Can you have our horses ready at ten o'clock tonight if I show you our animals and gear?"

"Yes, sir."

Dan nodded. "Try not to let anyone see you going into the stable, either. If anyone who works here asks, tell them you're serving a guest, but don't give out our names."

"Yes, sir. I'll keep mum. No worry there."

"Good," Dan said. "When do you finish in the kitchen? I'll come down and go with you."

"I could slip out for a few minutes around half past eight, sir."

Mudge left the room, and Dan locked the door behind him.

Anne had set the sandwiches and cups out on the table near the window. She looked over at Dan. "We're putting an awful lot of faith in that young man."

"Yes, we are." Dan could only pray that their trust was not misplaced.

They gathered at the table and ate their meal. Ernie had included a plate of raisin tarts and a dish of sautéed apples. Afterward, Anne sat quietly on the sofa, mending one of David's socks, while the men settled the details of their escape.

"I expect Peterson knows what rooms we're in by now," David said.

"Just the same, it doesn't hurt to exercise caution." Dan sat and studied him, thinking. David's height and bearing made him difficult to mistake for anyone else, and once he started talking there was no question. "When we leave, you should go out separately from us. Maybe through the kitchen door. We could meet you a short distance away with the horses."

David frowned but nodded. "All right. Less chance of him getting on to our plan that way. You and Anne get the horses, and I'll meet you down at the junction."

"I think that would be best," Dan said. "Even if Peterson sees Anne and me leaving, he won't see you. But stay out of sight."

"I've learned to sneak through the shadows." David's wry smile lacked any mirth.

Dan glanced at Anne. "Is this plan acceptable to you?"

She nodded, but her face had paled. Dan wished he could reassure her that all would go well and they would soon be away from this place and safe. Together and safe.

They waited in the hotel suite with the drapes drawn through the afternoon. At first all was quiet, but David became restless again. He paced for a while, then sat down on a chair facing Dan.

"Adams, I've decided what I want to do."

"Tonight, sir?"

"No. In the future."

Anne gazed at him in dismay.

Before she could speak, Dan said, "And what is that, sir?"

"I want to start a stagecoach line from Eugene to Corvallis. Heaven knows we need one."

Dan nodded, considering the idea. "If one was in place, Anne and I could have gotten to your farm much quicker. I think it's an excellent idea."

"They're bringing the mail up from San Francisco overland," David said. "Why stop at Eugene? The roads need some improvement, and we'd need better ferries and a couple of stout bridges, but whoever had the mail contract could get money from Washington for those things."

Having seen the hazards of the route firsthand, Dan began to warm to the idea. "You could offer daily service between the two cities. Or at least three coaches a week each way."

"Excellent. We'd need a station halfway, where they could change horses, or possibly two swing stations. But one driver could easily make the full run."

"I wouldn't mind being a station agent," Dan said.

David blinked at him. "Wouldn't you? I thought you were set to grow wheat."

"My brother's more keen on it than I am." He tried to imagine what the station in Corvallis would be like — hustling whenever a coach came in, changing out the teams of horses, loading the mail and freight. The passengers would go in to eat dinner.

That stopped him cold. Who would cook dinner for the guests? Before he could check the thought, he imagined a small, dark-haired woman in an apron standing over an iron cookstove. She looked uncannily like Anne. He glanced over at her. Anne had stopped her darning and was watching him.

He smiled. Anne hadn't known the first thing about cooking, or even how to light a fire, a few months ago. But she had a quick mind, and he figured she could learn to cook for a crowd if she put her mind to it.

"What's funny?" David asked.

"Nothing, sir. Not funny exactly. I was just thinking how our perspective changes over time. I never thought about freighting or driving a stagecoach before, but I think I'd like to be involved in such a venture, especially on the organizational end. Buying horses and making sure things run smoothly down the line."

"You could do it," Anne said. She turned to her uncle, her face earnest. "Daniel has a good mind for seeing problems and finding the solution."

"Hmm. Well, I'm about done with placer mining, and I may decide to sell my farm, too. Or I could use it for the home station on the southern end of the line, though a place in town would probably be better. I wonder if there's a good spot available in Eugene. I'll have to talk to Skinner about it."

"But —" Anne frowned. "Won't you be going back to England, Uncle David?"

He sighed and burrowed down in his chair. "Haven't decided yet."

That surprised Dan. Stone could finance a stagecoach line here and go back to his position of wealth and power in England. He'd thought that much was a foregone conclusion. From what Anne had said, the estate must be large, with a sizable fortune entailed. Who would turn down such an opportunity?

The other side of the coin was the danger

such a position brought. Why would a man take on the responsibility if it meant others constantly tried to kill him?

"I'll admit I'm ignorant in such matters," he said, "but it seems to me that accepting this earldom would be dangerous to you, Mr. Stone."

David turned languid eyes upon him. "I doubt it would be more dangerous than what I'm enduring now."

"That's so," Anne said, taking another stitch. "Once you're established as the earl and settle down to run the estate and —"

"And marry suitably, thus providing a direct heir or two," David said drily. "Yes, becoming entrenched in British society is probably the best way to ensure my life if I decide to claim the peerage. But I can't help feeling I'd be much freer and happier if I simply said no."

Anne lowered her sewing and stared at him. "You couldn't. You wouldn't."

"I could, and I might. All it would take is a letter. And I might." He laughed at Anne's horrified expression. "Don't you see, my dear? If I stood before a judge and signed a letter saying I give up any claim to my brother's estate, no one would want to kill me. Cousin Randolph would inherit, and Peterson would leave me alone."

"How would Peterson know to do that?" Dan asked.

"I haven't figured that out yet. I suppose we could have a copy of the letter hand delivered to him, if we knew where to find him."

They sat in silence for a full minute.

"Please don't do it," Anne said at last. "I do value your life, Uncle David, and your liberty to do whatever you wish with your life. If you want to stay here and open a stagecoach line with Daniel, why, that would be wonderful. Yet I'd hate to see you make a hasty decision. Please think of all the people in England who depend upon Stoneford. And think of your cousin running the estate. I can't say I like that picture."

"Nor do I," David said. "He was always a selfish twit."

"I fear he hasn't changed much — and his wife! Always one to live beyond her income. Randolph and Merrileigh would run through the fortune in short order if their present spending is any indication. Then where would the tenants be?"

"And this is the man who's hired Peterson to kill you," Dan said. "This spineless, spendthrift cousin."

"So it seems," David said. "I can't think of anyone else with a motive. And it's like

456

Randolph to hire someone else to do the work for him. It's true I don't like to hand the estate over to him. It's not an easy choice."

"Then don't make it hastily," Anne said.

"How is this cousin paying Peterson?" Dan asked.

"Yes. He hasn't much spare money." Anne eyed the sock in her hand as though she detested it. "He must be giving Peterson a lot."

"Probably promised to pay out of the estate when he gets it, other than expenses," David said.

Dan shook his head at the waste, let alone the depravity of it. Imagine what an honest man could do with the money this cousin was spending to kill David. It boggled the mind.

Anne picked up her needle once more. "Well, I think you should take your time deciding what to do. And regardless of your decision, we should send a letter to the solicitor, telling him I've found you and that you are alive."

"So far," David said.

Anne frowned at that. "Please don't speak so. If we let Mr. Conrad know you are safe, I expect he will tell Cousin Randolph. Then perhaps Randolph will leave you alone."

"I doubt it," David replied. "For one thing, he has no speedy way to call off his hound."

"And if we found a way to prove your cousin's involvement," Dan said, "would he be disqualified from inheriting the estate? If so, who would be next in line?"

"A good question," David said.

"Randolph's son, I should think." Anne continued stitching, but she didn't seem at ease.

"He's got children, then?" David asked.

"Yes. Three of them — two boys and a girl."

"Well, he's far ahead of me in that, though he must be six or seven years younger."

"Spoiled and ill-mannered, the lot," Anne said.

David sighed. "I should have married sooner. Then you wouldn't have all this trouble I've caused you."

Anne clipped her threads and laid the scissors aside. "I rather hoped you had. Elise and I speculated on the wagon train whether we might find you settled and the father of several little Stones."

"There was a girl in Independence," David said with a faraway look in his eyes. "I thought she might be the one. But by the time I got around to asking if I could court

458

her, she was looking at someone else." He shook his head. "I didn't do so well at farming there, either. I'd done better as a shopkeeper. I sold out after a few years and got enough to stock three wagons full of merchandise to bring to Oregon."

"So that's why you left Independence." Anne's sympathetic gaze would have cheered most men, but David still looked sad.

"The only thing is, it's mighty hard to get a wagon heavily loaded over those mountains."

"Tell me about it," Anne said. "I sold a trunk of ball gowns in Independence."

"Really? That was indeed a sacrifice, my dear."

Dan smiled. "Wait until you hear about the fellow who told us you were buried out behind his house."

"What?" David arched his eyebrows.

"Oh yes, Herr Schwartz nearly had us convinced you'd died on the trail."

"Schwartz? I remember him."

"Well, Anne and Miss Finster saw through him," Dan said. "But your niece has undergone a great deal for you."

Anne reached over and patted Stone's arm. "I don't want you to feel you have to return to England, Uncle David, but at least inform the solicitor that you're alive. If you don't claim the estate and title within a few years, the crown might dispose of the property and appropriate the money."

"I suppose you're right." David's reluctance was obvious.

Dan stood. "I was thinking I'd make a quick trip to the mercantile for some extra ammunition. I could take a letter if you want to post one. It might be a good idea to have one on the way before we leave here."

"I agree," Anne said. "And I'll send one to Elise as well. I know we hope to see her in a few days, but if anything should delay us, at least she'll know our plans."

"Does she know you've found me?" David asked.

"Yes. I wrote while you were resting and recovering."

He nodded. "All right, I'll fetch some paper and write to Conrad. Heavens, he was old when I was a lad. He must be positively doddering now."

David rose and walked unsteadily to the desk, using the cane Dr. Muller had provided.

"May I help you, sir?" Dan asked.

David looked down at his arm, still swathed in a sling. "I believe I can write a few lines, but perhaps you'd best open the ink for me."

He sat at the desk for several minutes, scratching away with a pen. Anne borrowed a sheet of paper from him and composed a note to Elise. At last both missives were ready to post, and Dan put on his coat and prepared to leave for the post office.

"If you'd like anything from the store . . ."

Anne tilted her head to one side, sending highlights from the lantern glinting over her dark hair. "Rations for the ship, I suppose. Something we can carry and eat easily, without needing a fire. I've no idea if we'll be able to buy things like that when we reach the coast."

"Or have the time to do so before we sail." David reached in his pocket and took out a silver dollar, which he handed to Dan. "Get some jerky and ship's biscuit, if they have it."

Anne made a dour face. "I suppose that's practical."

"It's only for a short time, and only if we need it," David assured her.

"All right," Dan said, "and shall I inquire for your mail, sir?"

"Yes. Let me write a note to the postmaster, or chances are he won't give it to you."

Finally Dan set out, hoping the post office was still open. The sun had gone down, and the temperature had dipped. At least the sky was clear tonight.

The postmaster was coming out from behind his counter when Dan entered.

"Well, now, you just caught me," he said. "Adams, wasn't it?"

"Yes, and I have a note from Mr. Stone, asking you to give me his mail. He and his niece also entrusted two letters to me for mailing."

The postmaster scrutinized David's note and compared the writing to that on the letter addressed to Andrew Conrad, Esq., in Middlesex, England. He turned and dropped it into a box and placed Anne's letter in a mailbag. He scanned the rack of pigeonholes on the wall behind him.

"There's nothing here for Mr. Stone today. Anything else I can do for you, sir?"

"No, thank you. But we'll all be leaving Scottsburg tomorrow by the steamer, if anyone should ask."

"Ah, then I should forward any incoming mail for Mr. Stone to his home in Eugene?"

"That's correct."

Dan drew on his gloves and went out into the dusk. A flicker of movement at the corner of the building drew his eye. Had someone just ducked back into the shadows? The back of his neck prickled. He'd never been fanciful, and he didn't for an instant think he'd imagined it.

He turned and strode quickly toward the general store, where several lanterns burned brightly inside. If Peterson or his hirelings lurked about, Dan wouldn't give them a chance to work mischief tonight.

CHAPTER 26

Anne had a nap after Dan returned from the post office. He came and knocked on her door as promised when their supper was delivered from the kitchen. She freshened up quickly and was only half surprised to find Dan coming up the stairs when she opened the door to the hallway.

"Your uncle sent me down to settle the bill for all of us," he said.

"Oh." She tried to read his face. "That was kind of him."

"Extremely. He had me tell Mr. Reed we'll all leave in time to make the steamer in the morning."

Dan seemed uncomfortable with that statement. He'd probably worked hard to word it so that he wasn't lying about their departure time. She started to close her door.

"Want to bring your last bundles over to Mr. Stone's room?"

"All right." She went back in and placed her hairbrush and gloves in her bag and looked around to be sure she hadn't left anything. Dan leaned against the doorjamb, waiting. He smiled when she turned toward him.

"All set?"

"Yes." They went out, and she locked the door. "What should I do with the key?"

He held out his palm. "I'll slide it under the door on our way out. But not until then, in case you want to go back in for something."

"Daniel, you've been so good to me and Uncle David. I'm sorry for the discomfort we've caused you."

"Think nothing of it. If I can just deliver you safely to Eb Bentley's house, I'll be satisfied."

His tone brought a wave of regret, and she touched his sleeve. "Satisfied, but not happy?"

He started to speak but shook his head slightly. "Come. Let's eat, and I'll take the last of the bags down. Mudge will be coming before long for instructions. I'll show him exactly where our stuff is in the stable, and we'll pack all of your uncle's gear and our extra baggage on the pack saddle."

"I'm so glad you were able to find a mule

for his things," Anne said as they walked down the hall toward David's room.

Dan grimaced. "I traded his sluice box and other mining gear toward the price of the pack mule. I just hope I didn't attract too much attention doing it."

"Peterson, you mean?"

"Yes. Something tells me that man doesn't miss much. If he sees we've bought an extra mule, he'll figure out that we're not sailing from here on that little steamer."

"I hope not. And we'll be much more comfortable without having all our bundles hanging about us on the horses."

They reached Uncle David's room, and Dan looked back toward the stairway then knocked on the door. A moment later it opened.

"Everything's ready," David said. "Past ready — getting cold."

"I'm sorry," Anne said. "I should have moved a little faster."

"Forgive me." David bowed his head in contrition. "I'm afraid I left some of my manners at Stoneford."

They sat down to eat. Ernie had sent his best, in Anne's opinion. The cook had shown himself a true friend to her uncle. The roast beef, baked potatoes, corn, and squash went down well. She'd asked for tea, and it was there in a silver teapot. Dan drank it with them, though she knew he preferred coffee.

He smiled when she handed it to him, already laced with milk and a little sugar. For a moment she wished they were in England, in the parlor at Stoneford — but the image of Dan calling there at tea time didn't fit. How many times last summer had she put a tin cup of coffee in his hand at the end of a long day on the trail? That was Dan, not high tea and evening dress for dinner.

Or was it? She'd seen Uncle David in both worlds now, and he seemed as much at home here, in the raw West, as he had been in England. Perhaps Dan could straddle both comfortably, too. Did she want that? The idea startled her. She'd spent many hours mulling the possibility of staying in America. Always she knew she didn't fit in his farming future. But Dan in England? He might blend in very well. But he'd probably disdain the wealthy people she'd always associated with and befriend the tradesmen and village folk. Her old friends wouldn't abide it and would cut her cold. What was the use of thinking about it?

They talked quietly through the evening, and it seemed to Anne that the two men had their stagecoach line planned, almost down to the last horseshoe nail. She tried not to take it too seriously, yet her fears strengthened as she listened. David might actually do it — and never leave Oregon.

Mudge came on time, and he and Dan went to the stable for half an hour. Shortly after Dan returned, Ernie came to get the tray.

"I thought you'd have gone home by now," David said.

"I should've. We had a lot of folks in for dinner tonight, but I wanted to say good-bye, sir. It's been a pleasure serving you and your friends." Ernie nodded at Anne and Dan.

"You've been very helpful," Anne said, "and tonight's dinner was wonderful."

Dan murmured his thanks, and David stood and shook the cook's hand.

Ernie picked up the laden tray and rested one edge on his shoulder. David walked with him to the door.

Ernie paused and looked back at Dan. "Mudge says he'll do everything just the way you said, sir."

Dan nodded. "Thanks. We appreciate it."

David let Ernie out and secured the door then checked his pocket watch. "Well, another hour."

"Yes." Dan fell silent. Everything had been said. If they could only get away clean . . . but speaking of it would make Anne anxious, so he said nothing.

"About that stagecoach line," David said, ambling to his chair.

"Yes, sir." Dan sat a little straighter.

Anne caught her breath. Here it was again. Her uncle was obsessed with the idea.

"Whether I go to England or not, I think it would be a good investment. Now, I figure I've got to stay here over the winter anyway. Don't want to sail this time of year, and the overland route is impassable now."

"Well, yes," Anne conceded. "I thought I'd stay with Elise, or —" She looked hesitantly at David.

"You can stay at the farm in Eugene with me, if you like. Or I could winter in Corvallis. Let's see what the wind brings when we get up there, shall we?"

"Of course," she said.

He turned back to Daniel. "But we could get a lot of things in place this winter. I want to talk to someone in Oregon City about this. I'm pretty sure the mail coach only goes as far as Corvallis right now, but if we had a plan ready for taking it the length of Oregon, why, I think we'd have a good chance of getting a contract."

They talked on for the next hour. Dan had an idea how much livestock would cost, and David, having run several stores, could figure fairly close on harness, grain, building supplies, and other commodities that a stage line would need.

"It's certainly doable," David said. "And I think I can sell my mining claim. That would give us some working capital."

Anne noted he'd said "us," linking himself to Daniel. Uncle David seemed serious about the venture, but what role would Dan play? Would he be a hired station agent, or would her uncle make him a partner? Dan wouldn't have nearly as much money to invest. But he looked utterly content, discussing the business as if it were a fact.

He gazed over at Anne, and her heart fluttered. Ever since that night in the hills, when he'd lectured and bullied her, she'd sensed a change in her feelings toward Dan. They hadn't talked about it, but he'd saved her life — no question about it. And he'd called her "dearest Anne" in the tenderest, most endearing way. She would never forget it.

Yet since then, they'd ignored what had passed between them. They'd rarely been alone, it was true — first with Whitey's presence and then Uncle David's, but still . . .

She could not deny that she was closer to loving Dan than ever before. His friendship went deeper now. He'd seen her at her worst.

Did he still dream of marrying her? Why would he, when she'd told him no so many times? She wondered what she would say if he gathered his courage and asked her again. But maybe he was past wanting her now. Had she annihilated his love up there in the hills?

He'd kept his politeness since then, and he'd always been quiet. On the wagon train, she'd caught him staring at her several times with a moon-calfed, lovesick gaze. She hadn't seen that in a long time. Did that mean he was over his infatuation with her? Or had it solidified into something else? Part of her hoped it had, and part of her was repelled by the thought. It would only be harder to return to England if his love was the deep, true, forever kind. Last summer, she'd taken his admiration for a boyish crush and thought he'd be over it by winter. But if he knew the real thing, did she really want it to pass?

He smiled and looked away — back to her uncle. Anne took a shaky breath.

"It must be time for Anne and me to go out," he said.

David extracted his pocket watch and opened it. "Ten o'clock. Go then. I'll see you in ten minutes at the junction."

They all stood. Anne stepped toward David, suddenly loathe to part from him.

"Uncle David —"

"It's going to be fine," he said. "And I'll be careful."

She smiled. Even though they'd been apart so long, he knew her thoughts.

"You're very like your grandmother," he said.

Anne barely remembered her grandmother, the countess before her mother. "I like that," she said. "Please tell me more about her next time we're at leisure."

"I shall." He stooped and kissed her cheek.

Anne went to the table near the door and retrieved the bonnet that matched her riding habit. She put it on while Dan and David shook hands and Dan put his coat on. He came over and held her cape for her.

"Good-bye, Uncle David," she said.

"Godspeed."

David waited until they had gone down the back stairs. They would sneak out and make their way to the stable, trying to avoid being seen by any other patrons or the hotel staff. Three minutes found the limit of his patience. He put on his wool jacket. Anne had mended the tear where the bullet had pierced it, and he could barely tell where the rift had been. Bless her heart, he hoped she didn't get killed for coming to find him.

He clapped his hat on, turned out the lamp, and grabbed the last bag — his small crocodile leather kit of personal items. He still wondered what had become of his Bible and his onyx cuff links. Probably the chambermaid had taken a fancy to the cuff links, but a Bible seemed an odd choice for a thief.

In the hall, he locked the door and slid his key beneath it. The Miner's Hotel had been mostly good to him. If he ever came to Scottsburg again, he'd probably stay here. He flitted quickly down the carpeted corridor to the back stairway door. As he opened it, a door farther down the hall opened. No time for indecision. He ducked into the stairway and pulled the door closed behind him, taking care to do so quietly.

The stairway was pitch-dark. He ought to have brought a lantern or a candle. Had Anne and Adams gone down here without a light? He found the railing and clung to it. His heart pounded as he felt his way, step by step, down the narrow staircase. It curved near the bottom and apparently had a few triangular treads. He nearly plunged downward before he realized it, but he caught himself on the railing and managed to reposition his feet in time.

After the turn, he could see a sliver of light shining through the crack at the bottom of a door. Why hadn't Ernie or Adams or someone warned him about this treacherous avenue of escape?

At last he felt the door panels and fumbled for a knob. Instead he found a thumb latch. It lifted, and light bathed him. He squinted and took a moment to orient himself. It was a pale light really, coming from the next room — the dining room, he supposed. He was in a large kitchen and could make out the bulk of a cookstove, tables, and cupboards.

He edged toward what he assumed was the back wall and slammed into the corner of a table. He sucked in a breath and gritted his teeth. Why on earth hadn't he come down when Anne and Adams did, or asked Ernie to show him the way out?

At last he found the back door. Adams had left it unlocked. A fine mist was falling outside. Next summer it would be bone-dry and hotter than a griddle, but for the next few months, this chilly rain would stay with them. He shivered and turned up his collar.

He was tempted to walk around the hotel

and look toward the stable to see if they were in there. But he'd promised to go straight to the rendezvous, so he ambled out to the edge of the street and stood for a moment, looking all about. Far down the road, near the smithy, a couple of people were walking, but they were headed the other way. David turned to his right and kept to the shadows of the buildings as he worked his way to the meeting place.

A narrow alley ran between a boarding-house and a feed store. He slid into it and leaned against the wall of the feed store. He could see the junction, and there didn't seem to be a better spot to wait where he couldn't be seen from a distance. He folded his arms and slumped against the log wall. He could hear the river in the distance, soft but insistent. An occasional voice called out indistinguishable words, and a couple of dogs traded noncommittal barks. An owl flew overhead, so low he heard its wings flap, and he shivered. This was the sort of place where that thug would gladly kill him. Was he a straight-out idiot to come out here alone?

He looked up at the sky. Still cloudy, and black as the inside of a hat.

"Lord," he said softly, "I sincerely hope we know what we're doing. Seems to me we maybe ought to have prayed about this plan before we settled on it. Something doesn't feel right."

Anne waited while Daniel opened the door to the stable. It creaked so loudly she was sure everyone in the hotel could hear it.

"Let me light a lantern," Dan whispered. "They have one hanging just inside the door here."

He stepped inside, and Anne paused, holding the door open to give him a little light, though that was meager. The moon was either hidden by clouds or not yet risen. She hadn't kept track of it since they'd gotten to Scottsburg. Dan probably had — didn't farmers always know the phase of the moon and when it would rise, the way sailors and fishermen knew the tides?

He rummaged about, and soft pats and rustles came to her. A horse nickered. At last Dan scratched a lucifer, and the flame spurted. He lit the lantern and adjusted it. Anne squinted and looked away from the glare. After a few seconds she could see the inside of the barn, and she moved inside and shut the door behind her.

"You get Bailey and Captain," Dan said. "I'll get Star and the mule."

Anne could see all four animals, tied in

straight stalls on the right. Their hindquarters and flowing tails showed, all in a row. The last one's tail didn't flow, however. It was scruffy and short. The mule, no doubt.

She walked into the stall with Bailey first. The chestnut gelding greeted her with a soft neigh. Her sidesaddle was in place. She patted his neck and shoulder.

"Hello, boy," she murmured, raising the saddle skirt so she could check the girth. She tightened it then fumbled for the fastener on the short chain that held him. "Are you ready for a midnight ride?" She got the snap off his halter and let the chain fall. Putting one hand on Bailey's nose, she backed him slowly from the stall.

"Is there a place to hitch him?"

Dan, in the next stall with his bright pinto, looked around and pointed. "There's a ring in that beam."

On the other side of the center aisle, iron rings were mounted in the thick, square, upright posts that supported the roof. Anne led Bailey to the nearest one. She had no lead rope on him. Mudge had put his bridle on over the halter so that he could leave the horse bridled but hitched up in the stall. She looped Bailey's reins through the ring and went across the aisle to get Captain.

As she entered the stall, the horse shifted

and snorted.

"Easy," Anne said. Dan was taking Star out of the stall next to Captain's. "What's the matter, boy?" The bay gelding moved over as far as he could away from her.

Something else moved, near the horse's head, and Anne jumped back with a gasp. She was not alone in the stall with Captain.

"What — ?"

A firm hand closed about her wrist and jerked her forward, toward Captain's head. The horse squealed and strained against his chain, trying to get away from them.

"Daniel," she screamed.

A man hauled her close to him and clamped a hand over her mouth.

"Hush," he hissed in her ear. Her heart hammered. The man pulled her closer, an unyielding arm about her waist, until her body pressed against his. Horrified, she struggled. The hand that had silenced her released her, but he reclaimed her wrist and twisted it.

"Let me go," she gasped.

Another voice stilled her struggles.

"Put your hands up, Mr. Adams." She jerked her head around. Dan had dropped Star's reins and was halfway between his pinto and her position. He stood stock-still now, staring at her with a tortured expression on his face as he slowly raised his hands above his shoulders.

Two paces behind him stood a young man with a revolver pointed at Dan's back.

Anne's heart plummeted. "Mudge."

"Quickly," the man behind Anne called. "Tie him up, and make it tight."

It had to be Peterson, Dan decided, though the man was hidden in the shadows. Captain snorted and pulled against his halter chain. The man shoved Anne out past the horse, and Dan saw him clearly at last. Peterson held Anne before him with his right arm, and in his left hand, held to the side of Anne's slender neck, was a long-barreled pistol. Her lovely face was a stark white, and her dark eyes loomed huge and pleading.

Peterson turned sideways and aimed squarely at him. "Snap it up."

"Let her go," Dan said.

Peterson laughed.

"Please." Dan held the man's malevolent glare. "I'll do whatever you say. Just keep Miss Stone out of this."

"That's rich," Mudge said as he patted Dan's coat. He found his revolver right away and removed it. "Gimme your wrists. Put 'em behind you." As soon as Dan complied,

Mudge began wrapping them with some type of cord or light rope.

"She has nothing to do with this," Dan said, never looking away from Peterson's stare.

"She has more to do with it than you do." His lips curled and the mustache twitched as he spoke. "Somehow I don't think her uncle would run as quickly to rescue you as he would his darling little niece."

Dan thought for a moment his heart had just plain stopped, but it kicked and raced on, faster now. Peterson would use Anne as bait — he should have foreseen that. And where did that leave him? Most likely shot and dumped in the river.

"Where is Stone?" Peterson asked.

Dan eyed him in silence.

Peterson tightened his hold on Anne and ran the muzzle of the pistol up to her ear. "Tell me where he is."

Dan tried to swallow the boulder in his throat. *He won't kill Anne,* he told himself. *He needs her to get David in here.* But he didn't dare trust that instinct completely.

"We left him in his room," Anne said.

Dan wanted to applaud her. He gave Peterson a grim nod. "He won't come down until we give him the signal."

"And what's the signal, dear friends?"

Anne stared at Dan, panic in her dark eyes. Silently she pled with him, and Dan read the message as clearly as if she had it painted on her forehead. *Don't betray my uncle. If one of us has to die, let it be me, not the earl of Stoneford.*

"We're to take the horses out front," Dan said, amazed at how steady his voice sounded.

"Watching from his window, I suppose," Peterson said. "When he sees the horses out by the hitching rail, he'll come down."

Dan said nothing. It was as good an assumption as any — and it would get them out of the stable at least. David should be well away from the hotel by now, but maybe if they got outside, they could attract the attention of Mr. Reed or the desk clerk — even one of the other guests.

"No, that's not right," Mudge said.

Dan could have kicked himself. Mudge had heard the whole plan. Or had he? If he knew they were meeting David at the junction, why hadn't he told Peterson?

"They were talking about meeting someplace."

Peterson scowled. "Tie his feet, too."

"Sit down, Mr. Adams," Mudge said.

Dan sat on the dirt floor, and Mudge found a short piece of rope. He looped it around Dan's ankles, but the rope went over his boot tops, so it didn't feel too tight. His hands, however, had been bound in an uncomfortable position, and he was beginning to lose feeling in the fingers of his left hand.

"Are you fond of that young man?" Peterson asked in a dangerous voice, so low Dan barely heard the words.

Anne choked out a yes.

"I assumed as much. I'm sure you'd hate to see him suffer."

"What do you want?" she asked.

"Only a chance to talk to your uncle in private."

Anne grimaced but said nothing.

"Now, Mudge is going to take a couple of these horses out in front of the hotel," Peterson continued. "When your uncle comes down and sees him, Mudge will tell him there's a little holdup and some of the gear needed to be repacked. And Mr. Stone will come out here where I can talk to him. And you — you just be ready to greet him as though everything is going forward, you understand?"

"N–no," Anne said.

Peterson sighed. "And I thought you were an intelligent young woman."

"Anne, don't listen to him," Dan said.

Peterson turned his head and glared at him. "Gag him."

"Yes, sir." Mudge looked around stupidly and patted his pockets. A moment later he knelt and stretched a sweaty-smelling bandanna across Dan's mouth.

"Open."

"You want to kill me? I won't be able to breathe."

"Not sure it matters," Mudge said.

Aghast at his apathy, Dan said, "How could you —"

Mudge slid the cloth between his teeth and pulled it tighter.

Dan gave up and tried to keep from retching while his captor secured the knot. When Mudge had finished, he shoved Dan down on his side.

"Drag him into that last stall," Peterson called.

As Mudge took hold of his boots and jerked him over the dirt floor, Dan caught sight of his revolver, lying against the divider between two empty stalls.

He could only be thankful that the last stall on this side was used as a tool room. A feed bin and a couple of barrels stood on the straw-strewn floor. Saddles, harness, and small tools hung on nails, and a shovel, a pitchfork, and a dung fork leaned against the outside wall. He couldn't see Anne or Peterson from the position Mudge left him in. The pungent earth and musty straw smells mingled with the scent of the filthy rag in his mouth and heady whiffs of manure and leather.

"Take those two," he heard Peterson say, and a moment later, hooves clumped on the dirt floor. The big front door was rolled open, and a wave of colder air swept through the stable. Horses shuffled, and the door moved again on its metal rollers; then the barn fell still.

What was Peterson doing now? Did he still hold Ann against him, with the pistol touching her head? Dan was consumed with anger and the need to see them, to know Anne was all right. Another question ate at him. Had Mudge picked up his gun, or did it still lie there in the straw a few feet away?

They waited without talking for what seemed eternity.

The drizzle let up, but that was small comfort to David. What was taking them so long? He'd expected them to be along by now. He pulled out his watch, but there wasn't enough light to read it. He shoved it back in his pocket and patted the Colt revolver in his coat pocket.

"Come on, Anne. Where are you?"

He ought to have gone with them. This slinking in the shadows didn't suit him. Even as he considered jogging down the street to the hotel, he remembered the night he was shot. Sometimes clinging to the shadows was best.

His new resolve to wait patiently lasted all of two minutes. Something was wrong. It had to be! He tiptoed out of the alley and huddled behind the steps to the feed store, peering down the street. He couldn't tell exactly where the hotel lay, but he suspected the highest roofline he could make out belonged to it. Maybe it was time to take a risk.

Hauling in a deep breath, he rose and scrambled around the steps, trying to run stealthily. He was getting a bit old for this sort of thing. Hurrying past two more closed businesses, he flattened himself against a jutting front porch. Only one more building between him and the Miner's Hotel. Lamps gleamed in several of its first- and second-story windows. The third floor, where he'd stayed, was dark.

Leisurely hoofbeats clopped on packed earth. Were they leaving the stable yard at last? David squinted into the darkness and made out two horses. They passed through a square of lamplight cast from a window casement. The first horse had a rider; the second bore an empty saddle. David waited. The rider didn't look quite right for Dan. And where had Anne gotten to?

The rider stopped near the hitching rail and gazed upward, toward the hotel's top-floor windows. What was he looking at? David followed the fellow's line of sight upward, but the rooms on the third story were still dark.

It hit him suddenly, as though a steer had kicked him. The man was watching his window. Dan wouldn't do that. Dan knew he was waiting at the junction — or should be. David's hand crept toward his revolver, though why he wasn't sure.

Who was that man? It couldn't be Peterson. This one slouched in the saddle. Peterson might be a rogue, but sloppy he was not. Impeccably dressed, well groomed, and superior in posture, from all David had learned about him. Quite the gentleman, until one got to know him better.

The rider slid to the ground and walked quietly up the hotel's front steps. Something about him made David tense. It was Mudge, the kitchen lad. Why was he out front with two horses? Something had gone awry.

David drew his revolver and slipped from

his hiding place to the edge of the hotel's porch. All was quiet. He bent low and slunk over to the horses. Captain whickered softly.

"Hello, old man." David ran a hand along the bay gelding's flank. "What's going on, eh?"

Hitched to the saddle by a long lead rope was Anne's horse, but Anne was nowhere to be found. And what about Adams and his paint horse? David eyed the closed door to the hotel lobby. Had they gone back inside? One thing seemed likely — Adams's horse and the pack mule were still in the stable out back. David tiptoed to the corner of the building and peeked around it. Light from a lantern shone through a narrow opening at the stable door.

"Sit there." Peterson gestured with his pistol toward a keg near the door of the stable.

Anne walked toward it slowly. The big, rolling door was nearly shut. She couldn't possibly open it and get out before he would catch her — assuming he would scruple to shoot at her. Not knowing what else she could do, she went to the keg, sat down, and arranged the skirts of her riding habit.

"Do I need to tie you up?" Peterson asked.

She frowned up at him. "What do you mean?"

"I mean, will you try to escape if I don't?"

"Of course."

He sighed and looked about for rope. She almost laughed at the ease with which she'd distracted him. Unfortunately, his search took him between her and the door.

"This will do. Hold out your hands." He came closer, carrying a short length of manila rope.

She raised her hands in front of her. He didn't force her to put them behind her, so she didn't protest. He pulled the rope tight enough that she winced and tied the knot a couple of inches above her wrists. She wouldn't be able to reach the short ends. Now she'd be helpless if Uncle David needed her.

Peterson planned to kill him — she had no doubt about that. And what would become of her and Dan afterward? Surely he wouldn't just turn them loose to testify against him. Maybe he didn't want to kill them all here in the barn. It would be easier to dispose of them if he took them all away from the hotel.

Would he really kill three people to ensure that David never claimed the peerage?

She shivered.

Peterson stood near the crack in the door, not two feet from her, peering out toward the hotel. She gazed along the length of the stable. Star was still tied in the center alley, where Mudge had tied him up before he left, and the pack mule remained in his stall. The butt of Dan's rifle stuck up out of the scabbard. If she could reach it . . . but would that do any good? She seemed to recall that the gun wouldn't fire until a cap was applied to the action or some such thing. She should have paid more attention when her father hosted shooting parties.

She'd heard nothing from Dan since Mudge had dragged him out of sight. Was he all right? Maybe Mudge had bludgeoned him before he left.

She swiveled her head and eyed Peterson again. He was still looking out the doorway. She measured the distance to the horse with her eye. How long would it take her to run the five or six yards?

"Don't even think about it," Peterson said drily.

She swallowed hard. The beast couldn't really read her mind, but he'd like her to think that. He probably thought she was considering braining him with something. But what? Nothing small and solid enough was within reach.

Again she gazed longingly at Star. The pinto snuffled and strained against his lead rope. He couldn't quite reach the straw on the floor.

Between the horse's feet, Anne glimpsed the sheen of lantern light on metal.

David kept to the back wall of the hotel as much as he could, tiptoeing around a pile of firewood and a two-wheeled cart. The stable loomed ten yards away, and the soft lantern light still spilled out the crack at the front door. Someone was in there, probably Adams and Anne, but he had to be sure. He crouched over and ran to a haystack near the barn. For a full minute, he stood still, waiting for his breathing to slow and listening. All he heard from within was a horse's occasional stamp.

The clouds overhead parted, letting the moon peek through for a few seconds. He took a good look around the yard, then hustled toward the rear of the stable. He'd just spotted a back door when the clouds drifted over the moon again. If only it wasn't locked.

The thumb latch clicked, and David froze. Even a sound that small might carry to his enemy. He tried pushing, with no success, and pulled instead. The door moved reluctantly toward him. An odd sound caught his attention — a pulley? He realized the door had a weight attached, so that when a person let go, the weight would fall and the door would close itself. No curious horses would accidentally get out the back door.

He held it open about three inches and peered inside. The glow from the lantern at the front of the stable barely reached back here. Was he looking into a back room or tool shed? Another few seconds of scrutiny told him he was looking into an end stall used as a feed room. David listened but again heard nothing out of the ordinary — which in itself was odd. Shouldn't Anne and Adams be talking as they prepared to leave? Shouldn't he hear them moving the gear or leading out the mule and Adams's horse?

He moved the door outward a couple more inches. It creaked softly, and the rope on the pulley moved. He held his breath. Nothing else seemed to change.

Slowly, he eased the door open a bit more, until the gap was wide enough for him to squeeze through. With agonizing slowness, he let it come back to the frame with the thumb latch depressed. He kept the fingers of his other hand against the jamb at the risk of smashing them, to be sure there was no sudden *thunk* when the door moved into place. He let go of the thumb latch and exhaled.

For a long moment he stood in silence, letting his eyes adjust and trying to determine what was around him and how best to proceed. The glow came from ahead and to his left, where it seemed a wall stuck out, shielding him from view of anyone in the stable. He stepped forward gingerly, feeling for obstacles on the floor with his feet. When he reached the edge of the divider wall, he eased forward and took a quick look, then dodged back.

Midway down the barn aisle, Dan Adams's horse was tethered, saddled, and ready to go. So why hadn't Dan left yet? David had received a hazy impression of a man standing by the door at the front of the barn, with his back turned to the stable. He pulled in a breath and held it, then looked around the wall again.

The man's build was too slight for Adams, and he wore a neat, town-gent's suit. Peterson. The scoundrel moved his head, and David swiftly drew back behind the board wall. Where was Anne? Had the blackguard hurt her?

A soft noise reached him from immediately on the other side of the flimsy wall. There must be a horse in the stall behind it.

David bent his knees and searched for a crack through which he could spy on Peterson, but the only one he found didn't give him a view of the far reaches of the building. He was mulling whether or not to risk peeking around the edge again when he heard the man say, "Stand up." Cautiously he peered around the divider.

Peterson moved to the right of the big door and returned a moment later, holding Anne by one arm. Her hands were bound in front of her. Peterson spoke to her, but David couldn't make out the words.

Behind him he heard a soft grunt — or more like a muffled groan. He turned and squinted into the inkiness of the stall. A barrel, the long handle of a tool, a dark bundle on the floor. He went over and felt the dark lump cautiously. A boot. A leg. A man.

"Adams?" he whispered.

Another soft grunt. David patted along the figure gently until he reached the man's head. A gag was tied in his mouth. He helped the poor fellow sit up and fumbled in the darkness until the cloth fell away.

"He's got Anne," Adams croaked out in a whisper.

"I saw," David replied. "What should we do?"

"Untie me. Do you have your gun?"

"Yes."

"Give it to me," Adams said. "If you go

out there, he'll kill you."

"Oh, and he'll welcome you like a long-lost chum."

Adams sighed. "What, then?"

David fingered the knots in the twine that held Adams and gave up. He pulled out his pocketknife. "Hold still." A moment later he'd sliced through the twine. Adams's hands fell to the floor with a quiet thump. They both stopped breathing.

After a moment's silence, David whispered near his ear, "We need to hurry. I saw Mudge going into the hotel." He pressed the pocketknife into Adams's hand.

"He was going in?" Adams began to saw at the cord around his ankles. "We told him you would meet us out front if we took the horses out there."

"Mudge must have got tired of waiting for me."

"All right, I'll go out the way you came in and see if I can keep Mudge away. You wait here and see if you can get the drop on Peterson."

David couldn't think of a better plan. "Has he hurt Anne?"

"No, she's the bait."

Adams crept on all fours to the board wall and peeked around it. He rose to a crouch and ducked toward the back door. David wished he'd warned him about the weight and the noisy door, but it was too late. He winced and waited, pointing his revolver toward the opening of the stall.

Adams had apparently paid attention when he heard David enter; he opened the door slowly and almost silently. When he'd disappeared through it and let it come gently back into place, David let out his breath.

The paint horse shifted around so that he stood sideways across the aisle, and David couldn't see Peterson well — only his feet and a bit of Anne's dark skirt showed under the horse's belly. Hoping the horse would also hide him from their view, David crept forward and across the center alley to the divider near the pack mule's stall. He flattened himself against the low wall. When he stole another look, Peterson still held Anne. Maybe he'd attribute any sounds behind him to the animals.

David checked his revolver. He wouldn't dare use it unless he had a point-blank shot. Otherwise, he might hit Anne. But he was sure Peterson wouldn't hesitate to fire on him.

He peered around the divider again. Peterson was rolling the door back. When it was open about eighteen inches, he stopped.

"Where is he?" he called.

David shrank back behind the wall again, certain the "he" Peterson inquired about was himself. If the assassin knew he crouched a few yards behind him, he'd sing a different tune. But now his accomplice must have returned. Mudge. They never should have trusted that boy. Ernie had proven himself, but the kid only saw the money he was promised.

And where was Dan Adams?

Anne flinched when she heard quick footsteps on the driveway. Peterson's breath tickled her neck as he stared out into the darkness, and she shuddered.

He shoved her aside suddenly and rolled the door open wider. Mudge must be back; he wouldn't give Uncle David such an open reception.

"Where is he?" Peterson called.

"Beats me," came Mudge's reply from outside.

Anne glanced down at her bound wrists. Was this the time for her to attempt a move?

Peterson leaned toward the doorway and let his hand, and the pistol, dangle at his side as he listened to Mudge.

"I went up to his room," Mudge began,

and Anne took quick stock of Star's position.

The pinto was broadside in the aisle now, his head drooping as though he dozed. She pulled in a deep breath and ran.

"Hey!" Peterson cried.

She didn't look back, but grabbed as much of her heavy skirt as she could, hiked it up, and flung herself under the startled horse's belly. Star grunted and shuffled his feet. Anne ducked her head and rolled on the dirt floor in a swirl of skirts, right underneath the pinto and out beyond him. Star whinnied and pranced, pulling the lead rope taut. Anne crawled on her knees and elbows and at last grasped the prize.

She turned awkwardly and rose to her knees with Dan's revolver clutched in both hands. Movement to her left caught her eye, and she flicked a glance toward the mule's stall. Her throat tightened when she saw her uncle crouching behind the wall that separated it from the adjoining empty stall.

Dan could see them both talking in the shaft of light from the barn doorway. Mudge was giving a cursory account of his search for David Stone. When Peterson jerked around and yelled, he knew the game was over.

Dan used the only weapon he had — a

stick of firewood he'd snatched up on his stealthy trip around the barn. He ran from the corner of the stable to the partly open door and swung at Mudge's droopy hat. The young man took a step into the opening as Dan delivered the blow, so it landed with less force than he'd intended and glanced off. At first he thought it had done no good, but Mudge paused for a moment then dropped like a stone in the doorway.

Dan looked over him. Star gave a shrill whinny. The lantern hung near the door, and its light showed Star, his white markings prominent, still tied in the middle of the barn, but backing and pulling against the rope. Between him and the horse, Peterson stood with his back to Dan, his pistol raised and pointing toward Star. Dan's throat went dry as he scanned the stall openings and brought his gaze rapidly back to Peterson. The killer took a step away from him, heedless of Dan's presence.

Stooping over Mudge's body, Dan grabbed the young man's belt and rolled him over. As he'd hoped, a pistol was stuck in the front of the belt. Dan grabbed the butt and worked the gun out of Mudge's clothing, praying Peterson wouldn't look back.

"All right, Miss Stone," Peterson said in a

voice like granite. "You're too old to play hide-and-seek. I see your dress plainly. Now come on out."

Dan swallowed hard. He was after Anne, not her uncle. Perhaps he still had no inkling that David was in the stable.

Peterson walked forward, leading with his pistol, until he was next to Star. He patted the trembling horse's flank behind the saddle and pushed Star's hindquarters aside.

"Come now, Miss —"

Peterson broke off as David rose from behind a stall divider to his right. He swung toward the Englishman. Dan aimed instinctively and pulled the trigger, getting only a faint *click.*

He wasted only a fraction of a second absorbing the fact that Mudge's pistol either wasn't loaded or had misfired. In that moment, Peterson swung his gun to point directly at David.

"Well, Stone, so you came to me after all." The two men stood for an instant with their weapons poised.

Dan pulled the trigger again. It clicked, and he threw it to the floor.

Peterson caught his movement or the sound and looked toward him at last. The hesitation was enough of a distraction. Dan dove toward him, hoping he could take Peterson down before he gathered his wits and fired.

But instead of aiming at Dan, Peterson whipped back toward David and pulled the trigger. Dan slammed into him as another gun discharged, and they both fell to the floor. Star squealed and sidestepped.

Peterson wasn't moving. Slowly, Dan pushed himself up to his knees. Peterson lay on his back, staring at the ceiling. He sucked in a breath, his face contorting. Blood soaked his shirt and coat, the stain growing as Dan watched. He leaned down and grabbed the shirt fabric and yanked, ripping the buttons out. The massive wound was too great. Dan clamped his teeth together.

Peterson's eyes sought his. "It's bad."

Dan nodded.

"I would have got him."

"Yes."

Peterson gritted his teeth and moaned.

David straightened and came from the shadows to stand beside Dan and gaze down at his enemy.

"We'll tell Stone's cousin you failed," Dan said grimly, looking down at the dying man.

"Cousin?" Confusion clouded Peterson's gaze.

"Randolph Stone."

"I . . . don't know . . ."

"The person who hired you. Randolph Stone." Dan couldn't keep the anger out of his voice, and he hated that. This man still had power over him, even now.

"No." Peterson pulled in another breath. "That's not . . ." He went limp, staring sightlessly. Dan stared down at him for a moment, his mind whirling. He rose and looked over at Anne. She huddled on the floor close to Star, holding his revolver, her face set in shock.

"Anne, you all right?" David called. He nodded to Dan. "See to her." He knelt beside Peterson and put his hand to the man's throat.

Dan hurried to Anne and knelt beside her. "Anne, dearest, are you all right?"

She looked up at him with stricken eyes. Very carefully she held out the revolver. Dan started to take it by the barrel, but drew back when he felt its heat. Carefully he took it from her by the butt and placed it on the floor.

With tears swimming in her eyes, she held out her arms to him. Dan pulled her close and held her. For as long as she would let him, he would stay there with her, with his arms around her. She didn't cry, but her breath came in quick jerks. Dan rubbed her back slowly.

"It's all right, darling." He kissed her temple and folded her against his chest.

After what seemed like a year, and at the same time the flicker of an eye, David came over and stood in front of them, his feet planted a foot apart, hands on his hips.

"Is she all right?"

Dan nodded, though he was sure that on some levels Anne was far from fine.

"Good. I've tied up Mudge."

"Peterson?" Dan asked, but he knew.

David shook his head. "We'll need to get the constable. I suppose it's safe for me to show myself outside now."

"I'll go," Dan said.

"No. Stay here with her."

"You don't know where Owens lives."

"Tell me," David said.

Anne gave a little sob, and Dan patted her shoulders while he described the house to David. "It's not far. I think it's the third one past the smithy, and set back from the road. Clapboards, but no paint."

"I'll be back in a few minutes. If Mudge wakes up, let him rant. But do not untie him. You hear me?"

"I hear you," Dan said.

"Do you want to reload before I leave?"

David touched the revolver with his boot toe.

Reluctantly, Dan stirred. He'd be foolish to sit here with Anne, a dead man, and a trussed-up thug without loading his gun.

"I'll do it," David said, stooping to pick it up. "You got what I need in your saddlebags?"

"Yes."

David walked to Star's side. He was surprisingly efficient and brought Dan's revolver back a couple of minutes later. He rested his hand on Anne's head for a moment. "I'll be back, my dear."

"Thank you," she choked out.

Dan looked up at him. "Take Star. I know it's not far, but it'll be quicker if you ride."

"All right." David stepped over Peterson's legs and untied Star. He led him to the door and carefully maneuvered him around Mudge's prone form. He shoved the big door farther open and led out the pinto. A moment later the door closed, all the way this time.

Dan sighed and settled more comfortably on the floor. Anne nestled into his embrace.

"Daniel?"

"Yes?"

"I killed him, didn't I?"

Dan swallowed hard. "I'm not sure. It

happened so fast."

"Uncle David didn't reload. He never got a shot off. And I saw Peterson fall — the hole in the back of his coat. I did that."

Dan tightened his hold on her. "I'm sorry. We don't have to tell the constable."

"No, it's all right. We should tell him the truth."

The ache in Dan's throat was impossible to swallow away. "I love you," he whispered. She was silent for a moment, and he regretted his words. She already had more than enough to distress her. "I'm sorry. I shouldn't have said that. Forgive me."

"No."

He drew back a little and eyed her cautiously. "You won't forgive me?"

"No, Daniel. Say it as often as you want. I'll never tell you not to again."

He looked into her sad, dark eyes, still not certain he read her mood correctly.

A faint smile curved her lips upward. "I love you, too. I've been so foolish, but I expect I'll mend my ways from now on."

Dan bent toward her, still swathed in disbelief, and kissed her gently. Anne slid her arms up around his neck.

"When Uncle David comes back, will you take me to Mrs. Zinberg's? I don't want to stay in the hotel tonight."

"Of course."

Bewildered but thankful, Dan kissed her again.

CHAPTER 27

Two weeks later, Anne helped Elise Bentley set the table in her ranch kitchen for seven. Dan had ridden down to Corvallis from his brother's place, and Rob and Dulcie had driven over from their neighboring ranch to join Anne, Eb, Elise, and David for supper.

"I suppose it's unrealistic to think we could keep your uncle here any longer," Elise said as she laid out the plain, white ironstone plates.

Anne walked along behind her, placing the silverware at each place. "He said that as soon as he and Daniel settle the details for the stage line, he's going back to Eugene to look for a suitable building. He's serious about it, and he wants to get started before someone else does."

Elise smiled but shook her head. "It's wonderful having him around again, but I keep wondering if he's even thinking of going back to England."

"Not for a while, I'd say." Anne went to the cupboard for cups and saucers. "Of course, he can't until spring, but I don't know if he even wants to go then. He's having too much fun here."

"I should hate to see him go," Elise said, "and yet . . ."

"Yes. I feel the same way. I'm delighted to be with him again, after all these years, but I can't help thinking how much he's needed in England."

Elise smiled. "Now that his arm is getting better, there's no holding him down on this stagecoach business. If he took half the energy he's putting into that and put it into Stoneford, why, the estate would flourish and the tenants would prosper."

"Yes," Anne said. "I can't help feeling he's sorely needed there. But of course, he seems to have become quite attached to the freedom he has here. I believe he sees this stagecoach line as a challenge. He's determined to see it succeed."

"I wonder. . . ." Elise eyed her thoughtfully.

"What?" When she didn't reply immediately, Anne's anxiety mushroomed. "What are you hinting at?"

Elise smiled. "Maybe it's Dan that he wants to see succeed."

"I don't understand." The truth was, Anne did understand. She dipped milk into a pitcher and avoided Elise's gaze.

"I'm just saying, maybe he sees Dan as a good prospect for a nephew-in-law and wants to help him escape his brother's farm for your sake."

Anne tried to formulate a retort, but she couldn't. Instead, her cheeks began to burn. She put down the ladle and carried the pitcher to the table. Without turning around, she said, "I do love him."

"Do I dare hope you're staying and will be a somewhat close neighbor?"

Anne shrugged. "I hope that as well. But Dan hasn't —"

"Don't tell me he hasn't renewed his suit. Whenever he's around you, he can't take his eyes off you."

She smiled at that. "I'm afraid I'm as bad now. But he hasn't spoken again. Perhaps I put him off too many times. I thought before we left Scottsburg that we'd reached an understanding."

"Perhaps you have. Dan is a practical man. He probably wants to be sure of what he's offering you this time before he makes the offer."

That prospect heartened Anne. She strained to catch sounds from outside.

"I hear a wagon driving up. That must be Rob and Dulcie. Is everything ready?"

Elise opened the oven door, and a cloud of roast beef–scented air wafted through the room.

"Yes, I believe so." Elise closed the oven and took off her apron. Together they went out to greet the Whistlers.

Dulcie hugged Anne and Elise and hovered over Rob while he unloaded the dishes she'd brought — two pies and a pot of beans, though Elise had assured her she didn't need to cook a thing.

Anne went to the team's heads. Bailey was in harness with Dulcie's mare. Anne stroked the gelding's nose.

"Hello, friend."

Rob smiled as he passed her, carrying the bean pot. "He seems none the worse for his sea voyage."

They all sat down to dinner. Eb carved the roast beef, and Elise served up the beans while the other dishes were passed around the table. For the first few minutes, the talk centered on the food and life at the Bentleys' and Whistlers' farms.

"How are things at your brother's place?" Rob asked Dan.

"Going well, sir. Hector accomplished a lot while I was gone. He expects his fiancée to come by ship next year."

"Sailing around the horn? She must be a brave woman," David said.

"I'm afraid the things Hector told her about our journey here dissuaded her from traveling overland," Dan said.

"Our trip last summer wasn't half bad." Eb held his cup out toward Elise, and she rose and took it from him. She returned a moment later with a coffeepot and poured his cup full.

Eb took it and set it down. "Somebody asked me t'other day if we were going to take another wagon train next year." He looked across the table at Rob.

"Not me! I promised Dulcie I was done with wagon trains."

"That's right," Dulcie said. "I'm surprised you'd even consider it, Eb, with your new bride and all."

Eb smiled. "Oh, I'm not going anywhere."

Elise said nothing but smiled as she made her way 'round the table dispensing coffee.

"And what about you, Mr. Stone?" Rob asked. "What are your plans?"

"I'll be going back to Eugene City soon and settle up there," he said.

"Going to England?" Dulcie asked.

"Weeell . . ." David looked over at Anne. "I've about made up my mind to stay another year. Daniel and I have a scheme we want to try — stage coaching from here to Eugene. We ought to be able to tell in a year's time whether we can make a go of that."

"Mr. Stone's found a place in town where they want to have the stagecoach station," Eb said. "Personally, I think it's a good idea."

"Daniel will man the station here, and I'll set up in Eugene," David said. "I intend to talk to Mr. Skinner when I get back there and see what's required for a mail contract."

"Well, now. You're giving up wheat farming?" Rob said to Dan.

"Yes, sir. My brother can do most of it, and I'll go up and help him when I can, for planting and harvest. But Hector's agreeable."

"So, Anne, if I stay in Oregon another year and go back in the spring of '57, will you make the journey with me?" David watched her closely, and again she felt her cheeks warm.

"Well, I . . . I'm not certain, Uncle David."

He smiled. "A lot can happen in a year or eighteen months."

"Yes."

Dan cleared his throat. "I believe Miss

Stone may have other plans, sir."

David's eyebrows rose. "Oh? You believe, or you know?"

"Yes, tell us, Dan'l," Eb said.

Rob grinned at him. "You'd better make certain."

Dan looked from one to the other, seemingly uncomfortable. Anne decided anything she could say would only worsen the situation, so she busied herself with cutting her meat.

"There now, leave the boy alone," Elise said. "Eb, could you please pass the biscuits?"

"Mr. Stone," Dulcie said, "I've been wondering what would happen if you go back to England. Would you feel safe with your cousin still about?"

"That's a good question," David said, frowning. "You see, before Peterson died — that is, the man who wanted to kill me — he said that my cousin wasn't the one paying him."

"It sure seemed like that was what he meant." Dan shot Anne a quick glance and then looked away. He was just as glad to have the subject changed, she was sure, even if it was to a gruesome topic.

"But who else could want you out of the way, Uncle David?" she asked.

"I've thought about it a lot, and I've come up dry. Perhaps we'll hear back from Mr. Conrad in a few months, and he can tell us if there's any evidence that my cousin was behind it all. Meanwhile, I intend to go on living."

"Sounds like a good plan," Rob said. "Now, tell me, sir, will you be buying horses for the stagecoaches, or mules?"

The talk went back to the business for quite some time. When the meal had ended, the ladies cleaned up the dishes. When Elise went out to hang her dishcloth on the clothesline, she came back with a message for Anne.

"Dan says when you're done, he'd like to have a word with you. He's out on the side porch."

"Oh. I was going to sweep the floor," Anne said.

"I'll do it. Fetch your cape and go on. Don't keep that young man waiting."

Anne smiled at her. "I always did obey you, Elise."

"Yes, you were an exemplary child."

A minute later, Anne was out the kitchen door. Dan jumped up from his perch on the porch railing.

"Anne! I was hoping I'd get a word with you."

"Take several, if you've a mind to."

He smiled, and the worry lines eased out of his face. "I hope I didn't embarrass you too deeply at dinner."

"Everything you said was true."

He stepped a little closer, and her heart beat faster.

"Anne, I do hope you'll stay. I didn't mean to presume upon your thoughts about the matter, but a few things you said on the ship . . ."

She looked up into his gray eyes, usually so calm. Today they seemed a bit anxious. "I meant to encourage you. Am I horrid for being so bold?"

He smiled and reached for her hand. "I almost said, 'Do you mean it?' but I know you wouldn't say so if you didn't. Anne, are you truly thinking you might make your permanent home here?"

She chuckled, conscious of her own ingrained sense of propriety and his even stronger reticence. "That depends on so much, Dan."

"Oh?"

"Dare I say it depends on you?"

He caught his breath. "Anne, my dearest, if you would marry me, I'd do everything in my power to keep you happy. I wouldn't stick you off on the farm, away from your friends. You could be here in Corvallis, near Elise and Dulcie. And I wouldn't work you to death at the stage stop."

"I'm not afraid of hard work, Daniel."

"I know you're not. But I wouldn't like to see you worn down by it. I spoke to your uncle about it. He said we should hire a cook and a couple of tenders for the animals. He thinks we can do that and still make a profit."

"We shall see about that — about hiring a cook, I mean. Having extra help would be nice, though."

"Oh Anne, does —" He dropped to one knee and held her hand in both of his. "Will you, Anne? Will you marry me?"

She touched his cheek. "Yes, Daniel. I think we shall have splendid adventures together."

He sprang to his feet and pulled her into his arms. "Oh Anne, if it gets too tame, we'll take a ride up into the mountains."

"Lovely — so long as we don't encounter any cutthroats or grizzly bears."

He frowned for a moment. "I can't guarantee that. You and your uncle seem to attract swindlers and assassins. I've never seen a grizzly bear, though."

She eyed him askance. "Oh Daniel! Kiss me, or I'll retract my answer."

Without another word he complied, and quite handily.

On the last Friday in March, Dan's brother, Hector, rode down from Champoeg and stayed with him at the small house he'd bought in Corvallis. After breakfast on Saturday, they dressed in their best. Dan put on the suit he wore to church each week, a new shirt and tie, and the silk top hat Hector had persuaded him to buy.

They walked over to the little church where Eb and Elise Bentley had been married in the fall. The minister greeted them. They sat down in the back pew, talking quietly. Dan's stomach was a bit on the roily side. He got up and walked to the door and looked out. Two riders had just entered the churchyard.

"Here's Eb and Elise."

Hector came out and greeted the Bentleys with him.

"How's the farm?" Eb asked Hector, whom he hadn't seen since they'd disbanded the wagon train in late October.

The two were soon engrossed in talk of crops and livestock.

"Where's Anne?" Dan asked Elise.

"Her uncle's bringing her in the wagon. But they were waiting for Rob and Dulcie."

Dan nodded and took a deep breath.

Elise smiled and touched his sleeve. "You look fine today, Daniel. How do you feel?"

"Not half bad." He grimaced. "Well, maybe half."

Elise laughed. "Anne is very excited, but she won't let on."

"No, I don't expect she will." It gave him a perverse pleasure to know that his cool-headed bride was nervous, too.

"How are things going?" Eb asked. "Anne says the stage line opens next week."

Dan grinned. "That's right. We're all set, and we've had people buying tickets already. Mr. Stone's got the station in Eugene set up, and we've got two stops along the way where we'll change teams."

"I admit I wondered this winter if it would all come together for you," Elise said. "I'm glad it has."

"Thanks." Dan didn't mention his main motivation — he'd promised Anne to have their house bought and furnished and the stagecoach station operational before the wedding. She hadn't insisted on it, but Dan didn't want her to jump into marriage and the chaos of setting up the business, too. He was confident that with her uncle's guidance for the next year at least, the line would succeed. "David's been a really hard worker. When something didn't want to happen, he grabbed both ends and made it work."

Eb laughed. "What about those swindlers? Any word on them?"

"No. The marshal thinks Millie and Sam have left the territory."

"Good riddance," Elise said. "Anne got a letter from England day before yesterday, you know."

Dan stared at her. "No, she didn't tell me."

"The solicitor says Mr. Stone's cousin denies having anything to do with Peterson or the attempts on David's life. He said there's no evidence that Randolph Stone was involved."

"Huh." Dan frowned at Eb. "What do you think about that?"

"I think the cousin's lying. What other explanation can there be?"

Elise shrugged. "At least no one's tried to harm David since he left Scottsburg in November. I hope that's the end of the matter."

A team of horses pulling a wagon clopped into the yard.

"There's Rob and Dulcie," Elise said, waving to them. "David and Anne won't be far behind. Daniel, you'd best get inside now. Can't have you seeing Anne before the ceremony."

Dan grimaced at her. "That's silly."

"Come on." Hector laid a hand on his shoulder. "If the bride wants to follow some harmless tradition, what do you care?"

"That's right. It'll be worth it," Eb said with a wink at Elise.

Dan went back into the church with Hector. The minister met them halfway down the aisle.

"Most of the guests are here," Hector told him. "We're apprised that the bride is on her way."

"Oh good, good," the minister said. "Perhaps you gentlemen would like to come to the front of the church. I'm sorry we don't have an organ, but Miss Stone had me engage Harold Scully to play his fiddle. He just came in the back door."

A gray-haired man wearing a passable black suit and carrying a violin stepped forward and nodded to them. "Gents. It's a pleasure."

Dan and Hector shook his hand.

"Harold plays at all the dances," the minister said.

Dan eyed him with some trepidation, but Scully laughed. "It's all right, sir. I can play slow tunes, too, and hymns."

A flurry at the door drew their attention.

Eb, Elise, Rob, and Dulcie entered, along with several other women Dan recognized from church services and one man looking rather ill at ease. They all sat down on the benches, and the minister walked over to greet them.

He returned a moment later. "Mr. Adams, I'm told the bride and her uncle are ready. How about you?"

Dan swallowed hard and looked at Hector, who chuckled and slapped him on the shoulder.

"He's ready, Parson."

Dan nodded. "Yes, sir."

The minister nodded to Scully, who began to play a soft, sweet melody. The door opened once more, and Dan straightened his shoulders and looked toward it. David Stone held the door while Anne squeezed her voluminous skirt through the doorway. She smiled at her uncle through the filmy veil that hung from her bonnet.

Dan's stomach lurched. She wore a dress fit for Queen Victoria herself — white, with ruffles and flounces and bits of lace. And Anne's face shone. She held his gaze as she walked slowly the length of the aisle, holding David's arm. Dan hardly glanced at the tall Englishman, but he had an impression of an immaculate, finely tailored suit of formal clothes worn by a handsome man of substance.

They reached him, and David stood between him and Anne for a few minutes while the minister welcomed the guests and offered prayer.

"Who gives this woman in holy matrimony?" the minister asked.

David Stone took a deep breath. In his cultured tones, he said, "In the absence of her beloved parents, I do."

He moved aside and placed Anne's hand in Dan's.

Dan gazed down into her trusting brown eyes.

"Daniel," the minister said, "do you take this woman to be your lawfully wedded wife, to love and to cherish, to have and to hold from this day forward?"

"Yes, sir."

Behind him, Eb and Rob chuckled.

Dan said quickly, "I do, sir. I most assuredly do."

DISCUSSION QUESTIONS

1. Anne has devoted nearly a year to looking for her uncle. At what point should she decide it's time to give up?
2. Dan knows from the beginning that Anne does not want to marry him, yet he joins her on her quest. Give two good reasons for him to do this — and two for him to put it to rest and go home.
3. Millie's morals slither all over the place. Was she justified in selling Andrew's pies and keeping the money? Name two other unethical things she did in the story. If you knew she was wearing a stolen dress, what would you do?
4. Why didn't David write to his family? Based on this, do you think Anne's expectations of her uncle were overblown?

5. What did you expect transportation, commerce, and communications to be like in 1855 Oregon? How did the characters cope with the primitive methods they had to use?

6. Do you think Millie is redeemable? How about Sam? Peterson?

7. If you were Anne, and Sam stole your horse, would you turn him over to the constable, knowing he might be hung for the offense?

8. How is Anne's quest as much a search for herself as it is for her uncle?

9. Anne suffers a great deal of anxiety over the fate of Bailey, the horse she borrowed from Rob Whistler. How does this compare with Sam's feelings about the blue roan?

10. How was Millie affected by her theft of David's things from his hotel room?

11. Anne has gone through nearly all of her annual allowance, but she hates the thought of borrowing from anyone. Unlike Millie, she can't just steal a few dollars. What would you recommend she do in her situation?

12. Anne is surprised that her uncle

isn't eager to rush back to England. What is keeping him in America? In Oregon?

13. Why didn't Millie want to stay with Sam at the end of the story? What do you predict for Millie's future?

ABOUT THE AUTHOR

Susan Page Davis is the author of more than thirty novels in the historical romance, mystery, romantic suspense, contemporary romance, and young adult genres. A history and genealogy buff, she lives in Kentucky with her husband, Jim. They are the parents of six terrific young adults and are the grandparents of eight adorable grandchildren. Visit Susan at her website: www.susanpagedavis.com.